Down
the
Hall

and Other Short Stories

by Ron Anahaw

Printed in the United States of America

First Printing, 2015

ISBN 978-1508845584

Published through Amazon CreateSpace.

The author welcomes any and all comments or criticisms. For requests,
feedback, or information, the author can be contacted at
downthehallstories@gmail.com.

Cover Design by Courtney Chan

To anyone who feels alone: just knock.

"This is a small apartment, motherfucker, where you gonna hide?"
-Craigslist, "To the Fly I Just Killed in My Apartment"

AUTHOR'S NOTE

I hope you're ready for a healthy dose of metaphor.

From a young age, many of us are taught to build walls around ourselves. Whatever fear guides us, we box ourselves into our own personal rooms to keep us, and sometimes others, safe. Throughout my life, I've isolated myself in my room to try and protect either myself or others. But I'm lucky enough to have friends who won't just knock on my door, but knock it down. The core idea behind this book is that sometimes, the farthest you have to look for someone who loves you, is down the hall. But if you're as lucky as I am, you won't even have to look. They'll come back, again and again, never deterred by a closed door.

I can trace this idea back to a specific memory. In the summer after 8th grade, when I was a chubby freshman-to-be with flimsy glasses and an inflated ego built on a semi-impressive vocabulary, my family took a trip to the Philippines. I'd only been there twice before by that point, both times when I was extremely young—so the giant cast of a family who greeted us was almost a surprise.

Filipinos have a culture based heavily on the strength of family. Kinship and warmth runs through our blood—we treat our fellow countrymen as brothers, sisters, and cousins. But the love we have for those connected by blood burns like a Filipino sun. My father's side of the family burned more than two dozen strong. So, on the first night on those heated islands, in the stone home that the Anahaws all lived in, even in the dark, I could feel all my family around me. Their breathing filled the silence. I knew that the farthest that another Anahaw was, was down the hall.

That feeling echoes even now. At our school Carver, I can rest easy knowing that, even if I close my eyes, I know that someone who I love and who loves me is right there with me. I know that I'll never walk those hallways truly alone. And I know that that feeling will continue to echo throughout my life.

It takes courage to knock on someone's door. And it takes courage to open that door for others. I hope that you see that in this book.

Walk the hallways with my characters. Knock on their doors and see who opens, and who doesn't. Welcome to the Crossings at Wolf Hall.

CONTENTS

PROLOGUE

THE KEYS TO THE CROSSINGS

NOTE to self: the following is a compilation of tenant information for the Greens Building in Crossings. Made sure to save this to my computer rather than a flash drive (See Room 3D for "Norman Incident"). In case of a repeat of the Norman Incident, I've only saved their emails for contact information rather than phone numbers.

Room 1A: Lindsey Paperman and Micah Leif
Contact: papermanstories@gmail.com
Rent (per month): $850, due on the 5th of each month
Renewal of Lease: January 2nd, 2016
Vehicle: 1 2008 Honda Accord

Room 1B: Jason Goldman, Roland Gardner, and Ash Pineda
Contact:rgardner@lucida.edu, jgoldman@lucida.edu, dirtpunchers@gmail.com

Rent (per month): $850, due on the 5th of each month.
Renewal of Lease: February 5th, 2016
Pet: 1 puggle
Note: Possible use of drugs. Admissible.

Room 1C: Jessie Haller
Contact: email unavailable
Rent (per month): $850, due on the 5th of each month
Renewal of Lease: May 10th, 2016
Vehicle: 1 2000 Lincoln Town Car Sedan
Note: Parking space is usually vacant.

Room 1D: George Perran, Vin Perran, and Lee Perran
Contact: email unavailable
Rent (per month): $850, due on the 5th of each month
Renewal of Lease: August 30th, 2015
Vehicle: 1 2010 Toyota Sienna Minivan

Room 1E: Vacant

Room 2A : C.J. Turner
Contact: cjturner19@gmail.com
Rent (per month): $850, due on the 5th of each month
Renewal of Lease: Vacating within 1 month

Room 2B: Gary Young and Millie Young
Contact: theyoungs@comcast.net
Rent (per month): $850, due on the 5th of each month
Date of Renewal of Lease: December 20th, 2015
Note: Available at any time of day to assist these tenants.

Room 2C: Patrick Thompson, Melanie Wright, and Zola Thompson-Wright.
Contact: mwright@lucida.edu
Rent (per month): $850, due on the 5th of each month
Renewal of Lease: May 8th, 2016
Vehicle: 1 2006 Kia Sorrento

Room 2D: Alishia Siller
Contact: sillerart@gmail.com
Rent (per month): $850, due on the 5th each month
Renewal of Lease: June 12th, 2015
Vehicle: 1 Honda Rebel Motorcycle
Note: Offered an original painting as payment once.
**Note:* Accepted original painting as payment.

Room 2E: Kira Carpenter
Contact: kcarpenter221@gmail.com
Rent (per month): $850, due on the 5th each month
Renewal of Lease: October 22nd, 2015

Room 3A: Luke Thompson and Pablo Galvarez
Contact: rattletattle@gmail.com
Rent (per month): $880, due on the 5th each month
Renewal of Lease: January 2nd, 2016
Note: Galvarez recently added on as new co-tenant. Rent increased from $850 to $880.

Room 3B: Joey Maxworth and Dinah Albright
Contact: howyoudoin@gmail.com, itstoobright@gmail.com

Rent (per month): $850, due on the 5th each month
Renewal of Lease: November 2nd, 2015
Note: Maxworth has notified of possibly vacating soon.

Room 3C: Tommy Belmont
Contact: gutofsilver@yahoo.com
Rent (per month): $850, due on the 5th each month
Renewal of Lease: September 17th, 2015
Vehicle: 1 Moped (lol)

Room 3D: Norman Alexander
Contact: ???
Rent (per month): $875, per month
Renewal of Lease: June 20th, 2016
Note: Definite drug use.
**Note:* Multiple complaints from other tenants.
***Note:* Complaints were quickly retracted. Reason unknown.
****Note:* Norman Incident: I had left my personal flashdrive, filled with information privy only to myself, in the Crossings. Including but not limited to poems, tax information, and tenant information. Found Norman with it three days later. He was reading my poems. Quickly reprimanded him.

Room 3E: Vacant

THESE ARE THE THIN MINTS YOU'RE LOOKING FOR

Room 3D

SOMEONE keeps knocking on my door. I move my blanket aside and get up from the kitchen floor.

As I pass by my window I look through the pane and wave at the sun. When I'm at my door I stretch my arms and strum my toes against the floor. I crack my neck and then open the door.

A small, blonde girl dressed like a Girl Scout stands there.

"*Holy shit*, do you have Thin Mints?" I immediately ask.

She nods and I laugh. "Whoo, papa is gonna be happy today." She looks confused. "Papa is me," I explain.

"Is it okay if I say what I have to say first?" she says quietly, looking down.

"Aw. Of course, sweetie."

"Hi. My name is Bella. I am with Girl Scout troop..." She mumbles some troop name or number. "I am selling a variety of Girl Scout cookies to make money for..."She mumbles whatever cause she's selling cookies for. "Would you like to buy some?"

"Hell. Yes." I put a hand forward. "You use a cookie sheet, right? Where do I sign up? Gimme, gimme. When do they get delivered?"

"Um, actually..."

She moves forward and reveals a red wagon filled with boxes of Girl Scout cookies.

"Ohmygod," I say. I move forward and pick up a box of Thin Mints. I can't stop grinning.

"You know, Bella, I have a lot of questions about these cookies."

"O-oh," she stammers. "Well, the nutritional information for Thin Mints—"

I shake my head. "No, no. I mean, questions like, why're they called Thin Mints if I feel fat afterwards? What's the chocolate to mint ratio? And more importantly, what are all these white people doing on the boxes?" I lightly hit the box with the back of my hand. "There's like, only one black dude. I want some representation, Bella! I want to know that my demographic is being represented! I'm sure there are some Native American Girl Scouts out there." I hit the box again.

It's quiet. I look up and Bella's eyes are wide and she's looking at the ground. "Bella?"

She looks startled. "I'm sorry."

"No, no, don't be sorry. It's okay. You didn't do anything."

"So, um, would you like to buy some cookies, sir?"

She's wringing her hands. She looks real nervous. She doesn't look a day over nine years old. I step forward and peer around the doorway. No parent behind her.

"Bella, how many more stops do you have to make?"

"You're my first one today."

"What? Did no one else in the building answer when you knocked on their door?"

She shakes her head. "No, I haven't knocked anywhere else yet. My mom always says to start from the top and go down from there."

"And where is your mom?"

She looks uneasy. She opens her mouth to answer the question, but waits for a moment. "She's...home."

I bring my wallet out of my pocket. "Alright, here's the deal, Bella. I'm gonna buy two boxes of Thin Mints, and then---wait, how much will that cost me?" I open my wallet.

"Sixteen dollars."

"And then we'll—holy crap, sixteen dollars, that's highway freakin robbery—go make these stops together. I'll help you out, since your mom's at home. What do you say?"

We swap the goods and the cash. She tucks away the money into a small bag on the wagon. Then, she nods. "Okay."

Room 3C

I knock twice.

As we wait, Bella pushes the wagon to the right of the door frame. I raise an eyebrow but think nothing of it. I'm about to say something when Tommy opens the door. He looks at Bella then me; his face twists into confusion.

"Norman, what are you doing?" he asks.

"Helping my friend Bella here!" I clap a hand onto her shoulder and she winces. "Oh, sorry there, Bella." I grin at Tommy. "She's selling cookies. These are the thin mints you're looking for," I say. "Get it? *Star Wars*?"

Tommy shakes his head. "Nuh uh, no way Norman. Not after last time."

"Last time?"

"You know. With the—" He drops his voice to a whisper. "—With those *special* brownies?"

"Oh! Those !" I laugh. "Well what was wrong with that?"

"You didn't tell me they were special!"

"Oh." I hold up my hands. "Forgive and forget?"

"Seeya, Norman." He closes the door.

I sigh. "Sorry there, Bella. Guess we'll just have to move on."

"Okay. But is it okay if I say what I'm supposed to say this time?"

"Oh. Oh, okay. Yeah, that's totally fine! Sorry, I don't want to be in your way."

Room 3B

Dinah opens the door. Her eyes widen and her lips stretch into a smile when she sees Bella. She's about to speak but I silence her. "Sh!" I say. Dinah looks confused. I motion for Bella to begin.

"Hello," she says nervously. "My name is Bella. I am with Girl Scout troop..." She mumbles again. Huh, weird. "I am selling a variety of Girl Scout cookies to make money for..." And then she mumbles *again*. "Would you like to buy some cookies?"

"Of course! I would love to. Do you have Caramel DeLites?"

Bella nods and reaches for a box. I raise a hand. "Um, what are Caramel DeLites?"

Bella holds up the box she was reaching for. "These."

I look at it. "Uh, no, those are the world famous and my personal second favorite, the Samoa cookie."

Dinah asks for four boxes and Bella tells her the price. Dinah hands over the cash. "Actually, they have made a lot of changes, Norman." She gives Bella a smile when she hands over the cookies. "Thank you, love. But yeah, Norms, they've renamed a lot of the cookies and made some vegan. Thin Mints are vegan now, I think."

That last sentence echoed in my mind. *Thin Mints are vegan now, Thin Mints are vegan now, Thin Mints are vegan now.*

"Why," I cried. "Why would they dare even change one line on the recipe for those beautiful cookies?"

Dinah stared at me. "They're not gonna taste any different."

"Oh."

Room 3A

I bring my hand to the door, but stop short of knocking. I look down at Bella. "What exactly is your mom doing back at your home?"

"Um..."

Suddenly the door opens. Luke and some guy are leaving together, hand in hand. Luke is startled at the sight of us.

"Jesus!" He takes a breath and laughs. "You scared me, aha."

The other guy smiles. "Don't mind him, he's easily excitable. Is there something you two need?"

Bella repeats her schpeal and I'm not at all surprised that she mumbles those same few lines again. They exchange cash for cookies and leave to go on a date. Once they're gone, I put a hand on Bella's shoulder.

"Hey, Bella?"

She looks nervous.

"Yeah?"

"Can I ask you something?"

"...Yes," she says hesitantly.

"Is there a reason you always mumble the same few lines?" I ask.

She freezes. Then, she finally opens her mouth to answer when Dinah angrily walks toward us.

"Norman!" she says. "Is this you up to your usual crap?" she says. At the sight of Dinah, Bella bolts, wagon and all. She sprints down the hallway and then to the stairs. I'm about to run after her when Dinah firmly puts a hand on my shoulder.

"Dinah, what? You scared her!" I say.

"I want my money back," Dinah says.

"What? Why? Did Joey decide he's on a diet?"

"No, this doesn't have to do with my boyfriend." She holds up one of the Girl Scout boxes. "This is filled with cookies, yeah, but not Girl Scout cookies. She's selling rip-offs."

2nd Floor of Crossings at Wolf Hall

I have a lot of questions for Bella. Why's she doing this? Is her real name Bella? Where's her mom really? And does she have real Thin Mints that I can still buy from her, or is that a faded dream by now?

I find her alone, in the strip of hallway between 2C and 2D. She's hugging her knees, sitting by her wagon, alone. She sees me and grabs a box off the wagon.

"Don't hurt me," she says, hand poised to throw the box at me.

I hold my hands up. "Peace, peace." I walk forward slower. "I don't want to hurt you at all. I'm just really confused, man."

Eventually I'm standing right next to her. She looks up at me with her big, brown eyes—man, are those suckers adorable—and puts the box down. I sit down next to her.

"So. Rough day at work?" I ask.

She laughs. "Sort of."

"Can I ask about your mom?"

"I guess."

"Okay. What's up with your mom?"

"She works a lot of jobs."

"Oh. I thought she was treating you bad, or something."

She shakes her head. "No. She's a good mom. We just don't have a lot of money."

I nod. "Ah. I've been there."

"Yeah."

"A lot of people wouldn't give my mom a job just because she was Native American. It's like, w'sup man, you can't handle the fact that not everyone is white? I always admired her, you know? She's the strongest person I know."

"My mom is too."

"Psh, showoff," I say. Bella laughs.

"But you can't always be strong," she says. She frowns. "People get tired."

"Yeah. That's true. Is that why you want to help your mom?"

"Yeah."

Someone in either 2C or 2D turns on their television. From the familiar sounds of Gordon Ramsay's beautiful, gentle voice, Alishia must be watching *Top Chef* again.

"Listen, Bella."

"Yeah?"

"Let me get this straight: you sell people overpriced Girls Scout cookies, that aren't really Girls Scout cookies."

"Um, yeah."

"How do you do it?"

"Mom buys me cookies to pack for my lunch because they're real cheap. So a lot of the time I hide them away. And our neighbor eats a lot of Girls Scout cookies, so I just sort of...I don't know. I take the boxes from his trash and I just fill them with cookies and staple it back together."

"Wow. That. Is. Badass."

"What?"

I shake my head. "Nothing, it's just...wow. Does your mom know about this?"

She shrinks into herself. "No."

"Then what does she think you're doing all day?"

"...Girl Scouts."

I burst out laughing. "Ooh, I like your moxie, kid. I like you. You're like this weird combination of naïve and badass." I pause. "You're a lot like me. I can't really help you out with your financial situation, but here's what we'll do..."

Room 2D

Alishia opens her door and sees me and Bella. Bella and I smile real big.

"Alishia, boy, have *I* got some cookies for you."

MISS FOXHEART'S GUIDE TO ROMANCE

Room 2C

*D*EAR *Miss Foxheart,*

I've been having a huge issue with men lately. I don't know whose fault it is, mine or theirs, but trust me, someone's doing something wrong.

Zola raised an eyebrow as she read on. She scrolled down the page. The lost, the lonely, the lovelorn—love guru Miss Foxheart dealt in advice, and these were her customers. Zola didn't consider herself so much a customer as she did a window-shopper. She liked reading about these people's heartsickness and seeing what Miss Foxheart had to say about it. Zola was seven.

...And that's the whole story. So what should I do? And I will say now, I refuse to return his tomatoes.

                    -Sally

Dear Sally,

Normally I would be doing my utmost to help you remedy your issue. However, I must take this moment to advertise something I am quite proud of: Miss Foxheart's Guide to Romance.

I've compiled and analyzed all the advice I've given to all of you, my Cubs, and created a comprehensive Guide to Romance. Not only does it offer solid lessons on life and love and lust, but it also comes with a survey that will help you determine where you are right now in your love life, and what you need to do to improve it.

And so, Sally, I suggest you read my Guide. It may have all the answers you need.

-Miss Foxheart

(P.S. It's on a new tab called Guide)

(P.P.S. Definitely return his tomatoes)

Zola clicked on it.

"And why don't you want him over?"

Patrick sighed. "Listen, Luke, it's not that I have anything against him."

Zola watched her Uncle Luke jab a piece of salmon with his fork. She took her fork and jabbed a piece of hers in the same way, celebrating it as if she'd just personally found and hunted the fish. Her Uncle Luke smiled.

"I think little Zola would love Pablo," he said.

"That's not the issue."

"Look, where's Melanie? What's her stance on this?"

"She's giving some lectures at Lucida."

"Ugh. I could've used your wife's input."

"Only because you know she'd be on your side!"

"What? Exactly! Duh!"

"Hey Daddy, who's Pablo? Zola asked as she stuffed the piece of salmon into her mouth. She chewed noisily.

"Your uncle's boyfriend," Patrick said and reached across the table for more rice. "We've talked about that before, right? How you can love whoever you want?"

Zola nodded.

"Then what's your problem with this, Pat?" Luke asked.

"This whole, him moving in with you thing. You know this is too damn fast."

Zola jumped up and down in her seat. Her curly hair bounced up and down with her. "Uncle Luke! I have a question for you!"

Luke looked from his brother to Zola. He smiled again. "Yes, sweetie?"

"Okay, uhhh, wait here."

Zola left the table in a breeze. She ran to her room, swiped her iPad off her bed, and ran back. She sat back down at her seat at the mahogany table. Miss Foxheart's online love column greeted her.

"Okay, let's see. Number 1: Do you prefer A. long walks on the beach, B. short walks in the park, C. running in the forest, or D. staying home and crying in the shower?"

Her uncle and father laughed. Her father spoke up. "I think I'd prefer—"

Zola shushed him. "Not yet, Daddy! Everyone takes turns answering the questions."

"Well," Luke said. "I do believe I prefer...D." He laughed. Patrick rolled his eyes.

Zola tapped the screen and then turned toward her father. "Okay, Daddy! Do you, A. take your loved one for granted, B. appreciate your loved one very much, C. Are not sure, or D. Are so, so alone?"

Zola knew she swung the best.

That's why she made it a point to swing on the swings at Crossings every day. Nothing marked her territory more prominently than the swoosh of her light-up Skechers, a pink parabola curving back and forth as she swung. She was careful to keep the iPad balanced and hidden on her lap. Last time her father had yelled at her when he saw she was swinging with it.

"Hey. Let me swing."

Zola stopped. She craned her head back and saw Lee and Vin. Two brothers that held a shaky kinship that was slightly strengthened every time they picked on Zola together. Zola was pretty sure they just both liked her. Vin spat at the mulch. Zola was disgusted.

"Ew," she said.

Lee and Vin laughed. "Listen," Lee said. He pushed his glasses back up the bridge of his nose. "Listen, Zola. Let us swing, okay?" His glasses slid back down.

"I mean, one of you can swing on the other swing, but I'm using this one."

"Nah," Vin said, and pushed her off. She fell forward into the mulch. She made sure to cradle her iPad in her arms when she hit the ground.

"Hey!" she cried out. They slid onto the swings. Vin smirked. Zola stood up. "Hey!" she said. "Let me back on, you jerks!"

They swung. "Hey, check this out," Vin said, and stuck his legs out. When his feet hit the ground on the way down, it kicked mulch up onto Zola. Lee laughed and followed suit.

"Look, I know, okay!" Zola shouted. The two stopped laughing.

"You know what?" Vin said uneasily.

"You two keep picking on me because you like me!" She held up the iPad. "I read Miss Foxheart a lot, and I know that's what she'd say!"

Lee was silent. Vin started laughing. After a few moments, Lee nervously laughed along. Zola wiped away the mulch on her face and looked away.

"Hey, get away from her!"

Zola turned and saw a man shove Lee and Vin off. As soon as they hit the mulch they yelped, got up, and ran off.

"Zola, you're gonna be in so much trouble!" Vin cried out as they ran back to the building.

"Little lady, are you okay?"

The man's eyes were only half open but he had a friendly smile on his face. He leaned down and offered a hand to her. She took it, and stood up. Zola smiled when she saw the picture of a dog on his shirt. He saw her smile and laughed.

"What, this little guy? This is my actual doggy, Plato," he said, and pinched the cheeks of the picture dog. "Who's a good boy? Who's a good boy?"

"Mister—"

He held up a hand. "No need to thank me, little lady. I was only doing what the sheriff would have."

"No!"

The man looked surprised. "No? The sheriff wouldn't have saved you?"

"No, what I mean is..." Zola stamped her foot on the ground. "I didn't need saving! Besides, you didn't have to hurt them."

"Aw, well...well I'm sorry."

Zola gave her best smile. "It's okay! It really is. Could I ask you a question?"

"Sure thing."

Zola unlocked her iPad. She scrolled down the page.

"Do you A. have a lot of friends, B. have a few friends, C. have one, close friend, or D. are an agnostic?"

"Well, if we're talking ends justifying means and all, then, hmm, I'd have to say B."

"Thanks!"

"Sure thing, little lady. Now if you'll excuse me, I've got to mosey on over to the book store."

"Daddy! Do you wanna hear my test results?"

"Is this for the love test you asked me about at lunch?"

"Yes!"

"Well sure, but sit down at the table first. Uncle Luke is here again."

"Twice in one day? Wow!"

Zola ran over to the table and sat down. Her Uncle Luke waved at her. "Where's Pablo?" she asked. Her father walked over and Uncle Luke looked at him.

"Um, not here, Zola," Luke said.

"Look, I know you're mad, okay? You know I'm not homophobic. This is just moving so fast."

"Moving too fast," Zola said.

Her father and uncle turned to her. "What sweetie?" her father asked.

"Moving too fast, or moving too slow," she said, and read off the iPad. "It doesn't matter for you. For you, you are the best kind of person: you follow your heart. Other people try to...to look in on you, and see what you're doing, and judge, but pay them no mind. They are living in their own orbit, you don't need to enter their gravity. Follow your own path. Do what seems right."

"...Fine. Invite the damn man over for dinner."

UNEMPLOYED TRAGEDIAN

Room 2D

YOU wake up. It's 6 a.m. He's making noise again. You get out of bed and find your broom and jab it at your ceiling repeatedly. One floor above you, in 3D, he is making damn noise again. You think he's found his karaoke machine. You're about to open your mouth and try and shout at him, but it dawns on you that you feel like an old lady. You quickly stop.

You get ready for work. All the blank canvases and unused paint in your apartment taunt you as you pull on your uniform. You give them the finger. You leave for work.

On your way out you pass by others leaving their apartments for work—Melanie slogs down some coffee as she exits Room 2C; C.J. locks her door to Room 2A and fixes her collar. None of you say hello. It's too early in the day to say hello.

So you all walk down the stairwell in a straight line and at a slow, zombie-like pace. You lead the zombie line.

"Heads up. Someone spilled something. It's sticky. Blegh."

"Gotcha, thanks."

"Thanks."

At the parking lot, they part. C.J. gets into Melanie's car. You wave. They don't see it. Your eyes linger on your motorcycle but you decide to walk to work. The birds are singing. And the bees are mating. But hey, at least the birds are singing.

Work is Silver Sun Books, and right across the street. Cars rumble along. The engines belt their own song. So you walk and you walk, past the cars and the playground and the people. Past the monkey bars and dirt mounds and hungry seagulls. Some children chase each other on the playground. You smile. This is a small place. Small, but good. You look back at where you came from, the Greens Building. It's tall, it reaches high. It's got a gray face. Someone on the third floor shuts their blinds—the building is closing an eye.

Oh great. Now the birds are mating, too.

"And that'll be $9.50." You are a gear, a mouthpiece, an experience. Take the book, greet the customer, smile. Ring it up, get the change, smile. Give the book back, bid them farewell, smile.

"And that'll be $10.35."

"And that'll be $12.40."

"And that'll be $18.72."

And then, quiet. Like someone lingering on Chapter 5 after flipping quickly through the first few chapters.

You are bored. "And so," you say to yourself. "the hero finds herself stranded in the worst place possible. Worse than a steaming volcano, or blizzarding mountaintop." You pause, for effect. You love pausing for effect. "The hero is stranded...at work." You gasp.

You almost let yourself smile for a moment. Then you realize you're supposed to be miserable. So you shove a frown on top of that almost-smile.

"Hey, customers don't want to see that," your boss says as he sweeps the floor. "Give me a big ol smile!"

You find out you have the iron will of a fighter. Because it takes everything you can to curl your lips into a smile that didn't also come with a side of eyeroll and the finger.

Your boss grumbles. He is unsatisfied. Your smile has not pleased him. Your boss is a self-made man. After years of working as a librarian and swiping a dozen or so books every month or two, he decided to open up shop: Silver Sun. *And hey,* he thought. *I make a damn good heated-up croissant.* Voila, a bookstore with a cafe a la mode. (Eventually he started buying actual quality baked goods).

"Look at you, just standing around," he says. He keeps talking but you can't help but just picture it: Kauai. Cabo. Fiji. It seems that the best beaches were always wrapped in two, sweet syllables.

Ah, shit. Bora Bora is four syllables. Whatever, close enough. With each syllable you picture the soft sand, the gentle heat, the water bubbling around your toes—

"Hello! Are you listening?"

You snap back and your boss is shoving the broom in his hands toward you. His coffee breath attacks your noses. "Take this," he says. Two syllables never sounded grosser. "I'm going to take my coffee break," he says.

But hey, you do get paid for this. So you take the broom and you get out from behind the counter and you sweep. You don't watch yourself do it, though. You just kind of watch the shelves. The books line the insides of the wooden cases like colored, papery teeth. Your boss doesn't have the time or patience to organize the books. You thank god he doesn't ask you to organize them.

"Hello there, Alishia."

Pablo is here. Pablo, boyfriend of Luke from 3A. He waves, so you wave back. He walks over to you.

"Hey."

"Hi! It's good to see you. Can I help you with something?" you ask. Your boss begrudgingly nods out of approval—he can't deny that you're helping out a customer.

"Just looking around," he says. He crosses his arms. "I need a good book. I don't have much to do."

"Oh, like after work?"

"Oh no, I, uh..." he laughs and puts his hands back into his pockets. "I'm without work."

"So that's why you have a lot of free time."

"Yes. But according to my love, it has made me grumpy. He's been calling me an unemployed tragedian." He flashes me a smile. "Such a romantic pet name, no?"

You laugh. "I guess you say a lot of depressing things, then? If he calls you a tragedian, I mean."

"Ah, no, see, that's what I thought." He strokes his chin. Honestly, you didn't know people did that in real life. "But he explained what he meant by it to me: someone gets consumed by the bad parts of life." He shrugs. "I am guilty of it."

You continue small talk and then point him the way toward the stacks of F. Scott Fitzgerald in the store.

And then you look at the broom in your hands and realize you wish it was a paintbrush.

And then you look at all the clunky books around you and realize you wish they were canvases.

And then you close your eyes and sniff the air and—well, to be honest, you don't quite mind the smell of warm baked goods. So you're fine with that. That's actually okay.

"Alishia! What are you doin—"

Your boss was always too fond of his hand motions. He shoves his arms toward you out of protest for your unproductiveness. He has a cup of coffee in his hands. An open cup of coffee.

A small pool of coffee splashes onto your shirt. Not hot, or cold, but lukewarm. This is your third favorite white shirt. The brown liquid spreads across the fibers.

"...Alishia, I apologize, here, I'll get you a napkin."

He takes a step and you stop him.

"I quit.

THE ENDS, THE MEANS, AND EVERYTHING IN BETWEEN

Room 1B

"HAVE you ever read *50 Philosophy Ideas You Really Need to Know?*"

Jason squinted and thought for a moment. He exhaled and the smoke blew out of his mouth. He nodded and nodded and passed the bowl and lighter to Roland. He spoke as Roland lit the bowl.

"No... I haven't. Why?" Jason asked.

Roland coughed and sputtered out a few tails of smoke at a time. Jason laughed. A playlist filled to the brim with B-list rappers played in the background. Their other roommate, Ash, walked over to the kitchen. He muttered the lyrics to the songs as he looked around, determined. He quickly got excited at the sight of a jar of Nutella on the counter.

"Well I think Mr. Pent should read it," Roland said.

Jason raised an eyebrow. "You think our landlord should read a beginner's guide to philosophy?"

"Hear him out, Jason," Ash said, and dipped two spoons at once into the Nutella.

Roland brought his hands up, as if to shape some invisible thought into words—Jason stared at his forehead, mesmerized at how the sunlight filtered through the blinds and struck Roland's head in such a way to suggest the same as an Italian sunrise, or like the falling light of—

"Concepts. Ideas. You know I love those," Roland began. Jason snapped back to attention and focused hard on trying to listen to Roland's words.

"There's this idea in the book: do the ends justify the means? Humanity has been asking this question for at *least* 20 years. Politicians, librarians, firefighters—they've asked everybody and nobody can come up with a good answer. And who could? The only person who could is probably God and he's totally, like, busy?"

"Have you tried praying? It's like leaving a voicemail."

Ash laughed from the kitchen and Jason nodded as thanks.

"Shush, for a second. This is real, this is big. This is important."

"More important than God? Gee whiz!"

Roland rolled his eyes. "Jason. Jason. Back to my thing. So the ends versus the means...it's like...it's like you're in a hot air balloon. This is what the book says: you're in a sinking hot air balloon, over the ocean. And there are kids with you. All the ballast is gone. You look down, and you can see sharks coming up for you. And I *hate* sharks. I don't mind the razor sharp teeth, but why don't they have hands? If something's going to eat me, I want to at least shake its hand first."

"...If it helps, I like to think of their fins as little triangle hands," Ash said.

Roland sighed. "Thank you, Ash. Anyway, so, like, you can either do nothing and you and the kids die. *Or* you can throw one of the kids off, and the hot air balloon goes back up safely in the air." He paused. "You see what I mean? Do the ends justify the means? You can either sacrifice one to save all, or nothing."

Jason thought for a moment.

"So would you throw one of the kids off?" Roland asked.

"I'd make the sacrifice play and throw myself off. There, the kids are safe and I'm dinner."

"Ah, the personal sacrifice play. How noble. Isn't that noble, Ash?"

Ash nodded in agreement.

"Well...I was hoping you'd say that, Jason." Roland clapped a hand onto Jason's shoulder. "Since you'll make the sacrifice, you can be the one to tell Mr. Pent we can't turn in rent this month."

"What?"

"I'll remember you fondly," Ash said.

Jason took pride in being the most lucid when the three of them smoked. Roland and Ash trusted him to be the most coherent if they ran into other people.

"Do I really have to tell Mr. Pent?" Jason asked.

No one answered.

"I mean, how far off are we from $850?" he asked.

Roland brought his foot up. "Where's my other sock...?"

"Hey, I want chips," Ash murmured.

"Do we not have any?" Roland asked.

"No," Ash said. "We...we don't."

Jason sighed. "I'll walk to Silver Sun and get some snacks, maybe a book or two if I feel like it. Since you two aren't gonna answer me. Should take me twenty minutes."

"Is the café part of Silver Sun open?" Ash asked.

"Yeah. Don't worry, I'll be careful."

Roland waved a hand. "Yeah, yeah, we trust you." He perked up. "Oh! See if Silver Sun's got *50 Philosophy Ideas You Really Need to Know*! I've got some things to say to those sharks…"

Jason laughed and left the room, and locked the door behind him. He whistled and ran his hands along the dark green walls. The cool touch of the metallic "1A" ran under his fingers as he passed by Lindsey and Micah's room.

He swayed his hips as he walked down the stairs; he added a dance to his step, a slow movement that, in his mind, was what he would do if someone asked him to "mosey on over here."

Then, he was in the lobby. He jumped on one foot from white tile to white tile. To keep his balance he pretended to steady himself with invisible, yellow ropes that swung down from the overhead lights. He waved to Millie, who was on her way in. She clutched an acorn in her hand; she waved back. Jason cocked his head out of curiosity and put his other foot down.

"Hey there Mrs. Young," he said. "Love the hair. Whatcha got there?"

She smiled and touched her light gray hair. Then she pocketed the acorn. "Something for my husband. It's nothing to worry about. Where are you headed?"

Jason didn't press further. He recognized that Mr. Young was a bit strange. "Silver Sun Books. Gonna grab some snacks for me and the boys. Maybe, you know, look through the shelves. Oh and hey, thanks again for watching Plato the other day."

Millie nodded. She started talking about some foreign novel she'd picked up there—something whose title in English translated roughly to *The Waves Are Hugging*—when someone took Jason's brain and spun it around like a top.

"Woah," he managed.

"Yes, yes, woah indeed! It is quite the twist..." Millie said.

Each time he blinked he switched from thinking it was a dream to recognizing reality. He sat down and put a hand to his head. A few black spots touched his vision and grew and shrank in sync with his breathing. They swam around his sight. He felt warm.

"Oh my goodness, Jason, what's wrong?"

"It's okay, Mrs. Young," he murmured. "I just kind of feel like I'm dying."

She gasped and he shook his head as vigorously as he could manage. "No, no, see, I'm not actually dying. I just *feel* like I am. I'm totally okay."

"Do you need me to call 911?"

Jason closed his eyes and breathed deeply. He pictured his veins were filled with cherry Slushy and imagined his brain cooling down in the icy mix. Slowly, slowly, he felt better.

He moved to his knees and stood up. His vision cleared and he saw how Millie's usual pearly smile had drooped to a frown.

"...I must've stood up too fast or something, I'm totally fine," Jason said.

"Jason, I'm not that thick. I've seen my fair share of bad trips."

"...What, like vacations?"

She lightly slapped him on the shoulder. "No, I mean drugs. So what is it? LSD? Mushrooms?"

Jason inhaled sharply and she laughed. "Not to worry," she said. "I'm too old to be judging people for what they do. Whatever it takes to make people happy, am I right? So who am I to judge?"

"You should really talk to Roland about that sometime," Jason said. "It's pot."

She laughed and waved a hand. "Is it natural, or synthetic?"

"Natural."

"Then you'll be just fine. Everyone loses control sometime."

"Yes, ma'am."

"Good, then I'll be going along. Tell the boys I said hello. And be careful, would you?"

"Yes, Mrs. Young. Hello to Mr. Young, and thanks for being so understanding."

She waved her hand and walked on toward the stairs. Jason plodded forward toward the door. He breathed in the blue spring air.

He was walking and walking. He didn't look forward, and just trusted his body to move toward Silver Sun. A bad trip, Millie had said—Jason wondered if he wasn't as good at handling pot as he thought he was.

Smoking was like running, in Jason's mind. By the time he'd introduced Ash and Roland to it, he'd learned how to run a marathon. Those two were still trying to sprint the entire way. Jason always felt comfort with leading the way. And suddenly now in his metaphor he'd lost control; stumbled and fallen, and Dr. Mrs. Young diagnosed him with the smoker's shin splints: "a bad trip."

Jason was at the Crossing's playground. He took one step forward into the mulch. He felt a yearning in his chest. He wanted to swing like a monkey from the cartoonish architecture. He looked from the slide to the jungle gym. His eyes settled on the swing set—two boys were swinging. They swung back and forth with their feet stretched out and straight like the limbs of a tree. Whenever they swung forward, the soles of their feet kicked bits of mulch at a girl. She stood in front of them with a paper clutched to her chest and didn't flinch. They laughed. The brazen bunch of curly hair; the light tan skin; the light-up Skechers shoes plastered on her feet. Jason recognized Zola, the little girl from 2C.

He stepped forward. Then forward. And again. He wanted to help her. Why was she just taking the mulch to the face? And suddenly he was behind the two boys on the swing. He blinked and he felt hot again. The black spots festered on the edge of his vision. Their black fins dipped in and out of sight. He put a hand to his head, and breathed.

"What do you think Jason's doing right now?"

Roland shrugged. He kept his eyes on the screen and hands at his controller and watched his character fight through waves of monsters. "You know Jason. Probably doing what he's supposed to."

"I-D-K. he's been gone longer than I thought he'd be," Ash said.

Roland paused his game and looked back at Ash. "Ash, are you okay?"

"Why?"

"How long did you expect him to be gone? Because it's only been four minutes."

Jason's hands buzzed. He was afraid. The black warmth bloomed along his spine. A numbness crept along his fingers and suddenly, nothing. He felt like he had no hands.

Like the fucking sharks, he said to himself.

The boys kept laughing. Jason clenched his fist and imagined wringing control back into his body. He didn't want to fall into the ocean. He wanted to stop it all. He didn't want to lose control. He was desperate.

Jason imagined crushing and stuffing all the planets into his body to ground him for one moment. He needed to do this. The black spots faded for a moment, and Jason reached forward and pushed the two boys off.

"Jason! You're back."

He tossed a bag of chips toward Ash and flopped a book onto the table near Roland. He walked into his room and shut the door. Roland leaned forward and picked the book up.

"The Awesome Book of Sharks..."

DRINKS

Room 3A

PABLO unscrewed the lid of his flask and downed the drink. The golden tequila felt like it was stripping the lining of his throat as it went down. He sat on the left side of the bench. Then after a moment he frowned and moved toward the center of the bench. He was alone. He took out his flask again, and this time ran his gloved thumb over the surface, and smiled. The flask was small and ornate. Seahorses pranced along the bottom of it, and engraved into the skin of it was *PMG*. Pablo took another drink. With each swallow he felt himself growe. He pictured his veins bulging with the golden liquid.

"If only," he said, and pocketed his flask.

His grandfather laughed as he poured himself another shot. Pablo sat across from him, hands folded together, a glass of water placed near by him.

"Even a man with no fire in his blood will feel his bones burn after he drinks tequila! This is ambrosia, the drink of the gods. Have I told you the story, Pablo?"

"Yes, *abuelito*."

"I will tell you anyway!" he shouted, and Pablo rolled his eyes, but smiled nonetheless.

"The gods--based in Cabo--live above us, amongst the clouds, sitting as divine kings and queens on their puffy thrones. And they have always had the most delectable food, the juiciest *elota,* the warmest *sopa de pollo,* and the best damn tacos you'd ever be lucky enough to sink your teeth into."

He pointed at Pablo. "Way better than that Chipotle *mierda* you eat." Pablo opened his mouth to protest and his grandfather silenced him by holding up a finger and downing another shot.

"Let me finish, *mi nieto.* These gods, they used to roam as freely as they liked on our ground. We revered the gods as they should have been--with fear and respect. We knew our place. Their food, you remember my vivid descriptions, yes? Well our food was plain and simple. We picked berries and pulled crops from the ground and enjoyed simple dishes. It was how it was. One day, however, a man by the name of Polgua, saw a goddess, alone, strolling along the red soils of Guadalajara. And though we had grown used to eating and drinking so simply, Polgua felt a thirst in him that seemed unreachable through words. A thirst that seemed only possible through action. *'If I kill this goddess,'* he thought, *'I will have proven my worth, and I will be accepted as a god. And I will be able to eat and drink as they do.'* And so he followed her across the red soil, eventually sinking a spear into her divine chest. And as she crumpled to the ground, she bled blue blood, and it took shape: the blue agave cactus."

"The cactus we use to make tequila," Pablo said. His grandfather snapped his fingers.

"Pablo! You have heard this before!"

Pablo laughed.

"Many times, Grandfather."

"Ah, so then you know Polgua's punishment?"

"Yes. The gods let us keep the agave, and let us distill it into drink. And we enjoyed the drink--we were tasting something of godhood. And everyone was allowed to drink it--except for Polgua."

"Correct! That's my boy. Hotshot, eh? Thinking you know this story inside and out?"

"Well it'd be impossible not to. You've told it to me so many times!"

He downed another shot and Pablo took a sip of his water. His grandfather inched closer to Pablo. "My boy, then here is a question: how does this story help us find who our soulmate is?"

"...I don't understand, Grandfather."

His grandfather laughed and laughed and snapped his fingers over and over. "Oh, seems the hotshot *esta pasando frio*. Who knows the story inside and out now?"

"Alright, alright, I guess I don't. So how does one find out who their soulmate is?"

"That, Pablo, is my secret."

Pablo liked to think he saw a glint in his grandfather's eyes, a short but sure shine in those dark, amber eyes.

"Don't worry, old man, I'll get it out of you eventually."

"Is it okay if I sit here?"

Pablo was startled. He looked up and saw a middle-aged man. He had ruffled dirty blond hair and was decked in a leather jacket. Pablo nodded and slid down the bench. The guy nodded in thanks and sat down. He brought his hands together, rubbed them furiously, and then breathed into them.

"Winter, he is one mean bastard, eh?" Pablo said.

The guy looked over at Pablo. He grinned. "You call winter a 'he'?"

Pablo shrugged, and then gestured to all the trees. "Women bring life. Men bring death." He stuck his hand out toward the guy. "Pablo."

He shook Pablo's hand. "Nice to meet you, Pablo. I'm George. So what's this about winter being a man?"

"...Well, my grandfather, he used to make up all these stories about this group of gods. We both knew he was kidding around, but he loved making up his own mythology, and I loved listening to him. Anyway, there was a story that explains why the gods decided to give the season of winter to a man, a skinny and mean one by the name of Frioro." Pablo paused. "He wasn't ever too creative with the names. Sometimes he didn't name characters, but when he did name them, he usually just combined Spanish words to make a name."

George laughed. "He sounds like a cool guy."

"Yeah. The best."

"I ask because, well..." George hesitated. "I adopted a son semi-recently, and things are still tense. I don't know how to connect with him."

"Wow, adoption. That's big. Connecting to kids is hard enough, but adopted...I can only imagine."

"Yeah. Handsomest little guy you'll meet, a boy named Lee. Him and his brother, Vin—my biological son—they actually get along really great."

Pablo looked at George for a moment, then took his flask out. He ran his thumb over it again. "My grandfather told me the best stories. This was my grandfather's. PMG. Stood for Paolo Martin Galvarez. He loved tequila. Practically wished his blood was made of the stuff."

"Oh, so it was a gift?"

"...More like a keepsake."

"Keepsake?"

Pablo turned to George. He closed his eyes for a moment, and pictured his grandfather there with him instead, pointing out the pretty girls in the complex as he drank tequila and Pablo sipped water. Pablo opened his eyes. "Yeah. About a year ago, he was diagnosed with Alzheimer's."

"...Oh."

"He never wrote down any of those god stories, so the only way I can hear them again is from my own memory."

"I'm sorry, Pablo."

"It's okay. The reason I'm telling you this is because some of the most fun I had was listening to my grandfather tell his stories. So if you want to connect to Lee, try that."

"So you remember his stories?"

"Yeah. My favorite is probably about how he said tequila was made. You know, he told me once that the secret to finding your soulmate was in that story."

"Oh...I guess you didn't find out from him before he got diagnosed?"

Pablo shook his head. "No. But...my grandma, she did say something to me once. And I think that might've been it."

"What was it?"

Pablo smiled. "Don't laugh. But my my grandmother was telling me about how she met my grandfather. And she said, '*Nieto,* your grandfather, he was a bold man. We were lovers one night, and the next morning I was about to leave. But as I was leaving to go, he took my hand and asked me to stay.' I asked her why he asked her to stay. And she smiled and said, 'You know your grandfather, he's strange. Years later he told me it was because, when he awoke the morning after, he looked into my eyes and saw the color of *Los Azulejos* Gold Tequila. That's how he knew.'"

George gave a low whistle. "That man had a dedication to tequila."

Pablo laughed. "Yeah. But I think that was the secret. When you look into someone's eyes and see the color of gold tequila, you've found your soulmate."

"Do you have someone like that?"

"Well, I recently moved in here with my boyfriend Luke."

"Well have you checked his damn eyes? I need to know! Is he your soulmate? Shit man, that's like Paolo Galvarez 101 right there!"

Pablo laughed and shook his head. "I haven't checked, surprisingly enough."

George stood up and extended a hand to Pablo. "Well I've gotta get back to my sons. Listen, I still wanna hear about Luke's eyes. I'm in 1D, if you ever want to hang out."

Pablo took Luke's hand and shook it. "Will do." Pablo heard his name being called and saw Luke exiting the building. He waved. George bid him farewell.

Once Luke was a few feet away from him, Pablo squinted and looked at his eyes. After a few moments, Pablo snapped his finger, laughed, and drank from his flask.

WE'LL ALWAYS HAVE CORS GLACIES

Room 1A

LINDSEY Paperman, the young flash-fiction writer with nervous hands, awoke to a rumpled bed and a Post-It note stuck to the headboard. She peeled it off the board and read the curly, green handwriting: *There's tea on the table. Look at that, alliteration. I'm a genius. Love ya.*

Lindsey stuck the note back as she abandoned the bed. She went to close the white curtains over the bedroom window. She stopped to watch for a moment as the train passed by in the distance, a boxy, gray snake that rumbled along and along.

Room 1A was held together with parentless chargers, pens from everywhere from Georgia to Spain, and binders fat with manuscripts. Her boyfriend Micah had shelves bursting with music, everything from faded vinyl sleeves to plastic CD cases. A stereo system and record player sat side by side in the corner. Lindsey ran her fingers along cases, which jutted out like uneven, multicolored vertebrae; she lingered only for a moment on Kanye West's *808's and Heartbreak,* her sole contribution to Micah's body of albums.

Her mug sat alone on the table. The tea bag's string hung on the side of the mug like a half-hearted fishing lure. She took the bait. Micah had hooked her on tea on their third date, a riverside picnic cut short by rain. The drink was still hot to the touch--the mug radiated heat like a fresh coal, and Lindsey thought of Micah's dark, warm hands.

Mug in hand, she moved quickly and carefully back to her room. She sat down at her desk. A Macbook, long known to Lindsey's rapid and slow typing, sat in the center. On the desk was a framed photo of her older brother, Marcus; his messy mop of hair was covered by a hat, and he had his trademark goofy grin on his face. She smiled. Fingers to keyboard, Lindsey silently recited the words in her head as her hands tapped life into each letter.

She wrote:

He was manufactured and distributed under the authority of The Coca-Cola Company. Former employee Bill Perkins had recently renounced his humanity when he found himself drinking a can of Diet Pepsi. He had been a long-time employee of Coca-Cola, who had treated him well: they promoted him often, paid him handsomely, and sent his niece crates of Coke as an annual birthday present. Guilt was scraping away at his heart, however, and that guilt was laced with Diet Pepsi.

Lindsey heard a buzz. She stopped typing.

Lindsey and Micah had met as two clumsy strangers at the Cors Glacies Ice Rink. Neither were new to ice rinks. Both were strangers to grace.

"Linds, are you sure you'll be fine?"

Lindsey offered a smile to Alexei, a Cors Glacies employee with skin built for the cold and two frost-blue plates for eyes.

"Alexei, this isn't my first time skating. I think I can handle myself."

"Every time you come here you ask me to tie your skates for you."

"Not every time...whenever Marcus comes with me, I force him to tie my skates."

Alexei shrugged. "Have it your way. Just try not to fall too much. I'm the one who has to clean up any blood on the ice."

Lindsey hit him on the arm. "Jerk."

She took a step forward onto the ice. She fell.

"Klutz," Alexei said. "Here, let me help you up."

She held a hand out to stop him. "No, I'm fine."

Alexei shrugged again. "Alright. Call me if you need me."

He walked back to the rental stand, and Lindsey set about standing herself up.

"C'mon, Linds. It's like walking, but with blades on your feet. You can skate. Marcus taught you how to," she muttered to herself, and planted her hands on the ice to push herself up.

"Oh crap."

Lindsey looked up and saw a skater pushing toward her. She stared as he swerved, willed his body to the left, but failed as his skates ran into hers. He fell with a frosty smack right next to her.

Lindsey stared at the body next to her. Definitely not dead, but could most certainly have an injury. He was going fast, but not that fast.

Lindsey had scooted forward on her knees and prodded the man's shoulder.

"Hey, I'm really sorry. I really am. Please tell me you're alright."

He groaned and pushed himself back onto his backside. He and Lindsey sat facing each other, legs crossed together.

"Yeah...I'm fine. I think so. I think? Is there blood?"

Lindsey checked the spot where his head had been. "No blood."

"Great, great."

"Thank goodness."

They both took a moment to collect themselves back into coherence. Lindsey studied his face. He had a jawline that bordered on sharp, and handsome dark skin. Tiny shavings of ice collected on the curls of a possible beard. He put his hand forward.

"So do I get to know the name of my almost killer?"

Lindsey smiled. "Hey, you weren't going fast enough to get killed." She shook his hand. "It's Lindsey."

"Micah. And hey, who was the one lounging around on the ice like it was her bed?"

"Hey, I don't *lounge*."

"Then what was with you just staring while I barreled toward you?"

"...Alright, that was me lounging. But can you blame me? The ice is *so comfortable*."

"Like a pillow," Micah said. They laughed. Lindsey slowly stood up, then offered a hand to him.

He took it, and she pulled him up.

"Thanks, Lindsey."

"It's the least I can do, Micah."

Lindsey stared at the intercom box. She pressed the Talk button.

"Who is this?" she finally said, and pressed the Listen button.

"It's me."

Lindsey was silent. For a moment, all she could hear was her neighbor Ash's dog barking a scratchy yawp that pawed at her walls.

"I'm here. Like you asked."

"Okay. I'll let you in."

Her finger lingered over the Door button. She pressed it.

"I've been meaning to ask something."

Micah looked up from the picnic basket. He set the paper plates down onto the blanket and stretched his legs toward the river, a wiry blue stream that glittered like glass when the sun touched it.

"Yeah?"

"...Do you really think you can make a better whale noise than me?"

Micah shook his head and laughed. "Paperman, I thought we settled this one date ago."

"Yeah, with a ruling from your 12 year old brother."

"Look, even though we're twice his age, he has the wisdom of an old sage."

"Old sage, eh? Maybe he can take a look at my manuscripts sometime. I need the feedback. Writers' got to eat!" Lindsey said. Micah laughed.

"If you ever need fresh eyes on a piece of writing, let me know. I was voted 'Most literate' in high school. I have it on a plaque and everything."

Lindsey smiled and rolled her eyes. "Just get the food out. I'm hungry."

Micah handed her a sandwich and took one for himself out of the basket. They unwrapped them and ate silently and watched the river bubble and flow.

"My brother Marcus and I would sometimes just make animal noises to pass the time," Lindsey said.

"Marcus is going on a mission trip soon, right?"

"Yeah, he is."

"Are you gonna miss him?"

"Definitely. I'm going to miss him a lot.."

"He's that important to you, huh?"

"Very much. Our parents are very...Mormon. And I wasn't-- and still am not--very Mormon. So things like wanting to be a writer, even drinking coffee or tea or soda, anything that I wanted to do out of my own motivations, they didn't agree with. Marcus was different. He supported me...Besides, he also happens to make an authentic bear sound that no one else seems to be able to match. So yes. I'll miss him. I don't want him to go. He's always been there for me, you know? But in six months, he'll be gone. Gone for a year."

Lindsey set her sandwich down and put her hands in her lap. After a few moments, Lindsey felt a weight on her back. She turned her head and saw that Micah was sitting back-to-back with her. She closed her eyes and felt his warmth press into her, softly, and slowly spread from one point to every inch of their backs that were touching.

"Did I hear you say you've never been able to drink tea before?"

"Yeah. Mormons believe that any form of caffeine stains the body."

She heard him pull something from the basket--then she heard pouring. "My dad wasn't perfect either. He wasn't really an 'emotions' sort of guy. His 'I love you' was ruffling your hair and saying 'Good job.' But, as a kid, whenever I had a bad day or had a nightmare or just really needed some cheering up, my dad made me a cup of tea, sat with his back to my back, and said, 'You've got me right here with you, kid.'" Micah paused. "You've got me right here with you, Linds."

After a few moments Lindsey felt Micah's arm move, and she looked down and saw that he had set a cup of tea down next to her. She took the cup and sipped from it.

"...Micah, this tastes awful."

Micah laughed. "That's okay. It's an acquired taste sort of thing. It takes getting used to."

He smiled when he heard her drinking the tea in small and furious intervals, one after the other. "I will like tea," she promised in between sips.

A cold breeze shook petals from their flowers and small blades of grass from the field. Lindsey shivered and clenched the cup firmer as she drank the last watery folds of the tea.

"Thanks for coming."

"Micah's not home?"

Lindsey said nothing. He pulled his hood down and took his gloves off. "Do you have a heater?"

"It's not working."

"Damn, I'm cold. Winter's coming pretty soon. Here, let me take a look at the heater."

"No use. I already tried."

He shrugged. "Alright." He sat down on the couch in the living area. "Whose dog won't shut up?"

Lindsey walked toward the table and picked up her mug.

"Ash's dog. It's next door, so you'll have to put up with it." She turned her back to him and looked out the window. She drank from her mug.

"It's cool." He looked around. "You know. I haven't really had a good look at this place before." He paused. "There's a lot of...color." He pointed to the kitchen, a small pastel-covered area to the left of the front door. "That's cute." He whistled. "Wow, someone likes music, huh?"

"Yeah. Micah. Do you want something to drink?"

He shook his head. "No, it's fine. How's your brother?"

"Still on his mission trip. Won't be back for four months."

"Ah. Still miss him?"

"Very much."

The barking simmered to the long draws of an unsettled whine. As Lindsey drank from her mug again, the rumbling of the train returned, a persistent *one-two* as the train skated over the uneven, old tracks.

"So why did you call me here, Linds?" He stood up and shed his jacket onto the couch. He walked over to her as he spoke. "Have you missed me?"

She flinched when he placed his cold hands on her shoulders. He touched his lips to the back of her neck and she swore that ice had just touched her skin.

"Alexei, stop."

He stepped back and put his hands up. "Alright, my bad, misread the signals." He crossed his arms. "So, did you need something? Again, why'd you call me here? If you called me here just to get me to read another manuscript, I--"

"No." The train disappeared into the distance. "I wanted you to know that I'm telling Micah about this. About me cheating on him."

After a few moments Alexei shrugged. "Ah. Cool. Just let me know if he comes trying to kick my ass. Was that really it?"

"Yeah. Just letting you know."

"Gotcha. Later, then."

"Sorry for having you make the drive."

"No worries. I was leaving work, you were on the way."

He grabbed his jacket off the couch and headed out. After he opened the door, he stopped.

"Just to clarify: that means we're done, right?"

"Yeah. Sorry."

He shook his head. "Don't be sorry. It was only a few times, so I'm not too broken up. And don't be a stranger. Well, guess that's up for you to decide. Seeya."

The day Marcus touched down in Korea and began his mission trip, Lindsey had approached Alexei. She held a pair of worn-down skates in her hands by the tips of the laces. He stood behind the counter of the rental stand.

"Oh, hey Linds," he said as he shelved a pair of ice skates. "What's up? We're about to close. In fact--" he looked around. "There's no one else around. You need something?"

"I don't know. I'm just kind of, here. Mind if I stay here a little bit?"

"That's fine. I'll just be cleaning up a bit."

"Okay."

Alexei continued to clean the rental stand. "Oh, those some skates? Here, let me put those away."

He reached a hand outward and she moved forward. She dropped the skates and kept walking toward Alexei until her toes touched the stand. Alexei held her gaze.

"...Are you still with Micah?" he asked finally.

She leaned forward and pressed her lips against his. She placed her hand on the side of his neck and felt her clammy palm be chilled by his cold skin.

"My place or yours?" he asked when they finally broke apart.

She tiptoed around the chargers on the floor and turned on the stereo system. She slid her one CD in and sat down, legs crossed, head down. Kanye West's auto-tuned voice struck the silence in the apartment. She listened, and waited for Micah to come home.

DREAMING OF REMBRANDT

Room 2B

THE woman brings me tea and says I have to shower soon. I mumble something about staying up too late and the color of the sun at nighttime. I feel the handrests of the chair I'm sitting in and it doesn't fit into my palms right. It doesn't feel right. I don't feel right.

The woman is so beautiful. But she has gray wrinkles that snake all around her, like someone couldn't stop tracing their fingers over and over her skin. I don't blame them. She is so beautiful. Her eyes remind me of ponds in the wintertime. Her voice is like a clear bell.

She's helping me into the shower when she says, "I'm going to pick up some books later." She takes the ring off my finger and leaves me so I can wash myself, but for a moment I can't. What she just said slings across my brain like a heavy bullet. The water starts and slides down my forehead as I remember.

A little boy in the library is acting out. We bring him stacks and stacks of books, from *Thomas the Tank Engine* to *Leaves of Grass* to *Magic Treehouse* to *Freakonomics*; nothing is sedating him.

"No!" he screams, and kicks at the book of Rimbaud that I offer him. It skids across the floor and settles open on my favorite poem.

"No, no! It's all wrong!" he screams.

The words in the poem jumble and tumble and suddenly it feels like they're choking me so I grab the boy's wrist and I quietly manage to say that we are going home, right at this instant.

I reach for his wrist. No, I'm reaching for the soap. I am showering. I turn the soap over in my hand several times. Slippery. I bring it to my neck. I feel my Adam's apple, and it feels like a cold bruise.

The other guy lands a jab on my throat and for a second I think I've swallowed my mouthpiece. My trainer is screaming at me but all I can hear is my sweat. It's clogging my ears. But then—*ring*. A clear bell sounds from the crowd.

"Beat his ass, Gary! Punch back!"

And now my gloves are made of air and my joints are smoothed over with butter because, damn, I'm gliding across the canvas. My punches are landing, are hitting, his face is pink with anticipation and fear. I'm dancing a quickstep and punch combination that my partner just can't keep up with. Millie, my clear bell, my sole voice in the crowd—goddamn, I love her. She is so beautiful.

I'm crying. The shower tricks me, but I touch the tips of my fingers to my cheeks. I can feel the lines in my skin, the wrinkles, like sagging tallies that weigh me down. The water is hot on my scalp. I turn the temperature down. I bring the soap to my stomach. The water that hits my toes is freezing. Feels like snow. I remember my father making snow angels with me in the middle of the city. Folks passed by, clenching their purses and walking along, and we were just lying down on the sidewalks, carving some damn holiness into the streets.

The gallery is quiet. I am alone. I'm slipping. The light plays off my wet footprints on the granite. I am frozen in place. A self-portrait. The sharp moustache, the craggy face, the slight wilt in his eyes. So much detail. The artist has painted himself so beautifully. My heart rings like a bell, my veins throb along in rhythm.

I turn the shower off.

I wait for the woman to come home. I wait to hear her voice.

BARE BOTTLES

Room 3C

THE city lights are brighter than the moon tonight.

"Alishia," I said. "The last time I saw a sight like this--"

She smirks.

The last time I saw a sight like this, I: was skydiving above Utah at night and I saw the city lights in the distance and I felt like a desert bug in the wind. Was looking out the window of a fiftieth floor office party filled with drunk accountants in some high-rise, and swore I could pluck the lights off their stems. Was on the second highest ridge on Crowtoe Mountain and drew shapes with my finger, and used the lights like stars that waited to be played into constellations.

"--I was drinking second-rate beer with a first-rate friend and we didn't give a crap about anything else."

She laughs. "What, no grandiose line of prose? No memory so shiny it almost seems fake for *some* reason? You must not be drunk enough, Tommy."

I spin stories. I'm better when I'm drunk; Alishia is entirely familiar with all this.

"Just shut up and let's clink our bottles together."

"But that's cliche," Alishia says.

"You know I operate off of concept."

"Eh. Alright."

The necks of our beer bottles touch. I bring the bottle back to my lips.

Alishia and I are frequent visitors to this, the roof of the Crossings. Potted plants hanging on by thin plastic hooks line the railing around the perimeter. Tables and chairs reminiscent of bohemian furniture are placed equal distances apart from one another. A silver flask sits alone on the table right next to Alishia; I recognize it as Pablo's.

I point to it. "Hey Alishia, grab that for me would you? I want to return it to Pablo when I see him."

She turns to where I'm pointing and stretches her arm out to get it. As soon as she grasps it, she tosses it to me. "When do you see Pablo?" she asks as she reaches down to the six-pack of beer on the floor. A pink Post-It note hangs off the edge of it: "Mine!" written in light blue, wavy letters. Alishia brings the drinks; I bring the stories.

"The guys of the Crossings have got to look out for one another. That's just how it is, Alishia."

She laughs. "Okay, Tommy."

"What? I happen to be close with most of the guys in the building."

"There you go again with another one of your stories."

She's right. I follow the night sky's concept--fill the dark space with light, with stars. And space them out evenly. I'm not interested in spitting out reality every time I open my mouth. I prefer repeating what I want out loud until the words worm their way into becoming true.

I visit here often, with or without Alishia. Even if I make the trek alone, though, intent on sipping beer and telling stories to myself, some other resident wanders up here and strikes up a conversation. Norman leans on the railing and looks out to the city and eventually asks if I want pot. Sometimes I accept. Lindsey sits at a chair three tables away and coyly asks if I'll ever make a move on Alishia--I always say no. Millie gestures for me to sit with her and offers me tea and I gratefully share a cup with her. And they always ask me for a story. This is a storytelling roof. And that isn't for someone who's alone.

"Tell me another story, Tommy."

"Okay."

I can remember this. This is true:

I'm 10. It's August 2nd, 1998, and my mother wilts as summer ends. She has laid in this bed so long a garden has grown around her. The soil blankets her. It is a bed of shriveling petals. The green stems sag toward the soil. I pick up a blue petal from the bed-- it's coarse, and there's a thin ring of red-brown on the edges. The soil is dry.

"Mom," my sister repeats, and gently prods her shoulder. Our mother coughs and moves her hair out of her eyes. She turns on her side and looks at us--her hazel eyes are flat.

"What is it, honey?"

"Could you take us to the park?"

"Oh, I don't think so, sweetie. I don't think so. Not today."
She shakes her head and seeds shake free like flakes of dandruff.

She hides her arms underneath her blanket and slowly turns
back to sleep; she seems just a feature on the bed's face now. A flower
that retreats back into the soil.

Anna shakes her head and guides me out of our mother's
bedroom.

"When will mom get better?" I ask her.

"Maybe soon," Anna says. "Dad left a month ago. I think
Mom will be better soon."

"When will her flowers grow back?"

"Her flowers?...sometime soon. I'm going to make her lunch, are you
hungry?"

I shake my head and Anna smiles and punches my arm.
"Alright, just let me know if you change your mind and want
something to eat."

I watch my sister as she walks to the kitchen. I frown when I
hear the angry whisking of egg yolks; too fast, too harsh.

"Anna, are you okay?"

I go into the kitchen. Anna is staring up at the cupboard,
with an arm reaching upward, fingers splaying over nothing.

"I can't reach the pan," she says. "I'm not tall enough."

"...I'm not tall enough either."

"We can't ask Mom. She's too tired. And we can't ask Dad.
Because he's gone," Anna says.

"Do you want to use a chair?"

"Okay."

Anna and I drag a chair into the kitchen. She stands on it and reaches forward to open the cupboard. Then, a creak and a groan; the cupboards shoot upward, growing, like a tree striking against the sky. Two muscled branches shoot off from either side of the trunk.

I squint and I can see it. Etched into the wood is my dad's face. He's holding the pan, up high, clutching it in his wooden hands. We aren't tall enough to reach him.

"...Is that the end?"

I shrug and hold my hand out for another beer.

"Do you know what you need?" Alishia asks me.

"Another beer?"

She laughs. "No, a girlfriend."

I set my bottle down. "...Look, Alishia, I'm flattered, but I like how we are now--as friends."

"Don't flatter yourself Belmont. I'm not confessing my undying love for you."

"Yeah, what? Psh. Totally knew that. Totally...knew that." I take another sip of my drink and she laughs.

"C.J.," she says.

"C.J.?"

"Yeah. You know. Frequented my work a lot? Before I, you know, quit? Brunette? A skin tone that doesn't reveal ethnicity?" She waits for me to show some sign of recognition. "...You know, the one who dances?"

I snap my fingers. "Oh, C.J.! Of course I know C.J. C.J. is great. What, you want to set me up with her?"

"No, my friend." Alishia walks over and throws an arm around my shoulder. "You want me to set you up with her. And you're going to thank me for it."

"What, do you fancy yourself a Miss Foxheart?"

"No one mentioned Miss Foxheart," Alishia snaps.

"Woah, alright, alright," I say, and hold up my hands. "Won't mention her again."

"No, it's...sorry. Just don't mention that love columnist to me again."

"Deal. So, why on the setting me up?"

"Because you're my friend."

"Alishia."

"Because she's my friend, too."

"Alishia."

"No, I'm serious!"

"No, I know, but Alishia--"

"Okay! Fine! A small part of it is also because C.J.'s constant rambles about being single are starting to get to me, Tommy."

"...Alishia, I just wanted to say that I'll do it. I'll go on the date."

"...Oh, you will?"

"Yeah. I think it would be fun. I don't see why not."

"...Great! It's a date then. In return, tell me another story, Belmont. Make it a good one."

I remember this. This is true:

I'm 20 years old. It's June 30th, 2008, and my sister is taking me to Ravenhand Bar to celebrate her Bachelor's degree. This is a celebration just for siblings. She asks me to be 21. I comply.

This is important: she's wearing a green summer dress and her blonde hair is tied up in a bun. I'm wearing a black button-down with the sleeves rolled up.

We walk in with no trouble. The bar is shrouded in a soft, caramel light. Squint and it's like it's night. My sister stops.

"What's wrong, Anna?" I ask.

She points to a scrawny, pasty man wearing a black leather jacket. He's laughing and drinking with two friends in the center booth. "That's Gregory Nowell. He's the drinking champion of the city. Once drank fifty beers in one night." She turns to me. "And he only ended up needing three stomach pumps."

"So?"

She grips my arm. "Tommy. You know your big sister thrives off of competition."

I roll my eyes and gesture toward him. "Go beat him."

An hour later and Anna has Gregory Nowell on the ropes. His bony hand reaches for his fiftieth beer. He is trembling.

A crowd has gathered to watch his dethronement. Anna smirks and snatches the glass before he can take it.

"Final move!" someone shouts.

She gulps it down in one swig and wipes the back of her hand haughtily across her mouth.

"Bye bye," she says, and he faints.

"K.O.!" the same guy shouts, and the bar cheers.

This is big. This is important: a man wearing a green button-down with the sleeves rolled up and with his hair tied in a bun parts the crowd, shoves Gregory Nowell's body out of the booth, and sits across from my sister. He folds his hands together.

"Anna," he says.

She raises an eyebrow. "And who are you?"

"Anna," I say. I point to him. "That's dad."

"Oh. Dad." She shrugs. "What's with the dumb hair?"

"It's how the masters wear it."

"Masters of what?"

"Ten years and that's all you have to say to your father, Anna?"

"She forgot to say, 'Fuck you!'" I yell, and the crowd laughs. I am not laughing. She is laughing.

"Dad," Anna says. "There's something that needs to be done." She jabs her thumb toward me. "This punk needs to kick your ass."

He shakes his head and laughs. "You always put Tommy ahead of you. Alright. What is it?"

"Drinking."

She motions me forward and somehow I am sitting across from my father.

"Tommy," he says.

"Dad," I say.

His skin is tanner and his hair is lighter and I don't have to look up to his face to see his eyes anymore.

I start to open my mouth. He holds up a hand to stop me. "Save it. Let's do it this way: I know you haven't even had a sip of alcohol in your life so far. For every drink you finish, I'll answer a question. Deal?"

"Screw you."

"I guess I'll go then."

He gets up, as if to leave, and lingers. I stare ahead. After a few moments of him waiting for me to ask him to stay, I say, "I've lived 10 years without you. I can keep doing it. So leave, if you want."

He laughs and sits down. "I'll accept the deal for you. You're interesting."

The First Drink: I hold the bottle by the neck with my entire hand and feel clumsy. I read the label: Verta Beer. I close my eyes and the crowd cheers and whistles as I crane the bottle toward my lips. Verta Beer tastes an awful lot like sour copper and dirt. I almost spit and sputter when the first drops touch my tongue. I clench my eyelids firmer and drain the drink. I set the bottle on the table and chase the taste with air.

"Why did you leave?" I immediately ask.

He looks at me as he slurps his entire beer in one sip. "I wanted to travel."

The Second Drink: I grasp the bottle by the body and stare at it. This seems harder than the first one. I tilt my head back ninety degrees and pour it in my mouth. The crowd laughs, but it works.

"Why didn't you come back?" I ask before I even bring my head back down.

He drinks his beer in one go again. "Forgot to come back."

I have to stop myself from kicking his ass.

The Twelfth Drink: I drink it in one go. But as I set the bottle down, I miss the table and place it on my leg. I am dumbfounded that my leg is not the table.

"Where's the pan?" I ask, and as my vision fades, he smirks, and Anna calls my name.

"What is it with you and cliffhangers?"

I shrug. "I don't like endings."

"Did you and Anna really run into your dad?"

I play with the lid of Pablo's flask. No more beer. I picture scooping up each of the lights in the city with the flask, filling it to the brim with those electric juices, and giving it to Pablo and telling him it's the white light from the stars.

"Yeah."

There is a fine line between storytelling and lying. When I tell people grand narratives about fighting lions or enjoying a drink with Clinton or scaling the Eiffel Tower, I spark laughter out of their lungs or gleams in their eyes. But my father didn't tell stories--he spun together lies and excuses to explain his disappearance. When he approached me in that bar, all I could think about at first was that insurmountable tree, taunting me.

His first words to me in ten years: "Tyler, buy your old man a beer and I can tell you all about my charity work. Which is why I had to leave. Sorry about that."

Alishia excuses herself; she has work tomorrow. She reminds me about my date with C.J., and after she's gone, I just look at the lights.

THREE NIGHTS:
OR, WHAT WOULD RASKOLNIKOV DO?

Room 3D

MICAH got drunk.

Night #1

He broke into the ice rink. No, no; he snuck in. No, better yet, he went to the locksmith and got a key forged and *walked* in.

Micah considered his options. He dragged his finger along the thin film of wet frost on the rink's front door. He rounded the shape into a crooked triangle and wiped his hand on his pants.

He wanted closure. That's why he had the bag of salt. He was indecisive and unclear about how he wanted to get back at her when, boom, he had it: what would Raskolnikov do?

He wasn't going to kill her, nothing nearly that insane. The bag of salt worked just fine. Granted, it was only half a bag of salt since Norman found it that morning and said he needed "some of it for something super important." But half-closure was better than none.

He just didn't know which way to go about it. Did he want to live an action movie and force his way into the rink, damn the consequences? Did he want to slink his way into the building, smooth and silent, like James Bond? Or like a puma? Or did he want to get the damn thing over with and just get a key made?

Well, it didn't really make sense to get a key made. It would take too much time and money. And he had no idea where a locksmith would be, too. And Micah had lost all ability to be any semblance of smooth after Lindsey broke up with him.

Right. So he'd break in.

"Micah? Micah, what are you doing here?"

Micah was staring. He'd lost himself in thought, and forgotten that he was standing in front of a glass door. A Cors Glacies employee peered at him from behind the door.

"How do you know my name?" Micah finally said.

The employee took a step forward. Micah recognized the blonde hair. "Alexei," he said.

Alexei nodded, but looked away. "Can you see out there?"

Micah shrugged. "It's only kind of dark."

"Ah. So what are you doing here? It's been an hour since we closed. Do you need something?"

Micah used his right foot to push the bag of salt further away from the door. He hoped Alexei didn't notice. "I think I left something here earlier."

"Oh. What'd you leave?"

"My wallet. Can I come in and look for it?"

"...Yeah. Yeah, sure, of course."

Alexei unlocked the door. Micah waited for him to turn his back before he reopened the bag of salt and shoved handfuls of it into his hoodie and pants pockets. He quickly went inside.

Alexei was at the rental stand, moving around skates and looking over and under everything.

"What's your wallet look like? Maybe we can find it quickly."

"It's, um, black. Yeah. Say, what are you doing here?"

"Oh, uh...well, sometimes if I'm free after work and I'm done cleaning up, I, uh..." He sighed. "I like to ride the Zamboni around. You know. For fun, or whatever."

Micah laughed. "Hey, that's funny."

"Yeah. Thanks."

A silence followed as Alexei looked around and Micah stood, hands in pockets, trying quickly to find an excuse to be left alone so he could find his half-closure. He felt a heat work its way around his body like a silent river streaming through his veins.

"So how are you feeling?" Alexei asked.

"...What, you mean after the break-up?" Micah kept himself from slurring his words.

"Yeah. Yeah. After the break-up."

"How'd you know?"

"Lindsey...mentioned it."

Micah grinned. "I forgot you two were close. Listen, Alexei, could you be straight up with me for a second?"

Alexei stood still for a moment before standing straight and looking over at Micah. "What's up?"

Micah let go of the salt and brought his hands out of his pockets. He blinked a few times. He looked back at Alexei and held his gaze. "Do you know who she cheated on me with?"

Alexei rubbed the back of his neck. "I'm not sure. "

Micah nodded and shoved his hands back into his pockets. "Ah, well, that's alright."

"Do...do you have any guesses?" Alexei asked.

Micah shrugged. "None."

"Ah."

Silence returned. Alexei left the stand. "I don't think your wallet's in there."

"Could you possibly check the bathroom while I check the stands, out there by the rink?"

Alexei nodded and headed off to the bathroom. Micah walked over to the door that led to the rink and sighed when the cool air greeted him. He traced the curvature of the rink over and over with his eyes, two pupils skating like ice dancers. He was torn—should he do it?

Then the pain hit him in the lungs again, like a heavy smack. And he wasn't torn anymore.

"We'll always have Cors Glacies, my ass," Micah muttered. He walked up to the entrance to the ice. He held on to the railing and took a tentative step onto the ice. And then another. He walked forward an inch at a time before he finally settled, a few feet away from the entrance. He took a handful of salt out of each pocket.

"Fuck you, Lindsey," he said, and threw the salt onto the ice. The small white flecks shimmered across the ice. He reached into his pockets again for two more handfuls.

"Fuck you. Fuck this place. Fuck us meeting here," he said with each toss of salt.

With each toss of salt he replayed the moment he met her here over and over. Tripping over her skates, falling down onto the ice, meeting her steely gaze with his own; he didn't want to hold onto that. He wanted to erase it. He wanted to take his frostbitten hands off that icy memory; he wanted to stop cradling it like some precious thing while it hurt him.

"I wish. I had. More salt," he said, punctuating each clause with the last of the salt.

"Micah, what the fuck are you doing?"

Micah started and fell. He hit his head on the ice. He looked up and saw Alexei rush over before slowly stepping onto the ice. Alexei tiptoed over to him and, once he reached him, knelt down to help him up.

"Again, what the fuck are you doing?"

Micah dusted the salt off his hands and smiled at Alexei. "Oh, I don't know, Alexei. Closure, I guess." He sighed.

Alexei watched his face for a few moments. "Listen, Micah…"

"Oh, and I didn't really leave my wallet here. I just, I don't' know. I thought that if I came here, and if I fucked it over, I'd be better. Because, I don't know if you knew this, but we met here. And, the salt, and sneaking in…I don't know." Micah sighed again and put his head in his hands. "Sorry, Alexei. I didn't mean to bring you any trouble."

"Micah, it was me."

"What?"

"Lindsey cheated on you with me."

Four seconds passed before Micah swung at him. Alexei fell back onto his hands and avoided being hit. He tried standing up and fell onto his front. Micah tried standing too and fell also. Alexei crawled back toward the entrance and Micah followed him, tucked toward the ground like a cadet under barb wire, inching toward his target quickly.

"Why the fuck would you tell me that," Micah said, breathing heavily against the ice.

"I'm sorry," Alexei said, and yelped out of surprise when Micah reached forward and grabbed his ankle.

"Come the fuck here," Micah said.

Alexei pulled his leg forward and they both tried standing up. They stumbled and slipped and fell. Over and over.

Micah slammed the door behind him as he entered Room 3D. The sight of Norman in Camel Pose greeted him.

"Hey there, roomie," Norman said. "Did you pick up the milk? And what's with that c-razy black eye?" He let go of his heels and straightened his back.

"Fell onto ice a lot. Tried to fight a guy. Salt."

"Ah, we've all been there, buddy."

"Listen, Norman," Micah said, and sat down on the couch. He looked around the apartment—almost identical to his old one with Lindsey, save for the lack of shelves of albums—and then back at Norman, who was sweaty, and bore a pearly smile.

"You have no idea how much it means that you're letting me crash here for just a little while."

"Mmhmm."

"But this isn't going to be a permanent thing."

"Mmhmm."

"Because, like, I've got prospects."

"Mmhmm."

"Living prospects, I mean."

"I hear you, man, I hear you."

"Good. I guess I just wanted to make sure we were both clear on this."

"Got you loud and clear, big man. Listen, can you see out of that thing?"

"I'm gonna go to bed, Norman. And please don't do your usual 'morning salutations.' I'll be hungover." He took off his jacket, bundled it up, and placed it beneath his head as a pillow.

"Got you loud and clear, big man."

Norman's salutations woke him up.

"Oh my god, Norman, why," Micah groaned, and sat up on the couch.

"The sun deserves to be greeted every day, roomie," Norman said.

"I asked you not to do your damn morning salutations."

"I'm not!...These are my afternoon salutations." Norman took a deep breath. "Salutations, afternoon sun!" he bellowed.

Micah rubbed his temple and checked his phone.

"So, this guy you tried to fight. Did you kick his ass?"

"No, he calmed me down and sent me home. Said we'll talk about this shit another time. Hold on, I got a text," Micah said.

He had a text from Ash.

Hey bud. I know we haven't talked in awhile, and a lot of that is my fault, and I'm sorry, but Jessica broke up with me. and I figured you'd understand what I'm feeling rn, so could you come to my apartment?

Micah was torn. He wanted to stay home and rest and get some peace and quie—

"SALUTATIONS AFTERNOON SUN, THE SON OF THE MORNING SUN!" Norman bellowed.

"Norman, I'll be back later."

"MMHMM."

Ash opened the door. Micah was there with two books in hand. He smiled and handed them to Ash.

"Hey, buddy. Brought you some stuff. How you feeling?"

Ash sniffed. "Not so good."

Night #2

"And the other one is *Howl*," Micah said. "There's some other of Ginsberg's poems in there too, but that's the main one."

Ash smiled and set it down on the table. "Thanks. Thanks so much, Micah. This means a lot."

"No, yeah, no problem. I just know that that poem really helped initially after my break-up. So, where are Jason and Roland?"

He looked around the apartment. An empty dog cage sat a few feet away. An Xbox was underneath their television, and on the dining table placed near the windows were piles and piles of papers. The sight of Ash's manuscripts reminded Micah of Lindsey's own writing. He took in how messy the place was, but didn't mind it. He'd just gotten too used to Norman's minimalist lifestyle.

"They're out of town for some research project."

"Are you guys still going to Lucida?"

"Yeah."

"So how long were you with Jessica?"

"About seven months," Ash said. He sighed and his glasses fell down the bridge of his nose. "Seven long months."

"These next few weeks are going to feel even longer, friend."

"I know."

"Listen, no matter what you think, we're good friends, okay? Whatever you need, I'm here. Don't blame yourself for us not talking that much lately," Micah said.

"I think all I really need right now is friends," Ash said. "You know? Friends, they make so much shit better and worth it. You get what I'm saying? There's nothing as beautiful—" He sniffed. "—As two people who can make each other smile."

"Yeah, buddy. I'll try."

"Thanks so much. And, Micah?"

"Yeah?"

"What's with the black eye?"

"Thanks for coming, man."

Micah nodded. "No problem. I had a lot of fun. I didn't think we'd finish all those *Top Chef* episodes, but, hoo boy, we...we sure did."

"Listen, Micah, before you go."

Micah finished putting on his jacket and looked over at Ash. Ash sniffed and rubbed the back of his neck. He muttered something.

"What was that?" Micah asked.

"Do you...sorry, this is kind of embarrassing, but...do you mind sleeping over tonight?"

"...Ash, we're both grown men."

"I know! I know. But with Jason and Roland gone, this is my first time really alone in the apartment for awhile. And they took Plato with them, so I really am alone. And I just really don't want to be by myself right now."

Eventually Micah sighed and took his jacket off. "I said I'd be there for you, so...no. I don't mind sleeping over."

"Thanks, man. I'll set up a place for you here on the couch."

Ash moved a few of his manuscripts from the cushions to the table and brought a blanket over to the couch. "Sorry, we don't have any more pillows. Roland and Jason took theirs with them."

"It's fine," Micah said and bunched his jacket together. He laid down on the couch and put it beneath his head. "Good nig—"

"Wait." Ash quickly went to his room. After a few moments he reemerged with a pillow and his own blanket. He laid down on the floor and wrapped himself in the blanket.

"Ash, what are you doing?"

"I thought it'd be easier for us to talk this way."

"I mean, I guess."

"So, how are you? After you break-up, I mean?" Ash asked. Micah adjusted his position on the couch and looked up at the ceiling.

"Shit man, I'm tired. Like, all I ever am nowadays is exhausted. I don't have the energy to do anything. And I don't even want to do anything. I used to love music so much and I haven't listened to a song in days. You know?"

Silence.

"You fell asleep, didn't you?" Micah asked.

Night #3

How does someone sleep for 19 hours? Micah stared at Ash's slumbering body. He checked his watch: 7:32 p.m. Yep, 19 hours. Micah scratched his head and sighed. He had to admit, he was annoyed. Not just because an old friend asked him to spent the night and swiftly fell asleep soon after, but also because there was a constant dripping sound that he could not find the source to.

Drip. Drip. Micah clutched at his head. He pictured getting an axe and cutting up whatever was making that damn sound.

He knew he was being extreme. It was just that kind of time for him right now.

He poked Ash's body. He groaned and turned over in his sleep. A smear of drool laced his chin. Micah recoiled. Gross.

"Jessica...why...the pans..." Ash muttered.

Pans? Micah mouthed to himself.

He decided to leave. He slowly got up and pulled his jacket on. He tiptoed over to the door and put his hand on the knob when, suddenly, it opened from the outside.

"What the fuck," Micah said, surprised.

Roland peered in. "Micah? Shit man, you robbing us?"

"Whatever you do, don't take Roland's stuffed bear that he talks to at night, oh please, not that, it's totally not a pain in my ass," Jason said from behind Roland.

Roland looked back at him. "The fuck man, you eavesdropping on me and Mr. Fuzzbottom?" He shook his head at Jason. "Can't believe you, man."

He looked at Micah and walked inside. "For real, what's up? What are you doing in our apartment?"

Micah pointed at Ash. Ash whimpered in his sleep. Jason walked in behind Roland, with Plato in hand. Plato barked.

Suddenly Ash's eyes opened and he shot out of bed. He saw his roommates and immediately laughed and smiled.

"Guys!" He said excitedly. "You're...you're back! You're back from your long journey!"

Jason let Plato down onto the floor. He and Roland stared at Ash. "Bro, we just were in the city for a conference," Jason said.

"I know!"

Micah stepped back and watched the three of them as they talked. Ash seemed better already. The smile on his face seemed like it'd always been there.

"Nothing as beautiful as someone who can make you smile, eh Ash?" Micah said, quietly, to himself. He left.

"Norman?"

Micah walked in. Norman looked up from the ground; he was filling empty Girl Scouts cookie boxes with the salt he'd taken.

"...I told you. It was super important."

Micah waved a hand. "It's fine. Listen, I 've got to ask you something. Do you..." He muttered the rest.

Norman got up. "What was that, friend?"

Micah rubbed the back of his neck and muttered it again.

"Jesus, w'sup with everyone mumbling things nowadays? Speak up, buddy! Let the moon hear you!"

"...Do you mind if we make this living arrangement a little more permanent?"

CRITIQUES FOR LINDSEY

Room 2D

FIRST, I'd like to say thanks for coming to me with your work. I was surprised. I almost thought you were messing with me. I guess someone told you I minored in Creative Writing in college. But when I asked if it was a joke that you wanted my help and you shrugged and reached forward to take the pieces back, I knew you weren't kidding! I'm pretty sure you called me Alyssa, too, so just to clear things up, my name is *Alishia,* not Alyssa. But I get that we haven't talked enough for you to have it down pat!

Second, I couldn't help but still think it was a joke when I finally noticed the sheer amount of work you'd given me. Micah said that your work usually spans only two to three pages, so 20 pages surprised me. I guess I didn't realize you'd be giving me several stories. But whatever, once I dove into it, it was so easy to get through all the work! Sometimes it was hard to get through it, but that's only because Norman lives in the room above me and that day he found his lost karaoke machine. I swear, if I have to listen to his screechy rendition of Poison's "Every Rose Has Its Thorn" one more time, I'll show him how many thorns I have.

Anyway, enough of that. I'll get right to your work.

Critique of "Manufactured, Distributed"

The hook here is fantastic. I mean, "He was manufactured and distributed under the authority of The Coca-Cola Company." That's just a great line. I wish I could hook people like that. You can really tell that this character, this Bill Perkins, is so cookie-cutter and yet so eccentric at the same time. He "goes through the same motions, the same people, the same sodas," and yet breaks that routine when he "found himself drinking a can of Diet Pepsi." You give us this character who is predictable and normal on the surface, yet continuously and unknowingly defies his own personal codes of conduct.

While I appreciate this, I don't quite understand the part when the piece moves from exploring Bill's unsatisfying home life to the interior psyche of his boss, Flummox Hayworthy. You spend about three paragraphs exploring the origin of Flummox's name, detailing the long trek his mother had made in Tibet, explaining to us both her mindset and how it was shaped by the epiphanies her journey had given her. And while those three paragraphs alone were some of the most tearjerking lines I've read in a while, it just doesn't make sense in context. You go into this piece reading about Bill and, in the middle of it, end up reading about how "Diane Hayworthy didn't find peace. She simply found something to give to her son. Two syllables that streamed in and out of her head as the snow blistered her fingers and toes: Flummox."

Personally I can relate. I can very much relate to both Bill and to Flummox. In Bill I see how I tend to remove myself from my actions. I tell myself I'm a certain person who acts a certain way when really I'm constantly breaking that definition of myself. Just the other day I was on Miss Foxheart's site—I'm not sure if you're familiar with her, she's a love columnist—and I was *obsessing* over her responses to people. I kept thinking, *What, why would you say that!* and *I would answer with something so much better*, and it surprised me when I realized how caught up I was in my dislike for this person. I always thought I was someone who loved everybody.

And in Flummox I can see how we're constantly being both lifted up and brought back down by our pasts. His mother's humble past is what helped him attain this tremendous level of success as an exec for Coca-Cola, and yet that same humble past is what drives him paranoid as to whether or not he's living life the right way. We're both young, Lindsey—I see what's going on there. In our 20s, and neither of us have "stable" careers. Neither of us are living the "right" way, so to speak. Writers and painters had their time; it's so much harder now. Just the other day I was staring at all my blank canvases and dreamed about what it'd been like to have thrived as a painter in the Renaissance. You touch a lot on how Bill's capabilities are, in the grand scheme, useless and forgettable—I disagree. If we dwell on calling what we do minutiae, why would anyone do anything?

But I think Bill brings himself, Flummox, and the reader peace when he resigns. It's not entirely logical, but it doesn't have to be to touch the reader in the way that it does. How he "entered that room. Told Flummox about the Diet Pepsi, the dreams, the guilt, all of it, and resigned. Flummox sat silently and absorbed the information. And Bill bade farewell to that silent room, and to that factory, and to Coca-Cola."

Beautiful stuff. Incoherent at times, but beautiful nonetheless. I suggest reworking the timeline of the work.

Critique of "Thermometer People"

I'll admit it: I was closed off to this story while I was first reading it. I'm not great at strange things. Truthfully, I am okay with strange content, but it's hard for me to enjoy it. My friend, with whom I like to carpool, kept playing an audiobook of a work by an author named David Wong—I'm pretty sure I avoided riding in his car for a while because he was still listening to it.

It's a strange concept, even for flash fiction, which is traditionally bizarre: thermometer people living in a world all too similar to ours, with the exception that humanity doesn't exist. It was a little jarring that you even came up with a new language; especially because you didn't provide any translations. I mean, when the dialogue is mostly "!!@!!!???@@huhuhuhu," responded with "GGGgggQQQ12," it's hard to grasp emotion or motivation from that.

I'll admit this as well: this piece taught me to be a little less high-strung, and to relax. Pablo and Norman and Tommy...alright, *everybody* in Crossings pretty much gets on me for those few times when I have a stick up my butt. But I think I'm slowly learning to accept things as they are.

I mean other than the fact that I had to make myself okay with reading this strange story, the relationship between Clinka and Tormoto is such a fresh spin on the classic story of love versus lust. It made me question my own romantic and unromantic priorities. He loves her, she lusts for him, where do they meet in between? It was fascinating, to say the least. Guess those thermometer people have a lot to offer. Other than what the temperature is, I mean.

The images were beautiful, too. You really showed us how "their slim glass bodies bobbed in the streets like bottlenose dolphins breaking surface to look at the sun," how "Clinka's red mercury shot up; a climb in the temperature, the climate, the heat between them."

I noticed that your narrator was very tough on Clinka for indulging her sexual desires rather than falling in love with Tormoto. I'm not too sure Clinka deserved that.

Overall, interesting read. Definitely opened my eyes to some things.

Last Critique, for "There Are No Towers Here"

I couldn't help but see a lot of residents here in this piece. I know the setting is different from the Crossings we live in—hell, a stranded island couldn't be more different—but in each of those survivors, I saw someone from this complex.

Geraldo, the fireman from California who handled the cooking and soothed all the kids: so clearly Pablo from Room .

Thomas, the forgetful old man, and Linda, his jaded yet loving wife: Millie and Gary from Room

On and on I saw parallels. (Don't think I didn't notice the jabs you took at mine! "Crystal sobbed into the sand. "How am I going to paint now?" she cried." Don't worry, I know it's all in good fun. Hopefully.)

I don't have much to say about this one. It so perfectly mimics this building and its people that there's not much more you could do. I can't help but chuckle at all their different attempts to escape the island. And it was even more amusing to see Chuck, the wandering mischief so similar to our Norman, be content with the idea of living forever on that island.

I think the last line sums it up perfectly: "To look at the sky, truly and ardently, to drink and smell and feel it, to know the people around you; to rest easy, and see that there are no towers here."

Thanks again for letting me read your work. Happy to do it again if you ever want me to. I always have my red pen ready!

-Alishia

REPROPOSE

Room 3C

Everything was perfect. All of our friends and family were in our apartment, hiding behind the couch or in closets. "This is going to be good," Aunt Ginger whispered to my mom. Aunt Ginger took a flask out of her shirt and took a sip. "So proud of you," my mom whispered to me. I nodded. Today was the day. On the dining table were candles and two plates of Dinah's favorite food: waffles. Roses lay across the waffles. "You look good," Dinah's dad whispered, peeking out from underneath the piles of pillows on the couch. "Thanks," I said, and took a moment to admire my clothes. I was wearing my favorite slacks, nice dress shoes, and on top, a cheesy shirt from mine and Dinah's fifth date; it had our names on it, with a heart around them. "She'll love the shirt," he said, and I thanked him again and he disappeared back under the pillows. "Is the hiding necessary?" my brother asked urgently, wobbling back and forth. "What's your problem?" I asked, and he mouthed the word 'hungry.' I chuckled. I looked back at the table--the candles were still okay. I heard the doorknob jiggle. I hushed everyone. Dinah stepped through and everyone jumped out all at once. "Surprise!" they shouted. Dinah screamed. We all laughed. "What is this?" Dinah asked. Everyone else just smiled, not answering. They all looked to me. "What is this, sweetie?" Dinah asked me. "Actually, more importantly: why are you wearing *that shirt?*" I got down on one knee. She covered her mouth with her hands. "No..." she said. "Yes," I said, and smiled. I took a deep breath. "Dinah..." I started. Someone screamed. I turned around and saw that the tablecloth was on fire. My brother stood in the dining room, waffle in mouth, looking guilty. "Someone put out the fire!" Dinah shouted. "What happened!" I urgently asked my brother. He chewed the rest of the waffle, swallowed, and mouthed the word 'candles.' "Your brother always does this," Dinah seethed. "I'll never be able to handle him, Joey," she said. I grimaced.

Everything was perfect. I was about to light some candles and put them on the table, but decided against it. "This is going to be good," Aunt Ginger whispered to my mom. Aunt Ginger took a flask out of her shirt and took a sip. "So proud of you," my mom whispered to me. I nodded. Today was the day. I double-checked the waffles, poking them: as fluffy as a cloud. "Those look good..." my brother said, and I shook my head. "Not for you, Mark." "You look good," Dinah's dad whispered, peeking out from underneath the piles of pillows on the couch. "Thanks, I said. "She'll love the shirt," he said, and he disappeared back under the pillows. I heard the doorknob jiggle. I hushed everyone. Dinah stepped through and everyone jumped out all at once. "Surprise!" they shouted. Dinah screamed. We all laughed. "What is this?" Dinah asked. Everyone else just smiled, not answering. They all looked to me. "What is this, sweetie?" Dinah asked me. "Actually, more importantly: why are you wearing *that shirt?*" I got down on one knee. She covered her mouth with her hands. "No..." she said. "Yes," I said, and smiled. I took a deep breath. In the background I heard someone loudly chewing; I ignored it.

"Dinah..." I started. Someone screamed. I turned around and saw my brother on the floor, He was convulsing, mouth full with something. "Your brother's choking" Dinah urgently said. "Joey, do something!" "It must've been the peanut butter in the waffle mix," I said. "Shit, where's his EPI pen?" I searched his pockets and found nothing. I looked into Mark's eyes. "You're going to be okay, bud, alright?" I looked away. "Someone call 911!"

Everything was perfect. I left the candles unlit and in the drawer. "Aw, no food?" Mark asked, complaining. "We'll eat afterwards, don't worry. I made a reservation at Honcho's." "This is going to be good," Aunt Ginger whispered to my mom. Aunt Ginger took a flask out of her shirt and took a sip. "So proud of you," my mom whispered to me. I nodded. Today was the day. "You look good," Dinah's dad whispered, peeking out from underneath the piles of pillows on the couch. "Thanks, I said. "She'll love the shirt," he said, and he disappeared back under the pillows. I heard the doorknob jiggle. I hushed everyone. Dinah stepped through and everyone jumped out all at once. "Surprise!" they shouted. Dinah screamed. We all laughed. "What is this?" Dinah asked. Everyone else just smiled, not answering. They all looked to me. "What is this, sweetie?" Dinah asked me. "Actually, more importantly: why are you wearing *that shirt?*" I got down on one knee. She covered her mouth with her hands. "No..." she said. "Yes," I said, and smiled. I took a deep breath. In the background I heard someone loudly chewing; I ignored it. "Dinah..." I started. "Wait, wait," Aunt Ginger said, stepping forward. She hung an arm around Dinah's shoulders and pointed to my shirt. She took another sip from her flask. "Aunt Ginger, what--" "Dinah! This man. This man here, he takes after my husband." She paused. "My ex-husband. That bastard. You know why?" She pointed at my shirt again. "Me and my ex, we had a shirt *just like that.* And with that shirt, that bastard promised me forever. Well guess what? We didn't have forever!" Aunt Ginger said, and started wailing. "Geoff, you bastard, come back here!" she said, shouting at the air. "Um, Aunt Ginger--" She vomited on Dinah's shoes.

Everything was perfect. The apartment was empty; there were candles everywhere; roses littered the floor. Paper lanterns were strung around the living room. The doorknob jiggled and Dinah walked in. "Joey, what is this?" she asked. I got down on one knee. "Dinah, will you marry me?" She looked at me. Then she looked around the room, and sniffed the air. She smiled. "Waffles?" "Yeah, waffles." Still smiling, she shrugged. "No one makes em like you, babe." She took a step toward me. "Yes. Yes. So many times, every time, yes. I thought you'd never ask."

Everything was perfect.

DOWN THE HALL

Room 1A

I'VE grown tired of counting.

Mr. Pent, who had a receding hairline and a kind face, was the first to offer his condolences. I let him inside and he spent a few minutes offering kindness and empathy in his open palms, but put his hands in his pockets when he saw I wasn't interested. He advised me to repaint the walls, to open the windows more, to fix the stubborn faucet he knew wouldn't drip properly. Told me I should fill the shelves Micah left. I thanked him. Then he left.

That was a week ago, maybe. I'd towed a half-dying mattress into the room and let it rest in the middle of the floor. The walls were an eerie red. I didn't notice it before when Micah still lived here, but sometimes, if I angled my view correctly, the sunlight would sneak a shine onto the walls and make it seem as if the paint were dripping down, streaks of red. It was unsettling.

Everyone in the Crossings has offered their condolences now. Pablo came to my doorstep with tequila and his warm, amber eyes. Melanie and Patrick baked me muffins and invited me to dinner. Their daughter Zola hugged me when I came over. Tommy told me a few stories on the roof to pass the time. Even Micah stopped by, to hug me, to talk. To ask how I was doing.

My routine has been this: open my eyes. Rise from the mattress. Put on coffee. Slip into the shower. Let the water bite my bony body. Throw on clothes and read. Write. Tap a few words onto a Word document then backspace until it returns to an empty page. Eat. Pour the stale coffee down the drain. And then I'd lay on the mattress, and if I couldn't sleep, I counted.

I didn't count stars or sheep. The stars pricked the sky like breaks in its blue skin. Hooves bothered me. Instead, I counted the normalities of my body.

I ran a finger over my nose and cherished the slender bridge of bone: one nose. I slid a thumb over my eyebrows, noting the gap between them: two eyebrows. I traced my lips with my forefinger, gently pressing in and out of the flesh: two lips. This would go on for hours: neck, two breasts, one stomach, two spindly legs, and a tailbone that poked against the skin like a surprise. The tips of my fingers climbed the notches in my spine and I would sigh in relief at the straightness of it all. I could only sleep once I had been sure that my health, my body, was assured. No changes. No breaks. A strange sameness that made the firm back of the mattress seem worth sinking into.

But I was tired of counting. I was tired of not having faith. I was tired of feeling like a fresh leaf waiting to be quietly torn to bits by the wind.

A confident knock came at the door. I rose from the mattress.

"Yes?" I called out.

"Yes, hi, is there a Lindsey here? I'm a neighbor of yours." The voice was cheery but hesitant, and came muffled through the door.

I peered through the peephole. It warped my neighbor's face, but she had a friendly smile.. I adjusted my clothes, straightening up. I opened the door.

"Can I help you?"

She beamed at me. I had to keep from slightly recoiling; her teeth were a stark white. I kept the door only slightly open. She held a small brown paper bag in one hand; it made me slightly suspicious.

"Hi, name's Jessie." She cocked her head toward down the hall. "I live four doors down, in 1C. Could I come in?"

"...Why?"

There was a silence. She shifted her weight between her feet. "I'd like to talk, if that's fine."

"I'd prefer if we talked here, if that's okay."

"Oh. That's fine. Well...I know you've probably gotten this a lot lately, but I'm sorry about your brother. I really. I know this is kind of weird because we pass by each other all the time and never really say anything, and we've only talked a few times, but I really am sorry."

"Thank you."

She looked at what she was holding and offered it.

"I was in Italy a few months ago and I got a bunch of souvenirs and, well, I happened to have some extras. I just wanted to give this to you." Her hand fumbled around inside the bag she was carrying and she brought out a small candle. It was a soft tint of purple. Her hand crossed the door, offering the candle. I took it and held it to my chest.

"...Thank you. That was very thoughtful."

"No problem at all. It's supposed to have been made using oranges found only in southern Italy, or something like that. I'm pretty sure there's orange, lavender, jasmine...I'm not too sure, all I know is it smells pretty good."

"Thank you, Jessie."

She stood there, staring at me. I waited for her to say something.

"What?" I asked.

"Are you alright?"

"Look, Jessie, thank you for the candle, but I really don't--"

"Sorry! Sorry! I'll leave you be. Hope to see you around."

"...Yeah. See you."

I closed the door as she started to walk away.

I dipped deeper into the bathtub. The tip of my nose touched the surface of the water.

The bathroom was small. The floor was made up of sterile blue tiles; there was a smudged window and I could make out the sun blurring into the horizon. The sun was a slurry of oranges and yellows, giving the sky one last flare of color before it would turn dark. I could make out the linings of the railroad, not too far from the building. It was strange to think that Miles would watch this sight as well. On the windowsill was a candleholder, and in that holder was the candle Jessie had given me. I was still suspicious as to why she would go out of her way to give me the candle, but I finally gave in and lit it. I sniffed it.

The scent was strong and fast and Marcus. It smelled like Marcus. It was citrus, it was lavender, it was beautiful, and it was Marcus.

I stared at the floor, at the lines of dirt in between the tiles. I wanted to hide there. I wanted to collect between two sturdy tiles and be kept in place, immoveable, against my own choice even.

The water didn't feel cold anymore. It felt warm. I clenched my fists; my skin was wrinkled, pink and old at the same time, warped and seemingly not fully formed. I thought of Marcus and how his skin would never wrinkle with age. My eyes and lungs felt heavy. My eyes were heavy with water. My lungs were heavy with thick, thick air. The warmth of the water surrounded my body. I hugged my knees tightly and bit my lip. I wouldn't cry.

The sun slipped below the distance and the light was gone. Suddenly a hoarse whistle struck the air. I recoiled, but immediately relaxed. It was the train. I sat, unmoving in the water, as the train passed by, the bumps in the railroad putting out a constant two-beat thud, a constant *one, two, one, two*. Steady. I closed my eyes. The scent of the candle was still present, and I imagined it snaking around the air, an orange and lilac cord that settled around me. It was comforting.

Eventually, the train rumbled into the distance. But silence didn't come back.

Voices and sounds filtered through the walls of my apartment. Ash's dog hammered at the silence with his barking. Above me, C.J. was watching the news with the volume turned up. People walked and skipped on their floors, their footsteps were so heavy. So loud.

I counted.

Two shoulders, two arms. I pressed my hands together before I tapped my fingertips against one another. Two hands, ten fingers. I rubbed my wrists together. Two wrists. I was still together. I was alive.

I had just finished writing when I heard a soft crumple at the door. I turned around and saw that a stack of mail had been slipped under the door. Mr. Pent must have noticed I wasn't going out to get my mail. I silently thanked him and went to retrieve the pile. I bent down and picked it up; it was thin, loose, sparse. Barely much. I flicked through the first few, uninterested. But then a letter from Mom caught my eye. I tossed the others to the floor and brought her letter with me to my mattress. I sat down carefully, very aware of what was in my hands.

She had scrawled my name on the front with rich blue ink: Lindsey Paperman. She didn't dot the i. The envelope was slightly thick. I was curious. I opened it and two pieces of paper fell out onto my mattress, folded over several times. One was written on yellow notebook paper; the other, crisp white printer paper. I picked up the former first, careful to not rip the yellow paper as I unfolded it. The writing was in red ink, and sloppy. Whoever wrote the note did so with shaky hands.

Mom and Dad--

Please send this to Lindsey. For some reason, I can't remember her address for the life of me. Thanks!

Lindsey--

Things are going well. Only nine more months and I get to see you again! We're heading to the city soon for our next stop. Hope all is well. I'll be sending a pack of Pokemon cards soon. I know you outgrew the stuff, but they look gorgeous. I'm sure they'll inspire some next writing piece.

Love,

Marcus

I didn't bother reading the other letter. I already knew what Mom's letter would say: *We miss your brother. We miss you. Please come home, even if just for a little bit.* Something like that. Something like that. I guess this was their latest attempt--I kept blocking their calls. I didn't want to sob more over my brother. Talking to them would only make it worse. I knew they would visit eventually, though, if I kept avoiding them.

I walked to the bathroom, clutching the note in one hand. I slowly turned the tub's spigot on. I turned it off when the tub was half-full. I undressed. I stepped into the water and lowered myself down until my back was against the porcelain. I stared at the note before turning on the faucethead. The water was hot. I held the note under the stream of water, watching as its form changed. The water made it limp. The yellow note sagged in my hand as I held it. Eventually it was drained of its color; the skin of the paper seemed like a yellow ghost. I didn't flinch once the water forced a rip in the paper. I let the water stream down until the note was unrecognizable, just soggy bits and shreds of my brother's letter.

The last light of the day struck itself against the bathroom's window. With the setting of the sun, my brother's last words settled at the bottom of the tub. The sun hit the horizon with a heavy thud, and eventually the sky went dark. I drained the tub and ignored the clumps of paper that stuck to the porcelain curves.

I lay flat on the mattress. I wanted to sleep.I didn't count stars because they were like gleaming cuts. I looked at my hand, at my feet, at my stomach. I was so pale. My veins were bundled in scrawny blue lines; it almost looked like they were poking out of my skin. I counted the parts of my body not to fall asleep, but to make sure I was alive. Sometimes I think I'm not alive, and that I've just forgotten I've already joined my brother.

I sipped at my tea and relit the candle. I watched the train rumble in the distance. I listened to the voicemail that Alexei left me: *Hey, just wanted to see if you're okay, if you need anything...*

A knock came at the door. I got up to answer it. When I opened it, Jessie stood there. She bounced on her heels, waved, and said, "Hi!"

I couldn't help but smile. "Hello, Jessie. How can I help you?"

"Well I had some takeout, and I ended up getting too much." She raised a takeout box in each hand and jiggled them. "Wanted to see if you wanted some. Didn't want it to go to waste."

"If you want to come in, we can eat here."

"Really?"

"Sure. Why not?"

"...Okay!"

I cleared the table and was about to get plates, but Jessie stopped me.

"Watch," she said, and quickly dismantled each box till two noodly piles of lo mein sat in the middle of the an impromptu plate.

I applauded. "Neat. Where'd you learn that?"

Jessie shrugged and passed me a pair of chopsticks. "It just sort of happened. I think I was in New York."

We ate in silence. She slurped at her noodles, guiding them into her mouth with her chopsticks. I ate slowly.

She sniffed the air and her eyes brightened up. "That's the candle."

I smiled. "Yes. Thank you. That's..." I cleared my throat. "That's why I let you in. That was a big kindness of you. Thank you."

She returned my smile with one of her own. "No problem at all."

"So...Italy. Does that mean you travel a lot?"

"Yep! All the time. I do a lot of charity work. Don't get me wrong, it feels great, but it's also an easy way to cross off every country on the world on my bucket list."

"Where have you been?"

"Every state in the U.S., Canada, Puerto Rico, Germany, France, Japan, both the Koreas."

"Let's go sometime," I said.

Jessie cocked her head, surprised. But Lindsey's unwavering stare confirmed it, and Jessie smiled.

"To where?"

"Anywhere! Anywhere. I mean, let's not go crazy, of course, but I think..." She hesitated, then beamed. "I think I'm ready to leave this damn building soon."

"You know, when I said 'let's go sometime,' I meant, like, Paris or Japan. Not twenty minutes into the city."

Jessie laughed and rolled her eyes. "Look, baby steps, alright?"

"Yeah, yeah."

Lindsey held onto the railing. The light-rail glided smoothly, effortlessly. Lindsey closed her eyes, and she felt weightless.

DAYDREAMING ABOUT YOUR DATE TOMORROW

Room 3C

BRING several pounds of washcloths. Hide them. In your pockets, your sleeves, anywhere and everywhere that they'll fit--you're prone to sweat, and no girl will kiss you when you're covered in sweat. Not even your mother.

Make sure you bring enough money to potentially pay for both your meals at the diner. If she wants to go Dutch, do so--either way, make sure you have enough to tip the waiter or waitress well. Meeting that 15% standard is a test of its own.

Don't be a cliche. When you compliment her, which is a must, stray from saying things like, "You're pretty," or "You're cute," or "Wow, you are so hot, I can't take how hot you are." That last one got you slapped. Hard. We both know you either talk too much or too bluntly. Say things like, "Your hips are the ocean's curves," or "Your eyes have stolen the stars tonight," or "*Te amo, tu tienes mi corazon.*" (Chicks dig Spanish).

Wait--scratch all that. Too creepy. Wait till you're married to say any of that. Dial it down. Don't overcomplicate things; "You look nice tonight," that'll do just fine. This is good. This is going smoothly. Oh no. You realize she has the kind of lips that wars are fought over. Calm down!...your hormones and your imagination are both going into overdrive right now. If you feel so inclined, create hypotheticals in your mind of you two pumping out two-and-a-half kids, adopting a dog, and erecting a white picket fence in the suburbs, but by no means should you verbalize any of this. She's trying to enjoy her salad. You're at a diner, for God's sake. This is not the time or place to have a salad thrown at you in disgust. Even if you feel like your souls throb at the same wavelength, even if your lips are itching to pull apart and let loose a "We'resoulmateslet'sgetmarriedrightnow," resist. Resist. Focus on your burger. It's nice, tender beef. The fries go well with ketchup. Bite, chew, swallow, nod, laugh at her jokes. Plate's empty. Dessert. Yum. Wipe the sweat from your forehead. The stars giggle while you try small talk. Only ask for water if she does too. You don't want to seem *too* thirsty. You want to seem the *right* amount of thirsty. Pay attention, she's about to speak: "*Are you enjoying the apple pie?*" Good, a question; it will distract you from her lips. Anyway. She has no idea the factors that affect your answer. For example: Is she enjoying the apple pie? Is it warm or cold? Have you used your fork or spoon or--God forbid--your *hand* to eat it? How big is it? Does it make your lips itch? Wipe your hands, you're sweating. Say the pie is fine, that's safe. Your tongue is so parched--hold. *Don't ask for water.* Dessert is done. She's still talking to you. She doesn't care that the food is done. *My god you've made it this far.* Keep it cool. Don't worry, you're smooth, you're slick, you know how to spin a few cool rhymes. "*I'm chillin in a diner / with a cool girl, I like her / almost as much as this apple pie / hopes she likes this nervous guy.*"

... What. Did. You. Just Do. Yeah, that's right, inwardly groan at the pure cheesiness of what you just said! In fact, outwardly groan! You idiot! You-- *"Was that a love rap?"* She's smiling. She's giggling. Wait. Maybe you didn't just screw up. My friend, you can do it. Lean in for the kiss. Do it.

ACKNOWLEDGEMENTS

To my family: thank you for the blazing Filipino fire in my veins. To you all, I owe an immeasurable debt.

To Mr. Flynn and Ms. Chambers: thank you for helping me cultivate my paper-thin drafts into some of the best work I've produced.

To Mr. Imbrenda: thank you for freshman year. My mind still wanders back to that musty, old Lit room.

To Mrs. Tenly: thank you for teaching me that poetry was more than just angsty lines, and thank you especially for *Catalyst*. It was a privilege.

To Mrs. Supplee: thank you for actively supporting and challenging him. You gave me the license to do this, this wonderful project that I'll never forget.

To my PB&J Sandwich Crew: we'll always have 1414 Art Center Avenue. Thousands of miles keep us apart, but I'm with you all always.

To Justin Bassett: thanks for showing me what it would've been like if I had a younger brother (so what if it's just a few months). It's all good from here, friend. I can see where your path leads—I hope you end up where you want to be.

To Joe Kim: thanks for being Asian, bro. Felt good. Once I learn how to Bboy I'll come back and destroy you. Thanks for always matching my sense of humor.

To Maya Leopardi: your perspective on life is beautiful. You're like a badass flower. I just know that if someone tries to step on you, you'll make them sorry. Thank you for showing me the human embodiment of the happiest and saddest thoughts we all have.

To Alena Lattik: you're one of the most creative and talented minds that I know. Not only that, you're one of the most fun and kind people I know. It would be a travesty if you stopped producing content. Thanks for always being eager to collaborate with me.

To Lisa Su: thank you, Sunami, for helping me hold my zen. Whether you're in Rhode Island or Maryland, you're a still pond. I look to you as a role model in many ways.

To Caroline Orth: thank you for being my cool friend in North Carolina. I hope your pen never dries out. Your drive for writing has continuously inspired me.

To Miranda: hey, go somewhere else.

To the Goon Squad: my brothers. Thank you, my brothers (and sisters). For the life lessons, the teasing, and most importantly, the friendship. I would not be where I am today without any of you. But there are simply too many of you to list. But you most definitely all know who you are. Thank you. I'm 100% sure I'd be super boring if it weren't for all of your humor and inability to not crack a joke.

To the Dirt Punchers: we few who punch dirt know the burden we bear. I'kei, my man, you're gonna be big. Like, 7'5 big. Reach for Neptune, my man. And hey, I'kei, HERE'S MY BOOK. You're holding it. Get out. Jordan, even though we were off and on, I forgive you. I'm not going to say much else—we're going to be like an hour away. But thank you—for nothing. Thank you both for being brothers (well, more like distant cousins). I always had a fun time around you guys, and treasure our friendships.

To the Slacker Crew: I spent a lot of time thinking about what I would say to each of you. But, in the spirit of the name, I'll simply say this: it was a pleasure procrastinating with all of you....damn, nah, I got too much to say. Thanks for keeping me sane in Lit. Thanks for being a safe space. Thank you, thank you, thank you.

To Team Booty Blast: All I'll say is this: I won't take no for an answer for a reunion.

To Tyler and Aaron: I hope you two know that, despite anything, I am always down the hall. Please know that. To the end, my brothers.

AUTHOR'S BIO

Ron Anahaw is a current high-school senior on the brink of freedom. He is one of 8 recipients of Scholastic's 2015 Portfolio Gold Medal Award. He has also won several Honorable Mentions, Silver Keys, and Gold Keys in his past of submitting to Scholastics. He plans to start attendance at Bennington College in the fall. He doesn't know where he's headed from here on out, but he's got a bag of metaphors and an armful of friends to help him along the way.

More Praise for *The Real McCoy*

"In *The Real McCoy*, Strauss lends another real person's life majesty and depth and sadness and sorrow...Strauss has many admirable attributes as a writer, but none more admirable than his incredible use of similes. They can be so pitch-perfect that they stop you in your tracks, so beautiful that their words stay with you like an embossed monogram on an envelope flap!"   —*Chicago Tribune*

"Just as he did in his brilliant debut, *Chang and Eng*, Strauss takes a piece of history and pumps it up with punchy prose and gritty period detail. Like E. L. Doctorow's *Ragtime*, *The Real McCoy* is nostalgic (and gory) without feeling like a textbook lesson...Get in on the con now, before Hollywood makes it into a crap movie."
                                              —*Maxim*

"Darin Strauss's *The Real McCoy* is a frenzy of a novel, its story coursing along with a literary style...enthralling."   —*Daily News*

"Prodigiously imaginative...Strauss is clearly a gifted, ambitious writer well worth watching."   —*The Washington Post*

"A tip-top humdinger!"   —*Entertainment Weekly*

"A muscular and entertaining novel about lies, scams, flimflams, and the inconvenience of truth."   —*GQ* magazine

Darin Strauss is the author of the international bestseller *Chang and Eng* (available from Plume), and his work has been translated into fourteen languages. He teaches writing at New York University and lives in Brooklyn, New York.

THE REAL McCOY

a novel

DARIN STRAUSS

A PLUME BOOK

PLUME
Published by the Penguin Group
Penguin Group (USA) Inc., 375 Hudson Street, New York, New York 10014, U.S.A.
Penguin Books Ltd, 80 Strand, London WC2R 0RL, England
Penguin Books Australia Ltd, 250 Camberwell Road,
Camberwell, Victoria 3124, Australia
Penguin Books Canada Ltd, 10 Alcorn Avenue, Toronto, Ontario,
Canada M4V 3B2
Penguin Books (N.Z.) Ltd, Cnr Rosedale and Airborne Roads,
Albany, Auckland 1310, New Zealand

Penguin Books Ltd, Registered Offices: 80 Strand, London WC2R 0RL, England

Published by Plume, a member of Penguin Group (USA) Inc.
Previously published in a Dutton edition.

First Plume Printing, June 2003
10 9 8 7 6 5 4 3 2 1

Ⓟ REGISTERED TRADEMARK—MARCA REGISTRADA

The Library of Congress has catalogued the Dutton edition as follows:

Strauss, Darin.
The real McCoy : a novel / by Darin Strauss.
p. cm.
ISBN 0-525-94651-9 (hc.)
ISBN 0-452-28441-4 (pbk.)
1. McCoy, Kid, 1872–1940—Fiction. 2. Boxers (Sports)—Fiction.
3. Swindlers and swindling—Fiction. I. Title.

PS3569.T692245 R43 2002
813'.54—dc21   2002023545

Printed in the United States of America
Set in Janson Text
Original hardcover design by Eve L. Kirch

PUBLISHER'S NOTE
This book is a work of fiction. Names, characters, places, and incidents are either the product of the author's imagination or are used fictitiously, and any resemblance to actual per-
sons, living or dead, business establishments, events, or locales is entirely coincidental.

For Susie

McCoy, or whatever his name in fact is, has been the herald of a new era. The fellow reveals that today a friend with a natty build can blaze a trail through the world of muscular sport. Notwithstanding the hullabaloo of his life and the mischief of his legend, threadlike McCoy with his wondrous speed and guile may be the first, greatest gentleman of this fresh age.

—H. H. Measures, the *New York Evening World*, 1904

To be believable, the story must first of all arouse our astonishment: only the astounding will be believed.

—Elias Canetti, *Selected Notes*

The one sincere confession is the one we make indirectly—when we talk about other people.

—E. M. Cioran, *The Trouble With Being Born*

'Zounds, McCoy

Here was a champion before he closed his hand into a fist. The boy's gumption was like the full steam of a locomotive. Plus he was a born liar.

In flat Indiana his father told him, "Virgil, falsity's in your blood"—with a voice deep and dark as a thief's pocket. "Go and make yourself someone finer." Before too long the boy made himself several someones finer.

However.

When we pick up his story, he liked to think he'd never been Virgil Selby, and he certainly wasn't yet St. Corkscrew LeFist, or the other empty title he'd come to call himself. In December 1899, on the happy morning he earned lasting fame, this top-notch fibber, "scientific" brawler, future political hopeful, sometime poet, jewel thief, and movie star was just about always McCoy.

McCoy had a wooer's slicked-up brown hair and the sweet temper of a lucky man. But even using that celebrated name the kid was slight, a cousin to the ribbed washboards women had in those days: not an ideal case for a guy intent on the welterweight crown. O, ambition!

"It's the hour for Kid McCoy." McCoy was laughing, and the look he gave the mirror weighed more than he did. "What he's been expecting all these years and here I am to delight in it." This was one of the last mornings of that century, and who'd have dared say the twenty-year-old flimflammer couldn't have taken the world before sunset?

Picture our milieu: Ronny and Ray's Sports Club on the Lower East Side of Manhattan felt about a hundred sticky degrees any season of the year, more or less suffocating, sweat heavy in its dead air. This was the gym the zealous went to—unpleasant enough to worry your skin and the one place in all New York McCoy felt relaxed. He had his own latchkey, and since 6:00 A.M. the battler had been waiting inside for the welterweight champ Tommy Ryan, the sort of pug whose head echoed if you tapped it.

By seven the gym was still mostly empty. A bunch of guys straggled in and out, though, trainers and towel boys and the fighter himself, and it was *all* of us who were responsible for spreading this story, even if accounts fail to mention that. Does the Bible tell you about the beetle who took note from the manger?

"You know something, fellows?" McCoy was shirtless and scrawny and all keyed up as he boxed shadows in the ring. Most people still knew him only as the sparring partner Ryan had given a humiliating lesson in prizefighting a few years earlier. "Come ten minutes' time," he said, "I'm going to start gathering the bricks to build my American Dream."

One of the towel boys said he didn't know lying was part of the American Dream.

"Where *you* been?" And McCoy gave the littlest of smiles, which a stranger might have mistaken for cynical, or a look of menace. I recognized it as McCoy's self-possession getting the better of his giant enthusiasm, and I fell in love with the man for the thousandth, the ten thousandth time.

The champ Tommy Ryan finally turned up with his pretty if plump new wife, Eleanor, on his arm. "'Zounds, McCoy" was the brawny champ's hello, his voice mild and innocent as the look on his face. His hair was a haystack. "Jab high," he said.

"Rabbit-punch low," answered McCoy—this was some dead language from a brotherhood long gone.

"What's all that to-do in your telegram? You get me here for a little of the old . . ." Without letting Eleanor's hand out of his, Ryan pantomimed the act of sparring. (Tommy Ryan was the finest welterweight breathing and floored by the soft of one woman's hand.) Over and again the champ blinked his left eye; at thirty he had a crushed duct. A tear waddled down his shaved cheek.

"Hello, Mrs. Ryan." McCoy could show a lot of warmth toward *any*one. "I didn't expect to see you"—although of course he had expected her. "Now, Tommy," he said, "I have a big proposition, Champ, that's why I asked for you." McCoy made sure not to look at Ryan's terrible huge fisted hand.

"Ooh, a proposition!" Eleanor Ryan gazed at her husband even when he wasn't looking her way. "It sounds an absolute pip, Thomas." Eleanor was a twenty-six-year-old schoolteacher who read poetry, and was therefore in a state of high romance all the time. (Don't *tisk tisk*. In my century an old pug could insult a girl and not have every female from Seattle to Miami take it personally.)

"'Zounds, McCoy," said Ryan, climbing into the ring in his street clothes, his smile a show of nothing more genial than some muscles in his cheeks.

"What're we talking here, McCoy?" Dukes up, Ryan began to circle McCoy absentmindedly, cutting off the space between the skinny kid and the ropes. Even wearing buffalo-hide ankle boots and an overcoat with chinchilla lining, the champ was at all times a fighter. Ryan's punching knuckles were clearly thinking: *Let me at that skinny McCoy.*

"A benefit exhibition," McCoy said, himself a source of bouncing energy. Imagine a whirlwind coiling this way then that across the canvas. "For charity and it wouldn't count. We'd stage the whole thing."

The champ stopped to stare into McCoy's bobbing face. "Hey, you got a black eye or some such?"

McCoy didn't quit dancing; more life in him than a congress of Ryans. "Who'd be fast enough to tag *me*, Champ?"

"You got like rings around your eyes, McCoy. Maybe it's you're so skinny."

"Skinny enough to give you a run for *your* . . ." Sometimes for

effect McCoy didn't finish his sentences. He'd borrowed the man-
nerism from the great Chinese flimflammer Johnnie Gold. "I've
gotten better than you know, Tommy," he said.

Other undersized pugs would find a lesson in McCoy's shuffle,
his spindle legs, in the spiral of his trademark coil punch. If every
ounce of the kid weren't in constant motion, pent-up energy might
have jiggled his insides off their tendons.

"If that's your say-so." From his sighing voice it was plain the
champ still saw Kid McCoy as the sparring youngster who caved at
the hint of punishment. Ryan had earned immortal renown with his
seventy-sixth-round knockout of Mysterious Billy Smith in 1895.

"Now, for real, Kid," Ryan was saying, "what benefit?"

The champ'd remained undefeated in forty-six fights over ten
years. (He, too, had taken a ring name: Ryan was born Joseph
O'Youngs, and for a short time he'd gone by "Nonpareil Andrew
Chiariglione." Now some called him "the Stinging Bee.")

McCoy said, "Raise money for immigrant literacy or some other
bilk. It's this show next week." The boy's cheeks had gone shiny
with the exercise. "A pretend fight, these guys are proposing for a
charity setup. Figure a little magnanimity on your part could make
the newspapers quit hating you. The ones who call you 'the Mick.'"

"'The Mick who's none too quick.' Ain't that what it is?" Ryan
looked around the dusky gym as if hunting for unfriendly journalists.
He saw only his schoolteacher of a wife and a few towel boys in unlit
recesses. "Ah, what'a penny-a-liners know about the ring game, huh?"

Eleanor, rising on tiptoes, cut in: "A fight with no payday, Mr.
McCoy?" She scrunched her little nose as if calling to mind something gone to rot. "I hope you'll take no offense, but I wouldn't
imagine 'free of charge' is your cup of tea." Her blouse sleeves
showed a peek of her bare forearms, and the skin was awful pimpled.

"Mrs. Ryan, it's not really a fight, and it doesn't have to be free."
McCoy bowed his head at her, as if at any time she might start treating him with respect. "Way I figure, we arrange it about as violent as
a ballet. But that's not all." He now stood still enough to put his arm
around Ryan, but his fingers still tapped a pulse on the champ's

shoulder. "The guys who want to organize this fuss are due here any minute, a Mr. Hill and a Mr. Overton," McCoy said. "They're talking a thousand for you, Tom, and five hundred for me. Together we could squeeze them for a lot more; scheme out a way to up their ante. Of course, Champ"—here McCoy smiled his widest of the morning, showing a set of surprisingly gray teeth—"it's up to you. But I heard Tommy Ryan could flimflam a little in the old days, and it'd be good press against those who say marriage has changed you."

Eleanor squinted at her husband. She chewed on her lip as if it were bubble gum. All the while McCoy eyed her. He had such acute sensitivity to the changeable ambitions of men—and women—it wouldn't have surprised me if he was of the same cloth as those balloons that tell specialists which way the wind's blowing in China.

Right before Eleanor next spoke, she inhaled as if she were about to walk through smoke and didn't want to waste air. "Thomas," she said, "maybe you and Mr. McCoy should fight, even if it's for free."

"*Free?*" McCoy said. "Oh, no, ma'am, I don't fight *boredom* for free. I just reckoned there was some angle—"

"Eleanor," said the champ, "darling." Another teardrop tiptoed the length of his cheek. "I haven't trained a whit since the honeymoon. I could barely spar out my own grandma next week."

"You're modest, Thomas, lovelily so," said Eleanor, the easy-grader part of her nature showing. "But it shan't be a real fight, isn't that right, Mr. McCoy? Playacting, so to speak. And for charity." She made sure she'd caught her husband's good eye. "Charity looks quite good, especially if there's no chance of anyone getting hurt."

McCoy saw his opening. "I suppose that's right, Mrs. Ryan." He scratched at his chin to appear contemplative. "Like a theatrical production, we could do it. At any rate, this pair of malooks Hill and Overton wants to pay us real money. If it's for a right cause, anyhow—"

"Who'd put up a thousand dollars to see me fight *you*?" The champ's voice crept on tolerant contempt. His genius for wearing down rivals in the ring had been unequaled in the budding history of this mad sport.

Here, I thought, McCoy would mention that he'd had his own big victories of late. Knocked out Honeyblast in six. Dago Frank in two. But his smile stayed relaxed—if a curious relaxed. Still, his light eyes clouded just a bit. The smallest reaction.

As McCoy turned again to Eleanor, the shadow had passed from his face. Eleanor still looked to be in favor of this "charity event"; the key to the whole flimflam was getting her approval.

"I can hardly fathom it myself," McCoy said. "The money's as good as the cause." (Later, when real success came, he would delight in a life Selby had only dreamt of: Selby had squirreled away cash, but as Kid McCoy he kept enough on his person after one joyous streak to add up his pockets and find $40,000.)

"Doesn't it sound *too* good, though?" Ryan said.

"Well, Tommy," McCoy winking, "maybe I mistook you for someone else. If you've still got that champion's belt of yours, check it. See if you aren't the winner I took you for."

"Listen," the champ growing heated, "I think I know who I am, McCoy."

"It's tricky, though. Could be today you find yourself a different guy?" And next, gently, "Tommy, you've forgotten more boxing than I ever knew, but here's a chance for us both to get the cash without breaking *a* . . ."

Ryan tilted his head. He breathed in through his nose and out again—his big eyes trained on McCoy. Then he started into the faintest of smiles. There it was: the Sucker's Smirk. It often turns up in the eye first, a flicky show of happiness. Next it skates down the jaw, wavering near the mouth like a bee around a hive, and soon it riffles under the flesh to shiver the chin. In a good flimflam the sucker's whole face will burst like a potato when it's cooked.

"Well, okay, McCoy. I guess that about says it." Tommy turned to his wife. "If you think, dearest."

"Yes, I suppose I do think." Eleanor was just woman enough to understand her schoolma'am smile melted Ryan's heart. "Why not?"

"'Zounds," the champ said, a once-wild pet near finished his house training. "Okay, McCoy—let's listen to what these fellows have to offer."

Eleanor clapping lightly: "Thomas, why are you so dear when you're agreeing with me?" There, now her heart had melted too.

A few minutes went by and then Ryan poked McCoy's shoulder. "Ever think of marriage, Kid?"

"Not for McCoy." As Virgil Selby, on the other hand, he was still married to a short person named Lottie. In ten years' time McCoy would be the most married man in America, with quite a few weddings to the same woman—the beautiful and fatal Susan Fields.

Both Mr. Hill and Mr. Overton perspired when they arrived. In truth, Hill and Overton were named Isley and Hewlett, button men of McCoy's and in on the grift.

". . . so very generous of you to agree to help our worthy cause," Hill/Isley was saying, his voice a little husky this still-early hour, but pleasant. "Thank you, Kid McCoy, and especially you, Mr. and Mrs. Ryan." Isley's was that style of enunciation well extinct nowadays, the ringmaster's cadence, an obnoxious inflection that in the last hundred years has gone the way of Zoroaster.

McCoy was standing in the ring, a few feet above everyone else. The schoolma'am wore her kindly smile, and the champ at her side blinked his crying eye and nodded like a baboon.

"Are these immigrant children very"—Eleanor ran her pointer finger the length of her neck as she searched for a benevolent word—"indigent, Mr. Hill?"

Isley didn't answer for a moment; Isley in his worn brown suit very near forgot his name was supposed to be Mr. Hill. "Uh, yes," he said at last. (Not that the Ryans caught his hesitation. Most who get duped see just what you want them to see. People don't put up a defense, or want to.)

"Oh, how sad and tragic for those children to be indigent, sad and tragic!" Eleanor patted her collarbone to show her pity, a gesture she probably thought was very touching. "These immigrant foundlings won't—actually be *present* that night, will they?" With her plump waist and her chest what it was, she cut a young girl's figure.

Hands in front of his body as if to start in on a hug, Isley with his mock-reproachful smile made a fair picture of a man of charity: fussy yet tolerant of what is base in people. The other imposter,

Overton/Hewlett, teetered like a Humpty-Dumpty egg in tight Sunday clothes. It was obvious Hewlett was drunk. The man hadn't spoken, and his cheeks rippled pinkly with each belch hemmed in. McCoy could guess the foulness of Hewlett's breath just by watching those flapping pale lips.

". . . Of course," Isley was going on, "we at Newcomer Goodwill will remunerate you for any and all altruistic efforts." (In reality good old Isley was an opium-smoking confidence man whose deceit had brought him within an inch of his life at least seven times—the worst being a stab wound from a swindled Irishman outside O'Shaugney's Pub on the Bowery.)

"Without this we're just degenerate sapheads in the wild," said Hewlett, his first words of the day coming thick off his tongue. He made a very large Humpty-Dumpty: tired, ashen, fifty-odd. "Sapheads in the wild attempting to keep some miserable campfire from going snuffed." The final, nasty *d* in that sentence bounced around the room for a time.

Tommy Ryan shot a bewildered glance at his wife, whose face— though too prim to display real confusion—did wrinkle a little. "Without *what* we're sapheads, sir?" Tommy asked.

"*Charity*," said Hewlett. He looked toward the ceiling and his eyes were dewy cue balls. "What I'm on about here is that." He brought his palms forward, then curled his fingers gently around nothing—a mime caressing the imaginary breasts of Charity. McCoy tensed. A flimflam is rehearsed like a stage play, and for one member of a con mob to crack out of turn like this was appalling.

"Well, Mr. Overton," McCoy said, and he winked at the Ryans as if there were some joke they were a part of, "I guess that's why we're set to do your little production, me and the good old champ here—charity." You can throw a cat however you want, it always keeps its head up.

"I lost money on you!" Hewlett crowed, his face turning the gray-green of an old pear.

"Lost on whom?" asked Ryan. Enjoying, at least, the chance to show grammar before his wife.

"Lost on youm." High-pitched Hewlett sounded like Dawn's

cock-a-doodle-do. "When you beat Mysterious Billy for the title in '95. Twenty bucks." The club's air smelled, as it tended to, from years of sweat and heat, cigar smoke, and urine.

Eleanor said, "I didn't know charitable men bet." And she blinked and blinked like some offended fairy.

"Isn't that why we're here, ha ha ha," said McCoy. I'd only ever heard him laugh loud, with explosiveness that would unnerve the deaf, but here his laughter was easygoing, of a charming kind.

A few hours later, once everyone had gone, it ended up just McCoy and a few towel boys alone in that old athletic club. He said, "I could kill Isley for bringing that drunk idiot Hewlett. How do you take a known sot to a grift?" He was laughing. "That devil Tommy Ryan punched the spit out of me when I was just a little shaver, and made a real neddy of me before a lot of people to boot." (Almost five years earlier, when he'd first traveled to spar Tommy Ryan, McCoy had been so nervous he'd donned his boxing trunks before leaving his hotel and worn them beneath his country clothes; he'd sat on the train like that. A fidgety prairiebilly locomoting toward his big break, is how McCoy described himself.)

"After it was all over, I was bruised up enough to pass for a piece of crow bait." McCoy was shaking his head. "And the newspapers still say Ryan took me under his wing, taught me a few inside moves. Ha!"

Shifting from foot to foot, McCoy said, "Listen up, fellows. If you're going to beat someone silly in the ring, at least be decent and declare him a real opponent who you pay." He was speaking quiet enough almost to conceal his excitement. "This double-cross is going to be sweet."

Ah, those times! In this new-fangled century of yours everything is well lit. If information today throws a spotlight, it was scarcely a candle in 1899, and in dark corners con artists had their chance to convince a half-wit to jeopardize his championship without knowing that he was putting anything at risk. Would it even be possible to pull that classy a swindle in today's gleaming world where everybody knows everything?

* * *

—But I've jumped ahead. Let me tell you how the scam played out in Ronnie and Ray's, how McCoy prevailed over Hewlett's drunken unprofessionalism in the turn of the century that this was. . . .

Midmorning. Hewlett'd finished his outburst about "charity." The daylight at the window seemed nervous to enter—it shied across the floor in little canary chicks of sun. McCoy was watching the scene with the concentration of a young boy stooped over a maggot with his magnifying glass.

If Isley was stammering on about indigent children, and Hewlett could barely stop his head from drowsing, and if Tommy Ryan (always a chump to endorse or mock something based on another man's reaction to it) could only wait for someone else to speak up—the champ's *wife*, her delicate hands like carnations curling under, leveled on Hewlett and Isley the kind of stare that took in more by the moment. She hardened up her face the way shy women do when they grow skeptical: their eyes biggen, their brows worm toward each other.

A scam is a fluid thing. Though it didn't seem so just moments earlier, McCoy and his mob had reached the grifter's stormy moment, the touch-and-wait when no one knows what to say to the suckers and the whole scam could unwind. The Ryans might not have realized it themselves, but they were about to form a united front against the flimflam—unless McCoy could find some switch to throw.

Time slouched along with mincing steps. Everyone watched everyone else. Even the windows were clouding in thought.

"My father, the coot, had a story." McCoy was addressing everyone, but he centered on Eleanor in particular. "Pa's uncle Michael—my great uncle—lost his finger as a boy, and that ninny kept that digit in an urn his whole life." McCoy leaned his head to one side, a youthful gesture.

"Everyone thought old Uncle Mike crazy. And he was. Mean as a bear, too, especially when he slugged it out against the spirits of the long dead. See, he had howling fights with the deceased every morning and most afternoons, being part Maumee Indian and all."

McCoy's eyes were no wider now than fingernail clippings. "When old Michael passed, my father said everyone in the family was secretly happy to be rid of the ding-dang grumbler who argued with his ghosts."

McCoy now smiled at the champ Ryan, who was doing little stretching exercises with his neck.

"But he passed away, my uncle Michael who argued ghosts," McCoy said, and even as he hated his mouth for being repetitive, he was calculating the effect his story had on everyone in the room, "—and the day of Michael's funeral, the headmistress of the local schoolhouse, Mrs. Dutter, came to pay her respects. She told us Uncle Mike had been visiting her classroom once a week. This was funny to me, though I can't speak to the rest of my kin, me being the clever one in *that* group. But it turns out that Michael'd hiked across Bluffton to the schoolhouse every Tuesday without any of us knowing. The old nutjob had let the children play with that finger in that urn."

McCoy saw that Eleanor was scratching her head like a country lawyer about to object. Was the con so obvious?

"The school," McCoy hurried, "had been paying Uncle Michael three and three quarters cents a week for this service, and at the end of each year he'd given back to those children every fourth week's pay, so they could buy books—yes, he kept that finger right in the urn his whole life. You understand why I'm telling you this?"

Tommy Ryan squinted and picked an imaginary piece of lint off his sleeve—a boy of ten or eleven hoping the teacher doesn't call on him.

"Charity." McCoy put a hush onto his words. "You never know who's going to be its keeper." He gestured sham-discreetly at Hewlett, for Eleanor's benefit. "That's my point." And didn't he wink at her, a little one? "Now, if your own charity can give you a little benefit—every fourth week's pay, say—then all the better."

Ryan, the champ, gave a nod in favor of charity.

"Well, lovely, then," said Eleanor, and a smile heaved onto her face like a wave over the beach.

"Wonderful!" said Isley. "You're wonderful for helping us,

madam!" He raised his arms. "Just wonderful, wonderful, *wonderful*, Mrs. Ryan." His rendition of a charity man was apparently a very encouraging person.

But Eleanor had spoken without thinking anyone would take hers as the final word; her eyes went timid. "Sirs, please wait," she muttered. "Are there not details to, to—"

"All right—Mr. Hill, is it?" McCoy was addressing Isley as if Mrs. Ryan hadn't just spoken. "You mentioned a thousand for the champ here, and five hundred for yours true?"

"Uh." Isley gave a worthy performance of an awkward moment, fussing with the handkerchief in his pocket. "No, sir. Our budget is nine hundred fifty for Mr. Ryan, and, gulp, three seventy-five for you, Mr. McCoy."

"Forget it." McCoy spat, maybe a little too quick and exuberant. "Forget that."

"Mr. McCoy—" Eleanor and Isley said it at the same time.

"Get someone else. You told me a price." McCoy was bouncing again. "Did you tell me a price? You told me a price."

"Wait, only nine fifty for *me*?" Ryan said.

"But, Mr. McCoy," Eleanor was saying, "what about your uncle Michael?" Then she spoke intimately to Tommy: "Nine fifty for doing next to nothing ain't bad. Isn't bad."

"Forget Uncle Michael, that story was bullroar," McCoy said. "Find somebody else. Hodge, for instance. You told me a price. Hodge's still in town, I'll bet."

J. K. Hodge, aka "Sweet Daddy Champagne," a fighter for the British Isles, was believed the most competitive spirit in the game; Ryan had battled him to a draw three times, finally knocking him out in the fifty-eighth round of their last fight, but not before the champ had broken most of his knuckles on the Englishman's face-bones.

"No, no, no, not Sweet Daddy Hodge," said Ryan. He gently rubbed his huge hand. A champion with feelings. He seemed more fitted to violence when he was whimpering. He rubbed those knuckles some more. "Come, now, McCoy," he said. "Money's not the whole of life. Ain't that what you just—"

"No, I don't know." And McCoy let the shiver of a wilting suspicion enter his voice. "I suppose I could use the notices." While inside him his spirit must have jumped for joy. "Well—I'll let you take me in sixteen, Tommy."

"Twelve," said the Champ.

"Sixteen," said McCoy.

"Fine, then." Ryan smirked as his dim eye wept. "It should be a pip, this fake battle." Had some photographer raced in to freeze the scene in black and white, it would've looked a tender meeting of the dearest of friends—smiles all around.

Nowadays you people merely stick the old flimflam days to the glass like some relic on a museum wall. Sure, people see the spectacle—but nobody gets a hands-on feel. Me, I live trapped inside my memory of old con jobs like a pistol under glass.

The date was set. Kid McCoy was going to fight an unprepared, unwitting moron and genius of the ring on January 1, 1900, for $375. And the World Welterweight Crown.

Now, I knew Kid McCoy and he got to know me, especially later. This scam would be one of a thousand heights in a life that in unequal parts I watched, heard from the horses' mouths, or read about in the papers of the day—not to mention spent the last many decades mooning over. McCoy's astounding weird story, as it lives in this old man's memory and guesswork, is what follows.

Book One

The Real McCoy?

You can't understand McCoy without this: The nation he hustled was closer in time and temper to the War of 1812 than to your automatic age. A backwater, America looked darn like the mind of the average flimflammer—blemished wild places, a hissing brier patch where dark fruit grows, serpents underfoot.

That was his era. Now picture the young battler almost five years before he conned Ryan—a boy locomoting one late night to his first-ever match as McCoy, across a stretch of Indian land dirty with sassafras and only recently made available for settlement by whites.

Eleven-fifteen P.M. on the Texas Oklahoma Railroad bound for Elk City, Oklahoma. Nobody aboard had any notion where they were headed, but anyway the train car was full to bursting. This redeye to Elk City never'd been so popular before.

He sat up front, just sixteen, a near-confident slant to his grimace, even with his gray teeth. Virgil Selby—oh, wait, he's McCoy tonight, he'd almost forgot again—held himself apart from the grown-up strangers on every side and he squinted, firing a pug's looks at these nameless men off hog farms or assembly plants, the

late-evening passengers carrying the work smells of wide home-
steads or of new industries, everyone looking forward to an event
that would lift his week a little—the factory night-manager on secret shift-break next to the suspender-wearing prairiebilly struggling to keep his eyes open, herdsmen and tilemakers, lawyers in
bow ties and someone who wore a janitor's blue livery, most of these
men hard faced in the fashion of that old century, sitting together
under the chance meeting of their enthusiasms, traveling God-
knows-where to witness a fistfight this ridiculous hour on a Tuesday.

And McCoy, barely there in his neat seersucker suit, not even the
145 pounds he claimed, sunk down among them but invisible as if
wrapped in a cloud, just a kid with money stolen from his sleeping
father, but secretly he was also the attraction that packed this train
full. His schoolboy straw hat shook around his skinny head, his
cheeks swelled with tobacco, and his shoe-leather boots frayed at
the heels—while beneath that hayseed getup were hidden boxing
trunks, the canvas footgear of the ring, and a mysterious urge to
mask any clue that he was the battler everyone was taking the trouble to see. At the same time he wanted more than anything to be
known by the whole world. Extreme oddness sometimes makes a
hero. His head ached. He'd been McCoy for exactly one day. Chewing tobacco had him nauseous.

Then someone said, "You're McCoy?" and the cloud around the
boy parted. Childlike McCoy shone in the electric light, head and
shoulders and youthful eyes all gentle.

Now again: "*You're* McCoy?"

The bald man asking was Dick Nibs, boxing promoter. Dick
Nibs liked to dance around the laws that banned prizefighting in
1895, and so was keeping the location of tonight's fight a secret—
even from the fighters themselves. (People had been told in a whisper to meet at 11:00 P.M. Tuesday at the railway station.)

"I'm McCoy, yes." The skinny kid's voice broke when it touched
the fiction. And the train rattled like a tubercular old man, coughing
its way down jagged tracks.

Dick Nibs patted McCoy's shoulder but kept his eyes down as if he were filching the kid's wallet; he missed the sight of a boy grace-less at spitting into a cup. Try as McCoy might to look collected, his excitement showed plainly across his sloppy chin and danced over the stage of his face.

Dick Nibs, meanwhile, owned a face with little use for features beyond the essentials—his drab smile had almost nothing in the way of lips to outline it; his cheeks slid into his neck just fine without the hitch of a visible jawline. This strict blankness helped call attention to eyes wild like spun gyroscopes. "Why're you dressed like that, McCoy?" Nibs said. "Dressed like a normal person?"

"Oh, well, I—"

"Look at that other guy." Dick Nibs pointed out a man some six rows back who wore only a robe and trunks, a man flanked by back-slappers. "The sensible way your opponent's dressed."

McCoy's shirtless rival was a deaf-mute whose ring name—and this is how 1895 treated a deaf-mute—was Deaf-Mute. An expert Oklahoma middleweight with experience, the mute was the bettor's choice, a local hero; even sitting he was taller than McCoy, thicker by half, scowling as if weaned on lemons. His huge fists hinted at what pain lay ahead. A blue tattoo tiger in fading ink roared frozen on his chest.

No one knows who I am, thought McCoy. *Not even the Selby I was yesterday, even he don't know in any real magnitude.* (Extreme odd-ness.) *I can beat this deaf-mute, or any man. Make myself someone finer.*

"I'm a fellow for the most lawful existence, truly," said Dick Nibs. "What I really do, I write steamship romances. I can see maybe you're like that, some other besides a fighter at heart. But Deaf-Mute"—here Dick Nibs lowered his voice and made McCoy feel far from home—"this guy fought a kangaroo once. Knocked him out in thirteen."

"Okay," McCoy said.

The promoter's eyes narrowed. "You're a reedy bastard, you are—all I'm saying." He scratched his hair. "You know, I seen you fight one time, seen you in Frisco, and I'm not sure. I guess—"

There were train lights flashing in the window. The far side of the blinking pane was a purple scene of swaying woodlands and little lakes sinking into darkness. Finally Dick Nibs figured out how to finish his sentence. "—I guess at that time you looked a much bigger man than you look now, McCoy. A much bigger man. Older, I would have guessed. Certainly you was older."

"I'm McCoy."

"Yeah, but are you the *real* McCoy?" First time anyone had said it.

They pulled into Elk City at midnight. None of the confused fidgety crowd knew what to do once they found themselves under the raw night sky. McCoy stood eyeing the freakish tall opponent beside him on the cold platform.

Deaf-Mute had the movements of a natural-born puncher—the loose intuitive shamble from one foot to the next, the lift of a muscled arm that cut the shortest path to scratch his nose—it made McCoy feel wobbled in the legs. What he failed to understand about himself was that even in those days he had more energy than most anybody. He'd been bouncing on his toes for half an hour without realizing. There was some mysterious delay, some problem Nibs wasn't sharing with anyone else.

The weather threatened. Low dark clouds were opening in strange contours. Angry men in the crowd started to call Dick Nibs "his nibs Dick Nibs," and questioned if there was even going to be a fight: "Rain's coming." "It's cold." "And late."

"C'mon, McCoy!" Dick Nibs grabbed our kid—and also the deaf-mute—and pushed the two fighters off the platform. "C'mon, boys!" Decades of fight promoting had charred Dick Nibs's bourbon baritone down to a single note.

"*That's* who's fighting Deaf-Mute?" This was the shrill voice of one stranger's doubt. Another: "That *skinny kid* is McCoy?"

And Deaf-Mute was smiling. His moldy slug-colored eyes showed an ember of life. Deaf-Mute must not have known he'd outweigh his opponent by at least fifty pounds. McCoy tried to empty his mouth of tobacco with a spit that was nearer to an upchuck.

Meanwhile Dick Nibs was shoving the fighters toward a wooden rowboat that bobbed at the edge of black Lake Pinckney. "There, right there," he said. In the boat sat an oarman who showed a long red scar across his jaw.

"Off you go," Dick Nibs said, then he started humming.

The promoter's plan had been this: As there were felony charges for setting up a prizefight in Oklahoma—in fact, known Elk City deputy sheriffs had been riding the 11:15 behind McCoy in flimsy disguise, following up on rumors of likely pugilism—Dick Nibs asked people to pay "for a ride across the river and nothing more." He'd provided several flatboats, and for two dollars fifty in this dead of night, spectators could buy a perfectly legal round-trip to Colorado, where a boxing match would happen to take place, "free of charge." Unfortunately most of the boats hadn't shown yet—none of the spectators could get across.

It was a damp half-past midnight. There must have been stars, and a guiding moon, but in McCoy's memory the night would always be a wondrous strange dark. He could barely make out Deaf-Mute now. Their rowboat shuddered with the rude current. Some quarter mile on the other side of the river, Colorado slept.

Holding on to both sides of the boat, Deaf-Mute leaned in to whisper to McCoy: "Crossing the river—to Colorado, or to the graveyard—the toll's the same." His robe didn't hide the violence of his body. "It's the same goddamn trip." And he winked, his huge packs of muscle jumping at even this smallest of gestures. The wet floor planks troubled young McCoy's feet through his shoes. The boat slogged in fits because the water seemed like quicksand.

McCoy shuddered. Maybe this phony mute would kill him.

Just off the Colorado shore was a long-abandoned amusement park, the years-dark Robert Kay's Famous Belmont Grounds, a set of wooden husks against the moon. Here a desolate, broken roller coaster looked like a dinosaur's skeleton in a museum, there a Ferris wheel without its benches was a giant dried dandelion with the seed-fluff blown off.

The old rowboat came to a hissing stop against the shore. A rotted tree near the waterline bowed in the wind, shy about its leafless-ness. Farther up from the beach, near boarded-up rides and the few standing ticket stalls, Dick Nibs had pitched a ring across an old dance floor, canvas over some hardwood that buckled as if the ring had crash-landed onto it.

(This was the state of affairs back then: boxers fought in barns across the nation; on barges afloat little rivers that traced county lines; in forests where it was warm, and inside closed-up resorts where it wasn't; in storehouses, deserted strip mines, back alleyways, in concert halls—one famous slug-out took place on a peaceable Long Island beach, so near to the water's edge that the boxers squared off thigh-deep in ocean after the tide rolled in to open the forty-first round.)

Inside the makeshift ring—with torch flames ducking in each corner—McCoy stripped to his trunks and started shadowboxing. He expected his opponent to make fun of his skinniness, badmouth his prominent ribs at least, but Deaf-Mute had gone back into his mute act. With his tremendous power Deaf-Mute waggled his head, showed the breadth of his shoulders, his great arms and legs, and threw punches against the turnbuckle.

McCoy shuffled on the balls of his wet, stockinged feet. He did this for quite a while. Oklahoma was far off, nothing to see in its direction but dark river—and he tried not to think about the sister, the half-sisters, half-brother, or the lonely father he'd just left, or about his mother who'd "departed," as McCoy called it. Some of his only memories of his mother: Her elegant hands wrinkled by the soap water of washing clothes for a large family. Her careful laying of a poultice, slathered in apple paste, along her weeping son's furiously bee-stung back and neck on a bright summer morning. . . . No, McCoy tried not to worry over any of this, nor who he'd become nor how he'd gotten here. But, oh, how stupid that *he* was going to fight Deaf-Mute, or anybody!

The promoter Dick Nibs arrived on his own skiff.

"The other boats are taking too long, boys." Nibs raked his fingers through what was left of his hair. "I got to quit this most shady existence and get to my romances." And he started moaning tunefully. Rumor had it that Dick Nibs had gone around the bend of late. He'd fallen into humming. Energetic, demanding humming—

operas and old polkas, little-known carols and popular ditties, and finally arabesque melodies of his own imagining.

An hour went by before the flatboats started one by one to bring ticket holders into the dim faltering torchlight. McCoy kept right on shadowboxing. The night was sunk so low in anticipation that the men who came off the boats propped the sky on their heads.

Everyone began to gather, stranger-to-stranger, edgy around the ring. Few of these spectators even acknowledged one another. But nearing dawn on a weeknight, they all pressed close, hours from their bedrooms, needing to be here, in the dampish air that promised rain. In this chilly darkish forgotten wreck of an amusement park. To watch the local hero Deaf-Mute beat to death a skinny nobody who called himself McCoy.

Among the crowd wandered a pickpocket hired by Dick Nibs, a fleshy kid about McCoy's age. And there was a woman—only one woman in the whole crowd, a redhead who, even tramping in the mud, showed a posture certain females can work at for years and never get right; she swayed at the hips like a human metronome. True, with those narrow shoulders and missing one side tooth, she was not half the woman that McCoy's three-time wife Susan Fields would be. But he fell in love with her right there—this redhead as welcome now as a blade of grass from home, as his backyard, as the wide prairie he grew up on. She was eyeing him the way an orphan eyes a home-cooked meal.

But the boy had other things to think about.

McCoy kept as quiet as his enormous opponent. He jabbed the air, summoning up pictures of targets: solar plexus, throat, head. He felt weary and cold and had almost no breath left. A kid like McCoy, however, didn't know to shadowbox half-speed. Some torchlight, shoved down by the wind, pointed at him like a shaking finger.

How could I have done the evil thing I did to get here, McCoy thought, *and not expect bad consequences for me?*

The men in this spreading crowd began to look one like every other—old and young, homesteader or city father—the same hot-eyed cruelty in each grimace. They were thick-coming now, these men like a tribe of nomads.

Some remark bobtailed from the general crowd noise—". . . what chance does a kid have against . . ."—but disappeared before McCoy caught the whole of it. There was more:

". . . don't even look like a real fighter . . ."

". . . just a rabbit trapped in a cage with a wolf . . ."

". . . *I* could take him, so what chance does he . . ."

Now, everything around was hateful, old, as from a strange part of the country, everything, and McCoy kept to shadow while the prefight chatter got even louder. The naked trees leaned back shivering as wind caught inside their cages. Men's faces, here and there topped by a hat, seemed to roll out into the fog without stop—

". . . blasted storm coming! If I came out all this way for a called-off fight . . ."

"But if they ever get on with it, it'll be old boy Mute in round one!"

". . . goddamn that pettifogger Nibs to keep us like this, goddamn . . ."

Yet McCoy and Deaf-Mute weren't being called for the bell. *Don't look at how big the mute is and maybe you'll be okay, McCoy,* McCoy thought. *And don't fret at the crowd neither.*

The anger riding the hubbub was bending restlessness into everyone's spine; the entire throng started to lurch and push: *This goddamn fight isn't even going to happen!* "Travesty!" more than a few were shouting. "Goddamn travesty!"

Dang these bastards! McCoy punching deeper into shadow. *Don't let them kill you, McCoy.* What hope of fair treatment does a skinny kid have when riot threatens? What hope of winning, when he's not even who or what he says? He tried to find the pale redhead among the angry mob.

It's 3:15 A.M., and raw. At last Dick Nibs jumps into the ring, calling for the first-round bell, his coattails whipping up. The wind is noisy, mocking, the night is spent charcoal far and wide. "Storm's coming soon, boys," Nibs screeches. "Let's go, let's go. . . ."

In the far offing a little tornado is a stood-up worm dancing across the horizon. Drizzle falls on the crowd. "Let's go!" Dick Nibs yells.

A loud cheer goes up for Deaf-Mute. The promoter Nibs tips an imaginary cap in the direction of McCoy—a taunt. A sideshow midget in small-scale fighting trunks circles the ring. He holds a placard that reads: "Round one."

Deaf-Mute rends the air with an unearthly howl.

As his name is announced, McCoy dawdles in his corner, dry mouthed even in the drizzle, his stomach shuddering up into his throat. His heart is calm, however, his mood mostly brave, this moment is exactly as he had dreamed it would be—but dancing on his toes, McCoy is weeping. The crowd roar has grown vicious, he has never heard anything louder. The redhead in the front row rears up her head and hollers for Deaf-Mute to pound this skinny bastard McCoy into oblivion.

But this is who our boy is:

When the bell sounds, McCoy is outweighed by fifty pounds that could pass for seventy, with a scrawny man's circles under his crying eyes, he's wincing as the night breaks open—there's a magnificent cloudburst, a bull-crash of thunder, deep-drumming rain echoing off the amusements and the ground and flattening the river—and the crowd curses McCoy even louder, tilting their faces back, catching the dark drops in their mouths, everyone soaked and wild to murder this delicate stranger if Deaf-Mute fails to kill him, all these men moved to some ecstasy of rage, their screams like an attack of bees stinging clear through the skin of McCoy's neck, right into him, and here's our raw-boned battler contesting all of it—McCoy rushes at his opponent, fist first and eager to win.

From the Dead

Let's fly ahead. Let's talk of McCoy and Tommy Ryan and their battle for the World Welterweight crown. What a fight it was. You can't imagine the blood.

Beforehand, in the challenger's makeshift dressing room in a huge icehouse called the Coney Island Athletic Club, reporters gasped at a shirtless McCoy. "I didn't know man had that many ribs," said the mustachioed Leslie McAdoo Jr., of the *New York World*. This was the frigid, very first morning of the twentieth century.

"Just watch me, boys." McCoy tried out a sneer and hoped to seem a mean one, menacing with fight craft. He punched the air, once, twice, quick. McCoy suffered the handicap of high good looks. "And count yourself lucky, Leslie junior," he said. "I don't often answer the questions of a man named after his mother." McCoy's chest was hairless, of course.

"McCoy, you got a build like some dolled-up corpse, and in addition the coloring." This scribbler, an H. H. Measures of the *New York Evening World*, talked into his notepad as he wrote. "You're all knees, wristbones, and such—except for your pretty eyes." In most quarters that would be an insult, but in old-time boxing the one-liner was nearly as regarded as the punch, and the press always liked to make believe they were in on things.

"I lack in bulk, but I make up for it in guile." This was McCoy winking, just about a hat rack with ribs. But tall, to an extent. "Boys, artifice is a dignified defense." (That being the same line he would give eleven years and about as many professions later, facing the lethal end of a policeman's pistol and near-certain demise.)

"You're as skinny as a shadow; you're just shadow." The *World*'s Measures again. Not many in the fight game liked McCoy's new-fangled "scientific" approach to boxing. He was a tactician and not a monstrous crude roundhouser.

In the cold air H. H. Measures's breath came spinning from his mouth like an evaporating cotton candy. "How does a man, skinny as you, have such a deep voice?"

"Routine," McCoy said.

"And what about that corkscrew punch of yours, McCoy? Where'd you come on such a cruel blow?" (It was McCoy's trademark; he'd turn his fist over 180 degrees, winding inward, beginning palm up and ending palm down, knuckles blasting into cheek or rib or shattery nose.) "Are you to bring out the corkscrew tonight, McCoy?"

"Patience, boys," McCoy said. "Have some."

And then the fight.

It was an early Sunday, the Coney Island Athletic Club largely dark inside and just about empty but for the few reporters (there hadn't been prefight ballyhoo because our boy didn't want to give Ryan any chance to figure out the flimflam). Ryan didn't have a "second" with him in the ring—in fact, the champ had brought no one here at all save his wife, and she wasn't allowed in his corner by reason of gender. McCoy had nobody at all. He wore black trunks with a green belt embroidered with "Kid McCoy" in dainty white calligraphy.

"Hello, there, Mrs. Ryan," McCoy said, catching Eleanor's eye as he touched his hand to his forehead—his easygoing salute. Mrs. Ryan fingered her glasses from slipping down as she nodded a smile.

The referee was the Italian hocus-pocus entertainer Francis Santoro, famous for his ability to guess what state of the Union you were from just by hearing you cough.

Kid McCoy and Tommy "The Stinging Bee" Ryan met in the center of the ring, ignoring Santoro as he spelled out what few rules boxing had back then—this was before gloves or decisions or knockouts of the technical variety. Both fighters' teeth clacked in the cold. There was one window in the whole place.

"'Zounds," said Ryan, "I see one or two who seem to be reporters here, McCoy, for a fake exhibition." A muscle twitched in his neck like a blinker from a part of him that wanted to turn left. "Whomever woulda thought. They know it's a fake, right?" And his veinsome right forearm was so overbrawned that his left, at first glance, seemed dwarfish.

"Yeah, that one looks like a penny-a-liner," said McCoy, all the while picturing his favorite targets: solar plexus, throat, head. Our boy threw four punches into the empty air—one punch for every year since Ryan had beaten him witless. "But isn't it great, Tommy, to take these suckers?" Even in the low light McCoy's sweat gave his skin the luster of a bedsheet under the moon. Ryan's chest and arms, meanwhile, were flabby in a way McCoy hadn't seen before on the champ.

"Listen, my friend—we'll put on a show for these guys, huh?" Ryan gave McCoy's belly a friendly tap. "And why not? These malooks who have no idea what it takes to do what we do, eh, McCoy?" At Ryan's amiable smile McCoy despite himself felt genuine warmth for the man. In the real world even enemies now and again step out of their roles.

"Just try to make the misses look like hits, Champ," McCoy said, "and we'll walk away richer and unbruised." And they both laughed, alike as apple is to apple. "Remember, Tommy, you're going to 'punch' first, a phony one to my head, then I'll come with a pretend shot to *your* . . ." Even back when he'd been Gil Selby, he'd dreamt of such a moment—and how did he feel having arrived here?

"McCoy," Tommy Ryan said, "is that teardrops in your eyes?"

There went up no cheer as the fighters walked to their corners.

I'm up against Tommy Ryan, McCoy thought. *I may not be in his class, but if I can scam a win, I'll be champ of the world.* There were three judges, paid for by Ronnie and Ray and McCoy himself.

McCoy, taller than Ryan, had the gangly man's advantage of reach. But gazing across the ring at the smiling champ, he had a moment of panic. Some dreams you can't help but wake up from: one day he might open his eyes to real life. He didn't want to guess what real life might be.

The referee Santoro, with his back to the fighters, bent to sound the opening bell. Ryan bullrushed over to McCoy's corner and he started clubbing our boy in the face. Brutal punches one after another slammed McCoy's head, glanced it, chased it, and missed it, and landed and landed and landed. By the time that opening bell finally rang McCoy had already been pummeled into the middle of the ring, bewildered, his left eye a glowing red balloon.

"What's the matter, McCoy? Huh?"

The fight was five seconds old and McCoy's face was severely cut. All he could see were fists; the pretty swerve of his cheek was worn raw as if by a pack of fire ants. Worse, he felt small. The champ had taken the measure of him.

Another punch to his face, a right hook with the sound of a gigantic water balloon bursting. The champ's foreknuckle bisected McCoy's lip.

This is the end of things, McCoy thought—

A swinging uppercut from the champ, a lightning bolt shooting against gravity into McCoy's skull. Ryan was hardly even boxing now, just taking aim. McCoy's head turned this way and that, his eyes bowling upward. He had yet to throw a single punch.

At least he was in pain; if he'd already suffered a knockout blow, he would have known softness like downy pillows at his ears—that being the mercy of total defeat. *If you don't get floored by this kind of punishment, you won't go down for a long spell,* McCoy thought. *McCoy might get clobbered all night.*

If he could last the round, he might be able to—what? Last one other? His legs felt like echoes of legs. He collapsed into the ropes, taking punches, his face a witless, absent simper. The corners of the ring bleared and then brightened: the world a white canvas. He felt the downy pillows, after all.

Ryan huffed through gritted teeth: "Try to flimflam me, McCoy?" And our boy at last managed to throw his first punch. . . .

Maybe it was the way Ryan had said "McCoy," like a hint into our boy's ear, or maybe because McCoy was fast slipping out of the conscious moment—but his mind began to paint over the white canvas with details from an old memory. The particulars came whooshing: All of a sudden he's sixteen again, and breathing the close beer-drenched air inside a Pillar's Saloon in North Judson, Indiana. He's simply Gil Selby, not yet McCoy—this before the Deaf-Mute fight, before *any* of his fights. The sixteen-year-old kid with small-town doubt is scared to be alone in this beer hall. Pillar's mirrored barroom is quiet, even the drunks at the gambling wheel are silent. Then, rolling in like the low note from a bassoon, a voice: *What's a skinny kid like you doing here?* The man who says this looks thickset next to the spindly Selby. *You got TB, or something, Kid? You look skinny as a TB sheeter.* And Selby's own voice, shy and slight: *You're the prize-fighter they call McCoy. That's why your posture's so grand. 'M I right, sir?*

The man—this man who is in fact named McCoy for real—is pockmarked; his black eyebrows are ferocious. All around the saloon, men turn their heads.

Kid, the man says, *who in damnation else would I be?*

Meanwhile, most of North Judson continues to make its way inside; they're here to see this thickset stranger who's come to fight in the boxing hall above the bar. And again Selby speaks bashfully, a bird addressing an airplane: *I could beat you, sir, in the ring.* Selby himself can't believe the strange words coming so gently from his mouth: *Maybe not today, but soon. Size I don't fear.*

The man's laugh reverberates: *Kid, you can't fight McCoy if you're frailer than a ghost.* His voice echoes as if he's right in our boy's ear, *Not today, not tomorrow, not even the tomorrow after that.* . . .

But these old memories of Selby as a teenager faded now as the welterweight champ Tommy Ryan's fists, the same fists that had clouded our boy's head with these memories, were punching him awake. It was as if the cloud had become filled with bees.

He writhed in pain, Ryan's straight lefts and huge rights landing to his head, and he remembered that, yes, his *own* name was McCoy nowadays. He was fighting for the championship.

Ryan panted like an old dog. After seventy or eighty punches, fatigue or overconfidence brought some recklessness into the champ's work. He was keeping his right hand below his waist. There was an opening at Ryan's nose—and McCoy gathered the energy for one wild swing, and hit the softbone at Ryan's temple.

For a moment neither man punched, and Ryan's face had the look of a bratty child's.

"I don't know how you lasted it, McCoy," McCoy muttered, as he hobbled to his corner after the bell ending round one. He stood supporting himself on the ropes, bent over like a man of eighty.

Across the ring Eleanor Ryan was heard asking her husband, "Why are you hitting McCoy for *real*, Thomas? Isn't this an exhibition?"

The champ, however, didn't seem to be listening. If Ryan had decided to fight McCoy at the last moment, he still hadn't trained for this match—while on the other hand, our boy was prepared to the minute. Ryan looked thoughtfully into the air, trying to catch his breath. He hadn't caught it by the time the bell rang for the second.

McCoy made his way to the center of the ring. He leaned into Ryan just to keep from falling over. This was not a winning strategy. You do not tip into Tommy Ryan to clear your head.

The champ punched and shoved McCoy back against the turnbuckle, and penned him in. McCoy had no room to work. He didn't bother to try.

Fantastic bombs burst in McCoy's ears. How many seconds? Twenty, more maybe. But Ryan was not at his sharpest. Trapped, panting, McCoy, still fighting on some shrinking deposit of instinct, kept his guard compact. His blocks began to limit the champ; Ryan missed one punch and then began in haste to throw another: such a small mistake. McCoy lunged, an overhand right to the champ's jaw.

Ryan wavered, they clinched like the Siamese twins, squirming, and the referee was there to break them apart. McCoy was off the ropes. Both men breathed in snorts.

Ryan was a wonder of the ring, but his method was old-fangled—sure, the champ was more gifted, but our skinny boy had a break-neck style that was utterly new. He had the modern zeal to make a quick end of things. This matched the exquisite boxing and finer strength of Ryan.

But McCoy was near senseless from the battering he'd already taken.

Any slug-out is a flow of chaos and brilliance. McCoy threw simple combinations now—most of them missing—to collect himself. He was tired in the ring for the first time in his life.

Ryan landed knuckle to nose, another four lively ones, their force gathering—pap-*pap*, pap-*pap*. McCoy's head ticked back. One of his eyes seeped pus. The fighters drew apart, then with the slap of clammy skin against skin they came together as if each had a magnet in his chest.

Ryan wagged his head like a baby with a wounded ear. He squinted to see how much he'd hurt McCoy, then caught him with an uppercut; the hardest punch landed so far. Now more hits, lefts and rights. McCoy's legs started to go; he felt air leaking from his brain. When Ryan dropped his guard again—McCoy wanted to punch before the opening vanished, but his body, like a stubborn pet, was slow to follow.

This is Tommy Ryan, he thought. Even his good eye was closing now. *I'm not in his class.*

If he could only clear his head and concentrate. *Wake up, McCoy! . . .*

Go down, McCoy! Go down, McCoy! The sixteen-year-old boy Selby in Pillar's Saloon in Indiana doesn't even realize it's himself screaming. It doesn't matter; he's a kid again and standing just outside the box-ing hall on the top floor, where the local fight is being held. He's out of anyone's earshot, staring at the violence through the glass panes of the locked doors. Inside, it's only adults with money. *Go down, McCoy!* Young Selby's lips close enough to the pane to cloud it every time he breathes. And the big man whose name is McCoy is getting beaten on the other side of the doors by a North Judson local named Billy Meyers. Surrounding the ring, a crowd of yelping prairiebillies waves money in the air like little flags. Young Selby breathes a silvery moon of his worry onto the glass: *Go down!*

The thirty-five-year-old McCoy is on one knee. The local boy Meyers is chopping away at his head, rocking back and forth like a man going at a huge log with a crosscut saw.

Go down! Selby's brittle voice again. *He'll kill you!*

This man whose name is McCoy finally does fall—collapsing facedown into the birdshit and dust of an earlier cockfight. A powdery cloud drowses up after him. Meanwhile the local kid Meyers swaggers around, his hands over his head, more like one of the insolent bastards of modern athletics than a sportsman of his day.

After a second the man named McCoy clambers to his feet. Meyers is too busy prancing to pay him any mind. This McCoy charges, shouldering Meyers in the groin while wrapping his arms around the man's waist. Meyers crumples, this McCoy falls on top of him punching and kicking—and the whole room is silent right before it erupts, an avalanche of locals at once set upon the stranger.

Don't let 'em kill you, McCoy! This is young Selby, of course, his skinny boy's cry going unheard. *Don't let 'em kill you!*

Then Selby can't bear it anymore; he runs away. Down the poorly lighted hall, panting, he takes the carpeted steps four at a time. The sounds of the gangfight at his back carry through the walls, glass is breaking, men are howling, Selby has never run so hard in his life, he's racing past the empty gaming table, he's the only soul in that mirrored barroom, his throat's closing, and still he's running, out a side door and into the alley and the frosty air.

He pulls at his hair. *Why am I such a mollycoddle?* He stops, getting his breath back, leaning against Pillar's cold brick wall. *Like a cockamamie mollycoddle.* He waits outside there, alone, digging his fists into his own toothpick legs. He thinks of Gilgamesh, the hero of the only book his father ever gave him, the dark fighter who appears in his mind whenever he tries to guess at the strange and terrible of his world. " 'Don't be afraid.' " He recites Gilgamesh's words. " 'There is nothing we should fear and even if we fail we will have made a name for ourselves.' "

Well, he thinks, *I won't leave, then*.

And so our boy waits in this narrow alleyway for ten minutes, fifteen, the noise of the barfight fading.

Selby thinks about making his way back inside, but he's afraid; he waits, he rubs his palms warm, he hops up and down, and it's now half an hour he's spent there. *What am I even waiting for?* he asks himself. *Nothing.* Indecision is the cage his hope is flying against.

Other boys have always called Selby "Bones," and also "Odd Duck" because of his tendency to play with invisible friends. He's learned that the way to get boys to stop making fun is to imitate the characteristics of the best-liked youngsters in town—winking, laughing loudly, telling stories. And he's gotten perceptive about how people sum up who you are before you even open your mouth. Selby now imitates McCoy's jab, his uppercut, as he begins to walk toward home. *Oh*, sighing, *why am I such a little mollycoddle?* But, hold on, is that—?

Mr. McCoy! Young Selby calls out to the shadow now drooping out the side door. The boy's voice is nasal and high pitched, even in his own estimation.

The shadow doesn't turn to look at Selby as it passes him. But over its shoulder it mutters: *I can say what Meyers can't, that is, I made it out of there*. The shadow coughs and coughs.

Mr. McCoy, I was—I was wondering if I—

The shadow stops abruptly as if it's come to the end of a yanking leash; it shakes its head the way people do after a long sleep. Then, the cursing shadow slouches against a wall. It slides into a puddle, sitting in it, breathing quick and hamsterlike. Selby lingers a safe few steps back.

Help me, Kid. Get me to my feet. A string of blood runs from the man's ear. *Please help me up.* The man moves side to side in the puddle for at least a minute. *I got another fight this week in Colorado.* Like a town drunk he struggles to stand, and he's failing at it, and Selby just watches.

Come, please, you little bastard— The man's voice is a carcass of a voice: *Help*—

Selby thinks about taking a small step to him, but doesn't. The man's eyes are big, one of them is entirely bloodshot and the other is getting smaller. Where he isn't bloodied the man is white as paper. He smells like the newborn horses that Selby has helped midwife from time to time.

Selby's been in awe of this McCoy, and yet he doesn't help the man now. It's not only that he's afraid. The boy is shocked to find himself lacking in pity.

Help me, you little whelp. Scrawny little cunny, help me—

The man's chest rattles and falls—shivery little breaths. A spume of blood gurgles out of his mouth.

The second-floor window of the bar flies open. Men from inside jeer and throw trash at the man whose name is McCoy—balled-up newspapers, bottles that burst as they hit the ground or hit the man himself. Young Selby flattens himself against the wall, shrinking from every bottle that breaks. Chips of glass hit his shoes, hold to his trousers and hair.

Once the men stop throwing bottles, once they've yelled their last insult, he shambles up to this McCoy—the fallen fighter in blooded-up clothes looking no better than anybody else in the world, in his too-tight green suit with a black vest and patches here and here—but the outfit and the man still look magnificent to Selby because it is McCoy, the almost famous fighter—

Here, Mr. McCoy, let me help you up. Selby sucks in air, getting under the dead man's shoulder, leaning into him, holding tight. But when he thinks about how best to help him, it brings an unpleasant stirring for reasons he can't figure.

Kid, I need a doctor. Speaking those five words seems to cost the man a whole week's energy.

Selby walks him out of the alleyway; the two are arms-over-shoulders like men posing for a portrait. The smell of the bigger man's breath is a punch in the nose. Selby doesn't know where he's going—this isn't the fastest way to any doctor's house he knows of. The unfamiliar stirring moves over the boy more strongly, together with a shame, a guilty fear of something not understood. *I'm helping this man*, Selby thinks to calm himself. *How can that be wrong?* The injured boxer's mouth is leaking blood. Selby carries him with a strange ease, as if all that he's feeling so excites him that he's moved beyond his own will.

Kid—the man's voice is a carcass of a whisper—*please, Kid, walk slower.*

Part of why Selby's going this way is that he thinks no local doctor would patch up this man who'd beaten the local hero Meyers with a cheap shot, and not at this hour—

Please—slow.

—But at the same time he feels as if kicked in his suddenly despicable heart. The boy has a few stirrings at the moment, and bringing this McCoy to assistance is only one among them. He tells himself that he's not as unmoral as this. It's as if there's something demonic at work. His heart is a crazy sprinter running five ways at once.

The street, a dirt street with a humped center and sloping sides, is empty. A star shows in the sky. It shimmers like a tear anxious to drop. Behind Selby and the limp boxer, a few prairiebillies have returned to the open second-floor window of the saloon, and they're yelling again: *Good riddance! Never come back!* But their shouting soon tapers off. *That's how North Judson treats strangers.*

Selby keeps walking. This McCoy is getting heavier on his shoulder. The night starts to rain. After a minute the street is all mud.

Selby walks the man across it, very slowly, staggering actually. The soaking muddy street is empty, the weight drags at Selby, and he thinks, *I'm not taking him as far as the woods, I know that much.* They pass through a gap in a fence onto a field. There's no moon tonight, just that star. After they walk some thirty feet, Selby can't see much beyond the rain-bleared silhouette of faraway trees. He keeps on. He knows the lights of the town must be visible behind him. His feet sink into the mud. His socks feel like tongues moist and heavy on his ankles and the tops of his feet. His heart has calmed. The ground is all puddle—rain just collects and collects in flat Indiana. It's work to carry a man twice your weight through the rain, at this pace. The spread of sky all around is sharp with cold rain that nips at his face. He sees his hands and the skin of the other man's cheek as glowing. His own legs spasm, urging the other parts of his body to stop. He doesn't stop, though it feels he's fumbling through an endless underwater with a boulder on his back. What is driving him on? *The best thing*, Selby tells himself weakly. *I'm doing the best thing.*

Why, then, aren't you taking him to Dr. Sachs?

But his heart is calm.

Come, now, Mr. McCoy, Selby says. *Please help me by not dragging your feet.*

They have reached the tree line. Selby takes a few stampeding steps, stops, then falls forward again into the woods, looking for momentum to help move them on. The man whose name is McCoy is now wet clear through, and he slips from Selby's grasp every three steps or so. It takes all Selby's strength to keep the man from falling. The man convulses. The man's eyes are closed.

The sound of rain hitting the leaves seems to echo: each leaf booms. By now an hour has passed, inches at a time.

Selby has to stop. In the dark, in his fatigue and guilt, he spends minute after minute pulling at the man, lifting him onto his skinny shoulder. He takes a step, grunts, and lurches before repeating the act at a wretched pace—all Selby's thoughts are dead in his brain. The roots at his feet trip him.

Selby and the real McCoy are deep inside the forest now. With his body going numb, Selby's losing his sense of where his hand ends and this other man begins.

I can't do this, Selby thinks. *I can't because it's wrong.* He resolves to take the man to the doctor after all. *I just have to keep going and I can get there.*

The man named McCoy doesn't care about this. The man named McCoy has died. Selby realizes this but doesn't stop walking with the dead body.

The path through the woods is narrow and difficult. Selby stumbles the corpse into the trees, or runs against them himself, his face and hands and the man's face and hands getting cut by the branches. Selby and the body are both bleeding; their blood runs together.

A burning pain shoots up Selby's spine. Flames rake out along the branches of his ribs. When he gasps for air it comes out like a dog's sob. He knows now exactly what he's doing: it is the act he'd considered but had been afraid to admit to himself when the boxer had still been alive.

Now he thinks dumbly that he wants to look strong, to impress this McCoy if the man is looking down from wherever it is that the dead go. Selby cannot catch his breath. Is that a snake underfoot? Or is it just the sort of snake his sister Anna has him look for every night under their bed?

His breath feels hot in his lungs, and he's desperate to stop, but he doesn't—he is not far enough into the woods. Even now, he has this energy. Maybe two hours have passed, three, the feeling that he is trudging across a swamp is still with him; the feeling that this is an endless chore. Our boy's stomach scrapes inside his chest. He is desperately tired. He hates the man whose name is McCoy, simply because he makes so heavy a burden.

Selby is numbed, and he can't distinguish between his own clammy smell and that of the mud or the sweaty corpse of the real McCoy. He trips. The dead man refuses to follow him and starts to fall. Selby catches the corpse in his arms. He holds it like someone dipping his dance partner. His nausea is brought about by weariness or maybe the stink vicious in his nostrils.

Again he gets under the dead man's shoulder. Selby's muscles twitch; his breathing has cracked. His mouth is hot and awful with bile. He marvels that he doesn't collapse. The lights of town may still be visible in the distance at his back. That's why he keeps walking.

His parents have always thought him lazy, and he, too, has mistaken his energy for shiftlessness—the dislike of working for others was thought to be an aversion to any effort at all. On all sides now the night is churning. His arms shake, but he doesn't slow. Tonight is the first time he's tested the limits of his stamina and it seems not to have any limits.

It's hot, the temperature really has changed, and also the smell, and he feels alone in a way he never thought possible, as if he'd walked across the world to a place no people have ever been. The smell is thick in his nostrils.

It is terrible—the smell, what he is about to do. He can't say if this was his plan all along. *No, I was going to take him to the doctor from the beginning*, he thinks, but he's too tired to concentrate on anything for more than a second or two. Any thought of guilt, any acknowledgment of it, even if to reject it, doesn't last. His shoulders have come out of their numbness into a deep ache, and his feet are raw, and the reek of the corpse gags him. He believes he could fight a heavyweight before carrying a dead load such as this again. *Yes, sir, this is the beginning of things*. And he keeps on.

He comes now to a steep, thicketed hillside. Carrying the body, he climbs. He staggers, almost drops the corpse. He reaches the crest where a little stream begins, its clear water fretting down a series of bouldered steps. The forest floor is slippery and dark; he is barely able to see the trees in front of his face now; the lights from the town could never reach this far, and so he stops—finally, he stops. Next to the little brook, within a gathering of high mulberry trees, he lets the dead body fall. It falls without much sound. He feels gloom on top of fatigue. In large part it's just that he's stopped moving, stopped his activity. The rain is letting up.

The corpse lies now at his feet. Its face, which Selby touches, is cold and hardly recognizable—pale and mindless—it could belong to almost anyone; its soul has flown off; Selby imagines it as a cloud of gnats. *Jesus Christ Almighty;* he speaks the words aloud, mostly from routine, from the habit of declaring his faith in the presence of adults. *I'm sorry about this.*

But I'll have my shot.

Panic hits him at last. He thinks dimly that maybe McCoy hasn't died. The corpse at his feet has dark shadow rings around its eyes, the sockets are depressed, and the cheek is mottled with a new-sprung mildew. And the gagging smell.

Selby brings himself to real remorse. This is an awful thing he did, a horrible thing. He starts crying. But he bounces a little on his toes too. The corpse who was McCoy looks years older. The sky is getting light. *Thank God, it's over*. After a while Selby drops to his knees.

Four trees surround this patch of flat, soft green, shaping a berth as if the ground had been intended to make a perfect bed, as if to help this act look normal. Tilting the body—yellow and black bugs already fidget across its shirt—Selby goes through the man's pockets and finds his travel plans, handwritten directions to meet someone named Dick Nibs on the Texas Oklahoma Railroad for a fight with a deaf-mute. He drops the body. Flies join the other bugs that drudge across its face. Almost without thinking Virgil starts to cover the corpse with leaves and with sodden earth. He digs with his hands. The dead man's cheeks have tightened up, his teeth are bared. The dirt covers the teeth, along with the rest of the body. Caterpillars wind around the corpse's earholes and a centipede scuttles across its open eyes. And our new McCoy is there until after dawn, the smell of dead body and *dirt bleeding into the skin of his hands. . . .*

The memory of that bygone night in North Judson flew away once more like a cloud of gnats as the champ Tommy Ryan—"McCoy, go down!"—had our boy close to knocked out at the Coney Island Athletic Club. The second round of the fight for the welterweight championship was not even half over. "McCoy, go down!"

McCoy felt his back to the ropes now—that's how he knew where he was.

Ryan hit him in the gut, and McCoy winced out of instinct, but his skin was dead to all feeling. He leaned back and hid behind his forearms. The ropes soaked up much of the force of Ryan's blows and shook like telegraph cables in a hurricane.

Still, Ryan landed.

Awful bile rose in McCoy's stomach. His pain woke up roaring. This was the lowest point. A rush of cold air whiffled McCoy's brain as if his forehead had been knocked clear off.

But Tommy Ryan was boxing right up on his toes now, like an amateur—or as if he were fighting an amateur—and behind his own knees McCoy found the strength for one last punch, a roundhouse right.

That punch didn't have much on it, but it hit cleanly. The champ bent double for a moment, and McCoy's mind cleared. He leaned back into the ropes, and before long he was able to work his reactions around the movements of Ryan's eyes and of his fists; McCoy willed his spent legs to dance, even if his left eye was oozing and closed shut. Even now, he found some little energy.

McCoy danced toward Ryan—a wounded cat jumping between two electric wires. As he leapt free of the ropes, he cut the ring off on the champ. Now it was Ryan on the turnbuckle, suffering jabs, tired lefts, weary straight rights to the head.

With every punch McCoy threw he shrank a bit. His punches quieted into taps. Ryan, scowling, elbowed him into the middle of the ring.

The champ swung his oversize right arm wildly and just missed McCoy's head. Both men were furious with McCoy's blood. It was then that tired McCoy saw something.

He recognized the look of the mark, the target, in Ryan's face. The champ's eyes, even in the ring, carried the slowness of the ever innocent. The Universal Sucker, blinking. And McCoy's worry left him. He was wobbly of body, but his brains had him at the gates of his own rescue. He improvised another flimflam.

Ryan grazed McCoy's ear with a vague jab, and McCoy staggered the way a man does when he's hit by a hammer. He unfocused his eyes for a moment on purpose, hoping to look like a sleepwalker.

The champ cocked his fist, but then held off, looking sideways at McCoy as if our boy had a weapon concealed in his trunks. This was the start of a *reverse* flimflam.

Because McCoy was really hurt—and because he understood that Ryan knew him for a flimflammer—he was acting *very* hurt, laying it on thick. The plan was to make Ryan believe that McCoy was only pretending he'd been worn out.

For a while the two fighters circled—partners at an old-folks' dance.

Frowning, Ryan backpedaled, staying clear of McCoy and trying to figure out what our boy was up to. McCoy continued to teeter, to overact. Ryan feinted, jabbing a cautious left, then a timid follow-up. Both punches fell short.

McCoy was breathing deep slow breaths all the while. Masking the truth of your condition is the enterprise of boxers and confidence men. He twisted and trembled his knees and he moaned. His legs returned, then the rest. And Ryan, flabby and tender—there was exhaustion in his grimace. McCoy, more important, had the mental advantage, and both men knew it.

Our boy had taken the worst of what the champ had given out. He had it all over Ryan now. There are certain children who come to control their households after shrugging off a second-rate punishment. McCoy'd made his way back from the dead in this fight, he'd waited *two* lives for this, and so now, heart thrumming, his wide-opened eyes looking as if they might roll out of their sockets, the immovable McCoy let fly his most miraculous punch of the evening, of his lives, a world-beater of a right corkscrew, a punch years in the windup, a shot to the head that made a comet's tail of the air behind it as sure as it made a zombie of its target. It hit with a sound like a watermelon fallen off a truck and splattering onto asphalt. In bareknuckle fighting McCoy owned the edge of being bony. And for the first time tonight this small, jaded crowd gasped.

McCoy hit Ryan again, in the solar plexus now, another corkscrew. The champ withered. McCoy landed again: to Ryan's head and his throat, in combination.

A second wail—a single hurrah—went up from the fifteen or so people in the audience. McCoy didn't see the tall woman who applauded from the back of the gym, the tall sharp-cheeked showgirl who, like a dancer just finished her spinning number, had tumultuous hair. That was redheaded Susan Fields and he didn't see her.

But who could have missed Eleanor Ryan whimpering just beyond the ropes; the champ's wife crying out behind her fogged glasses? Her husband looked like a man stumbling down an invisible staircase cut across the middle of the ring. He made it to the ropes now, Ryan did, and he cowered there.

McCoy walked to him at his own speed.

He gentled Ryan's head in one hand—the champ's welts gave him baggy eyes now, the cheerless baggy eyes of an ex-president living out the last of his sleepless nights (and picture one of those slack eyes dribbling tears)—McCoy babied Ryan's face in his soft left palm as he struck it with a right. Tommy's head turned ninety degrees in a painful direction—the champ lashing McCoy with a yarn of his own saliva—and Ryan went down like an old wino paid a dollar to perform Hamlet's death scene, Christ, he was long in the falling, and when he landed McCoy was the champion of the world.

J. G., Flimflam King

One scoundrel helped the sixteen-year-old Selby understand what it'd take to be McCoy: this was the princelike Johnnie Gold, Chinese con man, the "Buddha of Swindle," who radiated grandeur in bedraggled pants.

A live wire of a hustler, about thirty-eight, slicked up like a greenhorn's idea of an American, Johnnie Gold was huge, you might say hippopotamic, in a poor English-cut suit. Not like his countrymen with their plushy topknot braids and droopy jade coats, our approximate Occidental in 1895 wore a pompadour, under which more than a little genius of whim-wham got cooked up. His lapel forever held a daisy: the one playsome and untacky part of his person.

Oh, how did he and McCoy meet? How do any two people?

Gold showed a Cheshire smile of belly skin where his shirt couldn't quite reach to his belt. His shaved cheeks spread so wide, his face looked bigger than his head. "Your society's had all the nonsense superstition sucked out of it," he would say, "but all the magic too—a swindler such as myself is the mystery you people crave."

But first, back to McCoy, and a little context.

When he'd first taken the name, young McCoy figured: any

world west of Indiana will do. This was little more than a week after he'd buried the real McCoy—and just days after he'd fought Deaf-Mute to a draw under the Colorado sky—and now here he'd been sitting, almost seventy hours in a cram-packed second-class train compartment. He didn't know where he was headed. Quiet, nervous and still, he was slouching in his seat, a pale, pimply statue showing bruises. He'd run away from home with only one set of clothes, and not quite four dollars in prize money from Dick Nibs.

I'm a worthless stranger to these parts, he thought.

His money and therefore his journey ended in Elkin, Utah, where bare trees stood on guard before bare mountains, and near where a movable Chinatown advanced along with the construction of a railroad known as the Choctaw line. In Elkin, McCoy'd focus his ambition.

Picture young McCoy, that whippersnapper of twists and turns just stepped off the panting black locomotive in an overlarge straw hat, a boy homesick on the open plain, concern blanched into his skinny face, late-in-the-day underarm stains on his seersucker suit, some train smoke around his neck as an evaporating collar. If any of the slow-goers milling about noticed the pinched, goosey kid, they might've guessed wrongly at how untried he was, or how far from the glorified idea he had of his own courage. Now he stood watching a thin-hipped young girl cry her sweetheart onto a departing rail car, and felt as removed as a ghost from the world around him.

Elkin, Utah, was empty aside from a pair of tent cities—one home to white rail workers, the other to Chinese. Because the Choctaw Rail Company paid its whites thirty-eight dollars a month, it wasn't unusual to find in the "pale camp," among the roaming whores, a few lively teenage kids looking to fight each other for the prize of some pocket change. The pale camp was accessible by wagon road, and that's where McCoy headed.

After walking for half an hour he approached three shirtless, mud-daubed cattle-prodders playing at swordfight with pickaxes. They called our boy too scrawny to be the kind of fighter anyone would pay to see. "If you're going to die of starvation," one said, laughing (in those days everybody laughed at the rattle-boned kid), "then you might as well go home and do it among family." These giggling numbskulls chased McCoy out of the camp with their hatchets. Most Utahns were too grim to judge a pair of kids fighting as anything but an extravagance. (The Choctaw went from Nashville, Tennessee, through Oklahoma City to the eastern lip of Utah: all of it raw country then, populated by sons of bitches largely.) As McCoy fled the camp his shirttails lifted on air. That being the last time he ran from anything.

Skinny-legged McCoy tucked in his rumpled carmine shirt, flung off his hat and left it, and wandered down the footpath to the "little China" about a quarter mile away. He knew the Chinese would have to share food with him because of the white in his skin. Clouds snarled the open sky; the sultry afternoon was nearing its end.

In the "yellow camp" Chinese workers flashed by like fish busy in a still pond. They were everywhere spicing the air with lilac perfume and blinking under a glary close of day—little men in dragging robes of the same dark blue as their quick shadows. Their tent city was built on a flat expanse of dust and probably housed three hundred.

McCoy approached four Chinese who, emptying a crate of track joints, tossed curved irons very much like horseshoes. Sparks flashed up like bees. An increasing pile of irons listed next to a heap of threaded metal spikes worn out under ages of dirt.

"Hello." McCoy smiled, clearing his throat. When no one answered, he said it again.

"Greeting." This from a wiry trackman who was a few feet closer and older than the other Chinese. In a wicker hat like a big upside-down salad bowl, he seemed a kind of leader: his salad bowl was biggest. The other Chinese looked to their feet and pretended not to hear, but this old hat-wearer shook McCoy's hand—awkward as anyone who'd just learned the custom. With his tense-lipped smile the man seemed to be trying to erase all the differences between them. In 1895 America the Chinese were widely nicknamed "celestial monkeys."

"Deng Xu," the old trackman was saying, "I Deng Xu." His fingernails were groomed perfect. "Who you?"

McCoy struggled with himself before answering. "That's a tough one," he said at last. And, patting at the face bruises he'd gotten from Deaf-Mute, McCoy winked. Then he asked if it would be possible for him to sleep in one of their tents.

After some thought the trackman said, "All right. You staying one night, sir." He reeked of lilac. "But only *you* staying, sir, please." And he eyed McCoy's welted-up face as if first noticing how black and blue it was. He took a step back. "Only you. Bringing no one else, please."

McCoy nodded. All around men were pushing wheelbarrows. The sky had gotten almost dark, the sun retreating more or less to the Pacific.

Now Deng Xu blocked the sight of his toothless mouth with a shy hand. "You coming at the end of the day today, sir. If not, we eager to work." He was holding a tiny cup of tea such as a lady might enjoy.

"I'm a prizefighter," McCoy said, "I mean a celebrated prizefighter." He expanded his chest. "I fought Deaf-Mute to a stalemate over on the Colorado border this week. You ever heard of him?"

"We working hard and eager, so we allowed to break. End of day break, sir." Deng Xu had a low voice in spite of his smallness. Even at sixteen McCoy had to stoop to see eye-to-eye with him.

A dog sauntered up, an ash-gray mutt that cocked its head at this strange white McCoy. "Get along, cur," McCoy said, shoving the mutt's floppish head.

Old Deng Xu looked at him and sighed around his concealing hand. "Only you. You bringing no others."

"That's okay," he said. Along the stretch between the two camps, dry ravines waited for workers to fill them with tons of earth. "As of last Tuesday I'm all alone in the world."

Night fell.

This Chinese camp was composed of no more than fifteen tents—company-issue dwellings actually called "nigger wigwams" and what you'd expect an American concern would offer its least-favored employees: ratty unpatched canopies that tottered when carts rolled by. No women dignified this loose village, not even whores, American or otherwise. The men—their faces either crack skinned from sunburn or unwashed of the clay that blocked sun-light—the men drew wispy clouds from their long aromatic pipes. As careful as surgeons they played some sort of game with domi-noes. Above it all there was the smell ripening the air.

These men ate preserved oysters from China, preserved fish, preserved fruits, preserved mushrooms, preserved crackers and candies, preserved seaweed, and a hodgepodge of sweet-and-sour meats, dried meats, poultry and pork, rices and teas, everywhere barrels of tea. The fumes lingered in the air, along with dirt and the human smells, sweat and dung and muck, all the grimy troubles of life snaking together into McCoy's nostrils, flicking a tongue at his brain. But the camp's smell had another ingredient: the scented whiskey kegs filled with flower water. After a workday a Chinese worker would bathe in one of these makeshift tubs without fail. Every last one soaped himself like a queen, and got to smelling of lilac toilette.

McCoy put his single bag of possessions in the tent he was to share with some eighteen of these people and went back outside. He breathed in the oversweet air, biting a cuticle from his thumb, and waited to get his dinner from the cook: preserved seaweed and dried albacore.

An hour passed, and another, and a few more; McCoy talked to no one. He went over in his mind the shameful thing he'd done in North Judson, and the pain he endured in the Deaf-Mute fight, only to find himself here. A terrible feeling, as what it's like after a nightmare, came over him. He was very young, and not only ac-cording to the calendar.

Alone under the enormous overhead curve of midwestern sky after all the workers had turned in, he walked toward the edge of camp, head down like a dog afraid to leave his master's property. This was a vast dark landscape stripped of nearly everything. Far off, iron rails shone with the moon, veins of light in the ground. Farther, the straight leash of the flat horizon joined two of the Wasatch Mountains. The stars could've passed for floating dande-lion heads. But there was nothing else, and McCoy, never better than an unsteady actor in these matters, tried to put on a show of re-morse for how he'd acted toward the real McCoy, adopting regret-ful postures, first a little blustery, next timid. Lighted hazily under those yellow stars, he worked heavy lidded to call back visions of the dead man whose name he took, but he wasn't able to muster any real condolence.

"You ever think about notoriety, Mr. McCoy?" His care to hush his voice flattened it. He was Virgil Selby now, bashful as a stray fawn. "That's all I do."

The wind shook by. Selby traced the edge of his bruised cheek. He couldn't call up an image of the corpse.

"I'm sorry, sir. I should've said 'sorry' right off." But this was ridiculous—talking to a memory of a corpse that he couldn't even picture.

And then it was as if someone lifted a stopper from his mouth; he talked and talked, a crazy whisper, all of it a splutter, untamed brag-gadocio, articulate but a fantasy, a flow-over of ideas: mostly he imagined being a household name. (He'd never met anyone who considered fame as a goal in itself, and not just a by-product of some notable action or other. Imagine how odd it sounded—even to him—to need something so queer, really to need it, in the bygone isolated century that this was.)

"I'm not sure I want to be you all the time," Selby said, trying to sound convincing as he snorted at himself. "Just by calling my-self McCoy this week, a little of Virgil Selby died, whoever Virgil Selby is."

For years, whenever he'd stopped to think about the future, he'd filled with a gloomy distress like a sickness. This first had come on when he'd been twelve—it hadn't had anything to do with what happened with his mother that year, he was sure of that. But the dis-tress had gotten stronger and stronger, he couldn't deny it. Some days he'd feel wearied and crushed under his own skin. Other times it begged to be let out and he had energy to jump to the moon. Sat-urday mornings, when his half-siblings made merry down by the creek, he'd sit on the porch and imagine himself a king of Babylon, a Gilgamesh, making laws that would forbid anyone to call him a bad name or his mother a bad name. With his friend Inkidu he'd exile his half-brother Francis junior to outer Sumeria, and when the vengeful goddess Ishtar would beg for Virgil's love, the boy would say, "Oh? And which of your suitors has lived forever?"—stabbing her with his tree branch. While imagining this, young Virgil licked his lips and didn't even blink. Nobody would ask him what was wrong. If he believed himself especially empty, it was this feeling that steered him through the world. He couldn't express it any clearer, even to himself. Being navigated by a feeling he called the Why. If he ignored it—if he felt like the tired, cowardly creature he believed himself really to be—the Why demanded his attention, like a conductor tugging on a train whistle. And then, one day, he could have sworn his father had read his thoughts. Francis Marion had told Virgil to go off and make himself finer. . . .

Standing alone now among these shaky tents marshaled together on the Utah plain, in another burst of memory he finally recalled the corpse of the real McCoy as it had lain stomach-down on the damp forest floor, arms spread wide and bent, its face in profile, one cheek against the ground, the other bloodless as white tile. He pictured the wet glow of a black centipede scuttling over the corpse's face—the centipede that had shot our boy a twitchy accusing look.

At once he started to sob, but that was because he felt sad about where he was, almost as much as about what he had done.

Nowhere on earth was stiller than a Chinese tent city after every worker'd turned down his lantern. That's why, as old Deng Xu with the wicker hat ran yelling toward McCoy, the din he made carried into the quarter-mile interlude between the Occidental and the Chinese camps.

"Where you been?" cried the trackman. It was clear he'd waited for McCoy and hoped to turn in for the night.

For a while McCoy stared at him. *I've done enough apologizing for one evening*, he thought as he followed the old man toward one of the tents—a tepee dreadful, gray, and decked out in coily black lettering. When Deng Xu crouched inside the front flap, McCoy did the same.

It was pitch-black within and hard to make out the old trackman from motions of the dark air. But with Chinese bodies strewn about skimble-skamble, little foothills everywhere to be avoided, Deng Xu hopped around rabbit-style, and McCoy managed to follow.

Deng Xu fell onto the ground, then handed his blanket to him. "Here." Deng Xu whispered, very delicate, and this was the last thing McCoy heard before slipping into sleep.

He dreamed that an old ivory tusk was poking against his chest.

McCoy woke with a start. Deng Xu was kneeling over with one long finger extended above McCoy's stomach. Behind the old trackman stood about five Chinese workers squinting over dim candles.

"Up!" Deng Xu said. "You, sir, please up!" Three of them grabbed McCoy by the arms and jerked him to his feet. "Up, please!"

The early morning weather was cool and damp as McCoy was pushed into it. Across the dustplot from the tent, a crowd of at least fifteen Chinese workers stood around two pint-size brawlers filled with the pale light of daybreak. In their makeshift prize ring the boxers weren't fighting in any way Americans would recognize.

Lunging to close a distance quicker than fear, snaking their hips, stomping the ground and steeling all the muscles of their bodies at the very second of impact—these were Chinese pugilists, corkscrewing their blows with exceptional focus. They had command over movement and freedom from error; with their outlandish fistic choreography these pugs worked up so much power for little guys. Their punches sounded from a hundred yards away like the popping flash-bulb photography of that time.

Among the Chinese audience, one man as fat as a pork hog collected money. He dressed like a would-be Westerner: blue coat and pants; spats that had been out of fashion since the 1860s; and a pocket watch (only up close could you tell it was stopped and short a minute hand). He held his faun wachleather gloves close to his vest so you couldn't see the holes in their palms.

Oh, Johnnie Gold, deceiver of fools! He was a bush-league P. T. Barnum behind that daisy he wore most everywhere. He applauded

America and cursed Americans day in day out, and most of his life he romanced a Swede named Muff who saw nothing of the United States beyond whatever room Johnnie would manage to rent on a given week. He was thin lipped and pomade headed, a heavyweight-champion talker, a mountain stood up in a pair of ratty shoes but also light of step, a cocky know-it-all, and when—with his unexpectedly little foot poised on the bank of filthy clothes always at his bedside—he'd wax poetic about flimflam, his eyes would light like the morning as caught in a pair of his fake emeralds. Maybe that century had fixed a limit on how far guile could take a foreigner in America, and, yes, intelligence could be used for other than cunning—and a third plate of dinner could certainly be turned down—but no one ever convinced Johnnie Gold of these things.

And here now stood that con artist, speechifying like a Chinese Abe Lincoln as the fight ended.

The old trackman Deng Xu and his fellows ushered McCoy toward Johnnie Gold. The American-born boxer stood higher than any in the crowd from his shoulders and upward.

"I don't want to fight for free," McCoy managed. "I'm already pretty bruised up."

"Please," said Johnnie. He held McCoy with his glittering eye. "I would not expect you to fight *boredom* for free." He seemed to be attempting the accent of a Connecticut banker. "If you win, you will walk away well remunerated." Then, to the crowd: "You see him I have chosen, that there is none tall like him among all you guys?" He spoke next in Chinese—maybe the same thing, translated. Or maybe it was: "You see that there is nobody among all of us as weak looking and bony as this kid?" Johnnie then collected some money.

McCoy found himself squared off against a little Chinese fellow with stretched-down, shiny hair parted sinisterly down the center of his head (at least McCoy would have called it sinister, because back then what looked different seemed sinister). Days earlier McCoy'd fought bravely against Deaf-Mute; it'd been a delirious struggle just to eke out the draw. But there was something about *these* people, they didn't fight natural—

Among the gray tents the workers' ash-gray mutt marched out—

gray against the gray early morning—proud like some old general in shopworn epaulets. A wind blew but it settled, the sun was coming, the dog showed its teeth and barked at McCoy, stretching out its spine. *If I lose it's because of the consequence of things.* McCoy thought: *No one can get away from what he deserves.*

The Chinese punch's energy comes from the hips, and from the way the wrist turns to grind knuckles into target. What exploded into McCoy's jaw had to be one of the most exact human movements ever thought up. (Sure, a good American boxer has a jab as quick as any Chinese corkscrew. But an American jab ends by "following through" its target, which gives the punch its thrust. Thrust is not everything.)

McCoy went down, to the cheers of most of this betting crowd.

He crawled on all fours and tried to shake the banging pain from his head. Felled by one punch! He felt the consequences of things barking at him, and stretching its spine. He'd never been hit near so hard. His insides wanted to come spewing out onto the dirt, beginning with his blood.

Instead, McCoy got to his feet, set himself, and soon caught his opponent with a jab that didn't cause much harm. (Again, a Western-style jab with its follow-through is fifty percent push; a Chinese corkscrew is cousin to a viper, darting only to retreat in a burst. When there's no follow-through, when the fist withdraws at the moment of appalling collision, nothing gets in the way of the vibration that shatters bone or sloshes brain.)

McCoy had the longer reach, but the other fighter's ability to lunge ruined that advantage. The Chinese boxer, giggling to show brown teeth, hit him with another corkscrew. McCoy fell again. Even on all fours, imagination almost saved him; he could imagine succeeding; he stood. His nose and mouth were stained with blood and dust. His fear was vanishing like paper over a flame.

"C'mon," dazed McCoy said, drooling some gore, putting up his fists. Like most amateurs he let his energy tense the muscles of his neck and face. "Try that one another time, Chinaman." He gritted his teeth and tottered. And he leaned into the Chinese fighter in a kind of rapture.

Johnnie Gold squinted at McCoy. Who had such stamina? "Go down, sir," he said, for McCoy's own good.

The little Chinese boxer pushed McCoy back.

McCoy was breathing too quick. When he inhaled, his chest looked so skinny, you might have thought you could catch sight of the heart pumping.

Another corkscrew crashed against McCoy's head. The punch landed on a three-day-old welt just under his eye.

The Chinese fighter struck again, and McCoy fell. He was helpless now, but he had energy and he got up swinging. If he had nothing else, he had more energy than these people had ever seen. He found a kind of recovery in their jeering.

He was knocked down four more times.

But he gained his feet, imagining he had control of muscles he'd in fact lost to exhaustion. He tried to carry the fight. One more Chinese corkscrew, square to his nose, and McCoy collapsed like water tossed out of a bucket. He lay on his back, nose to the sky, and thought that this is what a corpse must feel—an eternity of being afraid and unable to move. Somehow he got up charging. One final lunging Chinese punch felled him.

He was unable to rise, at last.

You might think that was the end of Selby as McCoy. Though he was beaten shamefully in the middle of a Utahn nowhere by a man half his height; though he was too young and as skinny as some lepers are; though he had no plan or money; and though after two bouts he had no wins or discernible skills; though he was awfully downhearted; McCoy was on his way—really, his life was about to take him places.

Some two hours after that embarrassing fight, Johnnie Gold was smoking his pipe and lecturing our boy in a quiet nook between two tents on the other side of the camp.

"Do you ever contemplate the weave of a leaf, or what grants the sun its yellow?" Johnnie Gold was saying. "Or, rather—creation itself, is it not hit-or-miss?" He pointed at McCoy's cut elbow, his purpling face. Carted horses clip-clopped by.

Johnnie said, "Our every breath swims with what flimflammers in lab coats have taken to calling particles: bits, specks, jots. Particles between us right now. And each of these million flyspecks must have its insignificant family, *other* specks who depend on it, infinitesimal children, tiny wives, or as the case may be, a severely unstable Swedish mistress. Are *they* lucky? So many unfortunates live today! It is a marvel that our collective tonnage don't break the back of the world, eh? Now, however, think of yourself, pugnacious person. Do you remind yourself to be happy every day on account of you being born you? Do you see that it is unlikely that you would be such a lucky so-and-so? Don't bother about the luck of me being me—that is *im*material, and you'll soon see why." Johnnie Gold's sagging eyelids showed the weight of lifelong discouragement, and tent shadows fell upon the man's forehead. But he was always coming out from under shadows and discouragements to declare one philosophic tip or another. When you first heard him you were sure the words were just fluff.

The words were not fluff.

His insights jumped off his mouth like sparks, and these sparks took a while to burn their truths into your mind.

McCoy spoke thickly by way of his now-sausaged lips. "I'm sorry, but"—his eyes had been punched almost closed and it hurt to talk—"I don't get what you're about, mister." His cheeks felt held to his face by thumbtacks. "Can you teach me how to punch in that crafty way?"

About two hundred yards over Johnnie Gold's shoulder, Chinese and white men had started digging up a cloud of dust, drilling, exploding rocks and earth. And Johnnie Gold said, "Think, pugnacious person"—and how did that voice carry ridicule and affection at once?

"—Think of the drill, the rock to be exploded by Chinese and white workers. Think of Chinese workers! Do any of them feel lucky? Perhaps! But only because that is the way of most people and things: to see where they are as the place they should be. Not really." Johnnie Gold leaned in, his whisper faint as a seashell's: "Imagine for a moment if you had been the unfortunate ground that you fell upon when my countryman punched you from your feet! Wouldn't you then look up at the man fallen on you and say, 'Ah, if only . . .' True, you might have been born an emperor, and how many emperors have there been? Five hundred eleven, by last reckoning. Five hundred *twelve*, if you count Flavius Stilicho. However, I am sorry, you were *not* born an emperor. Still in all, here you stand, a person, pugnacious. Listen, Fortune is a trifler—she loves youth and is fickle. But at least she has flattered you above me, above all these hardworking people. You, a young tryer named, what—*McCoy*, did you say?"

At a distance, a group of Chinese built high trestles of logs, each cut-off trunk felled and tied by hand, and the men did it without talking. Johnnie Gold said, "If I were a boy like you, I'd go around telling myself, 'My life is one of the scantiest probabilities in the whole *wide* . . .' I'd say, 'Salutations, my solid gift of Fortunatus!' I'd say, 'Hello, answer to my prayers.' I'd say, 'Pleased to have you as mine, you good bet on ice!' I'd say, 'Don't let me stop you, roll all over me, Wheel of Good Luck!' "

Johnnie Gold opened his thready lips, between which that corn-cob pipe, dancing over his teeth, followed the bustle of his hand gestures—movements nervous and distracting.

"Is it not true that your family managed *not* to lose you, McCoy, to Cherokee ambush during your childbirth, or to elk in trampling migration? Further, the massacre of immigrant miners at Rock Springs, Wyoming, bypassed the likes of you. Further even more, you did not, I assume, live in the section of Chinese San Francisco that was put under harsh quarantine during the bubonic plague scare of '94. You, in fact, arrived centuries *after* child-killing plague struck the Western world. You have no trouble speaking the native tongue, have no boorish Scandinavian sweetheart at home. Don't slouch; listen. You were not forced to leave your country that was overrun with foreign guns and benumbed by opium. Yes! Contemplate of the luckiness of your existence! You don't have a rancher kicking his spurs into your side, or a train riding across your great length. And, oh, that the you that *you* are is *white*? And *American*—at this moment of manifest destiny? As an idea waiting to be given flesh and to be born, I had a Chinaman's chance to be you, as the saying goes."

"Sir—?"

"Basilides the False wrote that men were the near-perfect improvisation of a second-rate God. How lovely an idea, but is that too generous to man? Not all of us can claim that, eh? Not all." Johnnie Gold covered his pocket watch with his hand as he spoke, hiding a timepiece as dull as lead. "I may be the greatest flimflammer ever to lace on a pair *of* . . ." Fleshy Johnnie Gold looked middle aged, but this may have been because McCoy was so young himself, and because the boy was in the market for a mentor. "But what good shall it do me, McCoy? I boast conning technique such as you wouldn't give credence to. Jeff 'Bleeding Kansas' Roda? Eric 'High Ass' Salat, Esq.? What do these celebrated confidence artists, these so-called brilliant confidence artists, have on Johnnie Gold?"

Johnnie flattened his underslung double chin with an index finger, then: "Soren 'the Four-Eyed Mosquito' Gnatt? A softie, no bravado for the finale. J.C. 'the English Gentleman' Coulton? Patience of a two-year-old. 'Thank You Very Much' Brett Martin? A nervous nellie. Christine 'Betty Legs' Connor? Smart woman, a woman with a bosom so beautiful that the sight of her fairly compels me to poke out my eyes. But a woman nonetheless."

All the names and many of the words were unfamiliar to McCoy. He didn't understand how he could help Johnnie Gold anyhow. True, he was quick. And he had stamina. And confidence, for some reason. But his entire body spasmed now and ached to no end. *I'll never let anyone knock me down again,* he thought. *Never.*

"I'm Kid McCoy, a celebrated fighter," he spluttered, looking at his feet, at the dried-out choking unfortunate peanut-brown dirt he stood on. "Have you heard of my reputation, or—"

Johnnie Gold lifted an eyebrow at McCoy. "No," the Chinese con man said. "I am talking, however, about real things. You have an obvious desperation. I have schemes as extra-ordinary as cathedrals."

He didn't seem to notice that the wind blew his pomaded hair perpendicular off his scalp. "But—*but*—I live in want of the great flimflam. In view of the yellow color of *my* . . ."

There was not much of a real laugh in Johnnie Gold's laughter. "You, boy, on the other hand, own the whitest skin I *ever* . . . And real spunk. You are not the weave of the leaf, or the dirt at your feet. Or me. Or I, you. I've been needing someone such as yourself, I just never find him. Until now."

Yes, a partnership was struck. In exchange for lessons in twist-fist fighting and a thirty percent split of all swindles, flat-broke McCoy agreed to learn flimflamming under Johnnie Gold, the Chinese con man. He figured that, with his build, he'd need to know his way around a con or two just to get anywhere in the ring game.

So McCoy and Johnnie would travel together to Louisville, that rising New Orleans of the border states, because Louisville was the nearest big town empty of important confidence men, and because Kentucky had horse races. Johnnie Gold was a horse-race man. And our McCoy was now a scam artist.

The Lady and the Champ

If it was the Chinese con man Johnnie Gold who helped open the scammish part of McCoy's life, it was a woman who helped close it almost five years later.

Susan Fields was the first person the twenty-year-old McCoy met after he'd won the championship from Tommy Ryan in the Coney Island Athletic Club on New Year's Day. Right off he told her that he loved her. Nothing else had come to mind.

"Hmmm. That's a fine introduction," she said. "*Kid* McCoy, is it? I am not a big-city girl by birth, therefore I'll take you at your word." Her oval face looked so big and earnest, her cheeks undercoated by the race of her dancer's blood, that McCoy's heart quaked all through its cords and vines. Even though he felt sure that her wide-mouthed smile was changeable to something nastier.

"The thing is, Mr. McCoy, I would not try such sweet talk on any *Manhattan* broads were I you, as they will see through it like a window." Almost as tall as McCoy, Susan Fields stood the way a fox might, or a falcon or a high diver at the platform—audacity lived in that slight tilt. This made up no small part of the charm in her attitude.

"Yes, ma'am," said McCoy, pretty well beat up and unable to

think straight: he was the new welterweight champion of the world and in love, all at once. He'd KO'd Ryan, reporters kept taking his photograph, and this exquisite woman had approached him. If only he had a picture of this moment to look back on always.

"Here's my question," McCoy found himself saying. A cruel welt was starting to bud under his right eye. "Do you believe me?" His whole face was bruised the color of a raisin. He didn't feel it.

"Oh, pishy *pish*!" Susan said. "A thing I do not believe in is suspension bridges"—rubbing her goose-pimpled wrists. "But you, Kid McCoy, I accept." She had a slight British accent, or the false cadence of an American girl who fancied the English theater.

For a moment McCoy, of all people, forgot how to talk. He'd never attracted a woman this sophisticated.

Meanwhile, the club was a hive, with reporters and spectators and fight officials buzzing past. McCoy was wearing only his fight trunks under his robe. What didn't surprise him now was the drum-bumping of his heart.

Here, remember, was 1900—Susan Fields's heyday as a dance-hall luminary. You could buy silver-coated photos of her on certain corners of Broadway. In these early images, her sweet faint band of freckles showing from cheekbone to cheekbone, Susan looked as innocent as farm-fresh milk, even with her pouty lips. Pictures fib, though. (Besides, womanly innocence is like the sky: invisible and made up of many layers.)

"Aren't you standing awfully near to me, Kid?" Scrunching her gray eyes, Susan seemed to be trying to look unmoved, though the flutter of her girly hand told her real story.

Bone-weary McCoy, battered but very happy, felt her eyes all over the brusies of his body. It made him happier yet to be able to share all this happiness with her. Even the still-quivering ropes of the ring over Miss Fields's shoulder seemed to be laughing along with him.

"Maybe I'm pounded a bit, but I feel fine," McCoy said. And he knew he looked handsome, in his offhand way, slender and wide awake if all thrashed up—really, except for his teeth you could say he was beautiful, with his distressing blue eyes, his healthy chin. If the word beautiful could ever be used about men. "I'm the champ of the wide world!" His voice flying up to the ceiling to meet up with his spirits.

"That, I know," she said with a tepid tone. The way she poked her fingernail at her necklace tickled an invisible feather up the inside of McCoy's upper leg. "I am a follower of the fights, Mr. McCoy, as you may have guessed." Now she was hugging her own torso, a heart-robbing posture that reminded him of the redheaded beauty he'd glimpsed at the Deaf-Mute fight and never forgotten. "I know a champion when I find one, and not just from his welt marks," Susan said. "An actress is too often surrounded by a cast of characters. I like a straightforward gent."

Though they'd never met before, McCoy'd seen her once from afar, as part of the audience for her dance review *One More Go-Round, Grover Cleveland?* As in pictures, onstage she'd looked unlike herself. Behind lights and makeup and the span of the orchestra pit—beneath her blushful stage persona—she'd resembled the gangling opposite of the graceful sophisticate she now seemed before him.

Susan Fields's vaudeville nickname was "the Elephant of the Proscenium"—probably because when she walked she fairly stomped, and though too refined ever to lurch, she exhausted a pair of high heels every few weeks. Her hair—you might have thought any nickname would've described the fury of that hair—her hair was an adorable red tumble all over. She was sturdy (who could miss the fierce cords where her shoulders flowed into her neck?), with humid eyes that shone through their gray like lighthouse beacons through cloud cover. Hers was a face fantastic in its flaws—such as her small, uneven forehead; on pale days it resembled the underbelly of a crab, especially when her curlicues like red crawler legs arched in on both sides. But sidelong-glancing, with lovely lamping cheeks and those lips that always swelled out like pink bubbles overblown—this was the make of face that men who slept late on Sundays saw when they heard talk of angels.

And now she told McCoy: "I did not come here unaccompanied, you know." She raised her long, straight nose to what little prettying light came slumping through the window. Did such nose perfection really exist? "I am here with a gentleman."

"Of course you are," said McCoy. "I wouldn't have expected *any* . . ."

She waited for him to finish his sentence. When she shrugged, the unruly chest in her tightly buttoned basque moved just after her shoulders. "However, I sent him away."

"Who?" He was even more fidgety than usual.

"Never mind whom I came with, Kid." The tight skin on the back of her hands and the crinkles near her eyes let it slip that she was older than McCoy. Her ears were dainty for the diamond-and-pearl drop earrings she wore. "I suppose he didn't have the command of language that you seem to have."

He laughed. She could make him laugh too. But was this friendly teasing, or was she a bit aloof? Not since he'd become McCoy had this accomplished flimflammer been so clumsy a judge of behavior, so poor a charmer—never before had he worried he might lose the character of McCoy altogether. The soreness from Ryan's blows was starting to set into his arms, cheeks, eyes, and nose. Also, his mouth.

"Language command is fine," he said. "I use words like fists, sometimes."

"I have forever suspected"—she kept up her comical, bantering tone—"that certain muscles wither from lack of training."

He couldn't quit staring at her upcast nose or the way she hugged her torso, while back in the outdoor gloom of the abandoned Robert Kay's Famous Belmont Grounds on the Colorado border it began again to drizzle; he felt himself once more in front of the redheaded beauty in his first crowd, and squaring off against Deaf-Mute, and all the while Susan Fields was standing here, in the Coney Island Athletic Club, smiling at him.

She began her next sentence with a gesture toward the empty boxing ring. "It's said that Tommy Ryan is the most skilled fighter in the world. And yet, you—"

"He is. The best ever to lace on a pair *of* . . ." Later, months later, glum and *How'd this happen*–minded, McCoy would remember how flippant he'd been at this moment and want to hurt himself. "But, ma'am," he was saying, "Tommy Ryan couldn't find his own house if you gave him the street address. And you're so very beautiful."

"Oh," she said, looking surprised, "how kind of you." Naturally, she would've held it against him if he hadn't said that, or at least something in the compliment vein.

Now she inhaled as women do when they're figuring the tactful way to say something. "Mr. McCoy—or is it 'Kid'?—how is it that someone such as you became a fighter?" She eyed him up and down. "Yes I've *heard* of the notable Kid McCoy—I have read that you came through by fighting in hobo jungles, and that you once heroically rescued a child from drowning. Is that really the case?"

"Well . . ." McCoy was capable of blushing.

"Hmmm. Even with your championship bruises you are as thin as a famished rat." She stretched each word like a bow string before an arrow is shot. "And that doesn't match up with the stories I've heard."

"You don't think I"—McCoy swallowed—"look like I could have been a hobo brawler?"

"I did not say that," she said with a smile. "I thought it." And then turned sincere. "You certainly fight very well, McCoy. There's no denying that. You showcased an absolutely amazing punch to end the match." Her voice sounded all but contrite now. "Was it the fastest one you ever threw?"

"Miss Fields," he said, back on solid ground, "could you see it?" She told him that, indeed, she had been able to.

"Well, then, I guess I've thrown a few faster in my day." He winked.

"When is the rematch? I'm not sure I believe your legend. Cough," she demanded.

His confused expression made her laugh a little.

"Really, cough for me," she said. "I studied with Francis Santoro for *The Broadway Follies*. I can glean the world from a man's cough."

He did what she asked, trying to conjure up Hagstrom Street hobo jungles in Nashville and also to add grumble to his hiccough. *Rematch?* he thought.

"Hmmm." Kneading her temples, she said, "Nebraska—rural

Illinois? Lived at home most of your life. I'm close, am I not? You lived in isolation at a tender age, and were domineered by others." She looked carefully at him. "Is something the matter?" For he had gotten close to weepy.

Quick, he said: "I know everything there is to know about the knuckles business." He told her in his lowest, most McCoy voice about center of gravity, about the importance of keeping your guard up, and how to throw a punch: It's very important to close your fist, like this, see? . . . If you don't close it, not only do you lose power, but you could hurt yourself. . . . And you really have to keep your wrist straight, can I show you? . . . See, the wrist is the first thing that might break, after the concentration, that is. . . . Footwork is another key; yes, footwork is like a fight in itself. You have to know where you are at all times, and where the ropes are, and your opponent, of course, you've got to know where he is. . . . You have to breathe, also. You'd be surprised how hard that is in those situations, just remembering to do something you never would have to think about otherwise. . . .

With a hint of a giggle, she told him it all was *astonishing*. "Who would have thought the fights such a system of knowledge? How smart one has to be to be a brute."

"But I'd like to see if you know a nobler job or occupation." His smile was close lipped to hide his teeth. "You're making fun. There are so many things I could show you about it, if you'd let me—"

This is a jab, Miss Fields. . . . And this is an uppercut, may I call you Susan . . . and here's a straight right. . . . This is how you defend your head, your pretty head. . . . And you punch like so and you're the most beautiful woman in the world, and I love you, Susan, and I just won the championship from Ryan, and this is a world for people like me and I think you, it's filled with slow-goers and dupes and others who generally miss the adventure to it, and Susan you smell like a flower bed and I swear one day I'll say this and more to you out loud—

Before every modern man had become a calculator, making calculations in secret to decide whether to fall in love, in 1900 you could surrender your heart to someone without knowing her—this was even expected. But how to explain what happened next?

McCoy felt himself, as if drawn to do it, breaking into her eyes, darting right into the little black circles in Susan Fields's eyes. He didn't at all understand what was happening. Did she have her hand on his now? Was she talking softly into his neck, inside his ear? Maybe she was breaking into him as he, terrified and ecstatic, broke into her. How wet a world to lounge in was the inside of her mouth, how delicate her hands felt to themselves, and it was sweet to have her inside his skin, behind the caps of his knees. He was the tickle in her throat from having talked too often with her coy voice. Now with her eyes he watched his own alarmed face smiling back at her. Even as it ended—just like that he was McCoy again, standing a few steps from Susan—at least a particle of Susan remained inside of him.

Certainly she had felt it too. Hadn't she?

This was love! Old-fashioned love, odder and purer than what the world now knows. The feeling nearly razed him, he who had not loved anyone, kept still for anyone, been truthful to anything since he'd become McCoy. (As Selby, he was technically still married to a woman named Lottie Piehler in Louisville.)

Later that same week, after crying because he had everything he wanted and worried he'd never be so happy again, McCoy went to a party thrown for him by the American Sportsman Lodge in Manhattan.

He was glad for the time to plan, because Susan Fields would likely be there. He strode in like a conquering hero with his hat pulled down on his brow, and made a show of tipping the liveried doorman who took his coat.

The tuxedo McCoy wore chafed him a little. He still had so many aches, it took work not to hunch over. Still, he was confident McCoy again, cracking wise with purplish red cheeks.

He had with him a gold pocket watch that had, during the years after the Civil War, dangled from the vest of his father, Francis Marion Selby, who himself had worn clothes under his clothes to add bulk to the slimmest frame in town, and who'd had the "only Italian boots in Moscow County" (scuffed galoshes from New Jersey, actually), and eyes bright as a pair of gunshots, and who'd once traveled all the way to Manhattan with an unwed woman and her three-legged cat before settling down to a quiet life in Bluffton Creek with a God-fearing older bride—and who, by 1890, sat crouch shouldered on the porch of his far-from-the-world house like one of the tired slaves *his* father had owned, finger-combing at the few hairs left on his pale scalp, a remarried widower singing the praises of family and Christ, but mumbling, once in a great while, about the kind of woman and spectacle no one else in Bluffton Creek had ever laid eyes on.

Tonight, to celebrate McCoy, Manhattan's American Sportsman Lodge's banquet hall was brighter than a smiling noon. Candles and wall lamps everywhere—little and large, their silver sheaths done up with clinking, beaded threads—overshone to sting the eyes. The crystal chandelier blazed like some small-scale galaxy, packed dense and all the brighter for it. The mirrors on the walls looked as white as teeth, and maybe it was just his excitement, but blinking McCoy could have sworn that everyone seemed underwater, all the guests not just moving slowly but crowned by an unnatural glow like what you see around swimmers when you open your eyes beneath the waves. *This is what your world is like*, McCoy thought, *when you get everything you want.*

A crowd had come out. The men balanced cigars or long-stemmed cigarette holders in their mouths without care. They all seemed to have pocket watches, full whiskers, rheumy eyes. The women dressed in the mannish frills of the moment, dwarfed neckties, tight-against-the-bust shirtwaist blouses that ballooned at the sleeves, and flat straw hats. The hats featured upended feathers. Who were these people? Well, over here, wearing an obvious wig, sat the hopelessly half-dressed stage comedienne Kitty Sheppard; near the door smiled Charles Exleant, whose diamond-topped walking stick tapped at all the best gatherings. In the corner stood the editor of the faddish magazine *Clementine*, Jack Paris. He often performed feats of mesmerism that turned partygoers into beasts of the jungle. In short, these were the fancy of New York, and they now shuffled McCoy among themselves like a plaything.

McCoy was talking to a Christopher J. Keller—the shriveled German immigrant with a monocle and breath like hot trash who'd been a newspaper magnate, minister to Spain, and a member of the cabinet of our nineteenth president, Rutherford B. Hayes. It was then McCoy saw Susan Fields walking past a statue of Ulysses Grant. In all her immodest grace, she was laughing an olive-drab young man over to the bar. Over her back, a banner read: *The New Champion of 1900 Kid McCoy*.

"Are you as disturbed by the Philippines problem as I am, McCoy?" Keller asked. He spoke the way a man does when he understands the world bends to his own urges. It was a financier's version of how the new champ talked, low pitched and brimming with shadows. Keller was pointing his cigar at McCoy's chest. "I'm with Carnegie and Jennings Bryan on the matter. Any U.S. military involvement is tantamount to U.S. imperialism...."

McCoy saw that Susan Fields gave her hand to the young man by her side, who himself was about to plant in a kiss on that lovable knuckle of hers. McCoy's spirits were lowering like a winter storm—

"...Why, merely take a ride up Fifth Avenue on the electric bus"—Keller would not stop talking—"and you'll see we don't play by the old world's rules anymore!" The industrialist brought the cigar to its home in his mouth like he was doing it a favor. "Which reminds me, Mr. McCoy, as regards the bus. What say you about the lack of consideration shown pedestrians? The drivers of such monstrosities seem to consider their responsibility fully discharged by the ringing of the gong...."

McCoy kept trying to get Susan Fields's attention. Every time he thought he'd gotten it, he nodded in a breezy *hello*, but she hadn't noticed him. He was left jerking his head over and again like a chicken bobbing after some feed. This ached the bruises on his neck.

". . . Seeing as how the marquis of Queensbury has recently passed on to the other world, do you think the rules under which professional boxing is conducted today will wither?" Now it was a Miss Beverly Tyne talking to McCoy. He'd managed to get a few yards and snobs closer to Susan Fields and her companion at the bar, just not close enough.

". . . Not that crafty fighters like yourself care much about the marquis of Queensbury, I'd venture." The way the tubby Widow Tyne breathed through her nose made a crackly sound like someone stepping through a field of dry corn.

"The marquis of Queensbury was a great man," McCoy answered. He flashed the smile he'd worked on these last few years, which could propel a thousand electric buses. "Apart from William 'the Bard' Shakespeare, the marquis was the greatest Englishman ever to put pen *to* . . ."

"What are you going to do with yourself, seeing that you have become world's champion? Have you any political aspirations?"

"I'm a dew nut," he said, turning from Beverley Tyne to greet someone just behind her. There was no one just behind her.

The party din tore at what Susan Fields was saying, but McCoy could hear some of it: "That has nothing at all to do with my being young." She was raising her voice playfully. "It has everything to do with my being a *lady*."

McCoy moved closer and was stopped. Someone—McCoy didn't catch his name—started to prattle about how baseball teams from Boston, Philadelphia, Baltimore, Chicago, and Detroit had agreed to form the American League. "Now," the man was complaining, a faint tangle of purple veins following the slope of his chin, "now New York will never have any success in the sport of baseball. Ay, Mr. McCoy?"

"Excuse me, friend," McCoy said, stepping past him, "I never follow any contest where grown morons dress in pajamas."

And, finally, he slid to Susan Fields and her companion. "Who's he?" McCoy asked. He leaned his elbow on the shiny wood of the bar.

Susan Fields said only, "Hello, Mr. McCoy."

"Eh, yes," the young man beside Susan said, "Kid McCoy"—the man's complexion turning gloomy. "It's my bona fide pleasure to meet you. What's it like to be champion, McCoy?"

Even with his bruised, sore face McCoy showed Susan Fields his smile, as this was the moment for which he'd been building it these years. "Who's he?" McCoy said again. He hadn't taken his eyes away from hers.

"Hmmm. Is that very nice of you, Mr. McCoy?" she said, making a show of not picking up the thread of his flirting. "Is this your way of being polite to me? To my friend Mr. Todd and me?"

"I'm trying," McCoy said. The grin held.

"That's true. Just now I'm finding you *very* trying." But she was unable to hide the beginnings of her smile, the jitter of her hands, the greeting in her eyes. Unmistakable over her shoulder lived a corner of the banner that read *McCoy*. "Are your bruises from other women that you've talked to tonight, McCoy?"

"You know the worst thing I can think of?" the champ said, treating seduction as if it were a boxing match—jabbing, jabbing. "I think about how all this beauty is given out to people so ugly." He looked around, gesturing. "That's about the worst thing I can think of."

"Well, maybe your mind is as narrow as your shoulders." Susan Fields's lilac perfume reminded him of something.

"Hello, I'm Spencer Todd," the olive-drab young man said, getting that off his chest at least.

And McCoy smiled his smile even at Todd. What no one ever understood about him—even he didn't realize it until too late—was his delirious hunger to be liked. Now he just stood there, smiling. He caught sight of his own face in one of the mirrors at the bar. *All right*, he thought. *You are McCoy all right*.

The bartender approached, but looking at the three of them—noting the conversation they weren't making—he thought better of it and turned away. Then in a far corner someone dropped a silver tray, sounding a crash. Spencer Todd ran a hand slowly through his hair. He gave a long, lip-flapping breath. At last he said: "Well, smashing, *smashing* to see you again, Miss Fields. And, Mr. McCoy, a bona fide pleasure." Then he was gone.

"McCoy. That *happened* to have been *the* Spencer Todd." Susan rolled her eyes and sounded steamed up. "He happens to be working on producing an *American* automobile . . . have you heard of him? Don't you think that such a thing would be—"

"I'm sorry, really, if I was rude to your friend." He sounded miles from sorry. His professional flimflammer powers had returned; he knew about smiles and nervous articulate hands, and the rolling of eyes. Susan's signals were the kind people use when hoping to *seem* annoyed.

He threw out his chest. He had to argue with himself not to bring a caressing hand to her face.

"I really am in love *with* . . ." He was bouncing on his toes, still bouncing. When he saw she wasn't going to get his jist, he said: "You. I'm in love with you."

"So I hear." Her arched eyebrow looked like a baby silkworm yanked by a thread up the middle.

Even though he'd spent time with her just hours before and fallen into true love with her, now that she was up close he couldn't believe how he'd underestimated Susan Fields. The Saxon correctness of her face got softened by the little crinkles near her eyes that must have come from laughing; the breakableness of her wrists was agonizing to him, etc., etc. No one as sophisticated as she was would ever die, he thought.

"Hmmm. I don't take to being courted lowly, Kid McCoy." And to his surprise she was blushing up to her ears.

"Oh, no, never lowly, a woman like you."

Lust: he felt it even in the tips of his fingers. It's the lie of the elderly that those "old days" have been said to equal "innocent." And yet, McCoy was shocked by his next thought: He wanted *children* with this woman. He'd never before understood how lust itself could be bound up with its most wholesome payoff, but now it was, like a beast with a surprising, kind face.

"Well, pish, McCoy, I should hope it would *not* be lowly," she was saying. "Not from Champion of the World Kid McCoy." Then she fairly stomped off in her usual fair stomp, her bottom frisky as two little helium balloons inside her clothes. Lottie Piehler of Lousiville didn't walk like *that*. No one in the Midwest did. Love had him feeling flimflammed.

As she walked away, lighted by the quiet insanity of the glare in that place, she turned back to glance at him one more time. She was patting her belly absently as she went, and maybe that was because she could feel the kicking in her stomach of his child that she'd carry one day, one day—

She kept stomping her path over to Spencer Todd, who stood alone in the corner. Once more, she gave that fool her hand to kiss. McCoy's heart fell quickly from its recent height. That dandy's boot was enjoying a light touch against her shoe. At the moment McCoy believed a boot was a better con artist than he was.

Before he could storm up to Spencer Todd and the boot, a commotion upset the room. Everyone began muttering. Somebody unseen among the guests was parting the crowd; the disturbance rolled toward McCoy. When the excited throng opened, it spat out the pretty if plump Mrs. Tommy Ryan, flanked by H. H. Measures, reporter from the *Evening World*.

"Admit it, Mr. McCoy." Eleanor Ryan was huffing as if she'd run here. "You whim-whammed us." Her glasses slid down her nose and she didn't bother to finger them back up. "You lied to my husband to get the crown."

"Where's the ex-champ?" McCoy said, overdoing the act of looking around. Was Susan Fields watching? "Didn't Tommy want to come celebrate?"

"Admit it, sir!" she said, mad all the way to hopping. "Admit your trickery!" H. H. Measures had his pencil to his reporter's pad.

"I don't admit it," said McCoy, winking at her. "I *relish* in it."

H. H. Measures chuckled, and started to write.

"Wondrous speed and guile," McCoy went on, proud as any young bull or king. He saw himself for a moment as others might have—a dashing champion, his hat pulled low, his father's gold watch showing its chain, his narrow handsome face still bruised.

Once, a woman he'd known in Fall River, Massachusetts, told him he was more lovely than a butterfly, and that he was even farther from a caterpillar when he acted cocky.

"What about a rematch, Kid?" someone yelled. "Can you beat Ryan again?"

"Wondrous speed and guile," McCoy said, his heart gone hollow at the thought of Ryan a second time. "What qualifications beat speed and guile for a world champ?" He punched the air three times. People broke into applause. Even Susan Fields.

Golden Lessons

Right off with Johnnie Gold, Chinese con man, McCoy at sixteen had been sulky and, tossed like a feather in a whirlwind, humiliated. He'd begun his climb into the life of bamboozling and twist-fist boxing from the lowest step: he was a Kentucky snake-oil shill, at first.

A "tent barker," he shouted the virtues of Dr. Ping's Magick Chinee Elixir, a remedy for indigestion that brought as little healing as you might expect from its ingredients of well water, alcohol, and cascara (the latter being a "depth-charge" laxative). This'd been winter in Louisville, and a mean way to earn money. Nothing, though, was as degrading as McCoy's other task at those medicine shows: playing assistant to Dr. Ping (really, of course, Johnnie Gold) when the "doctor," wearing a hellebore-red Arabian turban, would perform his disgusting "additional ten-dollar tapeworm treatment."

"May I accept your gratuity, sir?" McCoy would say, upright as a young peach tree. This script was always followed. A medicine-tent flimflammer said the word *money* quite a bit, but never in the presence of a mark, not if he could help it.

"Sure, son," the dupe would say. The dupe was a rickety old

man, his spine a quarter moon of pain, or he was tall and mustachioed, or short and bald, maybe none of these. "I sure do hope this
treatment will give me help, son."

McCoy'd lay a little honey onto his voice to make friends:

"Have you had the indigestion long, sir? You don't say? Y'know, I
once had it myself. Yeah, this'll work great, *unless* . . . Oh, what? Nothing, nothing, just—unless you had what *I* had: tapeworm. Well, there's
no way of knowing. If only *somehow* Dr. Ping would let you try—but,
no, forget it. His special treatment is capital *G* great, but it's only for
Chinamen." McCoy'd smile, suddenly a coconspirator, and add:
"Well—maybe you could scare Dr. Ping into giving you some. You
know, show the yellow fellow who's boss in this country."

McCoy'd never be demanding; he learned how like a magnet to
compel people in a certain direction, even if they didn't see or feel
his hands on them.

When "Dr. Ping" came into the tent, he'd deny the dupe with a
tremble in his voice. "No—so*lly*, special treatment costing me six
dollar, I can no afford give you it." It was an elegant performance.
The character Johnnie Gold played was mindful of his low position
in society, but not subservient.

Here the rube, who never seemed to have his full complement of
teeth, pulled his money from his pocket or his hatband, wherever
he'd hidden it so as not to be ripped off. Next McCoy, smiling like
the Gates of Heaven, pocketed this week or two of the man's salary.

The rube would drop his trousers. Johnnie Gold, speaking only
in Mandarin-y chatter, drained him through and through with pig-
mented epsom salts. And in a flash McCoy, wearing a ten-cent
glove, holding his breath and kneeling, produced from the rube's in-
decent pile a conveniently placed, spiral peeled potato. "Look,"
McCoy said. "The evil parasite!"

This might not seem a great scam: it wasn't. But it was how
Johnnie Gold wet his feet that winter, earning some get-under-way
money to bankroll real swindles. Also it was easy and built McCoy's
technique. Two weeks at it, and he could make friends with anyone.
The world near at hand appeared pretty well clear and understand-
able when he was flimflamming. He felt safe from his usual error

and uncertainty, and took to conning like a bird to the sky. The young student of falseness and the corkscrew punch delighted in city life as well.

As a little boy he'd once traveled to Louisville by locomotive. He and his family had been off to visit buck-toothed second-cousin Phyllis in quiet Shepherdtown, but their train had stopped first at Union Station. There, out the window, draped in steam, bustled an atmosphere of fancy men and women come to watch the locomotives. The ladies held lorgnettes and sat on benches next to gentlemen who balanced canes over their knees. And the buildings stretched thirty and forty feet to the sky. How different from the flat nakedness of land he'd known! His nose to the window, Virgil fixed on one fancy-pants who wore a monocle and sat without moving. Virgil watched and watched, his face hot with sweat. The man with the monocle was sitting stock-still and staring blankly for such a long time. In fact, all of the dapper people outside looked frozen in place. And this is where memory gets tricky. Because whenever adult McCoy would look back, he could never be sure if he'd seen a set of mannequins. Little Virgil hadn't been to a waxworks before, or even come across a statue, and so maybe he'd been slow to recognize what that Union Station scene had actually been: an imitation of a bustling spectacle, a prettification by the railroad company. Or maybe the people had been real and memory was false. Either way, young Selby's train pulled out from the station and, in melting detail, our boy watched a city vanish, his soul feeling new and strange. For the whole of his life the memory of the contours of Louisville decreasing into that long brown-pink horizon remained his favorite. Watching it, the tingling under his skin had sharpened. This, of course, had been his first jolt of ambition, and it'd brought the fear that he wouldn't ever become fancy like the people out his window. He'd been twelve years old.

Now McCoy, when he wasn't with Johnnie Gold, found a regular job three days a week in Lester Wohl's Department Store on Walnut Street, working alongside a young would-be actor named David Wark Griffith. At work our boy was known strictly as Selby. He even joined the Young Men's Christian Association. Maybe he was a little scared of the Why, even as it had him whispering to himself: *As you have lived, don't live any longer.* (Extreme oddness.)

And so, given a tight red suit that buttoned to the collar, he spent his days as a part-time elevator attendant. Our boy never told Johnnie Gold that he had a name or a job—or a life—outside of his time as McCoy.

Weeks unfurled into months. He spent his nights at the YMCA, which had a gymnasium, a boxing ring, and a library of fight books. He boxed and sparred and studied boxing in his spare time. Not that he had much to spare, between Johnnie Gold's tent show scams and his job three days a week. Still, Johnnie did work with him on the Chinese twist-fist, which he practiced until his wrists throbbed like sore teeth. *The Boy's Guide to Boxing Footwork* taught him how to stand, and *The Basic Book of Boxing Defensive Techniques* to avoid getting clobbered. He also read from his favorite, *Gilgamesh:* it told him that men trying to be immortal can't always hold back their tears. But he'd already known that.

As hollow-eyed skinny as he was, McCoy took on small-to medium-sized comers in bars for cash, bettering his legs, his breathing, his guard, his pluck.

One working Thursday, Selby stood in his elevator with the blare of something like dawn all through his face. A woman named Lottie Piehler entered and asked to go to the sixth floor. Selby would marry her the next Wednesday.

"Well, hello, Miss," Selby had said as soon as she'd walked on.

Lottie had smiled, a timid one. Lottie Piehler was not the type men said hello to.

Selby pulled the brass gate closed. "Hello, again, Miss." He stood there handsome, calm, and of a strange innocence with his sixteen-year-old body of stretched ropes.

Lottie's white-gloved hands fidgeted. A brown stain on her left index finger made the shape of a *u*. She crossed her fingers to hide the *u* and stole glimpses at our boy working the lever. She probably found him beautiful.

Selby, meantime, looked and looked at the girl with her fair cheeks. She was wearing a yellow dress as if it had been thrown on with a pitchfork. "You won't offer a hello back?" he said, grinning carefree. She was that homely.

"I work in a millinery, sir." Her head appeared large enough to seem at cross-purposes with her body: Selby thought of those amusement-park novelties where you put your face through a hole to show against a laughable depiction of a runty headless figure.

"Okey doke, Miss. It's my pleasure to meet you." He glanced in the mirror and to his surprise he looked convincing saying it. The elevator had glass and polished metal that Selby'd scrubbed with delicate cloths.

"I make women's apparel for the head, I mean," she mumbled. This seemed a lie. Chewing away her underlip, Lottie Piehler looked a born counter girl.

Selby couldn't figure if what he felt for her was pity or a kind of affection. She reminded him of his sister's pet mouse that'd been born without hair. She might've been eighteen, but seemed both younger than that (the pitiful thinness of her shoulders) and a little older (her clayish neck).

"I don't like fresh talk," she said, her quick peek like the fidgety light of a candle. "I think some men are fresh talkers even when they say hello, and that they 'like to have met you.' But *you* aren't, I hope." She sounded two feet tall and shrinking. "Fresh, I mean."

Lottie Piehler wasn't a half-wit, but a woman strictly of her time, working around the narrow prospects and bigotries, the same pushes and pulls, that affected everybody in Louisville in early 1896. Few made more of themselves. Most made less.

Six days later he married her—a slouching mystified young bride clearly all alone in the world. (Her father had been killed by a falling grain silo, her mother by resultant fright.)

What made him do it?

For a while he told himself that living half his time married to a girl of simple plainness might pardon his own excesses. After all, he'd helped a defenseless man to die only to steal his name. That still shocked him, if he let it.

Not that he found Lottie Piehler ugly, exactly. In fact, mornings, when sunlight woke the soft down of her cheek, she turned a sort of pretty. But when her flatwormy lower lip vanished into her mouth, leaving a dot of saliva, his teeth set on edge with a sad tenderness. He told himself that he wasn't marrying her for cruel reasons.

"Did you say the sixth floor?" Selby had asked Lottie just before it'd been time for her to step off his elevator that first day in Lester Wohl's—his hair slicked, his shoes slicked, the only thing on him hinting at his capacity for violence the muscle action of his jaw. "Because we've come to that floor, Miss."

Weightless, shying her deflated body back against the wall, Lottie had said, "Yes?"

David Wark Griffith showed up for their justice-of-the-peace wedding, Johnnie Gold never knew about it, and nobody else came. The ceremony fell on a lovely Kentucky noon.

"I—I do"—Lottie's voice misfiring when it was her turn. She was delicate as moonlight and shivering, her thin hair pulled up tightly above her big ears, her feeble neck drawn out to steady her big head. Still, the bride looked all but lovely with the sun streaming in, her temples indented in shadow, those black melon-pit eyes in a glow because someone had saved her from the life she'd always been preparing for. And, of course, there were her pretty cheeks. "I do," she said, standing straighter, and loud now, "You bet I do!"—seeming surprised by her own pluck, like some homesteader-maiden who finds courage in fighting narrow-mindedness, her personal modesty, and the bandits who'd murdered her husband during the turn west.

Selby, meanwhile, was clenching a few gardenias he'd picked from a public garden. "I do too."

But even after he moved his one hobo's sack of possessions into his bride's water-heated loft on Bullitt Street, he peacocked around the Louisville brothels. He knew other women, but never his wife. He kept his room at the YMCA, and slept there many nights.

He stayed untroubled about this for the first week. His wife's attention and the overall familylike sentiment reminded him of those odd times when his mother had set him loose from the sneers of his half-siblings and, under the gray-white sky just after daybreak, she'd watch her young son toboggan down the steepest hill in Bluffton Creek. Looking back he'd come to recognize that he'd enjoyed those days, even if local kids sometimes had laughed at the "mama's boy" when he'd reached bottom.

One evening Lottie called to him as he was making his way out to meet Johnnie. "Please take a scarf, husband," she said in a low helpless voice. She was hugging a pile of faded dresses she was about to wash. "I don't know where you're going, but it may be cold." There was genuine concern in her voice, eyes, even her posture; marriage was no lark for Lottie. And, as winter came on with the sighs from dying leaves, Selby very quickly let go of his illusions about his marriage.

It seemed he'd snared this wife only to see if he could gull a susceptible young girl without even courting her. It brought him a sorrowful ache to own up to that. In his dim, unsuspected way he'd married Lottie Piehler merely to test his new powers of flimflam.

Meanwhile, he was spending three days and nights a week as McCoy, tent-barking and picking through what no man should have to pick through.

"Well, Johnnie," McCoy finally said one chilled March afternoon, "I have to ask: What's next?"

The two of them were walking past a medicine-tent show set up in St. Matthew's, a factory neighborhood on the edge of the city. McCoy'd long since stopped thinking of Johnnie Gold as a Chinaman—no, he hadn't—but he still felt intimidated by his older, wiser partner.

"Next, we're a pair of dew nuts." Johnnie Gold yawned and shook his head. Wave after fleshy wave rolled across his cheeks. "At least for a time."

They had a half-mile hike ahead of them, uphill toward a rented carriage that bore the legend *Chinee Magick* in chipping yellow paint.

"Dew nut, Johnnie?"

"Sound it out, McCoy. *Dew*," said Gold, "*nut*. This is a flimflam-mer's bantering way. 'What are you going to do?' Answer: 'Nut. Do nothing.'"

Always a man to step lively, Johnnie Gold was walking fast, with McCoy an almost unnoticeable step behind.

"Listen, Johnnie. I don't want you to take this hard, but I'm not gonna work with you anymore." Near their path, the branches of a few firs were already sprouting their leaves.

Johnnie Gold failed to suppress a burp and didn't slow his walk-ing. Like any respectable flimflammer he was a terrible boozer.

"I'm no con artist," McCoy said, edging up toward him. "I'm not cut out *for* . . ."

The Chinese flimflammer couldn't hide a self-satisfied grin. Mc-Coy'd just recently patterned his speech on Johnnie's.

"Johnnie, the way I figure it, a flimflammer hides from notoriety as a rule." McCoy had been planning this speech since his first spiral-peeled potato. Maybe if he could explain it in the right words, he himself would understand the Why better. "J. G., I guess the no-toriety is exactly what I want, I guess. And you already showed me the corkscrew punch."

Johnnie Gold started laughing. "I told you," the Chinese con man, mud dabs on his spats, said. "You wish to fight professionally?"

"More than that," McCoy muttered.

Old Louisville was the kind of place where the wind in the bare trees and the sounds of horses at their stables mixed with factory hum and the blare of passing locomotives and streetcars.

"Someone with your chest, your arms, is far too skinny to fight for earnest. We gone, *have* gone, over this." If you were going to argue Johnnie Gold, he would win, no matter which position you took. It was his harsh eyes, also the way his logic built on itself. "I'm not saying that you don't have nerve, or enthusiasm; you have those almost to superfluity. If I can be a flimflam virtuoso, you can be a champion boxer. In theory."

As hopeful as the first flush of morning, McCoy said, "Well, I was a celebrated fighter before I met you, Johnnie. I boxed in front of the most beautiful redhead in the world once—"

"It's not only that you are too skinny, McCoy. Also, you are imbecilic and dreamy." And here Johnnie Gold let in a silent moment for McCoy to think about the silliness of his own goals, and the odds against a boy who wore pantaloons and soiled ten-cent gloves—in short, a nincompoop.

"You not really *all there*, McCoy, if you take my meaning." It was very cold. Johnnie's lips were going blue. Wispy breath from his nostrils purled up only to vanish against his face. "I would be remiss, McCoy, if I let you believe that a crackbrained enthusiasm would get you through."

"Johnnie"—for all his ardor McCoy began to droop a little— "you've taught me the twist-fist, which I appreciate. Also, I already had a real fight once, with a contender—"

"Yes, yes, in Colorado, eh? A trackman once told me that the women are beautifully small breasted in that state." Johnnie Gold kneaded his brow. His forehead looked like it was frowning. "But give ear a moment, McCoy. Whatever one does in life, the ability to flimflam, the discovery, helps a fellow do it."

McCoy flared up. "What do I discover going through people's . . . people's . . . ?"

"What *don't* you discover? Oh, McCoy . . ." The Chinese flimflammer had spent years learning the psychology of the con, the philosophy of it, he had a grasp of the odd notions of Americans, but his skin had foiled him from really profiting—Johnnie Gold was able to assert such realities in a long sigh.

"Johnnie, when I fought Deaf-Mute to a draw, I didn't quit, even in the middle of a rainstorm," McCoy said, gently, "I ever tell you that?"

"In Hunan Province, my third sister knew a mute. I believe he was deaf as well. He used to eat his blanket and think it was dinner," said Johnnie Gold. "But pay attention, my friend McCoy. Real flimflams shall come soon. Do you know how many types of flimflam there are? Well, there's humbug, fraud, false pretension, quackism, false-pretension quackism, humbug quackism, quackery with fraud, humbug false-pretension fraud, bluffery with caprice, and subtlety ingenuous."

Next, Johnnie Gold detailed upcoming swindles, one involving a banker from Paducah. The wind blew this way then that, carrying inside it the scent of spring waking and a little rain. A few hundred yards up on the far side of the hill, men in gray and brown could be seen loping back to the Smithers Paper Mill from their breaks.

"I guess what I'm on about"—McCoy, his voice down to a whisper, seemed embarrassed to say it—"is the American Dream."

"Ha!" Johnnie Gold's shrill laugh came out like a rush of crickets. "Why does this place think no other country has people who dream? What you people expect we did all night in China? Tell me what you want, without empty speech."

McCoy would have to think on that awhile. There were so many things about McCoy even McCoy couldn't figure out.

Johnnie put his hand on McCoy's shoulder. "You remain with me, yeah? For a bit more." This was later, in the carriage back to town. "You have things to learn."

McCoy groaned. What he did know was that he was anxious for whatever was to come. At least spring was bringing an end to the cold days.

His days with Lottie, on the other hand, would always be cold.

The new Mrs. Selby was unsettled, she was all smiles, she was dumfounded; she often looked as afraid as a baby rabbit. He saw her only when he came home to eat one or other of the dinners she'd prepare for him each night of the week: potatoes like old bones and chicken boiled tasteless.

"Hello," she'd say, indecisive, careful. "Hello, Virgil"—this after she'd been eating at his side for an hour. Just looking at his wife melted Selby to grieve all through his guilty heart.

She never asked him where he spent his time.

Often, as he gazed into his plate of cooked potatoes, with the tinny sounds of his young wife's kitchen busywork jangling behind him, Selby considered his bride who was distracted enough to wear the same dress for two days without noticing. He considered her cowardly voice, and her courageous smile that failed to disguise her shame in having a husband who hadn't yet kissed her. Intense images of a miserable and possible future took shape for him in the lumps of his dinner: a stoop-backed old age, weekly churchgoing, home-building with her.

I hope there's some gentle way, he thought. *Maybe I won't break her heart.*

More than once soft-spoken Lottie said "this is the first happy time" she'd known. A bashful and wifely twitch would pass over her mouth, and then disappear. "All I look for next is some children, husband," which she followed with a barely hearable: "I've appreciated young ones all my life."

She always went to bed early before the end of the evening. She'd settle under the blanket with her back turned so as not to show her timid body. Then she'd wake him with the love sobs that she made in her sleep till dawn.

On the night of their first-month anniversary—when Selby'd fallen asleep as far from her in that narrow bed as he could—he was awakened by her warm little foot. It'd crept to his calf as they'd slept. Those unexpected toes, like little kisses, delighted his skin. Though he might not have asked for such a poke, and no matter if he felt sort of lukewarm about the person lying next to him, our boy was like most men; when the lights were out and little toe-kisses in that dark bedroom twiddled against his leg, or if fingers skated accidentally over the tiny hairs of his arm, he let himself think, *Well, maybe . . .*

Later on that week Lottie jolted him awake with "I'm not afraid of anything." He thought she was crying, or maybe there was just a sorrowful wind out the window.

He opened his sleepy eyes to Lottie's body rising and falling. It was only eight in the evening. They'd gone to sleep early enough to see dime-sized glitters of yellowy twilight wavering along cracks in the wall.

"I won't and can't keep anything secret from you, Virgil." Her speech was stiff the way prepared speech always is. "I want to know everything, and I'll tell you everything."

"Okay, wife." Even after marrying her Selby had failed to get his hands around the Why. At times he'd seemed near to it, but he never really made out any more than its shadow.

She spun over now and her chin quivered. "Husband."

"Wife." And he let the downhearted noise of the wind interrupt him. After a minute there was no more wind and he said, "You see, wife—"

Moving close to him, her face loomed tearstained, pathetic, sweet, and miserable. He'd caused that misery. In went her underlip. He couldn't avoid her misery now.

"I understand you, Virgil. I really do." Her voice was splintering. "I honor and obey, even if I don't really know you yet, I mean."

Selby felt himself blushing. She went on, "I know what you will like and what you won't. You just don't give me a chance to show you. Because what *you* like is then what I like, do you see?"

Selby had to look away, to the train of dime-sized yellowy stars in the wall.

". . . Because I'm your wife, Virgil." Lottie was groaning. But she groaned as though afraid to wake someone. If—when—he'd leave her, would he hear that weak gloomy voice in his mind forever? The air got heavy with his guilt.

No! he thought. His goals were inexpressible, illogical, but they didn't include that. Guilt was not what he'd allow McCoy to feel.

"All right, what is it, wife?" he said, sitting up to light the bedside lamp. He took her hand, he really did caress her mushy hand. How to explain something that he couldn't even put into words for himself? How to tell a woman that you're planning to try all the world with your own muscle? Or that you want to halloo your name all across the Republic, rattling America's windows but winking all the while. "What would you like to know about me, Lottie?" Or that you are McCoy sometimes.

"When were you born, Virgil?" she asked.

"Eighty."

"In Indiana?"

"So?"

"How—how do you like it in Louisville?"

"Wife," he said. "What is it you'd like me to tell you?"

"Anything." A tear strayed to the tip of her nose, where it flickered, dangling, a crystal with a shaving of gold inside it. "Tell me anything," she said. There were bags under her closed eyes. Maybe she hadn't slept for days waiting for this moment.

And so he opened for Lottie a window onto his past. This was all true, if not all of the truth: He'd been born in a town of two hundred, bypassed by road and rail and consisting mostly of his kinfolk. He'd had to share a bed with many relatives. ("I've slept abutting half-sister, half-brother, aunt, uncle, mother and father in turn, discovering firsthand how grown people scratch, wheeze, fart, cringe at imaginary snakes, touch themselves and others, and fake sleep to steal an eye- or handful of something they're not supposed to"—and Lottie's cheeks went red.) He'd been called an "odd duck," and always he'd had to make do with his own company. His mother's hands were always full of weeds she'd pulled or laundry or with one baby or another, and she hadn't ever noticed him much. He was not his father's favorite. And then his mother—well, never mind what happened to her. Selby told Lottie that he'd always been careful not to mention to anyone his dreams of being a fighter, never ever. But one day out of the blue his sister Anna said to him, "You're too skinny to be a boxer"—his secret had gotten out somehow—but at least Anna was the only one who knew. Another time, Selby'd been beaten up by three local girls who wanted his sucker candy. "Some boxer," they'd said. . . .

"And then I came here," he whispered. "And met you. And that's it." He wore a truthless smile and felt as low as the villain he was.

"A boxer?" she said. "You wanted to be a *boxer*?" And for some reason this made her cry even more—maybe she hated the very idea of fighting, or just that she was hearing this fact about her husband she hadn't expected.

She let out a whimper. Selby hated himself. He was ashamed of so much. But at the same time he felt glad at the idea of a woman crying next to him. The color on her cheeks and the shiny wet pout of her lips brought a gleam of near good looks to Lottie's face. Once, in Utah, Selby'd lost his heart to a thin-hipped stranger who'd cried her beloved onto a departing railcar. And here now was Lottie,

maybe crying because she loved him too much. He hoped that's
what it was. He started to cry himself.

"Oh, wife."

Lottie brought his knuckle to her mouth and gathered her lips
for what she must have thought was a real kiss. Selby had the unhappy realization that his wife had feelings to be crushed by how he
lived his life.

You married her. Her! he thought, and cried very much. *Oh, you
genuine jackass!*

So passed their first weeks of marriage. He felt sorry for himself
and Lottie when he was home, and disconcerted when he swanked
around with Johnnie Gold. Being McCoy *and* a cleaned-up version
of Virgil Selby was like setting out to learn two new languages. He
felt uneasy thinking in one language and speaking in another. Neither of these "languages" seemed near to who he wanted to be.

In this confused setting, McCoy pulled his first big con.

In the big filmflam, the bolder the fiction, the better. Preposter-
ousness makes a lie more believable. The trick to the most extravagant canard is imagination, having the imagination to build your
canard into something like a beautiful cathedral. Or, to put it one
more way: Ask for the sun and moon and stars, and you have a better chance than if you'd asked only for the moon. These were all
Johnnie Gold originals.

A big scam is terrifying for the flimflammer, especially if it's his
first. McCoy was sure that everything was wrong as he hid one early
morning behind the clubhouse of the newly built Churchill Downs
racetrack—a barnlike construction, modest and unpainted and
home already to an army of white ants. Beneath the overhanging
roof, his back pressed to the wall, he worried that not enough of his
body was blackwashed by shadow. He held a whip. In a spic-and-
span outfit of racing goggles, knee-high leather boots, pink jockey
silks, and a little black helmet covered with soft fur, he wondered if
he could survive jail, especially in this getup. He was no longer hus-
tling constipated rubes out of pocket change. This was to be a swin-

dle for thousands of dollars. This was genuine risk. What did he know about horses, about impersonation, about anything?

And here came Johnnie Gold, in bracelets and rings of hammered (fake) platinum and a vestment of green silk. He topped it off with a pointy "gold" hat taller than Abe Lincoln's. He was leading a man by the arm. This man was the mark, a gangly banker from Paducah named David Guion.

"Fred?" Johnnie Gold whispered in the direction of McCoy. "Fred, that you?"

"Yeah," said McCoy, patting dry his eyes before stepping from the shadows and making sure to look around stage-nervously, the way he imagined a thief would. "Yeah, it's Fred. But"—here he pointed to the mark—"who's this?"

"This a friend, name Mr. Guion," said Johnnie Gold, in character up to his ears. "He having money for half my bet."

"*What?*" McCoy said, reciting his lines. "Listen, Prince Chang, what did I tell you, I don't want anyone to see us here, and you bring some—*stranger?*" He couldn't stop his teeth from chattering. *Oh*, he was thinking, *they could take you to jail for this. And not just for this! Think on how you've treated Lottie and the real McCoy*—

"Hold on, gentlemen," said this Mr. Guion, smiling, making a point of smiling. So the mark was nervous, too. "Just a minute—Fred, is it? Fred, I'm a friend of Prince Chang here." Guion must have been sixty-five or seventy, he was gray and earnest and waterfall mustached, meticulous in a white shirt. He moved like someone who thought of himself as extremely handsome. But he had hairy earlobes, for one thing, and old yellowing fingernails and big black pores in his nose. Still, all through Guion's face you could just about see the young man inside the old, bleared like a coin that you spy at the bottom of a pond. His chin line had started to jowl over, his cheekbones slumped, and his eyes were milky and ringish. McCoy, taught by Johnnie Gold to be a watchful flimflammer, had noticed that, like most no-longer-handsome men, Guion was slightly embarrassed and docile.

"No, no, Mr. Guion," McCoy finally said, "*you* hold on, pretty boy." *Am I fooling anyone with this?*

"Fred," Johnnie Gold said to McCoy. "Fred, please let us show-ing him your horse. He a friend."

And the mark joined in: "Please, would you show me your horse, Fred?" And so the con game began . . .

It had taken Johnnie and McCoy a while to set this up. For weeks Gold had been playing the role of Cochin China's "Prince Chang." He'd told Guion—the local banker, married to a third cousin of J. P. Morgan—that he wanted to move the Cochin Chinese Royal Winter Residence to the Kentucky plains. The bluegrass, he'd said, was like the "magical lawn" that the Buddha used to dream about in the "Cochin Chinese Bible." The "prince" had then signed deal after deal to buy tracts of worthless crabgrass from Guion at exorbi-tant prices, and all the while he lavished gifts on the sucker, high-priced wine and silver cuff-links. Also, and this was important, he'd made sure to mention that he, "Prince Chang," had first visited Kentucky when he'd been profiled by a reporter from *Paradise* magazine in 1894.

Johnnie Gold called this "detailing the veil." There was a *real* prince of Cochin China, and he *had* been profiled in *Paradise* maga-zine (in fact, that's how Johnnie Gold first heard of Prince Chang). So the Chinese con man went to the Paducah Public Library, sneaked out all copies of that issue of *Paradise* magazine, and hired a master engraver to reprint each copy of the article, with Johnnie Gold's picture over that of the real prince (every flimflammer knew someone who could copy anything, from stationary to two dollar bills). Then Johnnie re-bound the magazines and returned them to the shelves. If Guion ever wanted to check that the prince of Cochin China looked like Johnnie Gold, now his proof was there waiting for him.

What's more, Johnnie Gold had been "switching" Guion. The Chinese con man, of course, had never intended to buy land. In act-ing as if he wanted to do so, and for such a ridiculous price, Johnnie was convincing the mark that "Prince Chang" was stupid; imper-sonate a moron if you want to swindle a moron. Likewise, Johnnie knew that a mark was most vulnerable when he thought he was rip-ping off someone else. Greed will make a mark "chase the scam." This was crucial. Always start a big con by hyping some decoy deal, only to get the mark interested in a *second* deal. This second deal is the actual flimflam, and the scammer's great gun is to have the mark anxious to take part in it.

Thus, during his visits to First Paducah Bank, Prince Chang had been making sure to talk casually about horses with Guion until the small-town banker had finally asked him if he liked the races. Suddenly animated, the prince had started to answer—saying something about a sure way to make *thousands* and *thousands* of dollars—then stopped. "Fo-geh *ih*," said the prince, quickly, disconcerted, his accent fogging over the words. "Jus' fo-geh *ih*."

Predictably, Guion urged him on—"Did you say thousands of dollars?"—squeezing the edge of his desk and tilting forward like a would-be suicide about to jump. "I always loved the ponies." Guion then admitted that his early life's fantasy was to be a jockey. He'd always dreamt of it. "Prince, I used to lie to people about my height, and as a kid I even told people that I was part Indian rider."

Prince Chang then related how he was betting in "fixed" races at the new Louisville racetrack. Johnnie's challenge was to convince Guion that a wealthy prince would bet on fixed races, and that he could have bet *well* on fixed races. Again, Johnnie Gold told the mark to "forget" it, but when pressed, he said that in Cochin China it was "sanctified" to gamble, and that one could earn his place in heaven by making sure a bet goes his way. Then the prince pulled out winning racing tickets, all for not much money (these had been acquired by sending McCoy to the track to bet twenty cents on all the favorites for days, until there was a nice pile of exclusively winning tickets. "Do you see, McCoy," Johnnie'd tell his protégé, "how a swindle can be gratifying and extra-ordinary?")

The prince had been betting small for a few weeks, he told Guion, just to make sure he wasn't being swindled. "And I winning every time." Then, the *coup de grace:* the prince said that next Tuesday he and his partner—a corrupt jockey—would split the take on a big wager. The prince, according to Johnnie's story, was expected to put up $16,000 on a bet of 20–1. The jockeys of the three best horses were throwing the race, and the 20–1 nag was being replaced by a breakneck thoroughbred. The prince said he had an "inside man," someone who would split the $16,000 up into many small stakes to make it look unlike a single, suspiciously large bet. The prince got excited just talking about it.

Guion said, "O-o-o, sixteen thousand?" He swallowed twice. "Such a lot of money. Of course, I am acquainted with several highly placed people, as my wife is dear to J. Pierpont Morgan. . . ."

Sixteen thousand dollars in the turn of that century was a life's savings.

"I no think I can include you," sighed the prince. "Though— since you and I are friend . . ." In those days a flimflammer was as expert a tracker as any foxhound; putting his nose to the trail Johnnie knew not only where the prey was, but where the prey was going to go. This prey was close enough; it was time to strike. "I take you tomorrow, Mr. Guion. I show you my jockey. *If* you helping me getting the bluegrass at cheap price."

The mark spelled out the scam himself. He offered to split the deal with the prince, with each of them investing $8,000. Which leads us to the morning McCoy'd been hiding in the shadows of the clubhouse at the racetrack. (McCoy played the role of a jockey waiting to meet Guion.)

While McCoy lingered under the overhanging roof at Churchill Downs, Johnnie Gold had taken Guion to the track in a rented carriage (automobiles with their putrid fumes weren't even allowed there until 1902), and he'd walked Guion toward the circlet where all the jockeys had gathered between races. The Chinese con man then had signaled to the area full of silk-shirted riders. Or at least, it'd appeared he had. Then he'd led Guion behind the clubhouse to meet McCoy, who emerged from the shadows.

"You can show me the horse?" said Guion, scratching the back of his ear as the three of them—he, McCoy, and "Prince Chang" in his finery—stood in the shadow of the clubhouse of Churchill Downs.

"Yes, we can," said Johnnie Gold. "Right, Fred?"

McCoy nodded. He did not trust his voice. *I'm a nobody.* Did he look at all like a jockey—or a fighter, or a con man, or anyone but scrawny Gil Selby from Bluffton Creek, Indiana, with the drab teeth? He felt he was in a dream. *Walk away from this craziness, from all of it*, he told himself.

Then, as if he'd fallen from one dream into another, McCoy discovered himself sitting in the back of Guion's carriage on the way to the stables. What had he been saying? He didn't know, but it looked as if he hadn't given the game away. Johnnie and Guion were laughing and smiling at him. Guion slapped him on the back. "They make you jockeys really skinny, eh, Fred? But you're a little *tall*, aren't you?" And McCoy's heart was galloping. Then he slipped back into the quicksand of his own mind.

What he heard next was his own voice speaking to Guion, explaining the fine points of horse racing. He saw the man's face, watched him answer—he was aware of that—but he could only register how difficult it was to breathe. Next he found he was in a barn, pointing to a horse. Time was passing as through a sieve. Apparently he and the other two men had made it to the stable. At any moment the prince would go on about the brilliance of this Thoroughbred. Or had Johnnie already given that speech? McCoy blinked and now they were outside, watching the horse run a little track on the Ohio River at what was called the Elm Tree Gardens.

The charging mare raised a reddish-brown, calm bale of dust. The air grumbled with nearing hoofbeats, the white sunk-railing that encircled the track shivered nervously, the morning was closing in toward noon, a few black workers across the field were digging in unison like slow-motion oarsmen, and the sun, now sitting white at the point of the whitish sky, looked caught in rippling tissue. And here was the running horse itself, black and fearsome with its terrible glorious nostrils, and it was fast, above everything *fast*.

"Is this a quick one, Fred?" said Johnnie Gold, as the horse blasted by. "This is good horse?" Some dust the Thoroughbred had kicked up was settling on Johnnie's gold hat.

"O-o-o," Guion said, "she *is* a runner, she is"—(wiping dust from his face)—"I know a bit about horses, of course, my wife does, too, but then, she's a third cousin to Mr. Morgan of New York. . . ."

As the finishing stroke to the flimflam Johnnie told Guion that a look-alike horse, a hopeless trotter named Sooty Saul, was set to run in the big race. However, the "fast" horse that they were watching—named Gold Coyne—would be entered in Sooty Saul's place on race day. What Guion didn't know was that Sooty Saul was a "morning glory"—quick in the early hours, but in the afternoon as slow as a lawyer on an unpaid errand. Really, there was no Gold Coyne. The horse that Johnnie Gold—having earlier bribed three Elm Tree Gardens stablemen—was now showing Guion was the nag Sooty Saul at the early hour when she ran at her best.

"Yeah, this horse'll do, anyway," said McCoy. "She only has to be fast enough not to look too obvious winning a fixed race." For some reason he thought of Lottie, alone in the small kitchen of her apartment that was now also his. At their wedding she'd seemed unable to look at him.

"—Yes, that is a *real* fast horse," Guion was saying, and wearing the smile that such bankers generally save for the inside of a vault. But how quickly a mark's faith can leave him! "Nonetheless," Guion said next, "it's hard to fix a horse race, I'll bet. How, I mean, how can we be sure that we—"

"Yes, maybe it best if we do not betting," said Johnnie, maybe too fast. Later, years later, McCoy'd realize that Johnnie Gold would never be as big a flimflammer as he'd hoped. The Chinese con man hadn't been fully at ease keeping up a seperate self. If you looked hard enough at Prince Chang you could spot underneath him another man at work, as when you notice a puppeteer's shadow behind a puppet.

"Listen," McCoy said now. Nervousness and indecision were still all over him, but marks usually didn't notice such things. McCoy took a breath. *I can do this, I can.* "I got plenty of guys waiting to lay out money if you're afraid, Prince." And he drowned out the voiceless howl of his own heart. "But don't waste my time, Yellow." He turned and walked away.

"That is fine, we no need this," Johnnie Gold spat at the ground near McCoy's departing feet. "Happy landing, Mr. Fred."

"Wait—" Guion said. "*Wait*." Johnnie Gold had gotten him to go after McCoy as sure as if he had said, *Go after him*.

"No, I'm not going to *wait*," cried McCoy, as Guion touched his arm. "Forget it, Mister, what is it, Gewlion?"

The mark looked hangdog.

"I didn't even want you to be *involved*," McCoy said. "No crazy Chinaman is going to ruin my twenty-to-one double cross, prince or no prince."

"Wait." In the morning sun Guion's face shone like the tear of happiness he'd shed if only he could be in on this 20–1 money. He held McCoy by the arm. "I think we shouldn't be too, uh, hasty here."

Skip the rest of this scene; it's boring, the minutiae of flimflam. A man is lied to, he is persuaded, and the event comes to the only conclusion possible.

"Are you insane? Are you? I'll *kill you*!" This was the shriek of someone who'd lost a life's savings. The yeller, of course, was Guion, at the suite of "Prince Chang" in the Maurer Hotel on Louisville's Main and Sixteenth Streets, after the 20–1 Sooty Saul finished dead last in the afternoon's race. Guion cried, "I have a wife who is cousin to a most important banker in New York!"

Incensed, petulant Guion was storming from bed to window and back, one big gray-haired flail, flinging teacups and papers and even an unlighted kerosene lamp. "Eight *thousand* dollars! We can't let him get away with it, Prince! You understand me, you fat yellow monkey?" He turned back to McCoy, hate faced. "What *happened*?"

"I don't know," McCoy said, his heart going out to the sucker, but not too far. "I swear, Guion, I swear I tried." The small cackle-bladder of blood that McCoy hid in his mouth warmed his inner cheek. "I don't even know where the other jockeys are! Maybe, I don't know, God forbid Frank and Charlie got busted!"

The hard part of the flamflam was over.

"I was in the stands, Fred! I *saw* you out there on the track!" Guion grabbed McCoy's shirt, but the mark's shaking lips gave his nervousness away. He went shy after his outburst, like a firefly all dark after its flash. "To me, Fred, it didn't look like you were trying to throw the race, you know?" His black-pored nose was pulsing. "Not to me, it didn't."

"True!" yelled Prince Chang, now grabbing at McCoy, also—shrewdly, for all the seeming clumsiness of his shoulders and elbows; he was pushing Guion aside. "You lie to us and you taking our money!"

"No, I . . ." McCoy said. Being no longer really afraid made it easier to act afraid. "I just—" He stopped talking, expecting to be interrupted. When he wasn't, the silence was startling.

"Out of my way, Prince!" Guion charged at McCoy again, smelling of cigarettes and hard liquor drunk quickly.

"Help!" cried McCoy.

On cue McCoy's friend David Wark Griffith blasted in, dressed in police-officer blue—a little blue helmet on his head, vivid stage buttons on his blue coat, and a gun in the blue holster by his hip. (This was the bailout they had decided on, and not a well-timed "heart attack" from Johnnie Gold.)

D. W. Griffith was young looking to be a police officer (the airy whiskers that hinted across his chin and girlish pink cheeks), but, again, there are things a mark fails to notice in the fever of excitement. "*Hold* it!" Griffith screamed, zealous as a missionary. "You! Are! All! Under! Arrest!"

Like McCoy, Griffith was one of our earliest fame seekers—he hoped to be an actor, though at that point America didn't have performers who dared share a stage with great talents of Europe and Britain. Now Griffith made sure to close the door behind him with his foot; no one wanted any genuine cops to show up.

At this point everything came so quickly that it would have been hard for Guion to say what really happened: the glint of a pistol suddenly in the jockey's hand; two gunshots; the jockey collapsing on the floor, panting, drooling blood; the policeman making a grab at Guion before falling himself; Prince Chang ushering Guion out into the hall, where random people were coming out of their rooms to see what the noise was; a mad run to the rail station; Prince

Chang putting Guion on a train to Indianapolis with the words: "Go, and stay at Hotel Baxter there. I meeting you tonight." Later, at the hotel, the mark would get a wire from Prince Chang: "Police officer is dead; jockey in hospital. Authorities ask questions. You being picked up in Indianapolis if you staying. Go Hotel Milan in Chicago. Where I meeting you soonest." In Chicago a second letter would send the mark to Gary, Indiana. There, another letter, and he'd be off to Cleveland; next to Detroit. By the time Guion hit Philadelphia, the letter from Prince Chang read, "Being chased by police—returning to Cochin China, be back in a few years to complete real estate deals." At this point Guion would probably go home and spend the rest of his life in fear of being arrested.

The success of this big con had an odd effect on our boy. In his own past, in McCoy's *pre*history, he'd been a worshiper of boxers. Not flimflammers, but strivers. Other kids had whiled away afternoons scooping frogs from the dead leaves of the stenchy muddy slope by his town's small creek, or they'd taunted each other in the watery Indiana snow, or chased the schoolgirls who wore billowy white dresses and hats whose tassels danced on nothing—motherless Selby against that grain would spend whole hours closing his eyes to moon about never-quitting in the ring. He had no friends, but he founded an imaginary gang of adventurers on Peach Street. Evenings he pored over his *Gilgamesh* and dreamed up a long string of images: cutting down great moonlit cedars and challenging the evil Humbaba. "Why worry? What men do is nothing; fear is never deserved!" Alongside the worn footpath in the pasture next to his family's house, he often punched air when he'd been sure it was too late for anyone but his pretend spectators to have noticed—this always in the darkness, Virgil shuffling and jabbing and pivoting, and scaring up a shock of dust that caked in his mouth. The girls under the white dresses hadn't ever known him. And now that he had abandoned who he was, was it worth the effort? Did he want to be the next Johnnie Gold? He didn't see how such flimflamming could help him secure his deathless fame.

Yet McCoy's heart expanded with resolve. After Guion left town,

McCoy started smoothing pomade into his hair at all hours. He spent free moments at push-ups, shadowboxing, staring into mirrors, bettering his carriage, his enunciation, his laugh and smile, deepening his voice. Almost overnight, like some hero in a fairy tale who wakes to find himself a prince, he felt at home with this language he called McCoy.

He said good-bye to Lottie, the YMCA, and his old self that foggy spring when he quit Louisville—a community, he decided, whipped by indecision and too much compromise. And worse, it was a terrible fight town. McCoy was going to slug it out for a living.

"You risk going away from me?" Johnnie said. "That is fine." The flimflammer kept his voice as cool as the air. "Where will you go?" But Johnnie's eyes held with a pitiful expression on McCoy's face. "Do you think you can survive without me?"

"Johnnie, I'm sorry," McCoy said, a little out of breath. For some reason he'd run all the way to Johnnie's camphor-smelling apartment.

Johnnie had educated him about scamming and twist-fist fighting and life in general. McCoy'd come to adulate his Chinese partner. But he didn't want to think about that too much, or that Johnnie might even have needed him. The Chinese scam artist had no more to teach, or so the new-minted McCoy believed. He saluted Johnnie, and left.

With his share of the big con money McCoy traveled around, scheming the best ways to join the skills of boxing and flimflam. He won a few five-dollar bouts, he wiped his wet nose, he made his way to the great Tommy Ryan, hoping to be the champ's sparring partner. He got pounded cruelly. That gave him a nemesis. He moved on, played possum in the ring, improved. He waited for someone to call him out, some cynic to say: "You're not McCoy." Nobody did. He corkscrew-fisted many, improved even more, and began to finish opponents in a hurry. He'd reek with their blood, sending to heaven some appalling cries. There was an Anthony Late, whom McCoy flattened in no later than one round, in Aliceville, North Carolina; a

Jonathan "Redress" Frankman in two and with a smirk, in a Park Slope, Brooklyn, dawn where the sunrise clouds were bloody footprints across the sky. In Normal, Illinois, braving his wounds, his many wounds, he went at someone named E. G. Emke like a tiger, and, his hair matted in gore, put the shine on Emke in the fourth round. "Skinny Bruiser Looks Like a Corpse, Wins Quick," announced the *Normal Bugle*.

If he missed Johnnie Gold, he almost never thought of Lottie Piehler. Newspapers, years later, always spoke of Susan Fields as McCoy's first wife. Because she was. A woman such as Lottie Piehler would never jibe with the growing legend of Kid McCoy. (After a while he learned that every legend matches up with a widespread want—or, to a kind of faith made up of a slew of wants. If the legend is recognizable, the legend is revered. An image holds up in the public's mind because it obeys the rules of its own game.)

This image building excited his fancy. He told any early sportswriter who listened that he'd run from home at seven, or sometimes at six. He concocted a history of hobo jungles, of having spent his youth (he was only eighteen when he told this lie) "living on the bum, riding the rails, fighting other tramps." Who could blame McCoy for not describing himself as a pretty, sensitive boy from a Christian home? His eyes did always look famished.

He could never figure out where McCoy was from. In Minneapolis he told the press Indianapolis; in Indy he said Muncie. Then he was from Cleveland, from Hot Springs, Arkansas, or Thomasfield, Iowa; from Roslyn Harbor, New York. He never mentioned Bluffton Creek, Indiana. He drank whiskey, went to the cineograph theaters, and relished the moving picture entertainments. When you live every day with a secret, when you think someone could turn you out at any moment, nothing is ever boring. Laughs come easily, at first.

In Fall River, Massachusetts, where his fight against someone named Dago Frank had been anticipated unlike any he'd had before, the local fans described him as their "discovery." After he won in three, they called him "the Kid McCoy of Fall River," product of Massachusetts, local idol.

In those days, when every town wasn't yet connected home-to-home across the world by electric cable, a rural community might as well have been its own continent. A local baseball team or bicycle racer or especially a local fighter caught love, often in the form of cash, from neighbors. Not that McCoy won much money, not right off the bat. In boxing's yesterday the purses were not counted in the millions, and often not in the thousands—even the great heavyweight champion Gentleman Jim Corbett began to box only as a sidelight to a career as loan manager of the Bank of San Francisco.

Tired of being from nowhere, McCoy stayed on in Fall River. He sang popular melodies in the village saloon. He listened to any local's foolishness and reworded it for her as a lump of insight. His loneliness got unfathomable.

After a month and two days—after he KO'd "Nashville" Billy Maber—McCoy of Fall River let it be known that he wanted to become McCoy of Nashville. "I'll make both the town and myself famous." In those days, you needed to be from a good fight town to get a real start.

This Nashville Maber had been a respected pug. He'd lost to Tommy Ryan, but only after twenty-two pitiless rounds. Skinny McCoy felled him in six minutes. "A quick knockout is polite, like a courtesy," McCoy told the *Nashville Commercial Appeal* in an article that named Nashville Kid McCoy the "quickest dispatcher" in the sport. "Otherwise," McCoy said, "otherwise these boys would waste years being propped up and thinking they might have real careers ahead. And fear is never deserved."

McCoy faked a sickness before his next fight. His opponent, Young Stoffo, said, "One good punch'll kill that anemic pile of bones, and I don't want no murder on my conscience."

After teetering and coughing across the canvas for the first round, pale McCoy skipped to attention to end the contest with a shattering uppercut in the second. *Thank you, Johnnie Gold*, he thought after that flimflam, and ignored as Selby-ish the guilt that came with cheating.

He drew up business cards that read a bold lie—"Middleweight Champ of the Middle West"—and he believed the unearthly still moment after a knockout and before the first peal of applause was the delightfulest split second possible. Looking out train windows, he never got used to the telegraph cables that appeared all across the country overnight—like a line of hunch-shouldered pioneers trudging dumbly from hill to hill.

He was carnal minded with women but self-controlled too. Many fell in love with him—poor-born country girls mostly, but on occasion: thankful widows at odd hours and with surprisingly young-looking hands; impish wives on respectable streets who were fed up with their starched husbands; unabashed ladies who wore classy shoes that seemed to give them little comfort; others, others—and a few even went as far as letting their little toes in darkened bedrooms twiddle against his leg, not necessarily because he was handsome and tough, or scrawny and vulnerable, but maybe because he was closemouthed about his past. Or, maybe there's something attractive about a young man with a deep bitter want. His mother'd once hinted that women love aggressors, dandies, oddballs, felons—and wasn't he a bit of all of these now? Of course, he laughed to himself that these ladies were enamored of an unfinished scheme called McCoy.

The thought of his old hometown or anything in it got him panicky. Two more years surged and passed.

He'd had thirty-nine fights now, mostly against nobodies of a higher weight class, but he'd never lost, or even been knocked down, or hurt, and he'd won thirty-two of these, twenty-three in the first, second, or third rounds. He read American frontier poetry and was sometimes moved to sigh. He met and drank often with Bob Fitzsimmons, the celebrated crook-kneed Australian title holder. He never boxed carefully; McCoy lived to blast through one bubble of frenzy and thrill to another.

Once on a train from Dayton to Scranton he sat four seats behind a theatrical troupe who wore capes and silk. When a pair of roughnecks began harassing the actors, McCoy curled his hands into fists. The roughnecks swiped one of the actors' hats and McCoy's fists were sent into action; he leapt at the thug who had stolen the hat, then at the other one. Next he watched the men tremble down to their feet. "If you want more," McCoy said, "come back."

With this same theatrical troupe McCoy started performing in a play called *The Pug and His Lady Friend*. The third act featured a simulated prizefight. Sometimes McCoy refused to die when the script said he had to. "What men do is nothing," he'd cry, improvising.

Next his fights were heraldized nationally in the best broadsheets, together with reports of the pretty contour of his cheekbones, the daintiness of his eyebrows, how he dressed in an 1897 double-breasted, didn't always finish his sentences, and had that queer twist to his KO punch. Also, they noted his laugh, which was very loud and a new trait. For McCoy, reading these accounts was not only like peeking trough a spy hole at a version of his life. It was like watching his own reflection in a moving creek as the reflection separated and varied: McCoy caught glimpses of the different angles of his life at once.

He got to troubling himself over his public presentation and how one act or another would affect it. He'd make decisions without any thought of right or wrong, or even of profit, but based only on what nowadays we'd call his "image." Nowadays this sort of motivation is common, but McCoy's attention to a public display that was separate from his private truth added a fresh twist to the way we behave. He'd done what his father had told him. He'd made himself someone finer.

In short, our boy had grown into McCoy to an extent not even he had foreseen. Going from state to state as a sort of one-man circus act, he found himself living in a cloud bank of spectacle. He would swell like a sponge with the admiration he soaked up. He had thin slight hands like a sculptor. After one quick knockout he felt bad enough for the audience that he invited a comer up to the ring and KO'd him on the spot too.

With the advent of the welterweight division—wide open if stocked with other dogged rookie contenders—McCoy found his perfect weight class (he natually banked the scales at 145). He crusaded to win the title. Then he turned twenty.

He settled in New York, an even wilder city in that doily-and-lace era than it is now. The buildings were lower, as were the people. And McCoy tipped his hat to children at every street corner. In the windows of the new stores, the couches for sale or the dining room tables and especially the wedding rings would seem at times to jeer at him, and he'd jeer back or just shrug them off. (Men from a town small as his usually got married well before their teenage years had ended. Men unlike McCoy.)

He wasn't alone in New York in having outsized and modern aspirations. That city in the pivot between those centuries seemed full to bursting with real strivers. Life itself was bursting. In the babel of Manhattan every joker had his own idea—talk understood only by him. You couldn't judge who was sane and who insane when *this* guy came up dreaming of photographs that would move and sing, and *that* guy of steam machines that could help build other machines; or of drifting above the North Pole in a hot air balloon; or of making a fortune by producing the sort of rubber that would improve the drive of the up-to-the-minute automobile that just rolled off some *other* guy's conveyor belt.

In this teeming world people multiplied, and McCoy won the welterweight crown; he knocked out Tommy Ryan thanks to real skill and the flimflam. He met and loved Susan Fields. And he knew his emotionless smile was an advantage he could wear outright and at all times. Soon he even stopped feeling queasy at his lips.

Then, just like that, great trouble would hit. Just months after he'd won the title, he would find everything that he'd worked for was in jeopardy.

In those dark times it'd seem the mysterious ambition that had been acting on him was contained in the image of the centipede that'd scuttled over the dead face of the real McCoy in the forest. Its antennae twitching a little, its tiny face looking right into his, this ambition had a hundred legs that, as plodding and relentless as fate, wouldn't stop driving forward. What McCoy didn't know was that an even finer glory would follow. I'll tell you how.

Book Two

Trust men, and they will be true to you.   —Emerson

Americans love so much to be fooled.   —Baudelaire

Trueloves

But, first: all champions are bound up in their love story, and the end of a love story hides out in its own beginning.

After their first night at the American Sportsman Lodge, McCoy courted Susan Fields like a farmer chasing a chicken. He left a note backstage at *One More Go-Round, Grover Cleveland*? She did not answer it. Imagine how that hit a man who hankered as hard as McCoy did. He went insane or close to it.

Walking, he sensed her around every corner. A few beauties with straight eyebrows and full mouths looked like Susan under spinning parasols on a breezy Sunday in Central Park; two or three men with one or another of her might have been Spencer Todd. McCoy even saw Susanish phantoms full of grace where there were no shadows at all.

"Ah, McCoy, you're a hard nut," the *Evening World*'s H. H. Measures told him, sounding disappointed, the scribbler's long fondness for McCoy at a low ebb, because our boy, having finally earned the belt he'd wanted so badly, acted now as if he didn't give a hoot, walking here or there in some kind of muddle and not even recognizing his favorite New York reporter at a banquet in honor of "the

New King of the Welterweights" (well, in honor of McCoy and a few other sports notables), provoking an insulted Measures almost to drop his free-of-charge newsman's plate of chicken *cordon bleu* in flabbergasted annoyance. "Don't overlook that you're the champ now, which carries expected behaviors," he said. "You want to keep that belt, you'll have to start thinking about a rematch with Ryan. Champs behave a certain way."

It had been hard enough to flimflam a victory over Ryan once. Maybe he could dodge him for a while?

"H.H., if I'm the champ"—downhearted McCoy knew blustery announcements needed to be made—"you have to change the subject if I want you to, right?"

But Measures had a point. McCoy was champ. Whatever had been true in his past, lately when he signed his name for street-corner admirers, or recited frontier poetry for them, or talked gently to some woman lacking Susan's polish—even when he wandered the avenues heartsick or just slept—he no longer felt like a scheme schemed by someone else. He was McCoy all the way now. For some time he'd enjoyed peering through the occu-sights at "mutoscope parlours" across New York, adding "motion" to pictures by turning a crank that flipped consecutive images before his eyes at a rate of fifteen frames per second. At times he saw Selby as one of the ghosts inside the optical glass. A flickery one, bloodless, but McCoy could see him and from all vantages—young Selby getting teased by his half-siblings, or punching air across the grass to the cheers in his head, or taking guff from his unfriendly father; teenaged Selby blushing away from schoolgirl neighbors or standing in profile next to his mother before she was gone forever. . . .

The new Champ McCoy took up residence at the Millhaus Hotel on Forty-fourth and Broadway, that sixteen-story dream in concrete that George Herman "Babe" Ruth would one day call home. Was that Susan waiting for the elevator in the great lobby? Or standing beside the potted plant at the front desk? One lip-sticked almost-Susan on a plush red settee even smiled as McCoy searched her face in vain. The lobby's ceiling was salted with baby lights to look, all day long, like the sky after dark.

McCoy left three more backstage notes at *One More Go-Round, Grover Cleveland?* "Yes, *yes*," sniffed the backstage usher, "the world champion Kid McKay, I remember from the last time." And Susan responded to exactly none of the letters.

The champ began to show up as a member of her audience, taking a seat near the back as the lights dimmed. The set involved monstrous sofas, crepe paper flowers, and electrical cell flashes; Susan hopped onstage to a wild rush of applause. Her performance showed a cocky, unpandering desire to entertain. She excited the crowd to see the play, the character, the song and dance—not herself. In short, she had real talent.

Almost bouncing in his seat, McCoy, suffering, watched the long artful sly stomp of her body. The memories of all the women he had ever known flew from his mind like unbound pages in a wind.

He considered trying to win Susan with a filmflam, and he asked himself, how would Johnnie Gold trick a woman into love? Had there been lessons he'd failed to learn from that master flimflammer?

Then one day Susan Fields in her beauty showed up knocking on the door to his room at the Millhaus.

"Hello, McCoy," she said, breathing through her nose with a *harrumph*-y kind of laugh. Under her suit jacket she wore a lace shirt that gave a peek at the horseshoe of her collarbone and the showy thimbleful of air it held. McCoy marveled that she must have similar secrets all over her body. Behind her, on the wall opposite his room, there hung a picture of a sleek brown horse with stormy eyes and startled tendons.

"Susan Fields." He kept most of the shiver out of his voice. Women rarely knocked uninvited on men's doors in those days, almost never. She was taller than he remembered. "Susan."

"Yes, I see you have conquered the pronunciation." She gave a reckless smile that showed perfect teeth. She stood a bit too close. "I began to get the feeling you'd had about enough of waiting." She wore a wide-brimmed hat, the crown of which was done up in a silk bow, while beneath that she was just a spell, an affectingly close-by, gray-eyed spell of loveliness in a lace shirt. Still, this thin beauty was known as "the Elephant of the Proscenium," and not the Dove, or the Rose, for a reason. She was reckless, a tall *harrumpher* whose typical entrance felt like a stampede.

McCoy wanted to ask her the obvious questions. But—no matter what Susan's excuse would have been—once she answered his *why didn't you respond* or his *how could you have denied for so long what we shared*, would it matter what she'd said? Facts were facts, but nothing was going to block the way of real love.

The important thing was that here she stood, stunning in the threshold and cheerful. He listened for a moment to the flapping of wings that was his worry leaving him.

"Your final note was sweet, the poem especially. You're sincere, aren't you? Not like the actors who call on me." Her voice gave under the effort of holding back a chuckle. "Although I didn't think it wise that you rhymed 'natty elephant's' with 'fat belly pants.' Tell me you're sincere."

(What he'd really rhymed was, "Thou, sly work of art!" and "Wow, my throbbing heart!")

"And you're funny." He spoke low and familiar. "Have a walk with me."

And so McCoy found himself taking Susan, very fine in her weekend coat of paint, for a nighttime stroll toward the Brooklyn Bridge, lovesick strangers hand-in-hand craving the pleasant aroma of the East River while ignoring that notable cologne of downtown Manhattan, that sour urban wind of garbage and sweat and foreign meat smells. They chose not to see the hoodlums in thug hats nor the brassy-mouthed women of easy virtue on every street corner— no, McCoy and Susan, as they walked under the elevated train tracks, looked overhead to give their eyes a snail-paced sort of mutoscope show, now here's the sky, now there it's hidden. In every glance between the slats, stars swam across the night like bright little goldfish. The Manhattan those two were in the mind to see rose out of its cheerful mist like the delight of sweetened lips to a kiss.

He didn't think about Tommy Ryan more than once. ("McCoy Afraid of Rematch!"—the *New York Herald*, February 27, 1900.)

With her thumb stroking his, as they stepped out from under the tracks, the dim streetlight and the shadow of a moony cloud chiseled new dips and ridges into the cityscape, making changes all the time, showing first an opening, then a ridge, showing and hiding as far as the eye could see. Something electrical from the train rails hissed like a sword being unsheathed. Soot fell between the tracks like black snow.

By midnight they stood no more than fifteen blocks from strange monstrous Brooklyn Bridge, that great triumphant stone-and-iron roar across the river that sounded of all the change that was then splitting the eardrums of our world. That's what the city was doing then, shouting up its colossal wanton future above the moldy smells and just under the swimming stars: vast warehouses and factories, town houses in marble, everything higher and higher. What couldn't you do, at that time, in that place of continuous rebuilding? Here our new trueloves stood, saying all the old things to each other. She had a lollipop in her mouth.

"Susan." McCoy's voice so tame now that it all but withered under his breath. He hadn't ever known a face to be noble like hers, framed so delicate by her collar and that feathered hat. He'd never known a woman's mind could take such odd turns. *Fat belly pants*, he thought, and laughed to himself. "I want to tell you something," he said.

A family of Italian immigrants stood a few feet behind her, small neat parents and round twin boys in knee socks taking in the view.

"Yes, Champ?" Up close Susan was freckled and her cheeks were an intense white. "I like the sound of it. *Champ*. Brave and true and unlike milksop theater men." Her face prettied with that touch of emotional thrill so lovable in fair-skinned women. Her lollipop made a rosebud of her mouth.

Her lips tasted of sugar. The snips of her teeth brushed across his mouth like an icy breath. People in 1900 rarely kissed in public, even in front of immigrants.

McCoy looked into Susan's face. Her closed eyes fluttered

sweetly as he kissed her. She had the symmetry you expect in your redheaded actresses: extraordinary if quick to change.

The little Italian boys chanted: "Mouth'a touch mouth!" They were laughing. "Mouth'a touch mouth." And McCoy and Susan laughed with them.

They turned back to each other, forgetting the immigrants, which people were free to do in those days.

"So that's how a kiss can cut a girl out at the knees," she whispered. For the most part Susan was different now, not as brash as she'd seemed when they first met—gentler, more modest. When she spoke there was trepidation in her eyes. "Your charm is improbable," she said. "Your skinny face is so very drawn and sad for no reason I can determine." Trying to make it sound light. "You're a terrible odd lone wolf, that's what you are, my dear."

"You must have me mixed up with someone else, Susan. That's not Kid McCoy. I'm no lone wolf." He took in a quick short breath through his nose. "Don't you know me?"

She watched him for a time. Her wide eyes were now among the smallest you ever saw. They were reading each other's faces. McCoy smiled—broad as he was able while hiding those gray teeth.

"Susan," he said. "I thought you knew me with the first look."

"Oh, I want to," she said, heartfelt if maybe stage-loud for the moment. "I want to!" The whole of that evening they never let go of each other's hand.

Their courtship was a regular whirlwind. Love bullrushed in with its chocolates and its poems, remaking, mystifying, not to mention honey-coating the whole damn world. McCoy had charmed a personality brighter, more successful and consistent, and more at ease than his own, a woman who promised an effortless sophistication above what he might have been able to manage by himself.

He proposed to her at his first boxing match after having won the belt.

This first title defense came in Nashville, against Wisconsin's Michael "Marmaduke" Grendelman. At ringside Susan fiddled with her silked-up hat. The trueloves had known each other six weeks and had just announced that they held each other more dear than anything else, any family member or memory or place or friend or God or pet or childhood sleighride or—

"Why, McCoy!" she spoke elegantly around her cigarette. "Are those tears in your eyes? Oh, you darling kid!"

". . . This Mr. McCoy, who is said to be quite thin, is said in addition to be an exemplar of pugilistic encounters, with his novel style predicated to quickness," read the *Nashville Daily Tennessean News*. "He is valorous, resourceful, moreover a popular favorite. The only question is if he'll have a chance against Ryan in the inevitable rematch." The Nashville Grand Opera House had never sold so many tickets for anything. Before the fight an ex-slave drove his fist deep into his own mouth for audience approval.

"—The spindly pugilist McCoy told this reporter, 'I'm never going to die.' Well, readers, we'll see if Grendelman has something to say about that. . . ."

Just before the bell Susan, the side of her face that was close to the candlelight going pink, hovered outside the ring as McCoy stepped through the ropes.

He swiveled around and said, "This one should be easy, Duck." Out of fun his sometimes name for Susan was Duck.

"All's easy for you, McCoy," she said, sweet.

Leaning over the ropes, he kissed her. "You're easy, too, Susan Fields."

"Say that again, you may develop a new limp." She pulled away, sour.

Really, he'd meant it as a compliment.

"Now, love," he said. "I just mean, I was trying to . . ." And like that he was dumbfounded. She was the only person who'd ever been able to affect him so quickly, except maybe Johnnie Gold. McCoy couldn't think of what to say. Grendelman stood across the ring at the edge of his vision, and clenching his muscles the man seemed close to bursting, like a human bean-pod.

McCoy just blinked at Susan. He was lost until she gave a smile. Around his Duck he no longer talked like a flimflammer. One thing that'd bothered him about their courtship: When he'd asked her recently if she'd also felt that weird breaking-into-each-other feeling when they'd first met, she hadn't known what he was talking about. Not at all.

"If you begin to behave yourself, I shall wish you luck," she was saying, sweet again. Her fleecy white cheek looked deserving of a kiss, and he felt the desire, standing right there in the ring, to quit this fight and crowd and concert hall—how much nicer to have been alone with her in their modest hotel room. . . .

"Fight well, and I shall be here when you get back," she said. He was pretty sure she didn't mean that she'd be there *only* if he fought well.

"I want you to be here forever, Duck." His voice going throaty.

"*If* you behave yourself." Still banterish. "I'm not the type for a hard day's work."

"Marry me, is what I mean, Susan. Marry me," he said. "Marry me."

"*McCoy*," she said. "Never to have been asked, and now to have been asked three times in succession." Then she smiled. "I am only joshing, you know." And winked. "I've been asked before."

He'd hoped and imagined she'd blush, or look away to hide happy tears. He did manage to get out, "Yeah, but which of your suitors will live forever?"

Kissing him she said, "Knock this opponent quickly onto his bottom, in order that I may see if you mean it." Her hair was honey smelling.

Sure enough, McCoy ended the fight in no time, flat. He hit his rival once in the head, and Grendelman cringed and drew away, but there was nowhere the Wisconsinite could escape in that ring. A tremendous welt appeared on Grendelman's face, and he started to weep. He couldn't go on.

"The McCoy-Grendelman fight," read the *Daily Tennessean*, "having been decided in short order, under the rank of shenanigan too characteristic of this rabid form of entertainment, assuredly will result in the decay of local interest in future events. . . ."

That was one of many McCoy stories the newspapers ran. In New York the broadsheets had started to fill themselves with features not only about McCoy and his twist-fist skill, but also about him and his "tootsie" Susan Fields.

Manhattan was at that time years ahead of the rest of the country, and, as every month in the Big Apple brought more changes than decades once had, overnight there appeared "gossip columnists" in the New York dailies. No one could say which came first, the talked-about romance of McCoy and Fields, or the columns dedicated to covering it. Either way, McCoy's social life was getting the kind of once-over unknown to men who'd gained their fame years or, it seemed, even weeks before he'd gained his.

Harper's Weekly magazine, April 3, 1900:

> Whosoever has subsisted in the good Christian life, and yet wanted now and again to kick up one's heels as Spring draws nigh; whosoever has sought to eschew the impelling force of those incompliant mores of the century newly-ended; whosoever values a punctilious chronicle of the deeds of comely womankind, he would have delighted in the doings this past evening, at the Mauer Hotel Banquet Room! There Susan Fields and Kid McCoy, better known to patrons of *Harper's* as the Elephant of the Proscenium and the newest notable of pugilism, respectively, were seen to hold hands in this public locality, making quite a fanfaronade in sight of all patrons, and not merely on the floor reserved for dancing! As if a tsar accompanying his tsarina, McCoy with a wry face shook every proffered hand, and Miss Fields received a kiss on her empyreal knuckle from any fellow stalwart enough to chance the indignation of the young champion of the young division of this young sport. Now, if only Kid McCoy will square off again with the great Tommy Ryan. . . .

True, McCoy *had* been to the Hotel Mauer with Susan, but hadn't shaken any hands—and Susan hadn't let anyone kiss her knuckle, at least not that McCoy saw.

Here was the *Brooklyn Daily Fox*, a publication that offered a "new process for language for the sensible American man"—functional

writing, stripped of "hindrances to pragmatic, Modern reading"—
April 10, 1900:

> Perhaps should come as no surprise two pugilists of neater
> build, Kid McCoy and Gentleman Jim Corbett, pair of pugs
> who cut a swath in world of sport, well-known to each-other.
> But of late Corbett, educated heavyweigher who more than any
> fistic brethren helping to lift boxing from paws of brawlers and
> goons, has according hearsay befriended new champion of Wel-
> terweights. Informed readers know McCoy, though unmarried,
> often in company of Miss Susan Fields, actress. (Miss Fields
> bosom chums Mrs. Corbett, patron theater arts, wife of Gentle-
> man Jim.) Barring Corbett, McCoy most artistic fighter we
> have, and needs be open to lessons from great heavyweight and
> gentleman, who is more established by yards. "Marry her, Kid,"
> Jim Corbett should vocalize, if truly gentleman; and McCoy, if
> blackguard wishes turn into gentleman, needs say, "I shall. . . ."

(That paper's motto, "The world is going to hell," was the new
expression on everyone's lips.)

Even the *Times* of London wrote about McCoy, on May 4, 1900:

> The nation of the New World that changes her monarchs
> perforce every four or eight years, and that builds railroads at a
> gait of a thousand miles in a week, and who accepts all the *residue*
> of every other country under the sun, this nation now gives the
> world yet one more specimen of her hastening of the natural
> way of things. The Kid McCoy, of New York via the vast empty
> middle of the continent, procures subjugation by knockout with
> more celerity than any other fighter here known. . . .

McCoy was in his time of contentment in the months before his
rematch with Ryan, famous, a "subjugator by KO," a friend of Jim
Corbett, and, together, he and Susan Fields were careless, charis-
matic, and extreme.

She'd grown up not far from New York City. Her family had lived in a manor house on the Hudson, with servants. Her father was princely, a forceful philantropist, related in some distant way to De Witt Clinton; for seventy-five years the Fieldses' money had come flowing out of the Erie Canal. Starting on her fifth Christmas, little Susan had performed a "Yuletide Dance Program" for her household every December 24, and she'd charged admission—parents twenty cents, servants fifteen. She was used to being doted on in a way that McCoy found strange; he took it on himself not to fall short of the pampering she'd known.

He'd ask things like "More tea, Duck?"—sounding a world away from tent barking in Kentucky.

"All right, darling darling."

He didn't just love her for her sophistication or her beauty. Or, he did—but in those simpler times men didn't separate out a true-love's beauty from her personality. Susan Fields's impulsiveness, her liberal temperament, and her humor—that was all tied up for McCoy with the pretty silhouette of her legs, barely seeable through the fabric of her dress as she strolled, his tall girl twirling her silked-up hat on her finger.

He often imagined her without clothes. In his mind, when she walked her thighs at their meatiest parts just whispered against each other, touching lightly skin against skin, a muted soft breathlike sound with each step. He adored the strength of her stride. Here was where the physical and the personal really came to a point: the endearing lumbered gusto of her stomp. And, when she stood still in his imagination, above those thighs came the pleasing triangle of air where her legs rounded gorgeously into the rest of her body. The littleness of her kneecaps he found delightful too. Love beautifies even kneecaps.

Anytime McCoy was alone after an evening with her, he'd bring his shirtsleeve to his nose, in hopes of catching the dying mists of her perfume. Of course it wasn't fear of a rematch that held him: how could he think of Tommy Ryan when he had this?

The Leaf and the Bird

She stretched out a few inches away and stared.

Susan's sagging bed was narrow for their bodies. Maybe she'd been watching him a long time. Lighted only by the moon and the little half-moon flame of a candle. Blankets all the way to her chin. The slopes of her body making snowdrifts of those soft pale bedcovers. From an opposite window, flakes of brightness swam down the stream of moonlight toward her mouth, which set in a frown.

She must've thought McCoy asleep.

What did she see when looking at him? A well-muscled dandy with custom English-cut waistcoats? A thin boy with ripped underdrawers and ripped socks? He thought she might say: *You have an expert haircut, McCoy.* Or: *Your belly button is by and large nap-filled. You're crude, Kid; your posture is top notch. . . .*

She sat up and the mattress sounded for a moment like baby sparrows. She was not dressed.

Or maybe it would be this: *McCoy, you have a long iron body like a locomotive but your chin's so often stained by Coca-Cola or cotton candy or other juvenile foods. . . .*

"What've you been staring at?" McCoy said.

Susan Fields crossed her lovable arms over her splendid disobedient bosom. She had alarming cheekbones. "Nothing," she said.

They were in her apartment far uptown, near the farms at the stay-at-home edge of urban progress.

McCoy reached to Susan's waist. She slid even closer. Among certain playhouse types, free love existed, even in 1900. (As long as it was likely to lead to marriage.) Out the window the city at night winked and rippled like a woman's hair after her shower.

"You don't have to worry," McCoy said, feeling Susan's warm foot against his calf. "I saw the way you were looking at me, Duck." If he adored her, he didn't know her well enough to talk very comfortably about serious matters. "Duck, I have a furious ambition, is all. But you can believe me, every time."

"Oh, pishy *pish*, McCoy, I don't care about ambition—in what way was I looking at you?"

They'd loved each other three months. And he'd never once mentioned the name Selby.

"Ever contemplate the weave of a leaf?" McCoy began now, swallowing. "Or what lends the sun that yellowishness?"

"No." She'd chosen to snort.

"Okay," he said. He could smell himself. "Well, Balisades the False—"

"McCoy—" She smiled, irresistible and tired-sounding. *She looks soft*, McCoy thought. *Yes, a pillow person; a* charlotte russe *with legs*. He kissed her shoulder, soft, soft.

"All trueloves when they first meet," he said, breathing these words into her neck, "are just like a particular bird and its leaf, the only kind of lucky leaf that the bird thinks it can survive on—"

"McCoy, where is this coming from?" She was nestled at his side. Her voice, too, was gentle. "I was looking at *you*. Thinking that you are exquisite. Not birds, or any leaf. Exquisite, and strange. Wonderful and—"

"I like that," he said. Of their own his quick-witted fingers took a graze over her. He thought he might find, in the difference between his hard boxer's fingers and the delicate cushion of her haunch, a lesson about what attracts men and women to each other. He hadn't overlooked that she'd called him strange; it made him feel sad, even if she'd wrapped it in those other words.

"McCoy?" She raised her eyes to him, bright as ice cubes in the moonlight. All their indifference, irony, even their calm, were gone. "Do you know what it is?" she said. Meaning: Do you know what is bothering me about you right now? Naturally, he turned to face the window.

She was concentrating on something hard enough to bring a little seam between her eyebrows. This he knew without looking.

"How we are with the lights out, you and I together. I mean *this moment*. It's wonderful just being here. My girlfriends never will know this, what I am like with you. My family will never know it. Maybe that's what separates a truelove from a friend. Lying here in bed, how our faces turn in bed. That's a secret we keep for ourselves." She was a little more eager than usual. "I just wish we had—more of that."

He turned to her again.

"Maybe it's enough," she said. "Do you think it is?"

The room was a minor ticker-tape parade, so many flakes of brightness swimming in the moonlight. Susan made a little moving-picture show of the shadows along the bed by swaying her hand between her face and the window.

At length she said what she wanted to, the words creeping out on little tiptoes like children stealing from their beds: "Do you think that what eventually happens to every man and woman who come together will happen to us, McCoy?" In those days, in that loneliest part of Manhattan, there was no street noise. "It must," she answered herself, and lay flat again. "What I mean is the monotony and distrust. No one meets a man thinking that she—"

"Duck, that's just what I'm talking about with the leaf and the bird." Until tonight he hadn't cared that there were extraordinary secrets he'd never told her about himself.

And he had this quick thought about his strange life, his entire boring, absurd, spell-caught and thrilling life. As McCoy he lived with more invention, he desired with more tenacity. Then why did he feel so very sad at this moment?

". . . do not understand the leaf and the *bird*," Susan was saying. "I do not know what you are talking about." For all its affection her truelove's voice seemed to have the wind's cunning for getting in and chilling his bones. "When I look at you, McCoy, there are things—" She stopped to choose another sentence. "You see, because I don't really know, it's that I want to know—" She stopped herself short again. Her hair was a red heave across the pillow. Her face was pale white, like the pillow, and part hidden by that heave of red hair. Maybe he should tell her the truth.

"I *saw* the way you were looking at me," he said. Over the past months he'd had some bouts of nostalgia when he'd tried to work the shy demeanor of his younger days, but he couldn't really spark a light that subtle anymore. Being McCoy was all or nothing. Especially if he wanted to stand a chance against Ryan in the rematch.

"Don't worry, Susan," he said. "I'm your chap, through and through." And why should he share with her the truth about Selby, if she hadn't admitted having felt the *breaking into each other* on their first meeting? Besides, how could he tell her about his past when he'd forgotten so many of the old details? (And here were some of the details he wanted not to remember: How his half-brothers and half-sisters called him "the son of the strumpet." How, after his mother had stopped taking him tobogganing, he'd set up rocks and sticks as an imaginary crowd of friends and admirers to watch him. . . .)

"I suppose I just do not understand what you mean a lot of the time, McCoy," Susan was saying, while the anxiety she'd been trying to hide bounced her knees. "I suppose I do not."

I don't care, he thought, which was a lie.

"Wait, Susan, I think I may know." His fragile little whisper was very different from the sudden hopeful swell of all the parts in his chest. "We don't have to be like other men and women." *We don't, we really don't.* "If there's one thing I've learned, we can change the normal way of things to fit our case," he said, and, lighthearted and suddenly sleepy, he smiled. *I see now we can change life and even death.*

"Can we?" She was shaking her head. "Just tell me how, McCoy"—her little night breaths on the plush of his neck. "Tell me how and let's do it."

McCoy didn't say a thing. Sleep was gathering just beyond the bed, but he fought to keep his eyes open and pulled Susan to him.

* * *

In those days a woman who conducted herself the way Susan had done risked the stamp of promiscuity. But McCoy told himself that all her past relations with men had just been the natural result of her curiosity. "Before you, men had been the puzzlement of my life," she told him once. "Some of the fellows recognized for alleged generosity ended up being misers, and so-called honorable men were sometimes the biggest cads. I viewed them as games or puzzles to solve, nothing more." That was it—she just wanted to know you, always and in all ways. Isn't that a kind of innocence? Sure, the desires of men on every sidewalk snapped at Susan like snapping turtles each time he took her out. But she was his now.

Two days after the Grendelman fight, he made it clear that he really did hope to marry her, during one of their romantic evening walks. Susan looked at him as if he'd spoken some language she knew nothing of. When he repeated himself, she seemed annoyed.

"Oh, pishy *pish*—and why should I want to do *that*, McCoy? Ruin the happiness we have, chaining myself to you, or to anyone?" Here she was being unkind before coming back with an unguarded type of self-insult, in the way of ladies from her time and class.

"I don't know why you'd want to marry *me*, darling." Her voice went very small, like a child's. "People say I am not of the cloth for it, as you've read and heard."

She was a free spirit, but a free-spirited woman in that America didn't have the luxury of predecessors. Even the freest were held by the self-doubt of the explorer.

It was dark now; McCoy and Susan found themselves by the wharf at the foot of Christopher Street, just in front of the Perry Brewery and facing water.

"Are we—agreeable together, Susan?" McCoy didn't mention love, because it was considered beside the point in a 1900 marriage. But love was there, thick in his voice under the word *agreeable*. The air was chilly for a night in April.

"McCoy, absolutely we are agreeable." They'd stopped walking.

"On our agreeability I should think we'd be able to agree. Look there, I've made a play on words."

"Be serious." Here came his smile. "Do you think I make you happy?"

"Positively." Susan pinned McCoy with a searching stare. "Absolutely." The air smelled sort of woolly: a factory's cough of yeast or hops.

"Tell me what you don't like, and I'll change it," he said. He remade his face into something thoughtful. "I'd punch myself silly, if I thought you wanted that."

McCoy squinted into the lights across Washington Street; a cemetery, in cold green, slept dreamlessly five or so blocks down. Some guard dogs were howling near the brewery. McCoy felt very lonely. He wished he'd asked for her hand far from any cemeteries. "I'd stop talking for a week straight, Susan, if you craved a little quiet." Rubbing his unwarm hands together. "I'd—"

"That, I don't believe. You're lying to me and you know I hate lying." Clean, gray-eyed Susan raised a brow at him, as she was known to do. "Listen, darling, don't punch yourself silly. Don't you have a rematch to worry about?"

"Don't you trust me?" he asked, turning even colder inside. "Is that what you're saying?"

"I'm *teasing*, McCoy." Starting in her eyes, her gray eyes that looked into his, something reached out at him, and he really believed that it wasn't the late wind that whispering toward them over the water rippled the smooth, glinting river-surface. How sad his love made him feel. And the smell of yeast all around. Maybe it was that smell that told of melancholy and worry in the air.

"Then I'll ask you again," he said, after a little pause. His voice seized up. "I will ask you again."

Folding her arms, Susan said nothing. With her solemn face so near, his teeth chattered. Even the way Susan's dress hung on her was heart-wounding. Now and then she had a surprising naïve grace, if not an outright awkwardness. At the same time she was so imposing. With the moon on her cheeks and burning the red in her hair, he went into such ecstasies. "Susan Fields, your beauty is—"

"McCoy," she said, her eyebrow arched, again.

"No," he said, choosing the words with care, "beauty like yours is, I mean—it's *real*. It's a thing a pug like me can almost touch."

"Not if you keep talking like that."

No jokes now. "I don't mean touching *you*," he said. "I mean it's something apart from you. How can you say you're not of the cloth for marriage? If you live alone with that much beauty, you're just wasting it."

She pursed her lips and looked angry—or was that her flattered face? He went on: "If you never have children, it's the world that'll miss out on having more of that beauty. Plus, you make me happier than anything under these stars." Bending now, dropping a knee to the cold cobblestone. "Will you be my wife and have my little Mc-Coys?"

She closed her eyes before responding, and her lips started to twist into what was either a smile or a grimace. There was a breath; the most perfect quiet; and then, just as she began to answer, it became clear whether she was smiling or not.

Here's to the Young Lovebirds

The *New York Record-Courier*, April 28, 1900:

Manhattan is on the smooth wagon-trail toward becoming a world capital, and no one who was present at the wedding of the Lady Elephant and the Lean Champ would oppugn our Empire City on the Hudson—oppugn it as did the Ambassador from the Austro-Hungarian Empire, Briano Tartine, when on May 27th of last year he called this fair municipality "still more Duluth than Paris." Nowhere in the world could have bested our Big Apple on the McCoys' night, excepting perhaps Paris or London or Rome, each of which is undeniably an attractive place. But Susan McCoy, née Fields, last Sunday's actress-bride, was as handsome as any wife of any king anywhere—not to slight the beautiful Alexandra, Princess of Denmark, who is said to be perfection on dainty feet . . . Kid McCoy, the thin bruiser of a groom, cut a dashing figure in his dress black and did not seem to note that our city and its responsible organs had beseeched him to acquiesce to this marriage for weeks. . . . In attendance were Frederick Huntington and Macaulay Johnson, the handsome central male characters presently gracing the stage of *One More Go-Round, Grover*

Cleveland? Also present to kiss the lady's decidedly nonmasculine knuckle was Spencer Todd, our notable automotive genius, and the entire Fields family, probably the loveliest ever to hail from Asbury Park, New Jersey. Another guest was Jim Corbett, who served as best man. Kid McCoy had few in his corner present to witness his happy day. The groom explained that both his parents died on the Oklahoma Plains, at the murderous hands of flagitious Chinamen. . . . Susan Fields wore a white silken veil, and one Reverend Mack Ernster presided. When the bride heard her smiling betrothed say the words "I do," she pitched up her veil and leaned over to kiss Mr. McCoy direct on the lips. The minister of Gospel laughed. "It is not time yet, my girl," Mr. Ernster said. "I could not wait," Susan Fields said. "I could not wait." Only a stone-heart would have had a dry eye at that moment. Or maybe an Austro-Hungarian.

Before bed on most nights, secretly McCoy watched through the half-opened door as Susan, dripping from her bath, flushed and glittery, rubbed off all the little rhinestone waterdrops with a slow, loving motion of the towel. She patted her breasts the careful way a maidservant would dry two pieces of valuable china, lost in admiring daydream. And why wouldn't she delight in the swerve of her own body? Arching her free hand—it reminded McCoy of the head of a swan—Susan brought a tracing finger up her leg, just ahead of the towel. When it was time to dry her face, she just about frowned into the half-steamed mirror as she leveled any wrinkles by pulling earward on her cheeks. The expression she then showed the looking glass was the same one she wore for her staged love scenes: *Kiss me, you fool!*

Mr. and Mrs. McCoy moved into a big suite at the Millhaus Hotel, eighteen stories up—you needed an expensive key just to drive the elevator to that fashionable floor—and their room overlooked small ornate brownstone houses and also the pale yellow work shacks that kept popping up around the city like an irritation on its skin. Across one of the walls they hung the banner that read *The New Champion of 1900 Kid McCoy*. "I'll stay champ, I swear," he said. "I'll beat Tommy Ryan in the rematch, on the square. I can fight better than anyone in my weight class and the two above it."

Around this time a small newspaper ran an odd story about McCoy, which he didn't see until years later.

The *Lawrence Daily Kansan*, April 29, 1900:

> Local boy Peter Baxter fought the famous "Kid" McCoy to a draw last night at the Lawrence County Gymnasoreum before a crowd of twenty enthusiasts. . . .

McCoy hadn't been to Kansas in years. And how could he have been in Kansas on the twenty-eighth—the day of his wedding in New York?

One night early in their marriage McCoy and Susan had dinner with Gentleman Jim and Martha Corbett at Corbett's restaurant, the Gentleman's, on Fourteenth and Broadway. The restaurant served fish. (Susan had a favorite pun: "We go to Jim's just for the halibut.")

"Oh, here's to the young lovebirds," said Corbett, raising a glass of French wine. The famous heavyweight, dapper beneath his Vase-lined black hair, was the kind of pug who acts like everything he says has some covert, humorous meaning. Corbett winked at McCoy, who didn't know what the wink was supposed to mean. He never knew what Corbett's wink was supposed to mean.

"They do look happy, a couple of kids," said Martha. She was a thick woman and ruddy, with fetching long eyelashes and long fingers, a fetching long nose, and a tall hat worn in a fetching, tilted way. "Yes, don't they look happy." She wasn't really asking.

"Maybe it's all that poetry which McCoy reads," said Corbett, maintaining his smile.

Corbett had just won a big, if controversial, fifteen-round decision against "Capering" Joe Choynsky. Many—including, some said, Jim himself—knew that he'd only beat Choynsky because the referee had had a healthy dislike of Jews.

"Of course you're happy, Kid and Mrs. Kid," Jim Corbett was saying. "Don't listen to what the papers go on about regarding your marriage." Sportswriters credited Corbett with high sensitivity for a pug.

"We don't listen," said McCoy, smiling. Susan's warm hand in his felt like something softer than a hand, like a baby's cheek. He didn't care about the papers. "What do the papers go on about, Gent Jim?" Susan's hand like a baby's cheek except for the ring on her finger that made him feel so glad.

"Oh, what do the papers go on about, you say?" Corbett asked— daubing at the corners of his mouth with a napkin. "What do the papers go on *about*, McCoy? Well, that, oh, every trolley car passing up or down Eighth Avenue was stopped over the weekend, any Negro on board was dragged out and beaten by the constabulary. That was Tuesday. The world is, shall we say, *going to hell*, is what the papers go on about, McCoy—"

"Here it comes," said Martha Corbett.

"On *Wed*nesday," said Jim, licking his sensitive lips, rejecting the fall of the world with that circling of the tongue, "the *Weekly True Talker* said that two men I happen to know, Leopold 'Poldy' McKenzie and Judge Ulysses H. Noyes, were arrested in Nome, Alaska, for running a fraudulent scheme to seize rich mining claims. A woman was found battered by her husband and kept in a steam closet in Boston for four days. A Brooklyn boy killed his mother with a pickax and brought her remains to Dogsbody Flats." (Dogsbody Flats being the hazardous wasteland on the west side of Manhattan Island.) "I don't know what's worse, being murdered or having to go to Dogsbody Flats!"

McCoy let out a pity-filled *tisk*. Imagine, four days in a steam closet! And killing your parents! He shuddered. The world was going to hell, which may not have been a bad thing for a survivor such as himself. He'd made himself someone finer, all right. Now all he had to do was not lose to Ryan.

"Oh"—Corbett was sighing—"and on Thursday, it seems that my hometown was having a *second* bubonic plague scare, and will likely quarantine its Little China again! *That's* what the papers say." Corbett was not finished. "Also, also, speaking of Chinese, the papers report that McKinley has ordered that the U.S. join the force of ten thousand going to fight a group of boxers in a place called, I believe, *Peeking*. I'll tell you, if there's one thing I know it's politics. I know politics. A man like me can't rule out politics as a career. People respect a champ, that's just the way it is, and a man like me just can't fight the love of the people." (All this because he thought it possible that Joe Choynsky had beaten him.)

"Oh, pishy *pish!*—my husband and I, the same as everybody else, know about all this ballyhoo," Susan said. "We read."

"How about that, McCoy?" Corbett had now widened his tone to bring in laughter. "We're boxers, right? How would we fare against ten thousand fighters who peek?"

"A half of an hour of talking, just for a punch line," said Martha.

Corbett, now picking at a hangnail, turned to Susan. "What do you want for dessert, Mrs. McCoy? We have quite a selection. The pastry—"

"I believe my husband's question was," Susan said, "what do the papers say about *us*." Then, to Mrs. Corbett, "Do all husbands prattle so?" And flashing a less than gentle look at Jim, she said, "You may as well forget it. I already know what the papers say. McCoy is not afraid of Tommy Ryan, is that clear? Also, would any man with a so-called 'black heart' have shown as much *compassion* during that little steam-closet story of yours?" She drew back, with a long breath. "And I do not care if they doubt that our marriage has what they call 'legs.' I can tell you without hesitation that we will be wedded forever."

The eaters at tables around them chomped and slurped. Someone in a corner was laughing. McCoy and Susan looked at the Corbetts, then each other, before turning back to their food.

"Sometimes I cannot endure him—Gentleman Jim, I mean," Susan said later, as the newlywed McCoys walked home down the lamped avenue. Susan licked the plump part of her thumb and went to rub McCoy's chin.

"You left some flakes of pastry on your face, darling darling." She mock-pouted, an action she knew he found pretty. "I cannot look at you until it's gone."

"You *like* Jim, Duck," McCoy said, jerking his chin quick, too quick from her thumb. He rubbed his chin himself, and muttered, "Thank you."

"He's not half the man you are." Susan took his hand and squeezed it. "Don't you agree about Jim, at least from time to time?" She seemed not really to be paying attention, even to her own point. Her hair caught a bright tinge in the lamplight, and her eyes did too.

McCoy said, "I don't know, Duck. Maybe the Gent *is* a little—theatrical, but he's always given me a fair shake." McCoy had forever been attracted to such pretty talkers as Jim and Johnnie Gold, and Susan was one, too. There was a subtle mist to the air, which helped the gray in Susan's eyes.

"And what of Martha?" she was saying. "She's kind of a *homely* beauty, don't you think? That woman's nose and lips wouldn't be so tolerable if she'd been born in a land without beauty aids."

"*Su*san," he said, not really a reprimand, because he knew she was half joking. Why was she being silly? "Mrs. McCoy," he said.

"Oh, darling darling," she said, with that almost Englishness, "wouldn't it—"

"*Mister* Darling Darling." He extended his pointer finger, a kindly scold. In a flash he imagined that he and Susan were some sort of mutoscope projections, actors playing husband and wife. Now *he* was being silly. Sometimes just thinking about being married to her spread a warm butter over his insides.

Why not just tell her everything! he thought.

"Darling Darling," Susan was saying, "wouldn't life be paradise if it were just us? What was it you said once? 'We don't have to be like other husbands and wives. We can change things to fit our case'? Don't think I've forgotten."

He smiled. What kind of marriage would they have as years went by? Easy or troublesome? Forever passionate? She was looking away now, too.

Here they were, husband and wife, and she had the same hair and eyes she'd had before, exactly the same. For a moment this lack of change annoyed McCoy as much as it pleased him—though he did adore her hair and eyes.

These last weeks as a married man, McCoy, like Christopher Columbus, had discovered a new world different from what he'd expected. Turns out he had a woman of endearing, often unfunny jokes and with a tremendous dislike of lies. And she preferred the company of men. "Most women," she said, "don't have minds trained for thinking. It is not their fault." McCoy'd also never thought Susan would be so untidy, leaving her dirty clothes where she pleased and never bending to pick up his. (The Millhaus chambermaid was summoned via the speaking tubes when *he* made the effort.) Mostly, she was stubborn. The real reason Susan was nicknamed the Elephant of the Proscenium was that she never forgot an argument. "McCoy, three weeks ago, that chilly Tuesday after my birthday, before breakfast, you told me that you didn't care about clothes on the floor as long as they were picked up in a few hours' time, but now it seems you do?") Still, he was happy. He and his wife made good roommates. They shared ambitions and biases and laughs, plus a flair for drama. "I don't much care what Mister and Missus America thinks is right once I've set about to do something," she liked to say. . . . He understood his new-world exploration was only beginning. He could picture a hundred possible futures with Susan, a thousand: when she touched her hand to her throat he saw one; another as she licked her lips all bashfully; and so on. One Susan evaporated; the next in line sprang into view, based on this turn of streetlight or that angle of her chin. Angelic; brazen. Good hearted; hasty. Fresh; sensible. How could he love someone so much and not know which of these she most was?

He wondered what Susan had learned of him.

Now, under the streetlight, she was lowering her chin and fixing her sweetest look on her husband.

She put her arm around his chest—she could get it all the way around—and he put his around her waist, and as they walked Madison Avenue, people, some of them anyway, began to point and smile. "Hey," they said, "isn't that the champ and his famous girl . . . Nah, it couldn't be."

And then came the rematch with Ryan.

Dogsbody Flats

He couldn't avoid it any longer.

Though the pride of a World Champion held McCoy high as a skyscraper above any self-doubt, he didn't forget that even skyscrapers have their foundation in the dirt. If he'd begun to think of himself as risen beyond the world of the flimflam, he wasn't too proud to set in motion a few cheats and scams for this rematch with Tommy Ryan.

The battle was to be fought at Ronnie and Ray's, and Ronnie himself, a McCoy backer and renowned accepter of tributes, would be the referee. If McCoy could knock Ryan down, if McCoy could last beyond the thirtieth round, then Ronnie'd declare him the winner. Easy peasy.

The crowd, too, would be largely for him. Our boy'd been given the right to sell the first hundred and fifty tickets to whomever he wanted. *Johnnie Gold himself*, McCoy thought, *couldn't have planned it any better*.

But maybe he could have.

A few days before the fight, one of Susan's actor friends paid McCoy a visit during his training hour at Ronnie and Ray's. Frederick Huntington had come with an offer to help fix the fight.

The actor seemed out of his depths, lounging before the ring, a pussyfoot too neat for that place with its forever mournful smells of cigar smoke, sweat, and urine. Still, the actor was friendliness on two feet. He stood pale and stout, and he carried a walking stick, though his legs were healthy. Like Susan, he had a straight pretty nose.

When McCoy, stepping sweaty and steaming from the ring, asked why Huntington'd come, the actor said, "I have a *big* proposition, Champ"—and this reminded McCoy of something.

Huntington waited for McCoy to ask him to continue, and waited. The actor shifted in place and dropped his cane by accident. He bent to pick it up, but apparently thought that position made him look silly. So Huntington stood with the cane across his feet, which looked even sillier. He moved to pick it up again—

"A proposition about what?" said McCoy. "And what's in it for you, if you don't mind *my* . . . ?" Contempt shaded his voice, and Huntington flushed.

"Well, I come here as a friend"—standing upright quickly—"of course. And, well, I also must admit I'm a messenger from an interested party who can guarantee you a victory over Ryan."

"Is that so?" Leaning over the ropes, McCoy breathed heavily; he'd been boxing shadows for half an hour. "*Can* he now? Who are we talking about?" McCoy's expression wasn't cruel as much as bored. Would-be fixers were as common as gym rats. "Why am I so lucky that he wants to meet me?"

"Well, about that." Huntington spit delicately into a handkerchief he'd taken from his front pocket. Then: "I only know that he contacted me with instructions when I was in New Jersey." (Huntington, like a number of actors, had started working for Edison's flicker studio out in New Jersey—work that usually required long stretches away from New York.)

Thoughtful, as the manner of flimflammers often is, McCoy said, "And some money for you, I'll bet."

"All I know," said Huntington, cane now in hand, "is that this man says he can help you."

Soon McCoy found himself traveling in Huntington's hired carriage, clipping off to meet the leader of the "Midnight Boys Gang," west of Twelfth Avenue. This was the infamous Dogsbody Flats.

They arrived at nightfall. McCoy looked out at the darkening landscape and felt uneasy. "Is it necessary to go to this place?"

The sun was a twitchy lip-color ribbon across the Hudson, but the evening was less than picturesque. If you think that hand-to-mouth, that beggary, is something particular to your times, or that what you call homelessness is a new-fashioned scourge, you're lucky not to have lived among the deep gloom and the garbage heaps and the rust-cankered huge iron casts of Manhattan's Dogsbody Flats in 1900.

Dogsbody Flats stretched out beside the shore, a marsh where the discarded cocoons of everywhere-sprouting New York, the shreds and crumbly oddments of a city bursting up, its horrors and malignancies, appeared like the ruins of some nightmare town. The twilight was melting across a hundred objects cut down at the knees: gnarled train wheels, half-buried in mud; cunning wire fence, rising and falling in odd wreathy angles; bank doors that stood alone without use.

What kind of flimflammer holds a meeting here?

McCoy and Huntington held their breaths from the smell of tar and garbage as they tramped across chance bits of junk, the black mud slurping up their shoes. McCoy's foot faltered over scraggly subway track joints and torn sponges and the stems of dead dandelions with their seed fluff blown off.

Everything about this chaff heap was roused by their coming: the underfed beggars staggering from dark corners, a few at first on the horizon; those five, six, ten children nearing, looking too small to be healthy; and that splayfooted teenager who pitched to one side as he walked; the cherry-cheeked hairless woman in a man's shabby brown overcoat who collapsed in the mud as she drew near, and the dirty little girls who ran over to hoist her to McCoy. Even the giant, hunched iron cranes far down along the riverbank looked in silhouette like beggars rising to their feet.

Twenty or more toothless families, their mouths as black as the soot on their skin, people naked or near it and silent, misshaped, packs of them, sickly, many deformed intentionally to earn a higher begging wage—these pitiful guttersnipes now fell in a violent swarm on McCoy and Huntington.

"Back!" McCoy said. Soiled, gouty old women rolled in handbarrows into his knees. Ash-blackened girls crawled to him. Chafed-up hands reached for his face, his eyes, coat, and his billfold, especially his billfold. With each touch came a transfer of fatigue. "Back!" Oozy boys with pupilless eyes the color of buttermilk rushed in; everywhere filthy faces without noses, or eyelids, hugely grinning mouths without lips. In 1900 there was nowhere for these unfortunates to go, no shelter to defend them from getting sicker, or poorer. At the sight of well-to-do visitors they swarmed, and swarmed.

"Please, food." Toneless voices: "Please, food." And McCoy swinging his arms hit crumpling bodies—"Back!"—his sympathy drowned by fear and revulsion. The air was sultry and clotted with shapes. Through the thicket McCoy made out the pale feebleness of a child's wristbone, then a torn white shirtsleeve with a fancy french cuff, the flat naked chest of a young girl, and dark streaks of blood on someone's neck. McCoy's hands sunk deep into everything he hit.

A few steps ahead, Huntington, wheeling and crouching, flailed his walking stick to a string of loud *crack-crack-crack*s and the bright, hollow noise of a little girl wailing out in pain. "Please, sirs," mewled some boy, a half-sized creature who along with everyone else grabbed for McCoy's pocket. Those with eyes had sad, bulging eyes.

"Come along!" McCoy heard Huntington cry. *"This way!"*

He could barely make out the actor as he jostled through the shifting curtain of bent bodies.

McCoy had to fight many little boxing matches now, jabbing, uppercutting—*Leave me alone!*—passing into the thick of the close darkness of all those guttersnipes. Some fell away, others fled, most were hard to shake off, their rotten gasps on McCoy's face, their fingers at his eyes. With a long gulping breath and all the life in his shoulder he thrust himself forward and started to run through the many-horrored cloud. He swatted away the clawing hands and kept right on ahead.

After a minute he opened his eyes and he saw that nobody had followed him. He didn't stop running through the mud.

"Where the hell have you taken me?" McCoy, upset almost to tears, caught up to his guide Huntington, who was straightening his collar and jacket sleeves.

They walked along the river shore, far from the beggars and approaching a landing pier that stood charred and deserted. The river looked as dark as the sky.

"Oh, Kid," Huntington sighed, "it wasn't as bad as all *that*," lifting his cap for a moment to flatten his already flat hair. "One or two riffraff and you look like you've seen the absolute *end*." But the actor couldn't keep the shudder from his voice. His clothes had gotten ripped and he kept looking past McCoy, back toward Dogsbody Flats.

McCoy took a fortifying swallow and then sounded a too-hollow laugh. "Fair enough," he said. He always found it more of a struggle to find his likable self under the eyes of famous friends of Susan.

"Always ungrateful," said Huntington, pulling at the silk of his cravat in a gratuitous adjustment. The actor talked absently, or imitation absently. "Young fighters are always ungrateful." He gave a wide smile that quivered along his upper lip. He had a long raw scratch and dirt on his cheek.

McCoy followed him into shadows and under a large slip on the water's edge that looked not unlike a stadium bleacher. A hidden rat made a rustling noise in the trash at his feet.

"*Men or Boys*," Huntington started to sing, "*Will make their noise*," his voice less than lilting as he fingered his cheek, "*And antipathy e'er surrounds them!*"

In this twilit moment the champ saw between himself and rich-outfitted Huntington his own ghostly image, helpless under all those grabby squalid hands. The feeling brought back a picture of the real McCoy's corpse and he shuddered again.

Say something, he thought.

" 'Zounds, Huntington"—working up a laugh—"what's in it for you to help me?" He'd sounded more curt than he'd planned to.

"I'd like to mention," Huntington, pressing, said, "that I consider you a chum personally, not just the husband of an associate—"

"Yes, thank you. But—"

"—A real chum." Huntington's voice was built on creaks and imploring.

McCoy realized that Huntington had not brought him out to Dogsbody Flats to be part of a money-making scam. Actors were like journalists, like *everyone*, in that they craved the thrill of the dangers that were wrapped up in something like the fight game.

"I'll stop that box of rocks in two," McCoy said now, "just like before."

"Who?"

"Ryan, who else?" True vigor came back to McCoy's speech. His urge to jab was plain in his now fisting hand. "And I'm leaving this awful hole this minute."

"Yes, yes—quite right." Huntington was a caricature of casual. He almost resembled a man with some choice to consider. "Maybe the two of us should just . . . leave. Let's head that way." Pointing in a direction far from the beggars of Dogsbody Flats. "That is, if you agree . . ."

With that they took off, just short of running. And neither noticed the large heavyset man of Chinese extraction who came up out of the gloom a minute too late, the self-proclaimed leader of the "Midnight Boys Gang" with his drab pocket watch and familiar faun wachleather gloves: the Chinese flimflammer who'd traveled all the way from Louisville to meet with McCoy and to change his life again.

McCoy continued to train hard for the fight. Leaving Susan early in the morning to run all the way to the Park Row building and then up every last of its thirty-odd flights; staying late hours in the gym, punching and squatting and jumping jacks until his heart convulsed and his lungs whapped across each other. Susan gave him a present of a silver heart locket, for luck.

"Thank you," he said. "But is it a bit . . . womanish?" She answered: "Well, I like it, and that should be enough for you."

On the eve of the match, even while he enjoyed the notion of defending his title and humiliating Ryan one more time, he recognized that pitapat of dissatisfaction, still, still. Not fear or apathy—certainly not *that*—but longing, as if even as champion he wasn't striving enough.

As he slathered his knuckles with the itching paste he'd bought, its lack of bite on his own skin told him that he'd paid for a weak batch.

* * *

Some in attendance called the second Ryan-McCoy fight the greatest they'd ever seen.

Many hundreds of punches were thrown, even thousands, two top-hole fighters standing nose-to-nose, hate-filled, brickbatting away for too long, McCoy unable to use the speed and guile he'd come to count on. Ryan figured how to cut McCoy off and trap him at the ropes. Capable and fit and brave and ferocious and expert as McCoy was, he couldn't answer the strength and dispatch of Tommy Ryan. He couldn't even knock him down to give Ronnie a chance to call the fight in his favor.

After twenty-four ugly rounds Ryan, his big shoulders straight and overbearing, knocked McCoy out.

The blows from both fighters came in so steady and loud that to sit near the ring was almost to hear a platoon's long march over a concrete road. During the fight's worst carnage McCoy missed a corkscrew and caught a reflection of himself in the hall's big mirror as he took a punch to his head. The image froze in his mind. What he saw was a man crumpled, as in death, blood jetting from his brow in an overhead curve like a ram's horn. The gobbets of sweat that flew from his wheeling face trapped the light and looked yellowish, like embers flying from a bonfire, or bees leaving a hive. He'd see that image for the rest of his McCoy days: the horn of his blood, the bees in midflight, and his long rodlike body, crumpled. McCoy swore Ryan would have fallen, had he himself not beaten the bastard to it.

"You're nothing without flimflam," Ryan said as our boy slumped. "Nothing."

When McCoy awoke, Susan kneeling over him in an emptying ring, the crowd mostly quiet save for the few Ryan rooters, and the reporters everywhere scribbling, McCoy had lost his championship.

Poetry

At this point, he turned to poetry.

Real Sorrows

Poetry: because without the welterweight title McCoy didn't know what to do with his days. Still the finest fighter in the modern "scientific" style, crafty, last week's world champion, handsome devil (save for those teeth), deflated as a washed-out balloon, McCoy threw away his mornings by reading the poetry of Maurice Maeterlinck and ticking off across sheets of paper napkin some light verse of his own. Well, he hadn't fallen totally to pieces. After the loss he felt despondent and listless and convinced his life was now fit for the dust hole—and that he had no way to fix it—but his surprise was that despair had turned out to be obedient, or at least isolated, like a yapping dog you barely hear on the far side of a thick window. *Put it from your head, McCoy*, McCoy thought. *Just put it—*

"Kid?" This was Susan at 7:30 A.M. "What are you doing, dearest?"—stomping by his writing desk on her way to her bathroom. (In their suite at the Millhaus, each newlywed had his own toilet.) "It's really quite charming that you're trying to be cultivated, McCoy." She spoke over her shoulder, her voice trailing her the way steam does a riverboat. "If you keep writing on napkins, you'll have nothing to help daub the excess food off your face, except that book of Maury Matterhorn's poetry." *One More Go-Round, Grover Cleveland?* had finished its run the day before. Susan was now out of work. "Was that a *thou* I saw dribbling onto your chin, dearest?"

McCoy, absently bringing a hand to his face: "I'm writing, Duck."

He didn't look up from where pen met napkin. Maybe the most important thing wasn't whether you lived thirty or forty or eighty years. All of those numbers seemed pretty small when you got down to it, McCoy thought. "A boxer uses naught but his fists," he muttered. "As for me, I would like—"

Oh, why hadn't he come up with a better flimflam for Ryan!

He poetized onto his napkin: "Let dogs delight to growl and fight/But let men rise above them."

Susan, who'd disappeared into her bathroom, now leaned back out into view. "Did you say 'naught,' McCoy?" That wasn't a laugh, exactly. She poked half in the room, her torso and higher. "*Naught?*" she repeated.

Susan's skin was pale as ivory. His heart still gave at the sight of her. Even more now than before. Was his affection bigger than hers? Was it too much? He hadn't really left this room since he'd, since Ryan had—

Poetry. He scribbled the finish to his verse: " 'Tis better to have a gal for a pal/Who really knows she loves him."

"I see you are spending the entire morning at the writing desk," Susan said. "Again." Lowering her chin. "Every day, all day. Certainly, I understand that." The top of her, following the lower part, had disappeared into the bathroom. "Do you want to try getting out today, dearest?" Neither of them had talked about the loss directly.

(The *New York Times* the Monday before: "History Turned on Its Ear, End of the McCoy Era!"; *Ring* magazine: "M'Coy's Corkscrew Science Done In by Brute Strength—What Will Follow, the Horse Vanquishing the Locomotive?" Others: "[McCoy] fills his vacancy with voluptuousness . . . he attends dances, drinks, wastes the night in reveling—he's no more manlike now than Mrs. Susan McCoy herself is!")

He turned to speak to Susan. "You know, I have to say that one day . . ." Poets weren't daring like boxers, but McCoy loved their lives of brainwork and beauty and immortal renown. "One day I'll be"—and his mouth got dry—"gone." He took a long breath through his nose. "Dead, I mean." Then he presented his wife a pause in which to cry *No! Not you!*

"Listen to me, McCoy." Her voice came out a little fragile, echoing off the bathroom tile. "You'll win your belt back, darling." (And that sharp edge in her words was love—of course it was.) "You *have* to." She, with the courage of being out of sight behind a doorjamb, had finally broached the subject of his failure. Now the *shh* of running water.

What he'd been feeling wasn't panic. He still had his wife, hadn't he? With her help and with poetry, even his pain was slight and mild—like what? Like the little plopping of rain that plays in country puddles and soothes Indiana prairiebillies to sleep. There: it was not even a panic at all.

But he doubted himself if he'd ever again—

Maeterlinck, he thought. *Maeterlinck writes poetry for the ages.*

"I'll send this rhyme to H. H. Measures at the paper," McCoy called toward where she was. "They'll run it." The sun was bright all through that apartment. A water glass on McCoy's writing desk got streaked through with gold, poetically.

After a minute Susan, her head tousled, her cheeks a just-washed pink, came around McCoy's chair to take a tight grip on his shoulder—the warmth of her body outflowing. She'd appeared wearing a white basque that made a show of her collarbone.

"Hello, Champ," she said.

"You know his name's not Matterhorn."

Susan brought her lips to McCoy's unwashed brown hair and kissed him above his ear. He looked to her already paling face. She kissed him this time on the mouth. But she didn't kiss him for long. "Mouth'a touch mouth," he said after she'd stopped.

Standing straight, she gave an almost-smile. "Yes, moutha touch mouth." Her voice was a bit husky, even with the little British-like accent pluming up the words. She was husky in general. Husky, he thought. Husk. Tusk. Ivory. My elephant. He wasn't feeling so hot.

"I need to get back to my poetry work now, Susan."

"McCoy," she said carefully. Her skin was taut. "Don't be worried."

What upset him most was her tone of forced calm. Their room probably always felt this cold.

"What do you mean, Susan?" Something rising in his throat.

"Never going outside." She gave off the bloodless smell of baby powder. "Never training. *Writing*—this simply is not you."

"Me? I'm fine." Not panicked at all. Just—

At least he still had her. He thought of their wedding night: those pale cotton bedcovers all damp, his truelove beside him in bed, when a noise had rattled out the window. He'd jumped up to look, and she'd said, "No, Champ, don't go": a beauty in the throes of something. Lordy, it felt so unnatural now not to be champion, not to be the man he'd been for five months. He'd stopped wearing the heart locket.

"—is that all right, McCoy?"

He'd missed what she'd said.

Tell her! He thought. *That I'm Selby, and that I buried the real McCoy*—

"Susan," he began in his deepest voice. "First of all, it's just that I'm taking my time before I come round." He felt his cheeks warm. Then he winked because he had no second of all.

"Of course, McCoy." She leaned over again and bought her lips to his forehead. "I just want for you to feel more yourself." He became aware of an affected note in her speech and her smile. Was she only acting the female lead in some drama in her head?

"Thank you, Duck." It occurred to him that she'd seemed stilted all week.

"Oh, you're very welcome, McCoy." And wasn't that the curtsy a nurse gives a just-tucked-in child?

"Very nice of you, Susan." He'd never heard his own voice so stiff before. If she seemed unnatural, how could McCoy be expected to sound any different? "Thank you again."

"Not at all, McCoy." She walked to her night table, opening a drawer.

She'd ministered to his feelings—actually, she'd nursed him—for days. Along the wall opposite the window, that banner still read: *The New Champion of 1900 Kid McCoy*. In honor of nothing. He just needed time, he thought.

McCoy felt his legs carry him up from his chair; in his slippers he wasn't much taller than she was. Where would he walk? To the mirror.

On his way his eyes went to Susan, who now looked for something under her pillow. Lately he kept coming back to something she'd once said: *I'm not the type for a hard day's work.*

He stood curling his lips, trying to look McCoy-like in the mirror. There probably were a lot of things Susan didn't reveal to him, he thought.

She came to stand at his back; her hands crept up his arms. She peered over his shoulder at her own reflection. For a second they both watched her lashes lashing in the glass.

"Oh, McCoy." She sighed. "Do you want me to have Robert"— their bellhop—"bring up the hot water for some tea? What's a wife for if not that?" She definitely was playing a heroine. Or else just being nice. Susan had acted a nurse to rave reviews in *Union Soldiers Come Home!*

He told her no, thank you, he didn't want tea.

She took her hands from his shoulders and started to move away. It seemed she couldn't or wouldn't keep her gaze on him. He was almost sure of it. Pipes were rattling in the wall, as pipes were then known to do. At least he hadn't been locked in a Boston steam closet for four days, he thought.

On a whim he turned to hug his wife. He loved her and couldn't imagine being without her, etc. He meant every word.

"I love you quite a bit, too, McCoy." But she listed subtly— nowadays you'd call that body language. She was looking right in his eyes. That was one victory, anyhow.

"It occurs to me, darling . . ." Susan stepped back a little. "If you never set foot outside again, if you never fight again"—she wavered, the tip of her tongue moving at her lips; she smoothed her shirt collar—"they'll hoist me up and show me to the whole chastising city. 'Here's the woman who ruined McCoy.' Ha ha ha."

McCoy didn't laugh along. "Why would they blame you?" (He knew she was right, though; true or not they'd fault the woman.)

But never to set foot outside again?

"Have you thought of nickelodeons, Duck?" he said, casual sounding. *Never fight again?* He hadn't known he was going to ask about nickelodeons until he had.

"Work the flickers?" Her face intensified and then restored itself. Apparently she *had* thought of it. Another thing she'd failed to reveal.

McCoy kept most of the unease from his eyes as he said, "I heard from Huntington that some fellows in New Jersey are approaching actresses for roles, if you're willing to spend stretches of time out of New York."

"Oh, well, I have heard that myself," said Susan, very mild. "I mean, I have heard from those fellows from New Jersey. And it's not only in New Jersey, you know."

The answer he gave almost sounded like: "Oh."

"Actually, it is a very new type of story these people have planned for me," Susan said, patting her chin.

"Oh, there's a . . . specific story they got to you about?"

Don't read too much into it, he thought. *Look calm into her eyes.*

"It involves a madman as my assailant, some rope, and an approaching train." Susan's gaze slid from his. "But it would require doing something I am not prepared to do. That is, to travel to North Carolina, to leave you for a little while, just to capture those scenes that occur outside. You see, winter in New Jersey—"

"I see." He imagined he could, in the rattle in the wall, hear Susan's brain at work, whirring quicker than his own. "I do see."

For weeks in his dreams he'd been watching himself as he'd looked in Ronnie and Ray's mirror: the horn of his blood and his long rod-like body crumpling in defeat. Maybe it hadn't been bees flying from his head but his own good luck leaving sparks as it skittered away to make room for the return of his humdrum, lonely, Selbyish past.

"Also"—Susan was holding her breath a little—"the financiers want to get away from the close surveillance of the churls in Princeton who own the patents on film, who apparently charge quite a lot of—"

"North Carolina," McCoy said, composed but not enough.

What was he looking for in her face? He knew it so well, didn't he? The full lips, the intelligence in her eyes. He was pretty sure there was nothing new to her now.

"McCoy, I am *not* going to North Carolina." She took his arm. "I've refused fifteen men in my life, accepted three, and none of them meant a thing, not like you."

Women, he thought. *Nature's born flimflammers.*

She was talking: "My stars . . . my heart"—going overboard, he thought. "I'm happy here with you, McCoy." She'd let go of his arm.

"You should be in North Carolina." McCoy straightened up. Vague but real emotion tore from a closed-off place in him and shot across his skin, inside her stare, and he found himself saying, "I'd like you to, Duck."

"No," she said.

They had one of those husband-and-wifely debates, where each person finds himself arguing against what he wants. She begged him to let her stay; he gently demanded she go. They didn't listen to each other so much as work on their performances. Not that it ever escalated into a real argument.

He knew she was asking a question, just under her spoken words: When are you going to fight again, McCoy?

He interrupted whatever she was saying. "Go, and I'll be here when you get back, Susan." *Not the type for a hard day's work*, he thought anxiously. The clean swell of Susan's skin brimming sweetly over the top of her dress reminded him of a cloud disappearing into the horizon. Eyeing her face again, he expected to see no sentiment there. Instead, she showed warmth, so much genuine warmth.

What a dunderhead I am, he thought.

Why hadn't he let himself enjoy her love? "Susan, it'll just be for a little while, so please."

"No!" A deep color spread across her cheeks. Sometimes there was a ferocity to her that was just about animal. "I don't want to leave you here! I don't!"

And for a while she didn't go. She allowed herself to be photographed for advertisements in New York, which paid well, and she even performed in a locally filmed "flicker." She really seemed to want to make him happy. But soon she made plans to leave for

North Carolina and the villain and the rope and the railroad. In the weeks before she left she smiled all the time, more than ever before. He was too smart to make noise about it.

"I'm going to fight again soon," he found himself saying. "I'll set up a fight by the time you get back, Duck." *And I'll never fight again without a rock-solid flimflam*, he thought. "Maybe I'll go against Choynsky."

He knew that once she left for Carolina he'd waste a lot of time in his bathrobe. Poetry was no consolation; he'd give that up. But he had a helping of optimism, too. He couldn't let himself forget: he'd made himself someone finer. First, he might mope a bit.

"Wonderful," Susan was saying. "I knew you would fight again, McCoy."

His wife kissed him on the chin and the hands. Her face was tenderness itself. "Show them, go out and show them." He held her and covered her everywhere with kisses, her head and neck and hands and—

Two days later she was gone.

Later that sad solitary fall, McCoy found himself out in the city for the first time in a dog's age. He'd gone months without the championship, spent weeks missing Susan, had no set confidence he'd return to the prize ring, and tonight the avenues, the season, and his mood were grayer than he'd prepared for. Worse, he wasn't alone.

Outside what had been St. Charles's Burying Ground, McCoy and his three companions jostled past laborers in black-spotted boots who carried heavy stones to the corner. Behind a nearby fence hired men with crowbars overturned markers or flung debris into a hole. And, snaking around Clarkson Street, a clanging tram eased a bit while its riders peered out the windows as the luckiest of the cemetery's bodies got removed.

Though the St. Charles had stopped its burials in 1850, some ten thousand remained in the ground. Tombstones were crumbling to ruin; weeds grew thick at odd angles. Workers were turning the boneyard into a neighborhood park. It was now seven o'clock, and few families had come to claim their dead.

I proposed near this cemetery, McCoy thought.

Meanwhile, the actor Macaulay Johnson was huffing at him through his whiskers. "A party at the American Sportsman Lodge, for *women* of all people." He was the thin and pretty actor who'd played opposite Susan Fields and Frederick Huntington in *Grover Cleveland.* "I never thought I'd see the dark day, fellows. What's the next? Jews? Chinamen? Australians?"

McCoy's eyes were dark-circled. Another tram clanged as it passed.

"Oh, it's not just that women are allowed," said Gentleman Jim. "Times must change, even for the lodge." But Jim's face was still red with annoyance. No heavyweight champion was used to indignity. "I just can't believe the jibber-jabber they showed us."

"Well," Frederick Huntington said, tapping his walking stick a little nervously, "the lovely Susan deserves this soirée, and bylaws are bylaws."

"Yes," said Johnson, and he started to recite. " '*Any social affair established by, or thrown in honor of, women, shall not involve alcohol or members of the opposite . . .* ' Oh, bylaws are poppycock!" Was his voice that loud naturally, or had there been throat exercise involved?

Having been asked to leave the the American Sportsman Lodge's celebration of Susan Fields, the "Actress of the New Century," on account of their gender, McCoy and these three male friends of Susan now walked toward the town common at the cross-section of West Eleventh Street and West Fourth, the best place to hire cabs in the entire city.

"The situation with the lodge is but *one* example of poppycock," said Gentleman Jim, sucking on his teeth. "The world is going to hell everywhere."

McCoy hadn't talked to any men in weeks, and he felt despicable now. Earlier tonight he thought these others had been watching him too much; now they seemed not to pay him mind at all. *Has my standing fallen so far?*

Huntington was speaking in a subdued voice: "Surely you don't object to progress, Gentleman Jim."

McCoy had a flash of worry that he'd left the lamps burning in his room at the Millhaus.

"Is progress men walking thirsty and alone," Corbett said, "while our women are drinking without the supervision of the mature sex? I can't fathom damn rudeness!" Maybe Corbett was still burned up about the Joe Choynsky fight. But at least he hadn't lost *his* belt.

"Draw it mild, Gent," Johnson was saying.

Corbett looked politely at McCoy as one would a little sister. "Of course Susan does deserve a party. I'm not saying that. She's a pretty actress, beautiful, and tolerably humorous. That isn't the point. Not to mention, it is ridiculous to throw a party in honor of a woman who is away in the Carolinas, and has been for weeks."

The world sees that Susan's humorous, thought McCoy. *We come here just for the halibut.* He smiled. But Susan could be harsh too: *And why should I want to marry you, McCoy? . . . If you never set foot outside again, if you never fight again . . .*

"I'll show you the progress to betterment, fellows—the best kind!" Johnson said, pulling a flask out of his greatcoat.

"Oh, ho!" said Huntington. "A nip for the road?" Ahead, already visible, stood the City Common. Huntington took the flask from Johnson and loudly enjoyed a sip.

"Halftime, fellows!" said Gentleman Jim. "On the topic of progress: did you see the new Brownie from Eastman in the *Post* today?" He held his pointer finger skyward. "Now, that, friends, is advancement."

"The camera?" asked McCoy. "Is it a camera?"

"Yes, I've heard that gewgaw is wondrous," said Huntington, handing the flask to Corbett.

"It'll be the end of painting," Johnson said, wiping his lips with the back of his hand. "Mark my words, you two. The end of portraiture, at least."

"A camera?" asked McCoy. He ran his fingers through his hair, which was a little sweat-damp.

"You deem *that* progress?" asked Johnson. "The end of painting? The end of theater—yes, Fred, we all know you've been approached for those Edison flickers. The machine brings the demise of fine arts, and you call it progress!"

"Times must change," said Corbett, just finished with his swig. "Man will adapt. Untwist your undergarments, sir."

McCoy opened his mouth.

"*Yes*, it's a camera, McCoy," said Johnson. He rescrewed the top on the flask and returned it to his coat. "*This* week's bloody revolution in science."

They passed the empty Lawrence Theater, where three Susan Fieldses smiled at them from old show posters of *One More Go-Round, Grover Cleveland?* Her smile brought about no comments.

"I will grant the world is going to hell," Corbett said now, as if lecturing little children or a pet. "Why, look at Hawaii, for example."

"Ha-wai would we want to look at Hawaii?" said dry-mouthed, drawn-faced McCoy, and he winked and waited for the laughs.

Everyone looked at him blankly.

I guess she's the humorous one, he thought. Without thinking he made his hand into a fist. *Stupid*.

"Honestly, Jim, not Hawaii again," Johnson was saying. "Gent, you've Stanford Dole on the brain." And they all laughed.

"My point, Frederick," said Corbett, "is that sugarcane money may not be worth trumping our democratic—" At that moment Corbett saw something: the Meadows Pub, on the near corner. "An idea, gentlemen! Thespians take to drink, no?" A laugh put some bounce into the Gentleman's words. "If the little Ladies Club will exclude us, well, I'll stand you a whiskey, gratis." And nimble Corbett, New York's last great "scientific" champion, skipped free and easy up the footwalk and under the pub's green awning.

"You're actors." Corbett swiveled back toward his friends while opening the door to the bar. "Act appreciative."

"Come along, Fred," Johnson said, " 'fore he changes his mind."

Johnson and Huntington followed Corbett; McCoy stayed in place. He couldn't decide if he'd been invited, so he waited, hands in pockets, just smiling. He didn't feel nearly as friendly with the celebrated Johnson and Huntington as Corbett seemed to. And hadn't Corbett only specified "actors"?

Exactly the types of goddamn puffed-shirt bastards Johnnie Gold and I used to flimflam out of their shirts! McCoy thought. *I'd scam the Gentleman, too.*

Johnson and Huntington, meanwhile, had reached the entrance. They were debating which one should hold the door open. Wouldn't it have been pleasant if someone had said, "Come along, McCoy!"

He just lingered in front of the pub, as conspicuous as a woman at a males-only Sportsman Lodge. Still, no one cried out: "McCoy, what's taking you so long?"

He could guess at how stupid his smile looked now. *Ha-wai's not funny like halibut.* He rocked on his toes a little, working up some momentum to start walking. The pub's door was just now swinging closed; Johnson and Huntington were hurrying inside. And with each of McCoy's hesitant steps away from the Meadows Pub and toward the horse-drawn cabs and the small number of new, motorized taxis at the far corner, he was positive that Corbett would become aware of his not being there, or maybe Huntington, but anyway that *someone* would call after him.

McCoy closed his eyes to his reflection in the pub's window. He actually worried he'd see the sixteen-year-old Virgil Selby there, a kid nervous and close to doing something amoral and foolhardy for some crazy reason or another. He couldn't really believe that this high disrespect could be his fate, or sad lowness of spirit. *What had happened to the cocky flimflammer who could do no wrong conning the championship from Tommy Ryan?*

When they yell out to invite you, he thought, *don't say yes right away.*

He needed to be more committed to being McCoy. Yes, that was certain—he'd lost the thread lately. Everything had been perfect when he had flimflammed Ryan. He'd had boldness and guile and real worth. *That was maybe the only time in my life I was a full one hundred percent McCoy,* he thought.

Huntington and Corbett never did call after him.

McCoy glanced at the gray sky for a second. Then, his head down, he walked home.

Francis Marion Selby

Of the two hundred people who'd lived in the pissant Indy town of Bluffton Creek when Virgil Selby was born, twenty-six or-seven of them had been Selbys. Semiliterate Laban, our boy's grandfather and one of the first homesteaders of southeastern Indiana, sunny as a meadow, had owned the gristmill and the sawmill. Virgil's uncle, a monocled runt nicknamed Weak'un, was the clean-smelling teacher in the first and only school in Bluffton Creek. Joyce Penelope Selby ran the store, and had done so ever since her husband, Charles Selby, had passed on. . . .

Everyone in the family had worked except for hollow-eyed Fran-cis Marion, Virgil's father. He'd helped a little at the mills, or run the counter or checked the books for his sister-in-law—even after he lost Virgil's mother. But mostly Francis Marion, starting at five-thirty in the morning, dressed often in his drab vest and gold pocket watch, his face kept a listless calm, sank into his chair on the porch of the family home and sighed at passing Peach Street traffic, as winter sighs for lost summer. If bony-knuckled, handsome Francis Marion had been healthy, his laziness had been healthier: as a worker he hadn't been worth a buffalo-head nickel. As a loafer, he'd been champion. His nickname was "Count No-Account."

When Virgil at six was the youngest boy in his school class,

Francis Marion filled in teaching for a stretch because Weak'un suffered consumption.

"Is your father a teacher like Weak'un?" the fat kid named Wells asked in a soft voice, leaning out over his desk.

"Yes," Virgil lied.

"Oh, ho!" Withdrawing, Wells spoke loudly now. "He admits his father's like Weak'un!" Other boys turned and snickered.

Minutes later, Virgil's father stood for the first time among these thirteen boys who didn't seem much impressed by the skinny person of their temporary teacher. Francis Marion had the students practice their signatures.

Virgil gave his a huge V and a tiny irgil. He didn't know why; he must have liked the way it looked. But Francis Marion would have none of that.

"If you write your name too large, it's as if you're asking the world to see someone who fancies himself a big stick!" Francis Marion lifted Virgil's book for the whole class to see.

" 'Oh, notice, notice, I'm so important! I'm just a big fool of a braggart!' " Francis Marion wouldn't look his son in the face as he yelled. "Or, if you write it too small, well, your neighbor, or the teller at the bank, or that girl you think you've picked out, she'll know you're small beer!" If his voice seemed angry, the quick eyes he finally turned on his son fretted with apology. "You're wrong on both counts, boy!"

Little Wells bit on his ruler to keep himself from laughing. Virgil felt gloomy.

Francis Marion went on: "This is your *name*, boy! Don't play about, it's not a goldern *antic* when you write it!"

A few days later after the end of lessons, Francis Marion stopped his son to talk alone behind the schoolhouse, for no reason Virgil could figure. Francis Marion seemed very anxious and spoke quickly, telling his son how he'd once worn a fancy pair of Italian boots from New Jersey and taken a trip to New York City with an unwed woman and her three-legged cat. "Boy, that was a *time*." The cornmeal drabness of his skinny cheeks, like what you often saw in anemic schoolgirls, had brightened into a touching show of spirit.

(Men in Bluffton Creek rarely spoke more than their few prudent words). But then the father came back to himself. "Course, son, I tell you only as a caution, seeing as how you wrote your name like some kind of big stick. Before I met my first wife I was hay headed. Don't be stupid in the ways I was." There was little tenderness in those words, but some tender sorrow—which is different. "Or, better yet, Gil. You're a little liar, aren't you?" The father's voice going as deep dark as a thief's pocket. "If falsity's in your blood, go and make yourself someone finer. But don't bother me about it if you don't."

That had been Indiana in 1886. Virgil's old school, like everything in Bluffton Creek, had been meager and unchanging. Nothing was jerry built. The town had none of the pulpboard facades of Manhattan, and none of the marble. Nothing shimmered there. Nobody had grand delusions. Nothing there was misleading, made of pulpboard.

Bluffton Creek remained unsurpassed in Moscow County for alfalfa production.

Years later in Manhattan, when his past came to surprise him at the Millhaus Hotel, McCoy's first thought was of that signature day in his youth.

Susan had returned from North Carolina not long before. McCoy had actually taken some important steps toward being more committed to McCoy—he'd landed the fight that would mark his return to the ring: a comeback in a few weeks' time against Capering Joe Choynsky, the "Jabbing Jew" who'd invariably been unlucky in "big" fights. McCoy was feeling good and hopeful. Then, at 7:00 P.M. on a winter Wednesday, he opened his door to the sight of his father, Francis Marion Selby.

The father, seeing the son, let out a gasp. And McCoy steadied himself against the door.

It can't be. It can't be.

McCoy's heart contracted. How had his father found him?

"Virgil," the crouch-shouldered Francis Marion said, five and a half years balder. "I made my guess, but I never believed it." His voice sounded changed. Something in his brow looked to be spasming. "Kid McCoy."

It took McCoy seconds to open his dry mouth to say: "Hello, Pa."

"Good evening," Francis Marion said. He was nervous—that was what sounded different. "Good evening, son."

How old would he be now? Fifty-nine, sixty?

Francis Marion lifted his smooth pocket watch from his front vest pocket and gently dropped it back. He was waiting to be invited inside; the older man fidgeted with his watch again and bounced on his toes a little.

"You know, this city still smells of muckety-muck," Francis Marion said, and just as during that day in class, he couldn't meet his son's eyes. "That's why, Virgil, if you remember, I always hated this ding-dang town. Smelling of horse filth. You're looking well," he said. "That Selby skin-and-bones complexion. How old are you now? I'll tell you a right good one about the last time I was here, Gil, in this jack-o'-bedlam place. Oh, it was a magic—"

McCoy, in a near whisper: "Maybe you can come back later . . . ?"

"Son?"—the older man looking hurt.

Coming up behind McCoy, Susan made a show of clearing her throat. "Darling, who is it?" She stood on tiptoes to see over her husband's shoulder.

Mr. Selby, also now on tiptoes, looked from Susan to his son, and back.

"This?" McCoy said over his shoulder. "Him? No one, Duck. I don't know. I mean. He's my father."

At first Susan let out a shocked ecstatic *"Oh,"* putting her hand on McCoy's arm and gently, happily squeezing. "Your father's not dead? McCoy!" He could feel her warm delighted breath in the hairs back of his neck.

She began to add things up. She let go of him. "You told me your parents were gone, McCoy." A dying hopeful note there, as she waited for a plausible explanation.

Francis Marion raised his eyebrows at his son. Already McCoy was suffocating. The room got dark.

"Dead?" the father said. "No, ma'am."

Francis Marion squinted into his son's face. "But the Lord above would be kind to take me any day he chooses." Francis Marion's voice starting to splinter. "Ever since Virgil's mother left us." Eyes down, shaking his head a little, Francis Marion looked as if he might cry.

No one had moved from the doorway. McCoy filled with a panic as heavy as water, a wide gurgling stream of panic.

"Well," McCoy said, or maybe just thought he said. He was drowning.

Francis Marion introduced himself to Susan. "Francis Marion Selby." The older man touched his hand to his forehead—his easygoing salute. "Virgil's pa."

McCoy turned to Susan; in her eyes violence was starting to take hold.

She invited Francis Marion in.

"Yes, come in," McCoy almost chirped, while his heart writhed, a boxer taking a pounding at the ropes. He led his father inside by the elbow.

"I didn't mean to disturb you young snappers," said Francis Marion. McCoy realized that his father was talking to him and not Susan. He was using a flunky's tone!

Francis Marion said, "I know young folks like you, such as yourself, must be very active, I mean very often *occupied*, as they call it."

Susan, wide eyed, bad tempered at the corners of her mouth, said: "You're—McCoy's father. And your last name is *Selby*."

"The thing is," said McCoy. All else having failed, instinct told him, of course, to smile. "Susan," he said.

And the three of them stood in the middle of the floor, fairly close.

Susan's stagelike calm now in effect—not without great cost—she said, almost merry, "It's a pleasure to meet you, finally to meet you, sir."

"Oh, stars!" Francis Marion blurted, smacking his forehead. He gave off a hay smell, or maybe that was McCoy's cruel imagination. "You're the Broadway actress, the *famous* actress I read about! Of course." Mr. Selby actually bowed. "A true honor, ma'am."

McCoy and Susan got a view of the top of Francis Marion's balding, stooped head. McCoy had no idea what would happen next. He tried to sound friendly. "How'd you find me, Pa?"

"What?" Susan said. "What did you just ask this man?" *That* question ruined her calm? McCoy felt bone tired and jittery at once.

"I just wondered how he found me, darling." Hard to smile when you feel nauseous.

"Ma'am"—Francis Marion appeared unsteady coming out of his bow; he could've used a cane—"if I fetch you a piece of paper, could you sign me a John Hancock for the folks back in BC? That's what I call Bluffton Creek."

She smiled at the older man, opened her mouth as if to say, *Of course*, but then she jerked her head toward McCoy. The movement was abrupt. She was quivering. That might have been out of anger, or a coming sadness.

"I want merely to get this straight." Her voice ran surprisingly flat. She tapped her lip with her fingernail. "You have a father named Selby who is," she said, "apparently, more alive than you'd mentioned."

"Saw you in the newspaper, Virgil," Mr. Selby was saying, nervously rubbing his hands together, "when you lost the belt to that fella Ryan, and I called to everybody—"

"I should tell you the truth, Susan, of course I should," McCoy said, reaching for and caressing his wife's hand, which didn't caress his. He decided not to let that shake him. "Do you want me to tell you the truth, Duck? About everything? Because I will, from now on." Behind her head was that poster. *The New Champion of 1900 Kid McCoy*. In honor of nothing. "If you want," he added.

Francis Marion, overlooking everything now but his fatherly pride, shook his head and giggled. "Yep, there was your face, right on page seventeen. I says, 'I don't know a McCoy, but that's Virgil, skinny Virgil all grown, or mostly grown, anyways.' I didn't see how, but it were you. Still, I wasn't sure, you understand." His wrinkle-cornered eyes were bright. "It all seemed so odd, so *doubt-*

ful. I won't ask if you've still got that pocket watch you took from me. I've let that out of my mind, as I wear Weak'un's now, God rest him."

Susan began to laugh and didn't stop. She covered her face with her hands, her wedding ring facing out. McCoy's father pawed the back of his neck and looked lost.

"I'm sorry, ma'am." Francis Marion cleared his throat and glanced around. Out the window sawtoothed Manhattan looked like the arm of a latchkey. "I've been so excited to elbow my way in here, I haven't acted right."

Susan slowly moved her hands from her face. Francis Marion was back to rubbing his hands together nervously. "The *Record-Pilot* says you're married to my son, and so I says . . ." He paused for drama—even him! "I'm proud and happy, proud and happy."

She laughed louder. It was a cheerful sound. Her long white thin neck looked like an exposed bone; it even showed that slight curvature.

"Ma'am?" said Francis Marion.

McCoy realized that he, too, was rubbing his hands together, and stopped. *Well,* he thought, *I did make myself someone finer, I did, I did.*

Susan breathed a loud, snuffling nose-breath as she slid her hands down her throat. Her blotched cheeks looked like a red-and-white map of the world. Though she hadn't cried, her eyes had gotten puffy. What was that slightly curved bone called?—a femur?

"Duck—" he said. "Oh, Duck."

"You know, I knew it." She walked, calm as you please, past McCoy toward the door. Each red curl flying at its angle across her forehead showed a reedy black filament, its dark vital principle like the head of a match at work below the flame. McCoy may not have noticed that before.

"I could never put my finger on it," Susan was saying, "but under it all I knew I didn't really know you." She didn't look over her shoulder as she stomped off. "I'll leave you two to dwell on the past."

"Ma'am," called Francis Marion, "please, please don't go on my accord." Once she'd fully left the room, the old man called out, sounding dispirited, "Ma'am, it's frosty out there. You'll be needing to dress warmer than that!"

But she was gone.

Before long father and son left, too. They walked together into the city of Manhattan.

Mr. Selby and Mr. No-Longer-Selby strolled Madison Avenue. The father rubbed his yokel's eyes at the sight of electric street lanterns, and the few motorcars, and the holy mess of white and brown and tan and yellow faces about in foreign costume.

"This place has changed, I'll say that." Francis Marion whistled, smitten by lamplight. In times of feverish progress, anyone out of date makes the world's changes look that much more clear. "I can scarcely recognize it." There must have been some older New Yorkers untouched by progress, too, but McCoy failed to notice them.

Father and son kept walking. Francis Marion didn't mention Susan. He didn't ask what'd made her angry—that being just one of the questions that the conversation danced around. A light snow half covered the ground, like a doily. And McCoy, just by looking at his father's nervous smile, could guess at the questions the old man wanted to ask. Francis Marion seemed so frail.

"I was sorry to read that you lost." That was all Francis Marion said. His gaze didn't seem fixed on anything. "Kid McCoy."

Father and son were on their way to Happenstance, a newfangled drugstore on West Eleventh that served famous chocolate drinks from its coffee counter. As if refreshments could make this evening seem normal. Francis Marion gave a polite smile to all the people that passed who were white.

Oh, Susan! What was McCoy going to do? How could he keep his life as it was? He'd been so very stupid. "Ooo" was the sound he made. A cool breath of wind felt like his wife's hair tickling across the side of his neck. . . . Here came his tears.

"Son," said Francis Marion, missing his son's distress entirely. Chin lifted, he was noticing his own reflection in a ladies' store window. He seemed skittish. "I'm sure you must have a lot of friends, Virgil." What little grass there was next to Madison Avenue looked like tent cloth, flat and dead on either side of the walk. Snow was here and there in piles.

"What I mean is, famous people," said Francis Marion, "celebrated people." He blinked at his son, nervous and hopeful. He'd never seemed nervous when the boy had been Virgil.

Three regally trimmed horse-drawn carriages scuttled by, each with gilded contours. The older man hadn't turned to notice. "Gil?" he said. His breath fogged the air a moment. McCoy felt worse than when blood had spurted from his head in the rematch.

"Pa." He overtook his father and seized the man's old shoulders. "Pa, listen." Even with the chill a sweat was breaking over his cheeks. "You cannot tell anyone, okay? Okay?"

"Son?" The father didn't understand. His face had fallen, so sad looking now, especially those lonely eyes, shining unsteady in the incandescent light. "Son?"

Francis Marion had often ignored McCoy's mother. McCoy couldn't stop thinking now of the way the old man had treated her.

He let go of his father's shoulders and started walking again. Francis Marion hesitated, then caught up. When the old man smiled, McCoy noticed the scab on his temple, as if he'd recently fallen.

McCoy said, "Okay, what do you want to hear?" Sliding his hands into his pockets. "And don't call me Virgil. Please." He gave himself several seconds to gain some calm. "I mean, what should I tell you?"

Francis Marion made a sly face. The old man was missing a back tooth.

"How'd you do it, son?"—Francis Marion's voice a controlled whisper, as if speaking any louder would work up his pride to swallow him whole. "Well, that's what I want to know."

McCoy kneaded his thighs through his pockets.

"I just did it, Pa." Each time he blinked his eyes Susan's face looked very angry. "I just went ahead and made myself someone finer. Like you said."

Susan Fields was the most beautiful thing he'd known in his life or ever could know.

"Like *I* said, Virgil?" Francis Marion was talking slowly.

"Yeah, yes." McCoy felt six or seven, no more than eight. "You told me once." He managed a smile. "You remember."

"I don't think so." Francis Marion's skinny old frame, impossibly, looked skinnier than it had inside and older. "When did I?"

"You did," said McCoy. "You told me to 'make myself someone finer.'" He caught the sound of his own voice, and tenderized it. "You remember."

Francis Marion's face made, finally, an expression McCoy recognized—that old nostril-widened, irked confusion. But the wires had rusted, so it was a pitiable, soft-joweled stare.

Taking a breath, McCoy asked his father if he remembered having stood in for Weak'un at the school.

"Course I do, Virgil." Serious browed. High and low, the undulating city was hushed at the moment and vivid. "I hated it."

"Remember"—McCoy was deliberate—"one day you talked to me behind the schoolhouse? You said you knew I was a liar?" And in a blast of memory McCoy saw the white sky and the shadowless fields, and his young father's neck going red with emotion all those years ago.

"Well, what was it you'd lied about, Virgil? That might help me remember." The whites of Francis Marion's eyes looked washed out. "Are you sure it wasn't when I caught you reading *Gilgamesh* in class? Because then I remember. . . ."

Our boy had to admit that he couldn't recall exactly what his lie had been. He swallowed. Finding a blank spot in such an important memory surprised and flustered him.

"The important thing, Pa, is you told me falsity was in my blood." He patted together his spread fingers. "And that I should make myself someone finer." Then he gave a short, desperate laugh. He needed his father to remember, the way a sea captain needs a compass. "So that's just what I did, like you said."

Mr. Selby scratched at the back of his head. Father and son were walking maybe two feet apart.

"If you don't know what you lied about, Virgil, how do you expect me to remember what I told you?"

Kid Virgil Selby McCoy pursed his lips. He didn't know he was going to moan until he had to tell himself to quit it. "Pa, you *said* that to me."

"I don't expect I did." Francis Marion shrugged and looked, McCoy thought, stupid. "Could be you imagined it."

"You did, Pa." McCoy's mind, like a sponge left under the hot breath of the sun, started to dry up and gnarl. "You just need to think on it, Pa."

Sounding just as grave as his son, Francis Marion said: "I sincerely don't—"

"Think!" What he was feeling was panic on top of panic.

"No," Francis Marion said. "I can't say I ever said it."

McCoy stopped walking. His legs felt as they did after a twenty-round fight. In his heart there was murder or something close to it.

It took Francis Marion a second to realize his son had stopped walking.

The bell from a tram going by, passing voices, the hum of a streetlamp—the sound of nighttime—closed inside our boy's chest like a fist. He stood taller than his father by a few inches. The old man's hair, what was left of it, looked dirty. The scab on his sunken temple was nearly black: his nose hairs were ashen. McCoy wondered if he might find in the delicate swerve of bone of that slender skull some explanation of the boy he'd stopped being.

Francis Marion was looking at his son straight on. "It doesn't even seem like words I'd say."

"All right."

What the devil had Virgil lied about as a kid? There'd been so many lies.

"You know, son, it's just not like me." Francis Marion seemed to shrink into his own body. "See what I mean?"

"That's fine, Pa." A life of lies. But he'd also owned a good pure heart. He was sure of that.

"Son?" Francis Marion in his homespun woollen, seen against the spectacle of New York City, lent even the skyline a look of futility. "Son?" Francis Marion was smiling now.

With the newspapers having added photographs—and with newspapers themselves multiplying to a newfledged degree—even an old prairiebilly had access to information about the world and who'd gone places in it.

"Yes, Pa, what is it?" McCoy really tried not to give his father a contempt-filled look. But there was something in the way Francis Marion tongued at the empty space between his teeth that told of how the old man had just sat on his porch all his life, looking out on a town that wasn't much of a town. And McCoy feared he'd lost Susan.

"Son, I'm glad to see you," Francis Selby said. "And, um, before I leave to go back home, um. . . ." The old man sucked in his lip. McCoy thought that maybe he was screwing up the nerve to ask for an autograph.

"Yes?" He nodded to hurry his father. He had to get back to his life.

Francis Marion opened his mouth; after a silent while it looked as if someone had shut off his vocal chords. A pushcart was clattering across the street.

"This is some city you live in now, son," Francis Marion said in an emotional whisper. "What I mean to say is, well, it's something."

"All right."

Gathering some of the old pluck, McCoy reached for and shook his father's hand with a flourish, like a robber baron after a cruel business deal. Francis Marion seemed not to notice the guilt and pity that worked over the muscles of McCoy's chin. "I got to say good-bye now, Pa," he told him, turning away.

He would never see his father again.

McCoy built up a greedy speed racing north and east in the blackish night toward the Millhaus. Shop windows flew by, multicolored. On the corner of West Sixteenth an organ grinder moiled with his dancing monkey.

McCoy's thoughts came fast, ideas popping up and being torn down, a Manhattan of the mind. A poet? He'd never been a poet. His bones itched, his skin was something he needed to shiver off. A goddamn *poet*?

He hurried completely unnoticed up Fifth with its immortal manor houses, running on and on, a man thrown open to the light and noise from the street and to confusion. He'd been champion and had the whole time been nothing. He didn't understand how all this was happening to him, and he'd always known that something like this would happen to him.

All-night workers hammered, swinging into the cobblestones of fast-passing Davidson Street. He hated himself. He felt his lungs starting to weary, and his legs, too—a few weeks without training, and already.

So many faces populated the streets now, people coming in and out of buildings, crossing streets in close lines like termites. He kept moving through the vivid flurry of Madison Avenue at night, past a trio of Susan Fieldses smiling from posters on a wall.

Ha-wai's not funny like halibut.

Could he try being normal? Stumble home and dolt around with the prairiebillies, people who worked and died and got no more attention than anybody else?

McCoy ran his breathless way through leafy Madison Square. An *ex*-champion! A "self-promoter" without a self! Past twin-turreted, white Madison Square Garden. A onetime flimflammer . . . champion and nothing at all. . . . Technically still the husband of a stranger named Lottie and, if you thought about it, not even married to Susan, not officially. Could he stay in New York, smiling, now that people had stopped looking? Time was running out. . . .

Everywhere he looked faces were flocking around, under top hats or bonnets or foreigner-type curls out in the autumn night. What a shameful thought for a manifest-destinying American such as McCoy: If you're just one of these termites, one of the unnoticed, you're nobody! But maybe the more that you *were* nobody—the more that people didn't see you—maybe the more complete you were, the more *everywhere*? Oh, now he sounded like Johnnie Gold. After beating Ryan in the first fight, McCoy'd let Susan break into him. Was that a mistake?

Do you realize you're crazy? This was the surprising voice of the *real* McCoy right there in his head, effortlessly deep pitched and lifted from the North Judson past.

His urgency ticktocking in his ear, McCoy reached the Millhaus to see Susan on the corner, trying to hail a cab while hugging a large suitcase.

"Duck!" He managed to ignore that she turned from him as he approached. "Wait!"

McCoy knew he had very little time to convince his wife not to leave him. How could he explain to her the inexplicable? To gain a few moments he bent forward and feigned exhaustion, hands on his knees.

Susan, breathing hard herself, showed only the pale anger of her averted face. She let her suitcase fall to the sidewalk. McCoy couldn't lose the feeling that they were both knee-deep in ice on either side of a cold world. The seconds hurried by, along with a current of passing strangers.

And Susan turned to McCoy her deadly stare. Even now—especially now—the gorgeous flush of her anger, the charm of her long nose and her fist that settled on the curve of her hip gave him that familiar excited feeling, as if he was whirlpooling down between his own legs. He tried to break into her eyes but didn't come close. Time was running out. The hands of anxiety in his head came together—*Brrrringggg!!!*

He wished pathetically that Johnnie Gold had been here to help him. His scowling wife, as frightening now as any vampire, had very slender arms, even in her green coat. *Not the type for a hard day's work.* . . .

"I know it's terrible," McCoy said at last. He wore a look, he hoped, as thoughtful as he felt. He'd been born a different man than who Susan had known. He'd anticipated how she might react to that; nervousness pushed him to smile. "I know it is."

Her voice came out like the brakes on an el train: "You can't even *feign* contrition!" Her eyes set to work on his. "Look at you, tapping your blasted feet! Content and happy McCoy, even now!"

And the muscles in her cheek were ticking. "I never admitted it to myself, but I always knew there was *something* I couldn't put my finger on."

A nearing carriage horse made a bell-like noise crossing Forty-fourth Street's trolley tracks—*ring, ring, ring, ring!*

"Oh, Duck, how can you say that?" McCoy almost added *Don't you know me?* but thought better of it. What he needed—for his own good and hers too—was to be more committed to being McCoy. "And, Susan, as for the foot-tapping, you remember I always have this energy, so I—"

She turned to stomp inside to the lobby. Picking up her bag, McCoy followed, shy as a rising snowflake.

"You don't want to leave me, Duck." The Millhaus's mostly empty lobby sparkled under the ceiling's baby lights. "I'm sorry." He wished he were wearing her silver heart locket now. "We're lucky to have each other."

"Ah, one of the many untruths you've told me." She lit a cigarette. Not all women smoked cigarettes in public then.

She sat on a davenport. "It's deceitful, this whole thing." Her cheek was still going, but more slowly than before: *tick, tick, tick.* "Deceit, McCoy!" she sound pretty dramatic. "Deceit!"

They'd never really argued before. Probably they'd been afraid to. *A fighter afraid of fighting,* he thought. Not that he could have called himself a fighter recently. What could he call himself? A husband?

"Duck," he whispered. Susan was pursing her lips as if she tasted some of the deceit she'd talked about. She stamped out her cigarette.

"Susan," louder. If only she'd look at him.

The wall clock over the front desk clicked: nine o'clock.

"Duck, please." In McCoy's teary eyes Susan's face appeared overlaid with blinky diamonds. He said, "I—" but what felt like a billiard ball in his throat stopped him from going on.

"How could you?" She was shaking. "We're *married.* Or, we were."

"Sweetheart, I think I understand what you're feeling." He knew it wasn't enough to look sorrowful; he had also to look moral, bona fide. And at the same time confidently McCoyish. "Duck, I can't explain, but I can account for myself." He hoped that his eyes could convey the message: *What is a lie to you is my truth.*

Her hands came together on her lap.

"Susan?" he said, wiping his eyes only after he made sure that she'd seen his tears. "Sweetheart?"

"What?"

"I love you" (picking his words very carefully) "so much that" (at this rate it might take hours) "I didn't dare risk that for anything. Even the truth."

Her shoulders relaxed a bit. And her cheeks: *charlotte russe.*

Now McCoy actually put his hand on top of her head. "You loved me as I am, that is, as McCoy." Showing the first rattles of a smile. "Virgil Selby was a stranger to us both," he said, "a dull kid even *I*'d forgotten about."

She might have been starting to give in. Her full lips curling upward—

McCoy gentled onto the davenport and kissed her. For a second their lips fit together like clockwork gears.

When Susan pulled back he was grinning. "Oh, Susan—"

"McCoy, I don't know who you are." Her face had gone as sharp as a bramble in the fork of a tree. "And I cannot stomach the sight of you now." She'd stiffened her whole body, down to the clench of her fists. "You poor fool." She moved to stand; McCoy grabbed hold of her arm.

He couldn't lose Susan. He'd shake off his skin if he had to, anything but that. And so, as he had no choice, he launched out on his own story.

McCoy's Brief History of the Selby Family

The near-empty lobby remained silent, and Susan's eyes were on him, as our heart-heavy McCoy began:

"Wait, listen to me. I had a sad thing happen when I was a kid named Virgil Selby from Indiana, more than sad. I actually shake at the memory of it, but since you're set on hearing about me, I'll tell you the worst thing that could ever have happened to a youngster. This was when I was twelve.

"They came out of nowhere. Mother was on the porch, rocking in her rocker, and I loafed there by her side, reading. I hadn't been in the mood to go to the creek. We weren't doing much talking, Mother and me. It was summer.

"They came up quiet. Before I knew it they were on us. One young warrior threw me to the ground, and he held me there. Two others chopped my mother in the head with a tomahawk ax. The killers who got her were adults. One was fat and old, and the other had a build like Tommy Ryan has.

"The inside of Mother's skull was out in the open, pink and gray and red. White, too, where the bone got caught up in it. I just couldn't turn away, and not only because the young brave's hands were holding me. He wanted me to watch, I think. I know he did. They had a lot of hate, I guess, for white farmers like us. Maybe they were crazy with anger that it had been just the two of us to kill.

I haven't even thought about this since, to be honest. I just put it away.

"Katherine, Francis junior, Anna, and my father were all out at the creek. My little sister Bea was still a baby and I guess she must have been inside, sleeping. But I can't say for certain where she was. I just don't know.

"I threw my guts up. I was on my back, mostly, and so some of the sick was still in my mouth even as I wriggled in that Indian's hold. I was crying, I'm not ashamed to admit that. I hated more than anything not being strong enough to break free from that little brave. He smelled like a fertilizer patch on a sunny afternoon, or maybe it was my own sick in my nostrils.

"Susan, I swear those older warriors were set to kill me, too. Like I say, I was just a boy and I didn't fight well, then. They were Maumees, I think, dressed in deer carcasses, using stone knives and such. There weren't many Indians left in Indiana, and the ones that were didn't often come to kill folks. But these three did.

"I was twelve. Their faces got stained red and pink from the blood and the brains of my mother.

"Finally, I was able to kick the one who was holding me. He couldn't have been much older than me, and when I kicked he fell back.

"I wanted to punch them out so badly, and take them all on. I wanted to kill the one who was. . . .

"I'm sorry. This isn't the most easy subject.

"Anyway, I ran. It was hard to breathe, not only from going so fast away from there, and also the upchuck I was spitting and all my heaving crying and my spluttering. Fear tires a person out more than anything. I was afraid, I can admit that, too.

"What I am ashamed of, I didn't run to get help. I just ran away. I hid in the grass in front of the woods near the house. I thought they'd find me for sure, being Indians.

"The day was especially hot, it was the middle of summer, and the grass was alive with stinkbugs. I saw the Maumees looking around for me, sort of halfhearted, axes out, wiping off their chins with the backs of their hands. Maybe they were drunk. I can't say for sure, but I heard that Maumee often were.

"I stayed crouched for a while and then the Indians left, and I still crouched there in the grass. My father and the rest of my family came home, and I was still laying in the tall grass. There was a bee at my head; I didn't even make a sound when it stung me. My father thought I was dead, and they called my name for hours, and I stayed there and didn't move. I cried until I had no water left in me.

"But I don't think about it that much now. Really. I don't. That's why I never talk about it, because I resolved to become McCoy. Her scream, Mother's scream as she was being scalped, wasn't a scream so much as a whine. It was like a trumpet in a union hall before a boxing match. I left Bluffton Creek soon after, and here I am. Your husband and champion. I guess that's all I can tell you.

"It's against my grain to talk much about it, as it's a story that happened to Virgil Selby. I just needed to be someone other than that motherless kid from nowhere."

McCoy fell silent, as he saw past his own words to the touch of her hand on his cheek, which would be a caress of pure forgiveness.

Book Three

There is no "real," and the modern age is about Becoming, not Being.   —Nietzsche

The King of the Self-Deluders

APRIL 1901

Did Johnnie Gold, Chinese flimflammer in a shabby suit, still sizely, his sly eyes bent to the cobblestones, follow our downhearted and now toothless McCoy—who lost even when winning—down bright rivulous Mulberry Street, by way of the volupty shadow that the Puck Building flung across wide Lafayette? Did he follow him through the door and down the weewowy stairs of 30 Crosby, where a dentist had McCoy's new incisors of fine china waiting?

But first: when had McCoy gone toothless?

In the spring. He'd fought Joe Choynsky and lost his canines, molars, and bicuspids, along with whatever had been left of his reputation. At the end of the bout McCoy had been called the winner, but the victory looked tainted by anti-Jewism, or outright flimflam. The *New York Times* named him the man who "loses even when he wins," and the "April fool" of the boxing game, calling into question even his first victory over Ryan ("Has-Been McCoy Pulls Rabbit of Victory from Hat of Frauds," April 1, 1901).

So, when Johnnie Gold found him, despondent McCoy was just leaving the dental office where he'd had the whitest porcelain teeth and their vulcanized rubber base installed. Along with everything else, McCoy's mind had been full of Susan concerns. After Choynsky, he had the victory and he still had his wife, but he was afraid he didn't have either of those things enough.

"An astounding coincidence!" cried Johnnie Gold, with too much heft against the rail of the sloping stairs where neighborhood drunks napped like corpses away from the eyes of the police. "As I live and breathe, McCoy. Is it you?" The flimflammer, mammoth if not exactly clean, held a box covered in red wrapping paper.

"Johnnie," McCoy said through sore mouth. "What're you doing here, of all places?"

"To repeat, it's an *astounding* . . ." The Chinese flimflammer's chin quaked with goodwill down into his collarbone. "As I live *and* . . ."

Thirty Crosby Street was a snip of an apartment building, four stories and narrow between a pair of wide six-deckers. Thanks to the inadequate respect dentists knew then, the tooth-setter's office sat in the basement, across from the boiler. Johnnie pointed at some mops and buckets and winos sleeping sideways. "Shall we avaunt, McCoy?"

Entering the light of the Tuesday noon, stepping among the Crosby Street peddlers, the pushcart pushers, those Eastern Europeans at the west side of the street, the Italians on the east with their candled shrines smack-dab on the sidewalk—1901's street corners danced to the weird musics of a hundred madman cultures—Johnnie Gold, daisy in his lapel, loomed large over these hard-laboring people, as would any man who had the mincing gait of a vaudevillian empress. Not to mention he was Chinese and three hundred fifty pounds. McCoy, too, stood out. For all his troubles, the fattedness of his lip and swollen jaw and the circle bruises around his puffy lids, McCoy still was an emaciated beauty with a diamond pin in his silk four-in-hand. And now he had his first set of pearly whites.

Johnnie Gold, his face soft as pudding, laid a hand on McCoy's shoulder. His eyes glowed like sun-splendid lizards. The eyes of a confidant: *Trust me.* "McCoy, I see you want to ask me something."

"Well," said McCoy, trying to ignore the small deposit of air between his gums and new teeth, "I was just wondering"—he felt a ripple of optimism—"if you also had your dentist in this building, or—?"

"You're curious about the happy circumstances that led us together?" Johnnie Gold tilted his heavy face up and to the side. A friendly gesture, a chuckle made physical. "To a sensible man there is nothing to chance. Can you see that?"

Johnnie burst into laughter. His mouth opened like an oystershell, bigger and bigger. And no street sound could draw off McCoy's attention, no savage car horns or trumpeting street musicians or horse coaches rattlety-banging. There was only McCoy's own heart. Gold was back, and maybe that was just what McCoy needed. His recent disappointments had already started to lose their grip over him.

"I was looking for you, Kid. I admit I was."

McCoy closed his eyes. The feeling in his soul was like a sudden gallop. "But why"—his words equal to faint little shadows—"why did you want to find me, Johnnie?"

"I underestimated you when you were in my employ." The Chinese flimflammer was halfway in smiles. "I acted like a *complete . . .*"

"Don't worry *about . . .*" McCoy said. Oh, yes: his heart was off and racing.

"Here, for you." Johnnie Gold handed over a gift. A Chinese box within boxes. Johnnie's hair was slicked black. An inky 'do.

The present seemed a bit much. McCoy raised an eyebrow. "You—shouldn't have."

A tram bell dinged, a street vendor cried out how fresh his noodles were. *Is Johnnie trying to flimflam me?*

McCoy tongued at his new teeth, which felt a lifeless cold. Johnnie Gold had often pushed his scams too far by a hair. "Why'd you come, J.G.?"

The fat old swindler was reaching now into his vest pocket. "An answer to that question might involve the history of the universe." He handed McCoy a few folded newspapers. "I have these to show, at least."

The headlines told of recent McCoy fights that had never happened, in places he'd never been: A McCoy knockout of a mulatto in Framingham, Mass; another described a sixteen-year-old Georgian lightweight, also claiming to be Kid McCoy, and how he'd lost to one William York Tindall; a third found McCoy a forty-two-year-old Irish-Navaho with a patented uppercut and a potbelly. One more McCoy was said to have traveled to South Africa to fight a barefoot Zulu so tall he couldn't reach the man's chin. Still, McCoy—this other, California-born McCoy of the news article—had beaten his African opponent, according to this report, by dropping carpet tacks across the ring during the first round. . . . Reading these, the only thing our boy could think was that his eyes had lost their credibility.

Johnnie Gold fixed his stare on McCoy hotly. "Such developments cannot hide in this world, eh?"

"So what," McCoy said, "some bums around the country are taking my name, dragging my standing even lower." But he felt terrible. This was as frightening as the ten-armed challengers he nightmared about. And smiling Johnnie Gold may have held any number of grudges against him.

"Guess you haven't heard the way my career has fallen off, J. G."

How could McCoy explain the dips of his life and even his marriage? If ever he put his ear to that marriage now, he was sure he caught a faint and forlorn heartbeat of Susan's disdain. Any foothold he'd gained with the story of his mother's death had begun to deteriorate, even before his shameful "victory" over Choynsky. (Though it may have been he was only imagining that disdain.) Now McCoy formed the confused idea that he should just start running away from the Buddha of Swindle.

"Don't underestimate yourself, McCoy. I saw you as a boy, and I see you here"—Johnnie took back the newspaper clippings—"with four faces." The flimflammer's voice was an instrument of surprising tenderness. In a few moments it would be raining, but now the sky was bright. "You've met the success I frankly did not think you capable of."

"Success?!" McCoy's mind skimmed over the last months like a stone hopping across the surface of an ocean before it sank. And each stop had looked like success's opposite. Susan, who hated lying, had pursed her mouth in revulsion after the *Times* had called McCoy a fool and a cheat.

"If your life's a mess around you," Johnnie said, "get a broom." He took McCoy's hand, actually took it. And he carressed the palm, as a suitor might. "I make a very fair broom."

"I don't understand, Johnnie, I don't." He was no longer even McCoy—people were taking that too! "How can this be any good for me?" His brain felt numb, as if he had an ice cube in his skull. The Chinese flimflammer's face looked strange and unintelligible. . . . McCoy never would have recognized him. . . . The sun tripped behind a wall of cloud. . . . The fast-clouding sky became a grotesque menagerie of strange animal shapes and cages of burnt-edged coral. . . . The street noise was just a single loud sob and it underscored the gasp that Johnnie's breath made from what seemed eager in his enormous chest. . . .

"Don't lose concentration now, McCoy. Why you?" Johnnie Gold snapped the fingers of his free hand. His diction had grown less clipped in these past years. "Ask yourself, pugnacious person: Why you, of all people, do they imitate? For all the differences in those news stories, each calls McCoy a fighter with willingness and spirit. A fighter who doesn't look like a fighter!" Johnnie Gold's laugh was natural. "Do you see how this can help you?"

McCoy, who didn't see at all, was repeating to himself: *You're Kid McCoy and not them.* But his heart was like his eyes, open to any possiblity.

"Let me talk of myself for a moment," Johnnie said. "I am misunderstood." And he took McCoy by the ears, gently.

It felt like just the two of them there, a lion with his cub deep in the green shelter of a jungle, commanding attention and forgetting the business of the wild. "My good McCoy, contrary to what a certain Swedish female may think, I am not a humbugger." Johnnie's power had grown massive; McCoy began to feel buried under it. "I do not slight Fact, homely matron though she is. What I do with her, I do out of affection. I dress her up, apply her a lacquer of lip rouge, add a little beauty powder to that craggy face of hers. You might say that my job is to ornament that apathetic moody strumpet day in, day out. What I *do not* do is lick her boots, as she avoids licking mine."

You have to understand the frenzy of immigration at the beginning of that century and how fearful and how nasty was the hate that most Americans felt toward the sunburnt and the narrow-eyed races. Yet Johnnie Gold, Chinese flimflammer, had awed McCoy for the second time in six years.

"This could be a lollapalooza," Johnnie was saying, his face getting bigger; his voice shrank. "Namealooza."

The 1900s was an age of Charisma, and some of the healthier personalities, those with a natural endowment of the stuff, radiated their own heat—a few seemed like walking planets. They had a gravitational heft that had nothing to do with physical size. McCoy'd recognized this in Susan Fields; her shadow now and again grew too big for her body. He sometimes felt himself drifting toward her without having moved his feet. But Johnnie Gold appeared fraught with more Charisma than any person McCoy'd ever met. The Buddha of Swindle, too, had come a long way since Louisville.

"McCoy, I don't really comprehend the whole truth of this either." He tapped his own forehead. "But that's the new astuteness I've come into about this country. For example, lollapalooza—the great Barnum's rallying cry. What does it even mean? Try spending the last few years on *that* puzzle. Then it hits you. The very vagueness is why it's a first-class American idea. No secrets are better kept, no ideas better accepted, than the ones that lack meaning."

Johnnie smiled, a wry one.

"But look at you, McCoy. Amiability? You have that, dear boy, part and parcel of your simplicity. Which reminds me, yours is the sort of wit that's enjoyable, but certainly makes no one else feel inferior. The irresistible grin of a rapscallion? You look charming with those new teeth. Your bang-up four-in-hand and its diamond pin twinkle like the eyes of a new bride. Has anyone ever pointed out that your very breath is like a vial of rose oil? The entirety of you is the purest package, a public notice on neat feet, announcing the decency of the Creator of All Things!" Johnnie spoke though a tightened throat as if trying to crush his words into a powder for wide sprinkling. "A package as bleached as the shirt of Sunday mornings, as pale as a lily flower. The only thing you are missing is what I can provide you.

"Claim your identity from those buffoons. You must accept who you were born to be—*you* are McCoy, not them! Show them it is *your* destiny. Take me, I was always Johnnie Gold, con King." He bowed. "You're thinking small, McCoy. Smallapalooza. That was my problem too. Whenever I thought big, it was still too small."

For the first time McCoy felt a need to come clean. "I'm passing you a bad check here, Johnnie." The words clattered over his new teeth like Morse code. "I'm not who I said I—"

"McCoy! The American Dream that you and everyone always talked about? Vagueapalooza!" It turns out a very fat man can jump with excitement and still appear agile. "In this country, if you mean nothing, you can get everything!"

Now Johnnie stood very still. "I'd have you know I sailed to America as a coolie, with my destination painted on my chest." He'd stopped yelling. "That is the truth. *C* for California. My old name was a sound a man like you could never pronounce. And here I am. I taken . . . I *have* taken as many steps as I am able." He actually pantomimed walking before going on:

"McCoy, I know a man named Jack Swilling. He was a stagecoach robber, an army reconnoiterer, then an army deserter. He was a teamster, a speculator, a card hustler. Basically, a minor flimflammer. In what is the territory now known as Arizona, he came across the canals of the Hohokam Indians and started selling their water as a kind of potion. A simple scam. One day, when the Indians started to make noise, Jack decided to found a town there and declare himself mayor, drafting his *own* . . . He called the town Phoenix. It is now capital of that bound-to-be state—a city *built* on flimflam." The Chinese con artist, loud and then quiet, high- and low-pitched, spoke in two and even three voices. "Make your destiny. Wonderment personified, that's what Mccoyalooza can offer people! Splendor with a human face! Think big and the world is yours. I speak of immortality."

If it's crazy talk, McCoy thought, *at least it's about me*. His blood ran fast in his veins and his body hummed like a train rail. "Darn tooting, Johnnie" was all he could manage. "Darn tooting." Maybe it would make sense to him later. He doubted it, but already his voice was back to that McCoy boom, a just-returned feature of the greatest scrawny fighter America had yet seen. "What next, J.G.?"

"We figure," Johnnie Gold said, calm now, removing a gnat that had flown into his teeth, "how to have you crowned King of the Self-Deluders."

And at that moment it started to rain.

It did so for three days, and before it finished McCoy and Johnnie Gold got to work.

"Fame is fame is fame," Johnnie liked to say. "The first stage of Mccoyalooza is to fortify your reputation, and then we'll see how to profit on it."

Letters were sent out, supposedly written by a "Connor Alterman"—one of McCoy's "safety net" names, invented for occasions like this—and these notes, along with Johnnie Gold's bribes, led the newspapers to prick up their ears.

The *New York Daily Salmagundi*, May 18, 1901:

Those who delight in uncovering examples of degeneracy in the sport of pugilistic encounter (and their count is uncountable) should find amusement in the most recent controversy surrounding and besetting none other than Kid McCoy, pugilist. Letters and epistles from a source whose name we are not at freedom to make known are now in circulation expressly to dispute the authenticity of the recent McCoy victory against the Jabbing Jew Joe Choynsky, pugilist. Neither is this page at freedom to impart our opinion as to the deserved winner of said fight between said pugilists. However, we presume that readers familiar with this page and with irony will infer our estimation of the truth from the tenor of our prose. That is, an ironical tenor. Be that as it may, the above-mentioned controversy (stemming from the letters mentioned above) asserts that McCoy never actually fought Joe Choysnky; that in fact the man whom people in attendance that night thought and believed was McCoy was in fact an impostor, and impersonator, and in fact a deceiver. This allegation is, if not corroborated, then at least made plausible by a number of irreconcilable newspaper reports from the evening of the contested contest which show McCoy in seven different cities at the time of the contested contest. "I'm sure that it was McCoy who fought Joe and no one else," says executive Patrick Clarkson of the Broadway Athletic Club. "I'm the one who handed him the check for $7,000, and I saw him pretty good. This whole hoo-ha is nothing more than a McCoy gyp." Never the less, one Prince Chang of Cochin China, a visiting notable in attendance, reports that he overheard the "impostor" McCoy talking about his "real identity," and about " 'pulling off the flim-flam and making the world think I'm McCoy.' " Reached for explanation, McCoy himself tells this page that he in fact did *not* fight Joe Choynsky on the night in question. "I would've come forward sooner," says the Kid, "but I truly did not wish to hurt the reputation of Joe Choynsky by letting on to everyone that he'd lost to some no-namer who pretended to be me. If it'd been said I'd *lost* the fight, I'd have shown my face right away." H. H. Measures, of *The New York Evening World*, a paper long friendly to McCoy's interests and welfare, says that he, Measures, and other reporters were too far off from the action to see the fighters clearly. Is there any way to suss out and determine the truth? We will keep you informed and steeped.

Imagining afternoons stretched ahead of him as a run of seven boiled lobsters and New York–cut steaks, McCoy spent a dollar on lunch each day for a week. Once again making headlines on his terms, striding the streets like the prettiest thing with pants, believing his name on the city's lips, dancing "the grizzly bear" on a Staten Island Ferry, performing handstands for applause and grinning his new porcelain bridgework at people whether they noticed him or not—McCoy about town was smitten by the return to form he saw reflected in his own smile; at home he found himself not yet fully back on his feet.

How cruel that his wife should trip him up just when confidence had returned. But the arrival of J.G. and the first stage of Mccoy-alooza seemed to italicize for Susan all the unpleasant things about McCoy she'd learned of late.

"The truth is, you *did* fight Choynsky." She seemed fond of descending on him, her sharp-cornered, genteel, and nimble face all hectic. "This is another lie."

Call my lies inventions, he thought. *My inventions show me at my best.*

Another time, as the couple sat on a buttoned-leather couch, lighted by a crystal chandelier at some banquet thrown by an old-timer with endearing large ears, Susan pleaded, "McCoy, you don't need some nonsensical, unformed *plan*."

With her hair of caught flame tall over her head and anchored by a little ivory butterfly next to her ear, glare-eyed Susan knew what her looks could do to McCoy. She added: "You don't need an overweight coolie to make you grand." The whole time an obvious emotion, a wind milder than outrage, started to breathe something like calm into her voice—he'd just given her his most soothing McCoy smile.

She must have at least liked the restored confidence that the First Stage brought him, if not the First Stage itself. She sat with her long legs crossed at the ankle, looking at her husband.

"As I once wrote"—he ran a finger along his wife's hand, wrist, forearm, as he knew she enjoyed—" 'We that are true lovers, run into strange capers.' " Just as his fingers made gooseflesh of her skin, so his words riled up his own spirit. "I can be who you want me to be."

If people love each other, he wondered, *why must they spend the time and feeling to work through special explanations?* (The "strange capers" line had actually been Shakespeare's.)

The worst of Susan's annoyance, if that's what it had been, was passing like a sigh. But a small look of embarrassment stayed on her face while she looked into his. "Oh, *pish*, McCoy, I just cannot imagine what this so-called 'plan' will bring next, and I would venture that you yourself have no real idea." The chandelier twinkled, and Susan's teeth and the fine crystal wineglass in McCoy's hand did, too.

"The thing is this, Duck." McCoy tried to feel the eyes of the room on him as he reclined into the pulpy sofa—an angle of success. "You have to let me be who *I* am as well." He welcomed, in the midst of this twinkling, the light of reclaimed energies. Thoughts came and went like echoes: Susan was an angry person and she was kind, she was blustery and was shy; she was loving and not; she was something else, he thought. No one woman could be drawn from all those traits. Maybe the Susan he'd chosen to shadow out from the jumble was just his invention. But if he was aware of this, he never really admitted it to himself.

With her or without, Mccoyalooza was going to work. Whatever it would be.

A Cranky, Arrogant Art

"True," said Johnnie Gold, misleader of men, "I don't know what we're going to do, exactly, other than see which cards we are dealt."

This was in a Chinatown restaurant that showed hanging browned birds in its windows, a curtain of carcasses. Two Italian immigrants had a juggling act by the door, the restaurant's gimmick to drum up non-Chinese business.

Johnnie leaned forward until his belly stopped him. "Thanks to me your name is news again, McCoy." He'd gotten a lot fatter since Louisville. "That will bring some value, Kid." The guy's body was like an outburst of meat, a jiggling eyesore, his eyes were majestic. "A palooza of an opportunity will present itself."

"I really hope it does." McCoy rubbed his eye with the heel of his palm. "I've been worrying lately you and I talk about the same thing without getting anywhere. I'm not the only one who thinks so, either."

Johnnie didn't hear this. He showed the concentration you'd expect from a man who thought himself close to the glory forever denied him.

The flimflammer pipe-dreamed aloud about founding a city (false-pretension-fraud), lending the McCoy name to a flimflam-esque product (false-pretension-quackism), or even—and this idea didn't go over well with our boy—franchising a host of McCoys, all fighting for profit (subtlety ingenuous). "My pugnacious friend, we need to keep our eyes open, our ears open. . . ."

By the door the Italians were talking and juggling. "Watcha you self." "No, *you* watcha *you* self." Patrons came and went.

Founding a city? McCoy thought. The food on his plate looked to him like roundworm. *Is this nonsense?*

"Something wrong, Kid?" Johnnie's sweaty-browed face seemed to show exasperation, then worry.

McCoy was working to quiet his own brain. Committing in this Mccoyalooza way to being more McCoy—what else could he do?

"My mother would have loved to hear talk of it, J.G., that's all." McCoy absently tugged his lower lip between finger and thumb, and his brow pursed as if he'd pulled a drawstring. "Me, a city founder, huh?"

"Your mother?" Johnnie regained what McCoy thought was the professional, Buddha of Swindle smile. "She is dead, Kid?" And he started to make a cigarette with fumbly hands.

"Both my parents." McCoy looked down. "My whole family, killed in an earthquake."

"'Founder McCoy,' your mother would have called you." The flimflammer wore an open face. Some queer brown sauce glistened across his lips.

One of the Italian jugglers was about to drop a bowling pin. McCoy felt impatient and restless. "Johnnie," he said.

The bowling pin hit the ground with a hollow crash.

McCoy fixed the most kindly stare on his friend; he, too, had developed a professional look. "Maybe we need to make sure we're not on different paths here." He wasn't a kid alone in Utah anymore. He had a wife to lose now and he knew he had worth. "Have I told you what Susan says about this?"

"A drop"—one of the juggling Italians was straining out his vowels—"is a just part of the act, people." This juggler wore a brown hat and a jacket very wide in the shoulders. His partner made a vaguely apologetic gesture with the back of his hand.

"You think a woman would give greatness its due, McCoy? Why

would she?" Johnnie's laugh sounded like the mucusy shudder you might hear from a prospector who's lost everything except the bit of poison in his brain that keeps him digging. "I learned something when Muff left me."

"Four or five guys say they're me, J.G., a few people in New York still know who I am. How does that mean anything as grand as we need?"

Though McCoy was sure he was about to tell the truth, really sure, the words came out wobbling as he said: "And I love Susan more than anything I could want in life. Don't say anything contrary about her."

Johnnie Gold tapped off his new-lit cigarette. "So what will it be, eh, McCoy?" He spoke fast. "Quackery with fraud? Humbuggish-fraudulent-false-pretensional-quackism? Bluffery with caprice? What card shall we be dealt, how d'you want to play it?"

A passing Chinese busboy almost tripped as he moved around the jugglers. The sound of a cleaver at chop carried out from the kitchen. And across the table from McCoy, Johnnie was breathing agitatedly. Once in a blue moon, pauses in a conversation with the flimflammer weren't intended.

McCoy sucked on his cold teeth. Ashes on the table fluttered and spun; someone'd opened the door to the restaurant.

"Hey! Watcha you self." "*You* watcha *you* self."

Now with fast hands, nervous hands, the Chinese con man gestured over to the Italians and what they juggled. "You know what? Societies can be set up and knocked over just like those bowling pins."

McCoy was tired of talking and to clear his mind he imagined Susan. He could only picture her huge fault-finding eyes; the rest was vague. At last she smiled.

Meanwhile Johnnie was staring at McCoy the way a caged hippo might have, wide eyed and wanting help from a friend. "You think it's some sort of fluke that other people have said that they are you? I don't pretend to know why, either. But it is no fluke. You look not much like a fighter." He wheezed, out of breath. "You yourself have told people that you are from any number of cities—yes, I have followed you closely since we were parted—and you will fight anyone, and you often win with a dispatch that—"

McCoy silenced Johnnie with a wave of his hand. "We'll figure something, J.G." The scientific twist-fist ex-champion sat up straight and cracked his knuckles. "I'll also fight again. That'll be our start."

In due course they set up a rematch with "Jabbing Jew" Choynsky, to be fought in Hoboken, New Jersey. H. H. Measures did some very public campaigning for McCoy, and not only because he'd been bribed; he still thought the Kid the best fighter of the new style. The *Evening World*, like many tabloids, supported its favorite athletes almost as a mother cheered her little tobogganing children.

Susan said, "You've become awfully meretricious, McCoy, under the effect of that Chinaman." She actually said meretricious. The *Poet's Wordbook* said it meant "false, gaudy, whorish."

He decided to train harder for Choynsky.

It would be the most reported-on American sporting event to date. McCoy vs. the Jabbing Jew, redux. The tale of impostor Mc-Coys, the possiblity of a flimflam avenged, and the spectacle of Christian versus Jew had attracted not just sportswriters, but also front-page newsmen.

"Which is the best way we can ensure victory?" Johnnie Gold wondered. "A little bluffery with caprice by some itching powder? Pepper sauce on your knuckles?"

"I can't, Johnnie." McCoy wiped the sweat from his face with a towel. He'd been jumping jacks for an hour. "Not in this match."

The night before, sleeping in the intersection of Susan's arms for the first time in weeks, he'd dreamed over this upcoming bout and finally come to understand what he was trying to do with Mccoy-alooza. In the ring of his fantasy McCoy had fought well; in the ring of his hopes he'd had no need to flimflam.

"Not to tell you your job, J.G., but for this whole thing to work," he said, "I've got to win on the square, unfortunately. Just this once. They've got to see it's me and not some bunko artist or some prairiebilly who's just taken the name." McCoy spoke as confidently as he could, though outside dreams Choynsky punched even harder than he did. "If I get caught flimflamming, with all the reporters who'll be there, it's over for McCoy." Later, fresh from the shower, he added in a friendly tone: "After, we can whim-wham all we want."

"Is this your wife?" Johnnie Gold was turning a curious pale color in the face. His frown edged on scorn. "Is she affecting you?"

True, Susan'd asked such questions as: "What about your dignity, then? Your pride in yourself?" But his decision wasn't about her, of course it wasn't.

"I have to fight Choynsky for real." The notion hit him now in its oddness. Whose dull mumpish voice was coming from his own mouth? But he didn't have a choice in the matter, though it might have seemed he did. "I just have to beat this pug silly." McCoy's head actually wagged a little under imagined Choynsky blows.

"I'm sure the referee won't let him win, anyway," McCoy added, "on account of anti-Jewism." And his eyes widened with relief at that notion. "It won't be *completely* fair. All I'll have to do is make it close, and my reputation will be top hole again, and we're off to the races."

Still, Johnnie Gold was shattered. Flimflamming was a cranky, arrogant art, but a life lived without it carried risk. "Our palooza, doomed before it starts," the Chinese cheat artist said, while McCoy gave what he wanted to seem like an indifferent hum, or a yawn.

What Is True, and What False

Much as McCoy believed Susan found his newbuilt confidence attractive, she was fighting him more and more. He strained under explanations he didn't have words for.

"Don't you see?" He'd get nearly as worked up as she would. "The coolie helps me, Susan, he's going to help me." A cloud of fatigue would settle around his eyes. Couldn't a husband work not to be one of the unnoticed termites of the world? Didn't she want him committed to being McCoy? "Why do you have it in to stop me, Susan? Why?"

She pulled away and stood with her back to him, her lovely thin back. She wore a mannish white blouse. "It is not the way people act, McCoy, that's why." Her hands were touching the windowsill and she looked out onto the street. "I did not marry a man who consorts with yellow swindlers. I did not marry a man who lies, who pretends for the newspapers"—when in fact that's exactly who she married.

McCoy felt just as he had in a nightmare he thought he'd outgrown: the boxer dreams a Tommy Ryanish opponent has let down his guard, and in his sleep the boxer throws a sure KO punch, but feels his arm slump, impotent as a noodle, and the frustration wraps him in his helplessness.

And Susan was continuing with her list: "I did not marry a stage actor, a milksop, or a confounded *story*teller. . . ." Listening to it strangled the breath in McCoy's throat. The nation's attention was coming back around, bit by bit, and where was her flair for drama, her ambition? A Susan without the independence to say, "I don't much care what Mister and Missus America thinks is right," wasn't the Susan of quick, wiry, once-again-beautiful McCoy's soul.

Still, he kept his hopes that he and Susan wouldn't give up their love under the push of these arguments.

The *New York Morning Telegraph*, August 17, 1901:

> To the bewilderment of no-one but herself, Susan Fields endured a frightful dispute with her husband Kid Mccoy, the boxer known above all for being married to said actress, as well as for having beaten the "Jabbing Jew" Choinsky under spurious circumstances. Susan Fields is handsome in light comedy roles, somewhat of an intellectual, a blue-stocking, and yet rumor has it that she has been abandoned by this miscreant! But in their divorce settlement, Kid Mccoy found that he had made a mistake. On Tuesday last, he asked Susan to remarry him. She refused, but after thinking it over, agreed to wed Mccoy for a cash payment of $10,000. He was offended, and broke off the courtship. But after he, too, pondered it, the Kid began courting Susan again, this time bearing a certified check, but not for the full sum. How do these people live? we ask humbly. "Ten thousand dollars," Mccoy is said to have said, "is too much for the return of a bitch."

The *New York Morning Telegraph*, August 19, 1901:

> Rumor is at it again, and she can't keep her mouth shut. Or get it right. The famous divorce case of Susan Fields and Kid Mccoy rages on, and is here clarified. Their dispute now seems to center on who gets control of their dog. What had been confused for Mccoy's offer of $10,000 to Susan to remarry him, now seems certain to involve a lovable pooch, whose breed could not be determined at press time. It seems that Kid Mccoy is being

held up to pay $10,000 for the return of an actual bitch. The New York *Morning Telegraph* apologizes for any vexation caused by our past error. However, if the participants in this connubial melodrama were not so perplexing a couple, this and other new-papers would not have to sort out what is true and what false from the ruins of their romance. All of this, of course, comes soon before Mccoy's highly anticipated fight against Joe Choynsky. One thing that is certain: the couple is no longer a couple.

First off, not much truth lived in what the "news" reported. Yes, McCoy'd quit Susan, the truelove of his heart. But there had been no talk of dogs or of money. There hadn't been much talk at all. The dying fall of a marriage sometimes is met with quiet helpless anguish.

The actual end had come as a surprise one morning after an argument. "Well, Susan!" McCoy'd said, blustering to the door. "If you won't leave off Mccoyalooza, I'm heading out for good!" He hadn't planned or even wanted to threaten that; what felt like an overflow of some outside force took his mind and carried his legs and mouth beyond his will.

Susan was sitting on her bed, unmoving and apparently un-moved, as if she were alone in the room and trying to decide what to do with her day. The only sound was a short and crushing grumble of the city getting built up and torn down out the window.

"You know, I'm not joking, Susan!" He understood that she was right about a lot of things, that he and Johnnie Gold had no actual plan in itself. At the same time he couldn't bear that she was stand-ing in the way. Hadn't ambition always been her wish for him? Oh, why wouldn't she say something now? "I really could walk out, end-ing our lives together, Duck!"

"Mmmm."

His own doom glistened in her cool-pearl eyes. A feeling of ruin dragged on his mouth and eyes; his cheeks slumped.

"If you won't quit hectoring me," he cried, "I'm actually going to walk out!"

"Yes, and the sky promises rain today." Her voice had come out hollow. So he'd left.

Afterward, sleeping on the floor of Johnnie Gold's tiny poor apartment on Mott Street, McCoy thought Susan had given him no choice. Should he live like his father, wearing homespun and a look of futility? The Why was at work, the odd rule of the Why. He had no choice but to serve it, despite Susan Fields's wild hair and stomp and humor. Besides, he did try to reconcile with her a few days later. But by that time she was already moving out and wouldn't hear him.

He'd never forget her piercing insults at that moment—"You fool"; "you backward child"; "liar"—or the sight of her angry burning cheeks, her face going wrinkled about her eyes and lips until she looked older by years.

A man like McCoy was unable to choke off his sadness without suffocating his other enthusiasms. To prepare for Choynsky he gave full play to all his emotion. Jabbing morning and night in Ronnie and Ray's practice ring, crying like a gutter in a rainstorm, McCoy got his legs back, his jabbing speed, and his tingling needfulness. He felt invincible, some days.

Johnnie Gold, meanwhile, thought up an excess of flimflam plans. He'd bribe the locker keepers to dope Choynsky's water. Maybe he'd hide a cackle bladder full of blood in McCoy's mouth so that Choynsky'd get overconfident early. Or, Johnnie would position himself in a prime location to shine a light into Choynsky's eyes. He'd—

But McCoy didn't want to think about scams—aside from the cackle bladder in the mouth, and the blinding light, which he thought pretty smart ideas.

The Real Mccoyalooza

A great reputation is a great noise; the more there is made, the farther off it is heard. —Napoleon

SEPTEMBER 9, 1901

Everyone who knew boxing showed up. Members of the press, gangsters and flimflammers, boosters and politicians (some of these were also gangsters or flimflammers), the actors of Susan's theater troupe, flicker folk, pilferers, onetime friends of McCoy, bookmakers and button men, the fraternity of boxers, a sorority of elevated ladies, Johnnie Gold's Midnight Boys, some baseballers and bicyclists, Jews—everyone but Susan.

High in the midst of a crowd, skinny Kid McCoy in pale majesty stood, all terrible in the ring. Under a canopy of some twenty silken banners like flapping cloud-cover, "[h]andsome as a god" (H. H. Measures, *New York Evening World*, 9/10/01), McCoy drifted alone across the canvas for twenty minutes, waiting for Choinksy to arrive. The elegant stir of McCoy's fists was followed by four thousand eyes. To himself grim McCoy muttered, "I'm feeling fine," clearly not, despite his impressive training. Without Susan or much of a flimflam his confidence was shaky.

The audience grew loud in the Mechanic's Palace in Hoboken— a towering hall built by a Masonic secret society, its deep red walls embellished with automobile grilles of chrome. And the ring, in the middle of the Palace's lakelike marble floor, rose from a sequence of carpeted steps.

McCoy was a two-to-one underdog.

Paul Armstrong, an unathletic writer of athletic melodrama, led the Jabbing Jew through the crowd to the ring. Choynsky, godlike as McCoy and looking pretty strengthy, murmured to himself, "I'm gonna win."

Then he shouted out for the crowd, "I'm gonna win!"

He didn't look at McCoy, as McCoy didn't look at him. Someone yelled, "Is this Jerusalem?" while another cried, "Jab him down, Jew!"

Choynsky softly muttered, "No one's going to take it away from me this time." And he burst out, "No one's going to take it away from me this time!"

Many in the audience cheered this. With Ryan's retirement unlucky Choynsky often got called the best fighter in the world, and here were thousands of spectators to see if—and many of them wishing that—this was the end for McCoy.

Blond-headed and pale (the light made him look paler still), Choynsky was a fleshy man and tall. Born Josef Chianki, this Jewish pug now showed no trace of a Yiddish accent and called himself Joe. His onetime handsome face showed a hilly topography, little knuckles rounding out in surprising places under his cheeks, that bulb by his nose, and also there was a sinkhole near his eyesocket. He outweighed McCoy by a fifth of a person.

McCoy charged at the bell, hoping to hurry the fight, his usual hope. Choynsky knocked him down immediately, the cackle bladder in McCoy's mouth exploding, red all over his face. After that the round was a dance of men in diaperesque waistcloths, each offering his cautious fists to the other.

Jabs marked out space. Light quick-flick punches. Both men careful with their—flick, flick—blows. And afraid of getting—here, there, flick flick—hit.

McCoy squinted at the crowd—where was Johnnie's blinding light? was that Susan who just showed up?—and he was caught with a Choynsky right that knocked him into the ropes.

McCoy charged a second time; Choynsky floored him. That's how it went for a while. Did the crowd cheer? It could be they did.

What McCoy knew was that he felt, taking the brunt of Joe's punches, complete happiness. Maybe his values had changed.

He wore a distorted grimace after a Choynsky left-hand lead bent the bridge on his teeth; his nose broke in the second round, and three ribs cracked in the fourth.

He tried a twist-fist, missed, and was canvased. He didn't even know he'd been struck until he was flat out on his back. And he passed through the most clear, easy, fluent state in the world. He was up before the count of nine.

But snarling Choynsky, trailing a string of drool, launched a haymaker that hit McCoy flush in the eyes. He went down like a buck felled by buckshot.

Choynsky had lacerated the bridge of McCoy's nose; blood gushed over his swelled-out lips and into his mouth. Loose porcelain teeth stabbed the back of his throat, on their way down.

". . . four, five . . ." The referee standing over McCoy was a short roly-poly man with a sober mustache. McCoy could see far up his nostrils. ". . . Seven, eight, ni—" The bell rang. At eight and a half.

Over and past McCoy in a jump, Choynsky ran to the timekeeper, his hands at his brow like someone with a terrible headache. A strong wind of confusion blew around the ring.

"Noooo!" Choynsky screeched like a pig half-sticked. "What are you *doing*?" The stupendous muscles in his back bolted with tension. There should have been at least half a minute left in this round. Choynsky was frantic. "What are you *doing*—stopping the round *now*?"

"I'm sorry, Yid," the timekeeper said, calm on the other side of the ropes. "I was counting along with the referee."

McCoy managed to roll over. He couldn't stand.

"This is an outrage!" Choynsky in tears. The crowd was all frantic voices and hysterical cheeks. Here came cries of "Fake!" "Thief!" "*Goniff!*"

"Enough." The referee pushed Choynsky's chest. His head reached to the Jabbing Jew's nipple. "It was an honest mistake, Joe, an honest mistake."

All the while McCoy was crawling to his corner.

"It's unfair! It's anti-Jewism, it's anti-Jewism!" Choynsky's voice snared inside his throat. A lump was caught there, a two-thousand-year-old tragedy. "Because I am what I am, should that explain why the *time*keeper counts a man out?"

"I agree, positively I do, but look at your opponent." The referee was humane. "If you hurry, you can knock McCoy out in the next round without any problem."

"Fake!" "Thief!" "*Goniff!*"

McCoy had just reached his corner. With the help of the ropes he might have had a shot to get to his smallish feet.

"Joe," the referee went on.

"Sir," Choynsky answered a little louder.

McCoy meanwhile pulled himself upright, and shook his head awake while the referee and Joe went back and forth. The Jabbing Jew was yelling himself a shocking pink in the face.

"Joe." The referee was smoothing his mustache. "Just go."

Choynsky receded into his own shoulders, aging on the spot. He went to his corner grumbling and scowling like a stormy sky. By the time the next bell sounded, McCoy'd had a total of almost two minutes to recover.

From here the fight was madness.

McCoy and Choynsky fell to the canvas twenty-six times in the next twenty rounds. Exchanging punches; landing punches, blood everywhere. McCoy with halting steps walked bravely into fists . . . a cold emptiness where his teeth used to be. . . . Second by slow second Joe Choynsky inched backward. Blood stung McCoy's eyes . . . the two fighters coated completely in blood. . . . McCoy fought like a demon. . . . He hit Choynsky flush in the jaw in the twentieth round, and he swore there was nothing he craved in life that'd be denied him. *I'm no fool, no backward child.* The ring felt like heaven, and Choynsky fell.

The sight of Joe on the canvas after such an effort touched all of McCoy's compassion. He bent to him, and with Armstrong he helped carry the Jabbing Jew to his corner.

The referee pushed McCoy aside—"Okay, that's enough" (the

poor man had awful breath, McCoy would think later)—while Armstrong worked over Choynsky.

Put the pity out of your mind, McCoy, McCoy thought. *Compassion is a Selby emotion.*

Soon the Jabbing Jew was awake, sitting up on his stool and nodding.

At the bell Choynsky lurched off his seat; after a few steps he sank onto the canvas. At the same time McCoy had muddled out to the center of the ring and found no sign of an opponent. McCoy's heart sank when he spotted Joe lying deadish, crumpled, and pale. He bent his knee to Choynsky. "C'mon, up you go, Joe. You're all right—"

The referee lifted McCoy's arm at the end of the greatest fight Hoboken had ever seen. McCoy had won.

But it was what happened next that proved Johnnie Gold right and changed the life of the nation to a small degree.

After McCoy's great victory H. H. Measures in the *New York Evening World* ran a headline that was picked up by newspapers in every last state and most of the territories: *NOW YOU'VE SEEN THE REAL MCCOY!*

How to describe the strangeness of what next happened?

Radio did not yet exist. The telephone was a luxury. Mail was slow. By and large people went about unhurried. With inconceivable speed, however, the phrase was everywhere to be heard and read. And the phrase, of course, was *the real McCoy*.

Phenomenon is too slender a word.

It was not a rumor, not merely news item, or talk, or fad. It became a palooza beyond even Johnnie Gold's desires—a wonderment scattering far and wide out of the spacious mouth of the sky, billowing everywhere and expanding forever. It was no mere phenomenon.

Overnight America had its national symbol for honesty: McCoy himself.

Why? Why did a headline become a phrase that meant so much?

People needed someone. The 1900s were a moment of unprecedented artificiality, of simulation and back-and-front dishonesty. Thirty-five years earlier, say, day-to-day life had been more or less as it'd been for generations. But now horses were being replaced by cars, candles by electric light, mailboxes by telephones, "live" theater by pictures that moved, serious journalism by scurrilous "rumor rags," painting by photography, stairs by escalators, the gold standard by god knows what. Buildings aspired to mountainhood. To offset the new parks at Coney Island—where history was reenacted daily as imitation battles and floods, and where people defied gravity on roller-coaster rides to nowhere, and where everyone was funhouse-mirror-reflected into a queer version of himself, and where folks actually drank from the robot udders of an ever-flowing electric cow—people needed someone. America had become a land of noisy forgery and wondrous pretense, of artificial food and salted gold mines, of phony stock shares and counterfeit money, of imperialism masquerading as democracy, of disenchanted young men living unmarried in cities with liberal-minded women philosophers. What had been a backward and isolationist republic was now a world power. We ate sausages stuffed with sawdust, with fake colorings, preservatives, sweeteners—people (without knowing it) needed someone true—we had frauds and flimflams and colonies and tenements and "more immigrants than Americans" and pollution and the normal man had no slogan to voice his longing for whatever was authentic in a world of terror-breathing falsity. Kid McCoy became the human rebuttal; he was truth in advertising, the genuine article, the real McCoy that was called for. There would be no more impostor McCoys.

Before he knew it, he got quoted in the papers regularly, on all kinds of matters.

"The real McCoy declares that 'the Hay-Pauncefote Treaty sounds like the real deal to me,'" the *Newark Star-Ledger* reported on December 22, 1901. And then, two days later: "Real McCoy says, 'Hay-Pauncefote is only bona fide as a treaty if amended to allow the U.S. to take complete control of the canal.'" Also: "Roosevelt seems like a true blue American to me"; "The mine workers' strike really is unfortunate for both sides."

Now *who's a backward child?* McCoy thought. *A liar?*

He took his new responsibilities very seriously. The opportunity had turned up for a grand flimflam.

Johnnie Gold's job was to dream up exploits: Maybe they could get President Roosevelt to choose McCoy as the face of the Pan American exhibition; McCoy could set up a national speaking tour with the people who'd made a fortune off the name of Wild Bill Hickock; or they'd set up a weekly column in Hearst's newspapers—

"I'm stuck thinking small small small," Johnnie told McCoy, and between his laughs, when the dull deepening shade of bafflement came to his face, it was clear that the man felt appalled at himself. "Something big will come to me, I'm sure." And he shifted in his chair.

This is who convinced me to leave Susan? McCoy thought more than once a day. He lived once again in their old room at the Mill-haus. He didn't know for sure where his ex-wife lived.

Other people, meanwhile, were thinking up McCoyish flim-flams. In an enormously popular motion picture—directed by one Leopold Lubin and marketed as the actual footage of "the real McCoy fight" under the banner BEWARE OF IMITATIONS—actors hired to impersonate McCoy and Choynsky counterfeited the gen-uine match down to the last punch, staging their movements based on news accounts. Though a fake, the Lubin film sold out every the-ater it played.

McCoy was far and wide celebrated. His nose had set after the Choynsky fight in a dashing upturned way. *Where is she now?* He thought every few hours or so. *Where is Susan this minute? Smoking a cigarette? Telling a joke?*

Much of the time, of course, he felt pretty satisfied. Or, he was full with emotions that were hard to sort out. It was like he'd been given a king's treasure in gold; it was like he'd been robbed of all he had; it was most like being alone on a great mountaintop.

One day Johnnie Gold had an idea. "I see an opportunity," he said—a shiver at play in the lowest part of his big noble face.

(The soaring inspired Chinese flimflammer had been in a bad way of late. He was driving himself crazy to figure how to profit on

Mccoyalooza. His intense stare was going weak and agitated. Maybe he'd guessed that McCoy realized a national symbol might not want a foreigner to tell him what to do.)

These, Johnnie said, were troubled times for Tammany Hall, the political machine that, under its leader Charlie Croker, effectively ran Manhattan and counted among its enemies such sages as Mark Twain and the vice-president, Teddy Roosevelt. The papers were guessing that Mayor Van Wyck would go, too, and—

"Mayor of New York, you say . . . ?" McCoy wet his lips with his tongue. "I never thought of myself as *a* . . . Plus, I'm not old enough."

"Surely, you are right," Johnnie Gold said quickly; his powers seemed to have abandoned him at the wrong moment. "It is dumbalooza."

"No. . . ." McCoy nodded and closed one eye in a way that all but said: Okay, go on. *What mayor has ever been called a backward child?* he thought. *Or a fool?*

Johnnie lifted his face. "We can pass you off as, say, twenty-eight?"—his confidence rising with his chin. He squinted toward where the wall of his tenement apartment met the ceiling, as if he'd never before seen anything so far away. "Listen to the ring of it: 'the Boy Mayor,' eh?" Once again the tone of Johnnie's voice *promised*. He gave McCoy an encouraging rap on the knuckle. "Yes, yes, trust in your imperishable good fortune, and in me." Now the flues of his nose went wide. "In my role as advisor, my role as *indispensable* . . ."

"Well"—McCoy searched for the word just beyond his tongue—"what do I stand for, what policies do I—?"

But McCoy'd already given himself over to the idea. He was always giving himself over to ideas. As Johnnie Gold wound his way to ten minutes of panting "new historical American" slogans ("Times are trying? Try men's souls!"; "Isn't it time you tried men's souls?"; "It's times such as these when a man could use a good candidate."; "These are days when people's spirits are stung painfully"; "It's times like these we should try McCoy."), McCoy had the shuddering awareness that Mccoyalooza was coming to its second act.

* * *

He performed the role of symbol of virtue publicly and to the fullest: cutting tape at restaurant openings as the breeze whispered in his ear, soft as a lady's secret; launching steamships on shorelines where leafless trees were dancing skeletons; and going to nightclubs and Broadway shows and flicker theaters, and bicycle races under fat clouds that changed shape very slowly across the sky; and at baseball games he'd toss out the ceremonial first pitch, his fastball free of curving deception. . . . He was well known enough that some of the many letters sent to the address "The Real McCoy, New York City" would find their way—like the hundreds of staring eyes he felt assaulting him every time he walked the streets—to him. All the eyes seemed to say, *We love you, McCoy!* On street corners little shirtless boys in beanies and girls wearing trash for clothes, all of them singing—"Aw, hey, McCoy!"—would swoop in bright like angels, basking in Mccoyalooza, and McCoy'd throw high all the change from his pockets. "We love you, McCoy!" But no matter if he'd come a long way since his Virgil days and the tame greenness of Indiana. He wanted for himself to have come a *longer* way. He craved ever more fame because he'd gotten much more famous; more grandness because he was pretty grand now.

Soon he met a woman who took his mind off Susan.

He met Rosella Bunker in Winston-Salem, North Carolina, the fifth stop on a slapdash barnstorming tour that he and Johnnie'd set up in late 1902 to bankroll greater ambitions. (On this roundabout lap south, McCoy knocked silly twenty-four fighters in seven weeks, local boys mostly, and he pontificated about fourteen topics.) In Winston-Salem, McCoy'd just polished off the small-town hero Edward Smithson in a single round. Rosella was the ringleted girl who'd stood on her tiptoes from the opening bell, and who'd clapped lightly at the finish, her fingers coming together, humble at their tips.

McCoy, glistening in sweat, not a scuff on his person, approached delicate Rosella just after the KO. There wasn't much swerve to her. But Rosella was the prettiest woman he'd met since Susan. She must have been nineteen.

"Hello," he said, looking round at her and grinning with his whole face. The fight'd happened in a shadowy barn; Rosella stood before a haystack.

"I'm the real McCoy," he said.

"I know."

But he hadn't finished. "America's true article."

"I know"—brightly, as if this hadn't been her second time saying it. Then, telling McCoy her name, she was singsongy as a wind instrument. Over her shoulder one of the animals in the barn kept going cluck.

"I—I know Eddie Smithson," she said. Her hands were pudgy but her eyes, her clear, quick-moving eyes beamed the same beaming gray as Susan's. Susan, the woman who said she'd always love him.

"You mean *that* fellow?" McCoy swiveled toward the ring where his opponent retched, smelling salts in his nose. "He seems a good man and true; genuine in my book."

"Yup." She half covered her cute little mouth with her hand.

Some more animalish gabble came from over Rosella's shoulder. Her features went stiff as she tried to think of something more to say. She gazed, lost for a second, at a bucket ladle.

"Yup," she said, a rise seeable in her posture. "I thought Eddie Smithson was a fine example of manhood, but now that you come around. . . ." The exact grayness of Rosella's susaneyes broke his heart. In her unsophisticatedness McCoy saw a vacation from the nagging of his true beloved.

Livestock breeders and stockmen and cotton pickers on their way out patted McCoy on the back. They were about as noticeable as whispers in an uproar. McCoy and Rosella were standing very close.

Finally he said, "Just because the Smithson fellow lost doesn't mean he's not good and true." And he smiled down into her turned-up face.

Rosella's pale skin showed a trace of color, like sand under the lightest snowdust. No, she wasn't Susan. On closer inspection, there was a gentle tug on the far ends of her almond eyes. (He'd find out

Rosella was one-fourth Siamese and the granddaughter of one of North Carolina's most famous twins from Thailand.)

Her face had the quality of a project outlined on a drawing board, all deliberate curves and right angles—as if her silhouette, her first-class nose, even the oliveness of her cheekskin, had been ruled on by some board of directors; but in laying down her mouth the day laborers had their fun: Rosella's lips had the stretch-across ambition of a railroad line gone too far. If her wide mouth threw off her symmetry, it charmed most everybody.

"You're sweet, aren't you, Mr. McCoy?" Rosella, grinning, seemed more comfortable every second. She had lipstick the color of blood on the sharps of her teeth. "You're also cultivated about the finer things, I'd put down a bet."

"Not as cultivated as some people I know back home, to be honest."

It's really quite charming that you are trying to be cultivated, McCoy, with this Matterhorn poetry. . . . Was that a thou *I saw dribbling onto your chin? . . .*

McCoy wagged his head as if he were trying to shake something loose. For too long he'd spent nights crying for Susan into his pillow at the Millhaus—

Meanwhile, a teenager at the edge of vision crossed the dreary emptying barn (like Rosella, the kid was the color of old newspaper). Behind him an open door gave on a green meadow. A gust of warm wind drove past the teenager and got to McCoy and Rosella just before he did.

"Hi, Mr. Real McCoy," the boy spat across his lips.

"Hello, there." McCoy shook the stranger's hand and continued gazing on Rosella in the chicken-reeking gloom. She wore no jewelry, no lip rouge or face powder. Her dress hung a bit shredded at the neckline.

"This is my brother." Rosella sighed, the corners of her mouth drooping with exasperation. "I reckon he's called Robert." She hadn't looked once at her brother. Innocence, greed, and desire all flared off her eyes as different specks of gray.

"I was hoping to see a better fight, Mr. McCoy," Robert said. The kid had the face of a ferret. "Surely, I was. But you took care of that one, really you did." Yes, with his pointed chin and whiskery mustache, a ferret for sure. "Mr. McCoy, for a Yankee, y'all really did go and—"

"Oh, hush, Robert!" Rosella porcupined up. "*Y'all really, y'all really*, is all you ever say. Now quiet yourself when I'm talking to the real McCoy!" Her hands spiraled into fists, and you could see terrible poverty in her face, the way you could sometimes see war in the faces of soldiers after a battle. No, she wasn't Susan.

Still, he married her.

T.R.'s Influence

Early the blue-sky morning January 17, 1903, the President of the United States Theodore "Teddy" Roosevelt came for a visit to Manhattan, while as evenly as face powder a light snow hid the city's flaws. Roosevelt was to dedicate the Henry Fairfield Osborn fossil exhibition at the American Museum of Natural History, and he asked that the real McCoy turn up to appear in news photographs.

This morning New York stood cold and free of its normal odor, the garbagey streets blanketed from the weak sun; a deep white spread across the opposite park, quiet and blinding bright. Shivering McCoy climbed the stairs to the museum, along with the other dandied-up guests. Reporters carrying their boxy cameras hurried at his back.

McCoy was tired. The feeling of being alone in his bed at the Millhaus had kept him up nights. And with whom had he felt alone in that bed? Rosella McCoy, his new wife.

She'd moved to New York to be with him a month after they'd met, and five days later they'd had a City Hall marriage. That was January 10. Sometimes she said things like "drug," instead of "dragged"; her hands would grope the air in sleep, her nightmaring face would warp, and she'd moan and gnash her teeth like a blind woman. Still and all, the bedside lamp, once McCoy'd leaned over and lighted it, reminded him—and he needed reminding—that Rosella Bunker had a real loveliness. Her neck and wrists, naked and pale dainty, put him in mind of things slight, like cobwebs or smoke. But her knuckles were red and scruffy.

Inside the Natural History Museum, under the artfully hanged vertebrae of an ass, Johnnie Gold in his sweeping royal Prince Chang duds carefully asked Mr. Roosevelt when it'd be best to stand McCoy for mayor. A pair of burly men in very tight suits came to push him away. (Secret Service agents had famously been assigned to protect the President after the 1901 assassination of McKinley).

"No, I *friend* with McCoy," Johnnie said, jiggling, delicate, and sad. The agents, their short-cropped heads at his chest, worked to shove him. And, dropping his fake accent, smile, red Arabian turban, his self-restraint, Johnnie yelled, "I'm with McCoy! I'm with McCoy, you oafs!"

"He is," said McCoy, his smile quick with embarrassment.

All week he'd been wild to meet the President, but nothing was going as he'd hoped. Waiting in his tiredness to be introduced to the famous man, distracted by thoughts of his pretty unexpected wife who wasn't Susan at all, McCoy sighed. His happiness didn't feel complete enough, in the same way that his affection for Rosella was—though sometimes big with desire—incomplete. It was not that he found her personality *un*pleasant. It was just unexpected. McCoy'd taken this girl in a Rooseveltian charge up the San Juan Hill of courtship because she'd promised to be an easier time of it than had been hardheaded Susan. But now he found himself in a marriage where he felt unsure whether to put his hand on his wife's unknown hand. He hadn't invited her to this event, or even told her about it.

The President's photographers, knees knocking, pushed forward and started to snap. "Please, would'ja stand still for the camera, Mr. President and McCoy?"—at which point this most walrusy President and the tuxedoed McCoy stood alone, shaking hands before a large glass case of very old rocks.

Or, they pretended to shake hands.

As the littlest motion would have looked blurred on film, McCoy and "the Great White Hunter" held to each other, motionless for the lens like two stuffed mastodons.

Teddy's big, unmoving hand started to sweat into McCoy's; the President's grip was fierce. His tanned-hide smile was frozen; his eyes, slightly pinched at their sides, also were frozen.

"Son." The stock-still President talked like a ventriloquist through his unbending lips. Shadows at the root of his nose came and went as flash powder whitewashed his face by snatches. "Son, it's perfectly easy to see from your reception here, there's a lot of fondness in this part of the world for you. I have but a word to say, and I shall sum it up with a bit of advice that I think those concerned in the development of your career will agree with." He hadn't loosened his squeeze, and McCoy's spirits were lifted, his drowsiness gone. *The President of the United States is here with me, he's shaking McCoy's hand.* . . . He hoped Susan Fields would read the papers tomorrow.

"Son"—the President's features tensed with enthusiasm; the great man really liked this speech—"you're in this life to work, and while you're at it, work hard. When you have got the chance to relax outside, play hard. Do not forget this, that in the long run the man who shirks his work will shirk his play. Now, you're a pugilist, so maybe these tidings of mine will not seem news to you, but the one thing I say to all aspirants: Never, never shrink from blows. Go forward. Face them."

Roosevelt's eyes were happy to tell what his mouth wouldn't: that the President found joy on this earth by governing you, bullying you, bossing you around, or disposing of you. "You look perfect for a career in politics. Athletic. That's what got me started, son. They said, 'That police commissioner's athletic.'" The President's cheeks twitched from the work of talking without moving. "I remember a professor speaking to me of a member of the Yale Eleven some years ago and saying, 'That fellow is going to fail. He stands too low in his studies. He is slack there, and he will be slack when it comes to hard work on the gridiron.' That fellow did indeed fail."

Sunlight coursed gold and churchly through the museum's huge windows.

"You are preparing yourself," Theodore Roosevelt said, "for the best line of work in this great world, so it is a safe plan to follow this rule—I once heard it preached on the football field. 'Don't flinch, don't foul, and hit the line hard.' "

The President fell silent, releasing McCoy's hand and fidgeting to move about as a live human being.

"Well, sir." The nearness of Roosevelt and his encouraging words puffed McCoy up toward that state where, moved by confidence and hope and he was pretty sure sophistication, he felt huge with victory, imposing and powerful as any man in New York. "I don't know about the gridiron, Mr. Roosevelt, but I can tell you I don't shrink from blows."

Though McCoy would have bet that surprises certainly did loom ahead—that his life would continue to follow the sure mode of zigzag—he stood up even straighter as he recited the great Gilgamesh to the President of the United States: "No novel kinds of hardship, no surprises, loom ahead, sir."

"That's fine, son." The President's voice was far off—probably his mind too—perhaps even as far as Port Arthur, China, and the predicament already beginning there between Japan and Russia. "That's very fine," Teddy Roosevelt said, starting away, showing McCoy the blond bristly hairs on the back of his sunburned neck. The room seemed to lurch toward Roosevelt just as he turned to leave: time to let someone else laze in the fullness of that presidential smile.

Mr. Roosevelt had what McCoy craved. Whatever Why the President answered to, it must have been pretty well satisfied.

Campaigning for mayor, or even beginning down a road that led to the possibility of making a sincere run, meant a lot of difficulties. McCoy put in the appearances, made the friends, actually perused the fine points of New York governmental realities and won, if not real political capital, at least some measure of respect that, without lying to himself, he could believe was worth the strain. Also, Johnnie got him thinking of founding some legitimate businesses to capitalize on his name. Editorials praised McCoy alongside Citizen's Union and Republican reformers such as Seth Low, who himself ran for mayor on the Fusion ticket against Tammany Hall.

The problem was there were at least ten Seth Lows hoping to challenge Tammany Hall, and ten like George McClellan Jr. on the other side, ready to carry the Tammany banner. A man with McCoy's makeup didn't like to wait. If Mccoyalooza now meant standing in line to take City Hall, when and what was next? Johnnie Gold spun new schemes nearly every day—more, it seemed, just to keep himself involved than to make the earth tremble. Once at dinner, he dropped his spoon to grab McCoy by his lapels; he'd read that the boxer had talked with another man known for political shrewdness. "We'd get there sooner if you trusted me! You don't trust me!" Johnnie's skin went a sickly shade like white bamboo and he coughed a lot now. "He doesn't trust me!" In a strained falsetto Johnnie called on the other Chinese diners to witness. McCoy didn't like to consider all this. "Get where sooner?" McCoy said.

Pluswhich, I'm a fighter!

Before Johnnie thrust his mayoral aspirations on McCoy, the boxer had had just one discussion about New York politics. It had been with Susan Fields, just before they'd ended things.

"Croker?" Susan'd said as she and McCoy walked in Central Park one morning a few months earlier. "He and his gang, why, those men are no more than hoodlums."

It had been a fair afternoon, New York enjoying a free and easy stroll in its Sunday best. McCoy glimpsed from over his shoulder what looked like a shadow rushing past. "Yeah," he said, and craning around—it all happened so quick—he met only sunshine on grass. "Croker *is* a hoodlum," he added (a little preoccupied, if truth be told). Then Susan quickly turned on him:

"Why do you always have to qualify my opinion?" If her voice was usually soft, now and then she used abdomeny, grating speech. "Can't you just agree for once, McCoy?"

"But," McCoy stammered, "I did; I agreed with what you said."

"I said hoodlum*s*." Susan gave the compressed smile of someone with a canker on her tongue. "Plural, with an *ess*." Not to mention she'd stopped walking.

"Isn't that just what I said?" McCoy's question pirouetted up at its close, a feeble turn of optimism.

"You don't even hear yourself." Susan sighed, but she'd put her hand on his arm, and not ungently. He'd loved Susan. He'd believed that he loved her more than his own life.

Two or three days later they'd parted for good. And he hadn't seen it coming! Real love is more blind than Rosella Bunker in her sleep.

The midnight after McCoy had met President Roosevelt, Rosella's sleeping face flickered oliveish and grieved under her ringlets. *Who is this girl against me?* McCoy thought.

"You're having a nightmare, Rosella."

She opened and closed her lips four times; she made a good-looking little grimace of her face. "I am, Yank?" Blinking. "I was?" (Yank was Rosella's nickname for McCoy). The next morning he woke to find that she'd left him.

I want a devorse, her note read. It was written on the sort of legal notepaper McCoy never kept in his apartment. *You trickt me up to the city and so Ill need money, besides. Rosella McCoy.*

Sitting dazed in his bathrobe, his heart going mad, McCoy was then served with an official document from a lawyer, Eric Salat, Esq. This memorandum asked for five thousand dollars on behalf of his client. Enclosed was a draft of a second note, "all ready to send to the newspapers." In it Rosella called McCoy a "cheater, a man untrue . . ."

Flimflammed!

He went wild all day, pulling his hair, in the bath and out on the street. This was a shock! Women didn't leave their men! She was so dishonest! On the eighth hour of his raging, when Manhattan's faint moon in turn dampened McCoy's light, he calmed a bit.

Sitting on a bench at Madison Square Park, dejected but still mad, very pale and hungry, he was trying to take it all in. No, women didn't quit marriage easily in 1903. Maybe that was why Susan, even fierce and modern Susan, had never really left him. Had Susan acted in her way to compel McCoy to leave *her* . . . ? Susan, who said she'd always love him. Maybe he'd been flimflammed twice. His teeth started to clatter.

"Hey, real McCoy!" "Yay, McCoy!"

He didn't hear them. The regret and anger in his gut, the taste in his mouth, and the scowl twisting his lips all belonged to saps, the people he'd duped in his life.

You're nothing without flimflam, Tommy Ryan had told him once.

Oh, McCoy had misunderstood everything since Johnnie Gold had come back! Yes, he needed to be more McCoy. But how stupid—he hadn't realized that *the meaning of being McCoy had changed!* He'd have to be "real in this age of artifice." (*Harper's* magazine, January 21, 1903.) He needed to be true, even if he had to fake it.

He mailed Salat, esquire, and had the marrage annulled quietly. Rosella Bunker may have been the first American woman to realize that divorce could make for a profitable living.

Forget Rosella—McCoy didn't like it at all without his real true-love. He'd say to the Susan Fields in his mind, "How could you have done this to me, you harlot?" Or, "Why did I allow you to let me leave you, my darling?" He hung one of her many photographs that he'd never thrown away. It showed her in a feathered hat in front of the Lawrence Playhouse. At the sight of Susan's picture McCoy could hear her smooth, sophisticated voice. It made him smile that she hadn't bothered to hide her cigarette from the photographer.

He'd have to find his Duck and show that he could embrace a spirit of perfect integrity, a life free of pretense.

With this in mind he decided something.

A Fool's Bolt Is Shot

"**N**ow, McCoy, tell me how you broached the news to Rosella—it's Ros*ella*, is it not? I admit I never *could* . . ."

Johnnie and McCoy were spending this winter dinnertime in Plume's, a street-level café on Broadway with brass fixtures, a tile floor, and a rule against photographs and Irish (but not Cochin Chinese royalty). Johnnie's eyes were baggy, the rims red, as if he hadn't gotten much sleep. And there was his lingering cough.

"You know, J.G., I hate even talking about this. I admit, I had to let her drop. I feel terrible, just—mmmnph. But. I've got to ask you about something."

For McCoy, telling Johnnie the news he needed to tell him promised to be very hard; he wanted to do it fast and without much thinking. Because he loved Johnnie Gold. He thought if he could numb his own mind, the way he did when watching some plays or flickers, he might tease out of himself what was required: hard detachment. If only Johnnie would give him an opening . . .

"Did she take it poorly, McCoy? I imagine the average American wife might bicker like *a* . . ."

"No, I don't know, she was almost—sophisticated, for her. I mean, she started out very calm. Before long I admitted I still loved Susan Fields."

"How very white of you."

"No, it was hard; I was in the wrong for sure. She told me, 'I don't want to be drug through the mud.' To be honest, I don't remember who first brought up ending things. When Rosella says it, it sounds like *die*-vorce. But she looked almost relieved, to tell the truth. I'd never seen her look so—"

"I must say, McCoy, I am a touch out of sorts about this. About what's happened—[*cough*]—to you."

"*You* are out of sorts? You?"

"Lend an ear. McCoy. A candidate for mayor of New York—should that man undergo a public parting of the ways? Now, don't. I'm in your corner, so to speak. Your personal life is and will remain your own, as a matter of course. Your comings and goings are not any of *my* . . . That's without saying. However—how*ever*. Let an old Chinaman tell you something."

"J.G., this is exactly the situation I want to talk about—"

"We, my pugnacious friend, you and I have obtained so much in the way of development of knowledge concerning the science of American government—which reminds me. Why, I wonder, do people of this culture always talk about the first impulse to worship one god, one single god, as a crucial moment in the development *of* . . . ? Take certain pagan systems, take the Greek: an assembly of more or less equal gods sitting on a council, flawed, arguing. Does that not seem a modern, more *American* take on divinity than the current single King of the Universe idea, which, to me, seems modeled after forms of government which the American experiment has . . . Listen. If America were true to herself, she would progress *toward* paganism, and her gods would be fallible, loud councilmen who back-door every decision."

"Johnnie—"

"Of course, I'm not suggesting you ever mention paganism as part of your platform! I only—"

"*Hello*, gentlemen. Sorry to interrupt. May I offer you fellows something in the way of dinner? Or coffee, perhaps tea?"

"Uh, coffee, please—and maybe some more tea for the prince here, thanks."

"No—so so*lly*, nutting fo' me, tank yu."

"All righty, sirs. Back as soon as the coffee's ready."

"Thank you."

"Tank yu. . . . Right, McCoy, where were we?—[*Cough.*]—More than anything I lament—"

"Johnnie, you once told me, uh . . . Hold a moment, okay? I—I don't think I need to have someone like—I don't think we should really work so close together anymore, I don't think I should pay you, I mean, anymore."

"What? McCoy?"

"I'm sorry."

"McCoy? *McCoy.*"

"Johnnie, I'm very sorry; I know that we've, that you've helped me a lot, but at this point, three hundred is a lot of money every month, Johnnie. Mostly, though, I'm just ready to move on."

"I—who will be your advisor? Who will decide the second facet of Mccoyalooza?"

"Well, the second facet is, I mean—one day it's South America, the next day China, or some government for the whole world. . . . You really think we could take South America? Isn't that—"

"Ah! Ah! Is this about your first wife? I know you better than you think. Have you been talking to her?"

"No."

"No?"

"No."

"No?"

"No."

"Fine. Without my guidance, what is Mr. McCoy planning to do? So, you propose just to neglect the chance to be mayor? My, you can lead an ass to knowledge, but you cannot make him think!"

"I have a plan, Johnnie."

"Oh? A fool's bolt is soon shot."

"I have a real plan. Not just talk, which is all you—"

"All right. I didn't mean to *suggest* . . . What, tell me your plan, then?"

"To fight Gentleman Jim Corbett for the heavyweight title. No one'll be able to miss me once I'm the skinny heavyweight champ.

It's the biggest prize in sport, bigger than all the other belts combined. What a great campaign boost: the heavyweight champion for mayor. Having both, that'll be true fame, and then I can—who knows?"

"What you do, McCoy, you do by rule of thumb, and not art. Kudos. You want to think small, all right. But I can help. I could have my indigent midnight boys break his kneecap. I've got it! Just this moment I figured out how we are going to flimflam this Mr. Corbett into setting up a—"

"I can set it up alone."

"You can set—? Well. Congratulations, McCoy, I say a bitter congratulations. One may not know it, but one can wake up as a flimflammer and return to his bed a dupe!"

"Johnnie, I'm sorry."

"But how do you plan to beat Corbett? Eh? Because the best thing, the very best thing for us to do—"

"I'll beat him."

"You have a flimflam for that already, as well?"

"Johnnie, I don't know if the real McCoy can be seen by the world to flimflam. Wouldn't that be wrong, considering everything?"

"Ha! I have been too skilled, I suppose, at my job. And so, what is it you are trying to tell me? That this is farewell again?"

"Well, yes, I'm afraid that—listen, Johnnie, I—sometimes a man grows up, he needs nobody but himself."

"And his first wife. Himself and his first wife."

"I'm full grown, and I make decisions for myself. I think you're tops, Johnnie, I appreciate everything. I really do. I'll pay you and always be your friend."

"I will demolish you. I will reduce you to ruin, sabotage you, I will pauperize you, McCoy."

"Please. Please, say what you think your help's been worth. We can talk over a figure. Don't act like this, Johnnie. It's just time for me to come to my own decisions, that's all."

"I will flay you. Ten thousand dollars."

"Johnnie—"

"I will break you all to flinderation. I will nip you in the bud."

"You don't need me. You're Johnnie Gold. The great Chinese flimflammer Prince Chang. Can't you rustle up your Midnight Boys again? What do you need—"

"McCoy—*still*, you don't see, you idiot. You moron. You nonexistence, you nothing. Naked, impoverished immigrant children are not known for their loyalty, or effectiveness. You were the white-skinned smile, the fair-haired handshake. But you need me as well. You *need* . . . I'll bring you to utter napoo, I'll ruin you. I will. Really, I will."

"Johnnie."

"I will!"

The Chinese flimflammer, his reddening jowls and pale lips quivering, got to his feet. He spat a big sticky reeking rheum that hit McCoy in the nose, and he blustered out of the restaurant, his hands moving wildly.

It was over. At least it was over. McCoy like a traitor felt heavy in his heart, but his mind reached something like relief. He'd said what he'd wanted to say. It was over.

The last that McCoy saw of Johnnie Gold out Plume's window, the flimflammer was rounding the corner of Broadway, looking un-well, gesturing in a huff to the sky and starting to glitter like a star: there surrounded the con artist a magnificent light—actually falling snow that passed under the streetlamp at the same time that Johnnie did—and it danced around his massive body like sunlit bees. McCoy watched him disappear from view, decked in what seemed the gleamy fancywork of heaven, and our boy thought he'd never hear from the Chinese flimflammer again.

Within weeks McCoy, along with an established jewel merchant named H. A. Goren, opened two diamond-cutting factories and storefronts: one on Maiden Lane, already the jewelry center of Manhattan, and the other on Broadway, near the Millhaus. This second store, standing handsomely among row upon row of ugly pawnshops, catered to the theater crowd. McCoy'd become a businessman.

Soon, the McCoy Company—capitalized at ten thousand dollars—launched a health farm in Saratoga Springs—the McCoy Sanitarium—where wealthy alcoholics would dry out and would-be fighters train, and where people of all stripes could pay to have their bowels absolved by the magic of bran.

"I'm not only a wholesaler or a mayoral hopeful or fighter; I'm very fond of my books too," he told the *New York Times*, which just happened to be Susan Fields's favorite daily. "My Shakespeare, Maeterlinck, my Longfellow and Tennyson, are great sources of delight to me. Poetry is fine." And of course he boxed again, and won again. He was even granted the middleweight championship by default when it was vacated after the retirement of "Punchdrunk" Sam Potts.

"When I'm mayor I'll hang up my dukes," McCoy told the same newspaper. And so it was that McCoy hobnobbed with Seth Low during that reformer's most important campaign rally—and also present at that rally, if McCoy's plan worked out, would be his ex-wife and only love Susan Fields.

The Possibility of Happiness

Two thousand people clustered as thick as penned chickens into the meeting hall at 350 Broadway on freezing March 19, 1903—the attractions were Seth Low, McCoy, and the writer Mark Twain. When Joseph Johnson Jr., president of the Order of Acorns, announced McCoy as first speaker, hundreds of sidewalk idlers tried to bully their way inside; their rush carried the six policemen at the doors off their feet.

"Ahem." McCoy took a little step forward on the platform. He'd forgotten to button his collar. "Thank you." He talked into his speaker's trumpet, though he hoped to boom his voice enough not to need any such devices. Men and boys climbed the latticework around the elevator just beside the stage to get a better view. Even the windowsills teemed.

McCoy said, "Tammany is—"

He could not go on for the cheers. Before him the crowd swarmed like flies; everyone sweat faced and upright and all brotherly with cheering. The stagnant air thickened moment by moment with heavy tobacco smoke.

After several minutes Joseph Johnson Jr. restored quiet. All McCoy had to do was to introduce Mark Twain, who wore a pitiless smile.

Then McCoy, on his way back to the wing of the stage, spotted Susan Fields. She stood in the front row, looking at him. (He'd had the Reform offices send her an invitation without his name on it.) At once that almost forgotten sensation of warm melting butter returned to spread over his insides.

Susan, unsteady and frowning, pushed left and right, looked about to cry from all the jostling. But her inmost nature, her *Susanness*, which overflowed even here, couldn't help but show itself in the haughty tilt of her head, the lively color in her cheeks. And also her eyes—which held McCoy's.

"In this campaign," Mark Twain began, "there is nothing very much simpler than to decide if we are to vote for the continuance of Crokerism or whether we shall not." As Twain spoke his mustache blew in and out like window curtains in a breeze. "I think we have had enough of a system of American royalty residing in Europe."

The crowd sounded like a single loud thundering typhoon. And Susan was standing in the middle of the bedlam. Her frightened eyes glared.

Oh, Duck, I've been so alone! McCoy forgot for the moment that he'd been remarried.

—If there's one thing I've learned, Susan. We can change the normal way of things to fit our case.

Just tell me how, McCoy. Tell me how and let's do it—

"Of course," Twain continued—while McCoy walked to the lip of the stage, extending his hand deep into a swarm of grabbing hands; he reached toward Susan. "Of course," Twain said, nonplussed by the commotion, "I cannot expect you all to know this, but it was only against my physician's advice that I came here!" The writer's voice rose to an extraordinary volume. "The trouble was, gentlemen, indiscriminate eating!" Twain's knotted hands were pulling Lincoln-like on his lapels. "I ate a banana, thinking that by doing so I might conciliate the Italians of this city to voting the Fusion ticket! But, as it was a Tammany banana . . ."

McCoy leaned down into the audience, ignoring the indignant stares of Seth Low and Joseph Johnson Jr. "Pull him in!" somebody yelled. "Sssh!" yelled somebody else. McCoy, his legs shaking, leaned even farther into the crowd, pushing away so many grabbing hands, every one of which thought he was reaching out to them. McCoy felt as if he'd lunged into a single body, warm and bumpy. And, about to fall off the stage, he found, yes! Susan's hand, her delicate clammy hand.

". . . a Tammany banana is a strange thing, folks." Twain's voice an alley cat's at midnight. He didn't even glance at McCoy, who panted and huffed, struggling to pull Susan up to the stage—

". . . One end of the banana"—Twain spoke loud—"is perfectly white! The rest of it is rotten! . . ."

Sweaty-handed McCoy almost dropped her back into the crowd, but pulling, holding her hand and pulling with all his strength—

". . . Now, I have the greatest respect for some Democrats personally." Twain grinned joylessly. "But nine tenths of the banana is rotten. The best we can do is to throw the whole banana from us. . . ."

There, a final McCoy tug; Susan wavered above the crowd, and with one foot no more than glancing the platform, she looked ardently into McCoy's eyes just before she was set firm, to the cheers of some in the front rows.

"The banana will make us sick, as if we had swallowed Tammany tigers that wrestled for supremacy in our interiors."

Susan radiated that beauty that comes with sudden relief. The exertion lent her cheeks the color of her furious hair. Just like that his Duck was actually standing right there next—

Don't look at her until you compose yourself, McCoy.

—to him, and she was just as he remembered her. The down on her cheeks brightened her face in the electric light.

". . . Do you want Tammany tigers fighting inside your belly, folks?"

Susan's eyes were deeper in their gray and brighter than Rosella's.

Twain raised a fist: *"No tigers!"* And Susan's ear looked to McCoy ripe for a nibble.

"Do you want Crokerism anywhere near the inside of your person? Do you want Tammany tigers growling forever . . ."

"Hello, Susan," McCoy whispered into that very ear.

"I think"—Twain twirling the ends of his mustache—"I think I can introduce you to a very good doctor too: Seth Low, who but lately was honored with a Yale LLD." And when Twain stepped back, the room went into a great booming spasm:

"Seth Low!" cheered the crowd. "Hurrah!"

Oh, the urge to nibble that little pink ear! Susan turned and started toward Seth Low as if he were the reason she'd come up here.

Mr. Low stepped forward. The two sloping halves of his mustache, his steep-angled eyebrows, and even his eyes gave the idea that someone was pinching him at his forehead and pulling upward.

No, Seth Low wasn't the type of man Susan would love.

"Hello, McCoy," she said finally, and had his heart.

Half an hour later our ex-marrieds stood alone onstage in the emptying hall at 350 Broadway. The capacity crowd and McCoy's fellow speakers were making their way out into the cold. And Susan largely failed to control her hair, even though she wore it in a bun. McCoy ached to touch the lock straying across her brow.

"Hmmm." She was shaking her head. "*Mayor* McCoy, eh?" She had one of her lollipops in her mouth now. Her fingers were ringless. "Mayor." Then she made a *tsk* sound. Caving, no doubt, to everything, McCoy didn't put up a reply. Instead, he grinned with all his face. *I don't like it without you*, he thought.

Susan had yet to show anything like a smile, but McCoy swore that goodwill sparked her eyes. "So," she said, "interesting things have happened to you, unlikely things." Her voice, however, sounded formal. "Wouldn't you agree it's unlikely?"

How silly, this small talk. He wanted to take her hand, bury his nose in her hair, to ask her to marry him again. He had oceans of promises to make, and he burned to kiss even the lollipop inside her lovable mouth.

"Yes" is all he said. He caught himself nervously rubbing his hands together. "Unlikely. And interesting, too." His anxious energy had him ready to go fifty, sixty rounds with Tommy Ryan. "What about you, Susan? You've been doing flickers?"

"You're a strange person, McCoy, to be an emblem for honesty." And she let that linger for a while. The air was still close with cigar smoke, the lights bright. "Yes," Susan said, "I've been doing flickers."

"You shouldn't wear your hair like that," McCoy said, taking a chance. His gaze fell to her neck and lower. "It's so pretty when you let your hair down."

McCoy'd forgotten about the dimple of her collarbone. Hello, dimple, hello!

He didn't realize how long he'd been standing there, his mouth half-open. Susan brought her hand to her neck. And left it there.

"How are the films?" McCoy said at last, trying to show off his new white teeth. "Enjoyable, I hope? . . . Oh, they are? That's good, that's good." And wasn't there a real reunion going on soul to soul under the words?

"We film them in California now," Susan was saying; she'd kept a little frost in her tone. But what about the goodwill in her eyes—

He said: "Duck," the word falling soft as snow on snow.

But she seemed prepared for this, and ignored it. "You know, McCoy"—and if she felt any tenderness, her face didn't reflect it now—"I've worked on a film called *Here Comes the Trolley* with a man who knows you, an actor named Griffith."

"David Wark Griffith?" McCoy knew his big smile wasn't believable, and his light tone probably wasn't either.

"Ah, but then," she said, "when Mr. Griffith had known you, you were a boy using a different name." When Susan was annoyed—as, for instance, now—her hair flamed the color of a bratty unspanked twelve-year-old's. "Mr. Griffith felt as surprised as I was, seeing you dubbed 'the real McCoy.' I wonder if the newspapers would find it as strange as we did."

"I knew D.W. in Louisville." McCoy swallowed hard. Maybe she'd start to go easy on him; once upon a time she'd given him the benefit of the doubt—though, often she'd just doubted him. Now he heard himself saying, "I've changed, Susan."

"Stop it." Even her cheeks were stormy now.

"It's true." He left off biting his lip. "I have." *Does she know I'd married someone else?*

Sure, he'd brought all this on himself, he could admit that. But wasn't she being unfair, in her high heels? He'd forgotten that her lips curled upward when she thought something over: another reason to love her.

Didn't Mother's lips curl up? He thought. *I think I can remember.*

By now a janitor had started to sweep across the emptied floor of the meeting hall. The man was looking at McCoy and Susan and wouldn't look away.

Time to go.

McCoy took his ex-wife to Plume's Café.

"Oh, pish." Susan sat across from him. "If you *have* changed, the assumption is that you're no longer going to allow people to think that your name always has been McCoy. Is that the case?"

Well, at least the fierceness is still there, he thought. But even her thorns tickled him.

After he didn't answer—she must've known he wouldn't—she laughed at herself and at him. It may've been a good-natured laugh. She wrapped the stick of her spent lollipop in a napkin, making even that look classy.

"I know about *your* kind of changed, McCoy."

"She knows!" he said. He was gripping his chair like a tobogganist.

Making a face, she raised an eyebrow and his hopes.

"What is 'McCoy'?" His voice went piercing. He took a sip from his coffee, as he hoped to draw strength from it. "It is not hand, not foot, not arm, not face, not any other part belonging to a man."

Even her nostrils were exciting. She said, "Is that from—?"

"I am myself, not a *name*," he said. Some substance like confidence fired and stiffened up his spine; like an underestimated general, McCoy set himself for a big-league offensive. " 'Tis but my name you're ticked off at," he said.

"*McCoy.*" She sighed—familiar sounding, at last. If not affectionate.

He scraped his thoughts together. Here he sat, a very famous champion and icon and political hopeful quoting Shakespeare to the woman who'd left him.

"I met the President, I fired Johnnie Gold, and I've been reading the classics," he said. "My vocabulary is top hole. And sometimes there are people who can't live without each other, despite themselves."

And there it was: some tenderness in Susan's face.

She worked to fight against it. "So now, McCoy, have you—oh, what was that ridiculous way you'd put it?" The motion of her lips was precise, the strength of her womanliness really something. "Have you 'built your American dream with golden bricks'?"

Susan'd turned her lively gray eyes to his. Maybe Rosella'd had that brainwork whipping around behind her stare too—if she had, McCoy'd never caught it.

His voice broke open. "Oh, Duck."

The muscles in her chin startled, and she looked into her lap. "Do you have any idea what it's like for a woman to feel devotion toward someone like you?" She spoke not without snarl. "Do you know that?"

If he'd have turned away—as he would a few moments later—he'd have seen out the plate-glass window all the sights of frozen Broadway where cement and brick and marble and wood battled it out for advantage, here the passing dray horses, here a skidding autocar, above it all the coming el train high on its tracks. But McCoy's eyes gave up the white spectacle of New York for the white length of Susan's downturned cheek.

"There's good in me, Susan. I think you know it."

When she lifted her face to him now it was a little girl's soft-shell timid. "You left me, McCoy." Pearl pendant tears hung from the edges of her eyes. "And you lied to me. I may be a professional actress, but I don't let people think I'm someone else after the curtain goes down." The tears falling now. "It's different, it is."

McCoy was beside himself. "Duck, I'll change, I've changed," he said. "Duck, Duck, my Duck," he went on. His tears had come also.

Susan's hands moved around the table. She wore the sweet face he'd seen on posters across Manhattan.

"Do you love me?" McCoy asked. How could she hold a grudge now? What did the past matter? Which would she be now, the duck or the elephant? "Do you?"

She was back to looking at her lap; the curls at the top of her head were bouncing. Had she nodded yes? Or was she just sobbing? His ears started to hurt as if from a great noise, as if a hundred baby ducks were breaking from their cages to quack across the floor all round his feet.

The possibility of happiness, like an el train shivering its tracks from way off, threw its rattling suspense as a ghostish tremor; nothing moved now but the quake on everything. McCoy was scratching at his hair; he would die if she didn't answer him now.

"Susan, Susan."

Her lips trembled, too. Her face looked whiter, and the noise of the café, the city out the window, all the mingling to-do of the night ceased: the shuffling waiters close by, the street musician trumpeting somewhere down the street, that rumbling sound coming from God-knows-where—McCoy left it all behind. He'd found an island of quiet. ". . . Oh, Susan," he was saying. "Oh, how I've—"

She brought a long, calming finger to his lips. She'd had to reach across the little table to put it there, and held it tender on his mouth. He caught his breath. She smiled, and joined him on his island.

The Real McCoy in Training

Let reason's bright light
Guide desire and appetite
Should happiness be your goal.
Don't scatter to the wind
The thoughts of your mind,
Those that come from the soul.

—Kid McCoy, "A Ballad on the Way Our World Works," last stanza, as printed in the *New York Times*, September 19, 1903

It was to be the culmination, the tip-top.

Not merely the riches, nor the heavyweight championship (the choicest prize in sports), and not merely the seizing of it from the great and arrogant Gentleman Jim; and not only how that triumph would help McCoy's political aspiration—no, it was that all these together would bring him what he'd been forever craving without having known how to articulate it. As the great reform gadfly Spencer Spinnell told the *World*, "A champion-candidate admixture may be impossible to beat come election time, most particularly considering the honest spirit, that real McCoy catchword, undergirding the whole package. Perhaps, *very* perhaps, he could be President!" Not to mention, such a brilliant McCoy victory would strengthen Susan's trust in him.

He could be the kind of American who lives forever in children's history books: President McCoy, who'd smile his way onto a five-dollar bill, pass a law banning Tommy Ryan, and maybe the Maumee Indians too.

McCoy's chance at real and permanent happiness was to come December 31, 1903, at Madison Square Garden. The "fight to end all fights"—literally, as the 1904 New Year would bring the revocation of the Horton Law that made professional boxing legal in Manhattan. (Unless, of course, a new mayor such as McCoy came along to renew the boxing law.) "McCoy-Corbett will be to New York what the Olympics would have been to old Athens if they had had a wire service and photography," wrote H. H. Measures.

The reporter wasn't exaggerating much. There remained a hunger for all things McCoy. Susan's friend the actor Macaulay Johnson, slated to play the fictional boxer and jewel thief Kid Garvey in the play *The Pug and the Pastor*, followed McCoy around as research. Before long Susan said, "I cannot tell them apart from half a block away—each has a puffed-out chest and a bounce to his walk!"

For a while McCoy attended *The Pug and the Pastor* nightly to see himself reenacted.

Not long before the Corbett fight, McCoy spent an eager week on the grounds of the McCoy Sanitarium, his new home in Saratoga. He and Susan entertained D. W. Griffith, as the actor showed up to make McCoy the subject of his directorial debut, *The Real McCoy in Training*, a flicker.

McCoy was now in impressive health. By dint of acrobatic exercise he added the weight and swell of muscle; he cut a thrilling shape for his try at the heavyweight crown. (He'd tilt the scales at 168 to Corbett's 194.) He forced himself to the outer edge of his stamina. He read a book about the training regimen of the soldiers of Sparta, and with that in mind ran up snow-packed hills carrying logs; he'd go and go until he'd collapse and each breath came sore in his throat.

At the same time he'd become a country gentleman, sprouting a neat little mustache. He bought mouse-colored clothes, replacing the bright and shiny things he'd favored in Manhattan. And he hired a staff: the shy pretty kitchen maid Anne Maxson; the lushy and doddering old butler Loret Sweet Fletcher; Geo Small the valet and his apprentice Li'l Amplee; a cook; and the housekeeper Edith DeBalls, who fancied herself mistress of the estate. Not least, there was Balty I. Beattie, the nutritionarian, who had his clients eat their bran, drink their sulphur-smelling spring water, and sleep in the gymnasium or in the fourteen cabins that, with the tall snow drifts and the bare maples, stood guard around McCoy's three-story Victorian home.

Days, McCoy trained, stopping only to read his new-bought works of "modern thought," and work on his vocabulary. He'd try to pepper his sentences with quotations from Hegel, Kant, Nietzsche. ("I have no knowledge of myself as I am, but just as I appear to be."—Hegel as quoted by the champ. And: "Ceaseless Becoming weighs on Man like a heavy illness."—Nietzsche.)

Nights, he was happy kissing Susan. (Once in a while he worried that it was under her influence that he'd abandoned Johnnie Gold just when the man had seemed unwell. But that feeling passed.) Sitting alone on the veranda, watching that moon pour its bleach on his acres, with the remindful white light in her feathered hat and showing now and then the secret freckles just barely on her cheek, McCoy'd find himself back to the romance of their first walk in the shadow of the Brooklyn Bridge.

D. W. Griffith arrived on this little estate with his cameras in mid-December. McCoy found being a film subject an exciting idea at first, then irritating by the second or third day.

Rather than spar with a real partner, McCoy had for posterity to pretend-jab an actor. McCoy shooed Miss DeBalls away as Griffith filmed him upbraiding strangers who pretended to be his valets. Next, after a call of *"Rolling!"* the director caught McCoy in a tender scene with Susan, the lovebirds walking together in front of the sanitarium's fountain. As cameras shuddered, McCoy took his wife's hand and said, in a spiny little sigh of irony, "Careful, Susan, you almost stepped on my foot there," and it looked for the world as if he were whispering a love devotion into his sweetheart's ear in flickery black and white.

"Remember, McCoy"—Susan chiding like a teacher—"this is going to help your image."

The flicker *The Real McCoy in Training* not only launched Griffith's career; it would make McCoy, for this one mythically successful film at least, a verifiable movie star.

How to explain McCoy's unnatural calm before the fight? It was the calm some people found suspicious. He wasn't stupid about it. His eyes weren't dreamy. With a smile of cool, prairie confidence he told his favorite reporter about a fierce, exhausting battle that he would win. "I really have no doubts about it, H.H."

They were sitting in the dining room in McCoy's manor house, which was also the dining room for the McCoy Sanitarium. McCoy had a plate of kippers before him; Measures his pad and pen.

"I'll stop speaking as an ink-slinger for a moment," Measures said, and he actually laid his hand over McCoy's shoulder. "Son, I know about you. I saw you beat Ryan, I know all the stories about how you'd 'play possum' in the ring, or lie about your health before a fight, all the *what have you*, the itching paste on the knuckles, all the guff. Now listen to me. You can't pull a scam-flam or whatnot here, not with this one. I'm sure you know that." He gave McCoy a questioning smile. "The stakes are too high, friend. The attention too great. Not to mention a lot of people have staked professional faith in you, you catch my meaning?" Though he stayed in his chair, Measures gave the impression of rising to his feet. "You're the *real* McCoy now—"

"I'll fight and win on the level. Gent Jim's good, but he's no Ryan." McCoy's chin jutted out, riding the current of his sureness. "Plus, I've got destiny on my side now, and the whole U.S. of America. Make sure people know that, H."

Measures bent over his notepad with a grumble.

One of the sanitarium's two-week clients, a seventy-two-year-old math teacher with the gout, came in holding a bowl of milky bran and sat down next to the reporter. "Hello, Mr. McCoy. Hello, sir." The man drew himself up like a peacock, but dropsical. He wore the bleached housecoat of the sanitarium.

McCoy jabbed his finger at Measures. "I beat Choynsky twice"—the newspaperman raised his eyebrow at the number mentioned—"and we all know what Choynsky did to Corbett." Just over Measures's shoulder, a portrait McCoy'd had made of Susan hung on the wall. She wore a blue hat in the painting.

McCoy's voice inched toward a sigh. "You don't think I'll beat him."

"McCoy." Measures hadn't looked up from his pad. "I think you have a good chance of pulling this out, I do, even with the weight difference." When Measures stopped writing, his eyes found McCoy's and held them. "But I've never seen anyone so calm before a big fight, unless the fix was in."

"Well," said McCoy. He punched the air three times.

He believed that his appearance of honesty, his show of goodness and authenticity, would protect him from defeat. Then he wondered if Susan would leave him if he lied again.

He turned toward the gouty client. "So, how's the oats, Mr.—?"

Plus, I've been training too well to lose, he thought. *And I can always punch below the belt in a clinch.*

"Shepherd." The math teacher had ten, twelve dabs of fiber across his teeth. "Ron Shepherd. This bran is really helping, Mr. Real McCoy."

At that, H. H. Measures turned up his eyes and, like an animal of the woods brought inside, scanned everything around him. He seemed as if he hadn't noticed the oak-paneled room before, or the painting, or the bran. The air had the dull flat inertia of an exhibit under glass.

"Well, you're not like other fighters, McCoy, I'll give you that," Measures said, as Anne Maxson stole from the kitchen to take McCoy's plate of kippers.

Susan came down to join them.

Mrs. McCoy wore a string of pearls and sat on McCoy's lap. H. H. Measures asked, "Everything is well?" Meaning as plain as day: is your marriage not a travesty this time?

"Oh, everything is wonderful." Susan kissed McCoy's cheek; her hair, which McCoy felt on his neck, was the color of wine enjoyed in the early evening, wine lighted with the sunset; but its color also held the shadows that lived in the wineglass and behind the sunset.

"Yes, just wonderful," McCoy added, quick. And though everything really was wonderful, talking about it now to a reporter hitched McCoy's voice up toward a liar's pitch. All the while Susan's backside was coming to a poking point on top of his thigh.

"Mouth'a touch mouth," he said, and kissed her.

"Well"—Measures again—"you plan on having children?"

"Oh, yes, *yes!*" For the readers of the *Evening World* Susan acted very animated. But under the table she patted McCoy's knee, a slow, private gesture. The pull of his affection felt like gravity.

Measures, changing tone: "Mrs. McCoy, you think McCoy's as upright as his reputation?" The reporter squinted at the lovely lady. "How does it feel to be married to our national beacon of honesty?"

Her gaze shot to McCoy before collapsing to her lap. "Oh, it is just wonderful," she said, flat. "Wonderful, yes." When she did next look at McCoy, she managed a tender smile that seemed genuine.

In two days would come the fight.

The night before the heavyweight championship match, warm Susan lay beside McCoy in their bed.

"You don't have any plans, do you, McCoy?" Susan looked pearly gray in the face, dark gray in the neck: a statue in midrestoration. "What I mean is, you hold no plans to . . . ?"

"No, Duck." The moon was a band of pearl on the bed, and McCoy more than ever knew who he was. "I swear I'm not like that anymore," he said. "I won't cheat, and I won't lose."

McCoy slept off and on that night.

In the Heart of the Fight

Yes, this is tough but I can do it, he thought, in the fifth round of the championship fight, *Joe's quick for a heavyweight, ah ah, that didn't hurt so much. There's an opening got it a jab. He's quick maybe that's why he's called a gentleman, ah, oh my ribs, well, he's not gentle, follow his eyes, eyes give away the moves of the body, hit him! yes, again, yes! his body softer to the punch than Tommy Ryan's, there, yes, his jaw! go down, go down you bastard, ah, ah, his punch is stronger than mine, he outweighs me by, ah, that didn't really hurt, there, back at you, take that. Ah, ah, it's true that you actually see little stars, get back into it now, McCoy, punch, there! How does that feel, you bastard, or that, don't think so much just punch, punch, punch, that's it, McCoy you've got him, corkscrew him, where's Susan there's Duck front row, ah, ah, ah pain is nothing if you don't let it get to you, ah. I've never seen so many punches not even in Choynsky or Ryan or where are the ropes I'm falling, there, the ropes, now block block, ah ah ah ah. Block. Jab. Block jab jab. Push him off, that's it, now to the center, hit him! just go back you bastard, there, combination, left right, left left right, left right, oh he can take a punch can't you Jim, ah ah jab jab uppercut, oh if that'd landed, you lucky bastard, ah, stop thinking, McCoy. There, I bet you never felt a jab as strong as mine, oh my jab is stronger than yours, it really is, look at your face when I hit it, punch!—you're like a corpse when I punch, like when the, ah ah, oh Jim's face sounds like a splash when I hit it, splash, ah ah ah, oh my* *he's strong and heavy and keeps coming, he smells like a ah ah, step away, punch I have him yes! In the face there goes his tooth so many people will see me knock him out! I'm going to do it! I have him! Punch punch there punch go down! Champion and President! Everything I ever wanted, there are more people watching than I ever how is he still standing come on I don't have anything more if he can take that, come on, punch punch, he's a goner he's mine, ah ah ah ah ah no ah ah ah ah ah, don't go down, McCoy, no one has energy like me don't ah ah ah ah ah, oh, Susan, I don't want to lose in front of Susan, Jim isn't so great, if I can just ah ah ah ah ah blood tastes like electricity in the mouth, oh no my new teeth, ah ah ah I'm done for it's dark don't fall. . . .*

The Fight to End
All Fights

But we've gotten ahead of ourselves.

Thousands upon elegant and not-so-elegant thousands—paying as much as twenty-seven dollars a seat—had come. Two scientific fighter-champions, "the match to end all matches," and picture the hopeful shrieking everyone had done for the twist-fister McCoy—the sentimental if not the bookmakers' favorite.

In bustling half-circles around the ring middle class and rich and very rich had brought Madison Square Garden into a state of bedlam. Teddy Roosevelt himself turned out, and common immigrants too. What a swaying city in that one building! Crystal and concrete. Faces as far as you could see. Uneasiness ran brilliant in the air. Science, wealth, bloodshed!

Just before the bell, between loud whistlings of support, McCoy in his corner nimbled around like a windup doll. The light was filmy under the gray ceiling, the grotesque brightness of the electric lamps, and in the irregular sparking of flash powder. Gentleman Jim looked like a gray ghost punching the air.

Jim had come in four inches, maybe five, shorter and ten years older than McCoy. He was powerful, if not enormous; he didn't charge, but advanced straight at you. "Steady as the surf," *Ring* magazine put it.

The fight started in the heart of a near-infinite crowd's yelling.

After four sweet-flowing rounds it would end in near silence. Most reports would call the fight a fraud. If the spectators had been as hushed as a grove of trees when McCoy went down, when he came to, precisely ten and a half seconds later, the loud boos came and came.

Even before the fight there'd been rumors. Letters had come to New York newspapers, claiming the match was going to be fixed.

"No, I hit the deck only because I lost on the square," McCoy, still steely at his core, told the *New York World* the day after. "What kind of honest man would I be if I went down otherwise? If it'd been pre-arranged, would I have all these bruises? 'Beliefs are more danger-ous enemies of the truth than are lies'—that was Kant. Besides, I have a good feeling as to who started this rumor-letter writing cam-paign. Look toward Chinatown, is all I can tell you."

McCoy hadn't lied: his bruises were bona fide. His eyes puffed out like matching bellies, the bridge of his teeth had broken (again), and his bruised hands were swollen wide as Chinese fans; his forehead looked washboardy. The *New York Times* declared, "The cruelty of the fight controverts any claims of contrivance," and added, "if it was rigged, Mr. McCoy received needlessly rigor-ous reproof."

Thinking it would quiet people, Corbett and McCoy worked to-gether on a motion picture simulation of the fight (they read a newspaper to determine precisely what punches they'd thrown, and in what order). The fake match, filmed, looked fake, which only added to the impression that the fight sure seemed fixed.

(Another film that claimed to be a record of the match—this one shot more professionally and employing two actors named Mog-gach and Stoltz to play Corbett and McCoy—won universal ac-claim. In fact, stills from *that* film that showed the nonfighters Moggach and Stoltz appearing not to be fighting very well were sold as authentic photographs and taken as further proof that the fix had been in.)

"Susan—*Duck*," McCoy, shaky and lumbering, with feeble eyes begged, "do I really look like a man who's taken a dive? Look at me!"

Who else would have sent letters claiming the fix was in but Johnnie?

The rumors would not be squelched, especially after Martha Corbett lost, for all intents and purposes, her mind.

"The fight was a joke, and every sport in town knows it!" Mrs Corbett told *The Standard & Vanity Fair*, looking on that magazine's illustrated page twenty-two more tousled than usual, and with her tall hat tilting almost off her head.

"McCoy did not train, I know for a fact," Mrs. Corbett went on, "because he was sure my husband was going to lie down. But half an hour before the fight, Jim refused the fix and gave the 'Kid' the double cross. You could all see how mad McCoy was. He wouldn't shake hands! Tell the world, that's why Jim Corbett left town and I'm not sorry he's gone."

What did Martha mean, *gone*? Well, "Gentleman" Jim Corbett disappeared from his home on West Thirty-fourth Street and set secret sail for London the Friday after the fight. That's when the scandal reached epic proportions.

"I don't know why Jim and I didn't shake hands before the fight," said McCoy, telling the truth, now his habit. "But the fight was honest. Honest." This being his third press conference in a week. For some reason it looked to everyone as if McCoy hadn't been fighting, when in fact he'd fought his hardest.

Jim Corbett, meanwhile, was said to have met up in London with Maribeth Batcha, a beautiful vaudevillean. For months Miss Batcha's "friendship" with Jim had been hidden.

McCoy's formal statement read as follows: "Mrs. Corbett's accusations are simply the hot answer of a jealous woman. . . . I am unable to see how either Jim or I would have gained any prestige by being defeated. I fought a bad and wrong kind of bout. I have no one to blame but myself. I still believe I can beat Corbett, and hope sometime in the near future to prove it." He ended with a poem:

"Be careful who it is you fight/Otherwise in time you might/End up looking a wee bit dim/When your opponent's as off as Jim."

Susan said, "I believe you wouldn't have lied about this fight. Tell me you wouldn't have."

"Duck, I've always been a man not to take a dive. I've had principles since way back when those Indians killed my mother and my sister."

"Wait." Her face fell. "It is your mother *and* your sister now?"

The following day Mrs. Corbett and Susan Fields sued their husbands for divorce simultaneously.

Susan's note to McCoy read, *Enough*, in an arching feminine script. That was it; no whereabouts, no explanation. Sometimes even blows that are expected can be leveling. He next saw her on the steps of the courthouse.

"You really have to believe me, Duck! Please—"

Mr. and Mrs. McCoy were alone in front of that municipal building, but Susan was a woman of the theater, even—especially—in private moments. "I shall never believe you again, McCoy. Never!" She wore her pearls and her hair in a high red surge. "You lied about your family once more!" That soft quality beyond description he'd loved in her voice had now gone, whether through emotion or art he didn't know. She had turned on him.

That was it, it felt like the end. His businesses all died at once. Forced to sleep—or not sleep—in a rented room in Grand Army Plaza, Brooklyn, with bright dawn staining his window, and that flat borough stretching beyond the glass as sleepless and humble as he was, McCoy lay curled up inside the cubby of his own terrible grief, haunted by details—how in *One More Go-Round, Grover Cleveland?* she'd sung to an entire audience but really only to him. *You can't!* he yelled in his mind. *You can't!* If only he'd never left her once Johnnie Gold had come back!

Susan's lawyers falsely, publicly accused him of adultery with Andrea Truncali, the star of *The Pug and the Pastor*. His sorrow had no bottom. It just kept dragging him lower and lower. How could Susan? And how dare people say *he'd* agreed to take a dive? He would never have agreed to *lose*! The bruises on his knuckles and one side of his neck didn't seem to be going away. He closed his eyes to a nauseating, skull-splitting headache.

One morning McCoy drove through thick snow to Saratoga without once stopping his Model K Ford. ("'*The Model K is A Okay'*—*a real McCoy testimonial.*") Any street-corner hobo standing in his stupor could have seen that McCoy was heartache and rage passing at twenty-six furious miles an hour.

McCoy as he drove failed to notice the passing forests or hours.

He skidded and clanged into the sanatarium's front yard at nightfall under a halo of dust and smoke. Other cars—blue and yellow and even a red Rolls-Royce with mahogany sideboards, glinting vehicles in childish colors—were parked outside. Jumping the teal-painted stairs of his porch four at once, McCoy thundered to the front door. It was locked.

He pounded his fist against his home. The sounds of some kind of commotion inside reached him through the walls and closed windows. But no one answered his knock. McCoy threw the full weight of his shoulder against the door, and it whipped open.

Inside, near where the dining room led to the kitchen, Susan stood at a podium before a scribbling crowd. The soon-to-be ex-Mrs. McCoy was holding a press conference.

". . . and he was *always* posing," Susan reciting a statement. "Why do you think he'd begun to quote Nietzsche and Kant and . . ."

She—a feverish glow to her skin, her eyebrows soaring in triumph high over her reading glasses—she looked up and saw McCoy, who was huffing. She gasped a little: "oh."

"What are you *doing*?" McCoy barely heard the rabid sounds coming from his own throat. He felt himself sweat from the armpits.

"McCoy, is it true you're actually someone else with another name?" This from the mustachioed Leslie McAdoo Jr., of the *New York World*. "And your whole life has been a sham?"

McCoy's rage was a horde of bees freed at once, buzzing thunder in his ears and stinging everywhere.

"Mr. Selby!" *The Herald's* Bill Jamison cried, just being malicious. Then all of the reporters: "Mr. Selby! Mr. Selby!"

Shattered McCoy charged his wife.

He couldn't help it. With a great sob he felt himself lunging and there's nothing more frightening than losing the last shreds of self-control—

As McCoy ran crazy at Susan and her image bounced and grew in his eye, her high-boned face he knew so well now shook with something close to fear—a kind of dumbfounded and questioning doubt. And wait, there was that lovely dimple in her collarbone. Hello, dimple, hello. . . . No, McCoy could never do harm to his sophisticated, spoiled, dimpled Susan.

He ran right past her, and had no destination, the way a decapitated chicken will continue to run.

But what if I'd hit her? Oh, how she would have bled!

He stopped, because he had to stop someplace, in the kitchen, at the portrait of Susan in a blue hat. He hesitated before the painting—the artist hadn't made the eyes gray enough—and then grabbed it by the frame.

"You shall not take that!" Susan was yelling, her shoulders high, her color high, her words aimed to stab.

"Oh, I will take it, Susan!" And the tears burst forth, and McCoy howled the only sentence he found. *"And all that's mine!"*

For half a second he just held the picture, before he headed for the front door. Susan frenzied toward him, her flush getting deeper—how dare *she* be angry!—and she grabbed him. Her clothes made an exciting rustle-sound against her body.

McCoy pushed her partway into the kitchen, his heart pounding up to his throat, and turned to leave.

One reporter started to clear his throat. Others shook their heads, *tsk*ed, smoked their cigarettes.

"You can all go to hell, you penny-a-liners!" McCoy hated the new goosey sound of his own voice. And on the edge of his vision he caught Susan beating toward him with a decanter of whiskey.

She threw her whole body into swinging at his head. McCoy lifted his arm to block; a *crack* noise sounded as the bottle split at the neck. Whiskey and shattered glass showered on his head, clothes, everywhere.

And so it's over? he thought. *Everything is really finished?*

McCoy blinked. He was all right. He looked at Susan. She looked at him. His elbow prickled where it had broken the glass; his face was wet and sticky. Susan's mouth hung open. She was blinking. The wet down of her cheek caught the light. McCoy grabbed her with his free hand.

He felt affection for the curve of her shoulder in his hand, and for the sink of his fingers into her skin beneath her dress as he squeezed. He was shaking her.

"M-McCoy," she said. "S-stop." Her reading glasses jumped across the room as if yanked on a string. With her fine crinkled hateful nose and her little pink ear nudging through her frenzied hair she was still gorgeous. McCoy's heart felt uncommonly still.

The timid hand pulling on his collar belonged to H. H. Measures. "Get off her, Kid!" The reporter's voice, like the dying gasp of a small animal, came out high and meager. And the punch McCoy threw felt almost like a clean getaway. It was all but pleasant to have a man's blood spilling warm on him, his fist having broken someone open, his strength having burst a face as if a grenade had gone off behind the eyes. The guilt would come later. Now Measures collapsed like an empty suit.

The room was very still. McCoy was afraid to look at Susan. He straightened his posture. Wetness trickled down his back. The stillness of the air was taut and unreasonable. His hand was covered in blood and whiskey. When McCoy did turn to his wife, to her wide-opened eyes and half-tilted head—had the situation been different he'd have been sure that her face was full of affection. He almost started to smile at her. But then a wave of embarrassment made him shake. Of course there was none of what he'd thought in her grimace. Standing right next to her, he began to miss Susan very much.

McCoy stood for a few seconds. He felt restless and flushed and athletic and his sorrow like an undercurrent behind his lungs threatened to swallow up his entire body, inside out, as he ran to the door.

At least he knew where he'd go next.

The Last Gasp of Johnnie Gold

In the early years of automoting most didn't, because it was less than safe, drive through the night. Roads were few and unsettled, cars were slowpokes, vulnerable and fickle. Motorists lacked experience. Cold or heat or rain always found a path to the driver by way of undercarriage and window gaps, or soft-tops. But the evening that McCoy fled Saratoga in his machine that breathed out a gas fume that smelled like burning gunpowder, he drove straight to Chinatown.

When he rolled to a stop before 268 Mott Street his watch showed 6:30 A.M. As McCoy made his way up the dim shameful ruined stairwell, a child's cry seemed like just one more surge of nauseous anger washing over him.

"Johnnie Gold!" McCoy was screaming now. The brutal surroundings, the peeling dirty walls and the knurly stairs earned none of McCoy's sympathy, not this time. "Johnnie Gold!" Chinese eyes were staring at him from out of the crack of door after half-opened door all the way up the stairwell.

It was cold. McCoy'd felt cold for hours now. He knocked on Apt. 53 and yelled, "Johnnie!" before shouldering open a door for the second time in two days.

Johnnie Gold's miserable little apartment was almost dark. Only the dim hall-light that sniveled in through the unhinged door made a faint yolky trail to the far windowless wall.

"McCoy?" Johnnie Gold's voice sounded awful now.

"You, Johnnie!" McCoy stepped slow into that shadowy room, fifteen feet by twenty at most. Johnnie Gold was seeable only as an Olympian silhouette on a narrow bed that looked close to giving out under the strain.

"Ah, McCoy." The obese shadow murmured, and the powerful current of McCoy's anger that'd swept him here was starting to dwindle already. Johnnie Gold coughed and coughed.

"Turn on a light, Johnnie."

"You came." The Chinese flimflammer leaned heavily to his nightstand, starting a lamp.

"You wrecked me, Johnnie. Do you understand?" In less than a minute McCoy's emotion had meagered into a little stream that lapped at his ankles.

Johnnie watched McCoy, his dim eyes empty. "I knew that you would come."

"Oh, is that right, J.G.?" No matter that McCoy was working at gruffness; it was impossible to keep afloat on such a quick-shallowing hostility.

Johnnie, with a twisted face, wheezed to a stand, leaden and naked: obesity pushed toward farce. "I wrecked *you*, McCoy?" And Johnnie Gold lurched forward. The grim naked totter of the crudest burlesque comedy.

"Put some clothes on," McCoy said. "I don't want to see that. The thing about you, Johnnie, is you were never anything but puffed-up with hot air. Maybe that's why you're so fat."

Johnnie's hair had started to thin and dinge; the bones of his hands twisted like an arthritic's, or a man much older than he was. "I read of your troubles everywhere"—he was laughing without breath—"but I did not cause them, ass."

McCoy slumped into one of the two chairs at the table fronting the bed. *Oh, my Lord. My gray-eyed Susan*, he thought. *I'll never see my sweet gray-eyed Susan again.*

He felt hemmed in by his own heartache, failures, mistakes, his lies. "Well," McCoy said, "*some* jack-of-bedlam was sending letters about me."

"I mailed no letters, ass." He faltered up to McCoy, twitchy and wagging a finger. "I could have told you—" His own coughs cut him off.

"Are you feeling all right?" McCoy said stupidly. Johnnie was puffy with probable sickness; in the half-light the Chinaman's gums were more pink than expected.

"You are a defunct entity, a flimflam stillborn." Johnnie's chin looked all bunched up. "Beyond my help."

"I didn't come for help," McCoy said, calmly. "I came here to crack your head off."

Johnnie cleared his throat—so much phlegm. "And I, McCoy, I am merely that which you have left to a sea of troubles," he said, going slack and bending forward heavily.

Years earlier, when McCoy was first coming up through Tennesee, he'd watched men dynamite an abandoned coal mine to ready the land for a coming railway. After the first internal explosion, one side of the little hill around the mine had given way before the rest. Fresh hollows had formed, crannies and new fissures, drops and unusual depressions, cutting the little hill a different face, a weaker chin, an overall slump.

"I was good to you, Johnnie." McCoy was trying to speak in an even voice but knew he was pleading, his temples going *rat-ta-tat*. "For a long time I was good to you, Johnnie."

Naked, coughing Johnnie Gold with his creased dough face looked like a baby seen through a magnifier. Inconceivably, he began to cry.

"Johnnie—" McCoy felt legitimately sorry for him. But under the compassion ran the idea that maybe the Chinese con artist was faking. A shiny fly passed humming between them on its way toward one or other of the stinks that reeked all along the stairwell. *I'm the one who had more to lose*, McCoy thought.

Johnnie lifted his face. Great red blotches crossed his cheeks.

And his eyes behind their tears burned like undersea fires. "Laundry?" Johnnie was almost gagging, a giant, washed-out man. "I will not do *laundry*!"

McCoy told Johnnie he didn't understand (but he did). The flimflammer's teeth caught on his lower lip. And he brought his plump fingers to his chest as if to smooth his shirt. He wore no shirt.

"McCoy, you are a blackguard, a bastard." His laughing tone was worrying. "Now that money will be less plentiful for you, will you be generous with me?"

McCoy thought of the red bruises covering the skin of his own knuckles and the left side of his neck, the little rubies that weren't disappearing, that might not disappear.

"You have no conception," Johnnie spat, "of the thousand natural shocks that yellow flesh is heir to." Johnnie's tongue clattered in his mouth like dice in a shaker. "You deserve what you got. Did that whelp of a wife leave you? I expect she would have, you fool."

McCoy caught himself curling his hand into a fist. A few sparks flared inside him; his heart like dry paper could go up very easily. "Johnnie, we're both of us sad, okay?" McCoy's chair against the floor made a throat-clearing nose as he stood to leave.

Johnnie Gold reached out a splay-fingered hand. "I ruined you," Johnnie said in a voice McCoy could barely hear.

He felt his mind start to strain. "You *did* send the letters."

Johnnie shifted his great weight, picked delicately at his fingernails. He seemed to be breathing more easy. "Youapalooza. My one big idea in a lifetime *of* . . . You came from nothing, and you'll return."

McCoy gritted his teeth. Days later he'd still feel soreness in his jaw.

"Yes, I sent letters—to everyone!" Johnnie now used a voice throat-tearing and remorseless. "Letters to your wife's lawyers alleging you were having an adultery, letters to the governor about invented illegalities in Saratoga, letters to the news outlets about frauds in each of your fights. 'The *real* McCoy!' Bah! I wrote letters and I wrote and wrote and you are done for."

McCoy now slumped into his own chest, ulcery, everything inside turning acid at once. "Johnnie"—almost whispering—"be quiet or I'll kill you."

"Mccoyalooza, it was genius, and you failed it! Before me you were a walking fiasco who couldn't flimflam or even beat up one Chinese rail worker. You think I don't remember who you were before you met your whore of a wife?"

McCoy sprang across the room and punched Johnnie in the face, a tap connecting just above the eye—not enough even to knock the flimflammer from his seat. There had been twenty, maybe thirty, evenings that McCoy'd just idled in this apartment with Johnnie, evenings of mild brotherly fondness at this very table.

"Is it unendurable, McCoy, to be Nothing after having been Someone?" He sighed, rubbing his cheek, calm like someone waiting on the slow line at the bank: McCoy thought he caught a false note in Johnnie's exasperation.

"McCoy, you're a doomed moron! Your wife and fame and money gone."

He punched Johnnie again—pitiful Johnnie, right in the teeth— and just after the last second McCoy thought that maybe he should've held back.

"I have wrecked you." Johnnie Gold, not surly or jolly, drawing his knuckles along his bloodied lip, showed calm and unlikely dignity: a milk cow eating grass by its own slow timetable.

Spasms of anger still fanned out inside McCoy, but beside them rose an uneasiness, like a seasickness.

"Oh, my eyes have been so sore lately." Blinking, Johnnie coughed a dainty one, like a bell going off mellow inside a purse. "McCoy, he who has fallen from a height is lower than his neighbor who has never climbed! And your life will be a sad echo of a sad shell of a past glory!" Johnnie's voice was able to creep like a thief through sighs and coughs; there was a melody of vigor moving between the words, even a baiting charm. "You are alone in this world, McCoy, an idiot. An orphan."

"Shut up!" McCoy screamed now, while part of him kept separate from his own anger. And yet he was inflamed, like a stage actor caught up in his script. "Shut up, Johnnie!"

"My genius is like lacework on cotton! You, McCoy, are not even cotton; you are *dung*!" The health of Johnnie's mind seemed to charge his body: McCoy was watching one of the very greatest flimflams of Gold's life. "Dung that thinks it has snared itself permanently to cotton only to be disappointed in the next wash! Your days"—the Chinese con artist now building toward rapture—gone were the coughs—"Your days shall be more helpless than you can imagine, and it is my doing!"

McCoy told himself to stop. He felt close to despondent, jaw-fallen, as he punched Johnnie, hard in the cheek, a side-thrown uppercut that hit with a noise like a plank splintering.

Johnnie Gold flailed, turning and turning as he toppled to the floor in a tail-high crash.

As the flimflammer lay there his breath hissed out of him.

McCoy knew he probably looked just as pathetic as Johnnie. His laugh came out a sob. *A poet? Mayor of New York? The husband of a woman like Susan Fields?*

Naked and facedown, Johnnie vomited at McCoy's feet—a thick green soup dribbling onto the floorboards. Johnnie's nude back rippled like a lagoon under the wind.

"Now will you shut up?" McCoy's voice was choked. "Now will you shut up? Johnnie?"

McCoy knelt to lay his hand soft on Gold's hair. Johnnie, rolling over to his back with his vomit at his side, threw a slow flabby jab. McCoy slid forward on his knees, blocked the punch easily—*That man in North Judson, Indiana*, McCoy was thinking, *that man was the real McCoy, him*—and he let fly a hard straight crunching right to the bridge of Johnnie Gold's nose. Johnnie's head hit the floorplanks and bounced. Dark blood trickled over his face alongside the vomit. McCoy bent closer. The flimflammer's moan had a whiff of the worst filth on Dogsbody Flats.

Johnnie, hardly opening his eyes, grabbed McCoy's neck. The squeeze that his fat fingers managed was surprising; McCoy lost his breath. He collapsed to his side with Johnnie's hands wringing the wind from his body.

McCoy could see Johnnie's wheezing smile only through pulsing black spots.

"I will ruin you in ways that you don't yet understand, McCoy."

But Johnnie's fingers had already started to lose their push; they shook around McCoy's throat. It didn't even really hurt. McCoy grabbed Johnnie Gold by *his* throat and squeezed as hard as he could.

"Are you afraid, McCoy?" Johnnie's oyster eyes drooled huge tears. "Are y-you afraid that your Susan is gone?" The bones in Johnnie's neck creaked like ice brought into the sun. Then the squirming was over: no life in the flimflammer's body except in his eyes, which moved side to side.

McCoy knew he had to stop, but for one more second he forced the base of Johnnie's head harder against the floor. Tears, spasms, whimpers. Lordy, he missed Susan and everything else.

"Ahh," Johnnie's face was greening, his eyes now rolling back, "*Ahh—*"

Stop before he gets really hurt. McCoy eased his grip, uncurling his fingers. He let his hand rest limply on Johnnie's thoughtless simpering face.

McCoy was calmed.

"Johnnie, I'm sorry," he said, "if I hurt you," and for a half-second, less, McCoy felt a little silly about the whole thing—a little sheepish about having actually choked someone like Johnnie. Then he realized that Johnnie Gold was dead.

The flimflammer's eyeballs stayed right in place, his drab face was calm and huge with wide-open nostrils. McCoy cleared his throat. Getting slowly to his feet, stepping over the naked corpse of his old friend—not looking down at the far-off palsied smile that set Johnnie's cheeks—he felt not much at all.

Well, his ears throbbed. He was confused, vaguely nauseated, not especially frightened, at the same time a little bored. This was a terrible thing and it had really happened. He paced the floor a little. Beyond this he really didn't suffer much, even as he started to cry gently. He still wouldn't look at Johnnie's body.

He turned instead to the little mirror tacked up over Johnnie's sink. Half in shadow, McCoy couldn't really see himself. "Maybe I'll suicide myself with alcohol," he muttered, almost casual, to fill the silence. But he couldn't stop crying. He closed his eyes. The tears felt warm on his cheeks. He wanted to sit down but didn't sit. In back of all of the nothing that he felt, all the not-suffering, the sadness of despair came slowly, too slowly for McCoy to have noticed at first. It rose up, late as ever, on the stink of the room. It was the goose bumps on his own forearms, it was in the chaos of his breath.

McCoy'd killed Johnnie Gold.

He'd never forget the sight of that dark puddle of blood expanding under Johnnie's lifeless smiling face.

McCoy agonized with warmth and sorrow for himself. *You Chinese milk cow, you tricked me into this!* Could he still be a good person if he'd killed Johnnie Gold? *No don't dry your eyes, don't because once you dry them then it might seem more true.*

Going breathless, he scratched at the top of his head with both hands, fast and violent. This was the fidgety horrible thrill that comes with looming up so close to death. Little dark tufts of hair peeking out from Johnnie's nostrils, like stilled pine needles, seemed profound. A chill flowed over McCoy's body to numb his feet and arms and his head—

Swaying with remorse now, gnashing his teeth, McCoy started to cry intensely. The apartment door that hung half out of its frame, the mirror, the whitish-yellow light of the lamps, Johnnie's grayish-yellow skin, the air itself, the world around McCoy as seen through his tears, shook and warped and flickered hatefully at him. He was frightened sick and by now crying himself almost blind.

In his frenzy of tears he ran out to the stairwell, knocking a loitering drunk into the wall. He faltered down the stairs and out into the street, where he stumbled past the police officers who were a few minutes too late on their way to Johnnie Gold's apartment. As the finishing stroke to the Chinese flimflammer's last scam, the law had been tipped off regarding a murder.

McCoy was already on his way to becoming someone else.

Book Four

Now I am ready to tell how bodies are changed into
different bodies.   —Ovid

I am falser than vows made in wine.   —Shakespeare

Prairie Life

After his life as McCoy in New York, Virgil Selby had trouble sleeping in his drafty childhood home in Bluffton Creek, Indiana. The third of the house's three bedrooms was all broken shadows and scooting flies. His wallpaper furrowed here, swelled out there, yellowing by catches. Spiderwebs flapped in high corners; lines ran the ceiling as in a broken mirror. His bedsprings whimpered every inch he moved. The company of creaks and thumps made for an old house coming to terms with its age. And every night a gasping Virgil Selby thought he might be a murderer. He was shy of twenty-five years old, and a failure.

Summer came to Indiana. Virgil worried that the gears of his personality had worn down. When he smiled his mouth scuddled weakly toward one ear, squinching an eye, and this set up his whole face to look woeful. He felt pretty sure his smile hadn't always tended sideways like that. The bruised skin on his knuckles and the base of his neck never really healed all the way, and wouldn't. He suffered that numbness you might after thunder roars an inch from your ear. That may have been sadness.

Sometimes he'd say, "Wait," rising out of his stupor; but then, a soft: "Ah, forget it." To put it in a nutshell, he'd become depressing and awkward. McCoy was dead.

Virgil accepted, of course, that it was over. His family's house, new job at the library, Bluffton Creek—these things were to outline his life. That was the choice he'd made, having fled who he was in utter defeat.

It'd been a weepy trip. Five cramped, hat-pulled-down days from Manhattan aboard the graceless Middlewest Flyer, then Virgil'd found himself alone on the wooden platform of the Moscow County Station in Indiana. He peered down into the hollow green bowl of valley that penned in his helpless hometown. Down there nothing moved except the cloud's shadow that swam over the two white mills, the store, the white church. Bluffton Creek's streets curved in on themselves dreamily.

He'd worn a tight-cut English suit he'd bought months earlier in another life. He touched the crown of his hat to stop the wind, not that there was wind, from swiping it. No one had known he was coming. He carried one large suitcase and let the softsmoke taste of the air onto his tongue.

"All right, Virgil," he said, and started down toward Mulberry Avenue, his heart empty. "All right."

His father's porch whined a bit from the bounce in his step. Selby hovered in front of the door, looking at it. It was a red door. He didn't know who'd be living there, other than Francis Marion.

"Yes, hello?" The tall young woman who answered had lightless blue eyes. Then all at once emotion gathered inside them like bright schools of fish darting straight for the surface. "Virgil?"

He went into the throatwork behind the McCoy rumble, but realized that never again would he try for that sound. He stood there with his mouth open like the end of a sawmill. All around, Indiana was tilting into noon.

"Anna." His voice came high pitched. His pant legs stuck to his thighs. The heart-shaped locket that Susan had given him was inside his suitcase.

"Well," Anna said, and seemed unable to stop rubbing her hands together. Virgil's half-sister was nineteen, looked older, pale and spindly. Inside the house, a gray kitten on a straw carpet raised its head for a skeptical look at him.

"Some Chicago reporters showed up here not long back about you." How Anna'd felt about this out-of-town intrusion sounded through her tight voice. "Come in, come in." She'd said this slowly. "Come in."

And so he had. Now McCoy was dead. Dead and gone.

Or was he?

Make no mistake, he was back in Bluffton Creek. It was a town of Selbys.

Virgil's people owned the store and much of the land around Blue River. His father had passed on a few years earlier, the old loafer's heart having given out not long after his visit to New York.

Now Virgil shared Francis Marion's old place with Anna and his sister Bea. Sitting near the center of twelve moss-grown acres on the skirts of town, the house was wide stretched but fairly squat—the Selbys had named the simple clapboard home with its tin roof "the Long and the Short of It."

Nobody raised in Moscow County would have called that plot a farm, in the way people in New York didn't see a ten-story building as a skyscraper. But the land had all the expected: some poultry and horses, pens and hay, and a small number of horse-dragged contraptions—saber-toothed hay-rakes and bladed harrows—even if no one in the extended Selby family of mill- and store-owners considered himself a cut-and-dried farmer.

Virgil's other half-sister, Katherine, had moved to Chicago with her husband in 1902; his half-brother and old tormentor Francis Junior now lived in Kansas City, where he actuaried for an insurance concern and had probably found a new scapegoat to bully and call a "bony lunatic," a "trollop's son." Isaac, a second cousin, stopped by "the Long and the Short of It" twice a week to help out with chores—or he *had* done. These chores were Virgil's now, caring for a few chickens they raised, and their small laid-by crop of oats. He didn't complain. New York was New York; Indiana was Indiana.

I should never have left Susan that time, he thought. *Who was I to leave her?*

Virgil felt certain that every one of the two hundred or so people in town was using his life as a cautionary tale. (If they'd only known the half of it.) That's why he didn't meet glances; he looked at the ground. It was a very humid summer in Indiana, which didn't help matters.

He spoke in a voice that showed little hint of grief.

Virgil'd found work quickly. (If his father had never really earned much of a living, his family had always been provided for, and continued to be provided for.) His third cousin Lawrence J. T. Selby had plans to retire, and needed a replacement.

Although everyone came to call Virgil a librarian, what he'd really become was the caretaker of the local book room. He swept up, unclogged toilets, a job that needed to be done often, and he had general run of the library, which no one visited much. This would pay $14.59 a week, or $758.68 a year.

And so this is what I am now, he thought one night, with Anna's skinny gray cat, Wilhamena, under his arm, a little engine whirring inside its chest. He looked back on his New York years as a bruise remembers a fist.

The library sat next to the store on Mulberry Avenue: the main street in town, though it had no shops, restaurants, or offices, only the store, the bank, the library itself, and a string of identical houses dreaming dreams of escape. All of them had porches; some were elegant. The town was thirty years from being wired for the kind of electricity that had flowed through Manhattan for ages.

Even after two months in Bluffton Creek, a heavy fog lay over Virgil's dealings with his sister and half-sister.

Anna had been, when he'd known her as a child, a life-frightened girl who'd shivered herself over the invisible snakes under the bed. Now, without shame, she worked counter at the store. Blond, tallish, cream-colored Bea kept the books and swept up at the grist-, or was it the saw-, mill. Bea was fifteen, pretty and thin, with her brother's sharp face-bones. Her eyes glinted black as beads. She was the one person in town Virgil thought he might find a little fondness for.

When they spoke it was a jumble of awkward feelings, *thank-you*s and *excuse me*s. But if her voice failed around him, and as her cheeks burned whenever he came out of his dullness to tease her, he felt something like brotherly affection. Other than this, he remained closer to a mannequin than to his old self. All his ingredients were there, the looks, the posture of McCoy—but there was no warmth of life, no Why.

If he'd only have become a *different* someone else, someone who'd had, say, elite credentials, a history of exceptional social and economic standing, he might have had access to anything in America. Instead, he'd become a boxer. And now, not even that anymore. His ambition now was to make himself normal. You people don't know how hard that was for him.

He and Susan would likely never see each other again.

At the close of Virgil's second Saturday working the library, Anna and Bea paid him a surprise visit. He was sitting alone reading *Anna Karenina* in front of one of the three shelves, and didn't hear them arrive. (He no longer read from *Gilgamesh* about that hero's fight for immortality).

"Hello, Gil!" Bea's slightly breathless voice roused him from Princess Kitty Shcherbatsky's first ball and he looked up at his little sister's bright eyes, which gazed nearly straight at him.

"Ah," he said, his voice lazy. Bea and Anna waited for him to say something else.

—No one had ever been fair to him, starting with his own mother, he thought; Johnnie Gold had treated him unfair, too—

"Come home to dinner, won't you?" Anna was saying. (Had he anywhere else to go?) "We're having a guest tonight." For once Anna showed a gentle calm expression.

"Yes, we thought we'd come and walk you home," Bea said, "and then we'll cook dinner and talk and—" Bea quieted when Virgil looked at her. They were now out the door and into the springtime dusk. Virgil locked the library's gate.

"Well, who's the dinner guest?" he asked.

"Did you know Father always liked to come home to a nice dinner on Fridays?" Anna said. She was rangy and her neck was stunted like an athletic boy's.

"Well," Virgil said, "it's really nice to be back home"—still a bit fumble tongued. He swallowed and nodded and feared he might start to cry for some reason.

Mess *is too kind a word for the way I left everything,* he thought. Not that anyone had found out the truth about the death of poor Johnnie Gold. That crime was just one more secret now.

"Indeed," Anna was saying. "Father always liked coming home for dinner." The three of them walked the threadbare grass beside Mulberry Avenue (Bluffton Creek wouldn't see a sidewalk until 1936).

"My schoolfriend Carol Abbott." Little Bea's voice was like something watery; it trickled out of her. "*She's* our dinner guest."

"Not"—Anna spoke with a finger pointed at the sky—"that Father ever was out and about." Her voice got darker. "Especially since *your* mother, the strumpet, ran out on the family and broke Father's heart."

Bea spoke in a hurry to change the subject. "You knew Carol's brother Bertram, Gil. I'm just about sure you did."

Virgil frowned. He'd thought he was making strides toward feeling at home with these people, but Anna had just ruined it. His mother, Jane Selby, had been church-going and far from a strumpet.

Jane Selby had been a good-looking country woman who'd tired herself fanning the flames of a marriage that had pretty much gone snuffed by the time Virgil learned to talk. She'd never replaced Francis Marion's first wife, not in Francis Marion's eyes or the eyes of the children of the first Mrs. Selby. Sometimes even young Virgil had felt that his mother looked at him and baby Bea just as she did her stepchildren—as two more frowns of fortune on her life. He'd only been twelve when she abandoned everyone. That's when they'd started calling her the *strumpet* and when he began to pretend she'd been killed by Indians.

Now he was feeling awful, from one thing and the other. "I'm not sure, Bea." He tried to smile at his sister. "It could be I knew a Bertram Abbott."

Bea was biting her lip and seemed distracted.

On the opposite side of the street a man pretended with his head down not to notice the three Selbys. Bea was about to call out a "hello" when Anna, her face going agitated, shot the younger girl a glance. A long silence followed. Or did Virgil imagine all this intrigue?

"Well, it's really nice to be home," Virgil said.

I have a feeling it came out sounding forced the second time.

"The Long and the Short of It" was the resting place of so much unremembered past. That evening, as he washed for dinner, his trip through his father's old bedroom spooked a pair of memories back to life, and like a haunted house Virgil was spell-caught even if he didn't show it: the calm facade, the inside that shook with ghosts.

When he'd been five or six, home on a Sunday after listening to one of Pastor Moody's grim church sermons, Virgil'd played with a pocket watch that belonged to Francis Marion. Thinking he was alone, impersonating an oil-rich swell from Indianapolis, young Virgil paraded in haughty steps before the mirror in his father's bedroom. Without warning, Jane Selby walked in, and dropping her often-at-hand *Ladies' Temperance Handbook*, she cuffed Virgil in the face—not too hard, but still a cuff. "That watch is not yourn," she said, looking tired already at 10:30 A.M. "Did your father tell you to fuddle with it?" Young Virgil felt his eyes getting all soggy; emotion knocked in his chest and up into his mouth; he was sure his lip quaked. But it didn't quake.

Sundays later, in that same room, he'd been about to try for the pocket watch again when his mother caught him a second time. "Virgil, what are you doing?" "Nothing, Mother, looking for a Bible is all." "Well, what is wrong with your own?" "Worn out from too much reading," Virgil said. She said, "Honor bright, Mr. Whippersnapper," then paused to think. "For entering this room unadmitted you can bet your boots you're not allowed to go to church with the rest of us today." Virgil tried not to give the game away, but he was sure his joy was plain across his face.

In both cases—when he'd been caught strutting with the pocket watch and later, when he'd made up the story about seeking out the Bible—he'd learned a lesson in the mirror: each time he'd made a considerate and still reflection, relaxed and sorry, not at all showing the emotion he really felt. How strange it'd seemed, that he could appear in all ways different from the heavyhearted or overjoyed boy he'd felt inside.

The dinner table took up most of the space in the Selbys' dining room, and on it rested a meal of roast chicken with apple dressing, mashed potatoes and gravy, churned butter, tea, and of course dinner rolls. The house as always threw a musky smell: tonight that was a whisper just barely made out over the full music of dinner aromas.

Eighteen-year-old, twitchy Carol Abbott sat just to Virgil's left, her face pregnant with freckles. The girl's cheeks bloomed so round, you couldn't make out any system of bones underneath. She smelled sweet with powder-room work.

Anna and Bea were frisking around Carol and Virgil, carrying plates, serving.

"Mr. Selby." Carol Abbott patted her chin with her hand. "May I call you Virgil?" She and the busy Bea traded meaningful, poorly concealed glances.

"All right," Virgil said, feeling wary but not sure of what. "Why not?"

The evening sun through the window and the candlelight on the table came together harshly to underline Carol's eyes. "Good." She gave him her serious gaze. "Virgil it is, then." Carol's family owned Bluffton Creek Trust, the town bank, and she had a rich girl's wide expectant smile.

Everyone, after saying grace, ate. But nobody seemed to know what to talk about. The room, the whole house, was calm and scrubbed: at rest. This wasn't a family for bookshelves, or a piano, or a globe. Or enough mirrors for Virgil. The windows looked east onto flaring green pastures that kept on as far as the clever cities of the coast.

Was Susan Fields now eating salmon under cream at Delmonico's? With whom?

Carol Abbott sucked in for courage and swiveled to him. "I don't care what people say, Virgil," she managed, a little awkward and quick. Her lips puckered a bit—a 1904-era, eighteen-year-old nowhere-town girl's idea of coquettish? Cords heaved up in her neck and her expression pleaded: *Save me, I'm bored.*

"I think it's terribly exciting, Virgil. *Terribly.*"

His meek smile ushered in a hurry of his championship memories. This was one of those times when the sluices fly open and happy images scoot behind the eyes too numerous and closely packed to distinguish. Followed of course by a stabbing pain of guilt and regret. The slowest-dying image was of himself, hunched over in pain and his own blood in Ronnie and Ray's mirror.

And that bastard Tommy Ryan never respected me. . . .

"Can you tell us"—Carol's hair, surging blond and long, caught in the little chain of her silver heart necklace—"what was it like to have everyone in the whole world know you?" Her fair voice issued out of her like more blond hair. "Can you explain about the real McCoy, Virgil?"

Bea coughed into her hand. Anna sat openmouthed, like a bird in a fit. The cat Wilhamena sat purring in the fifth chair at the table, where Francis Marion had sat.

"Well," Virgil said. Behind his lips he wiped his cold teeth with his tongue. He said, "Well—"

"It was like being in a small town, I imagine," Anna cut in. "Father always said, 'Everybody in Bluffton Creek knows me. That's why I like it so.' Remember, Bea?"

"Oh, with all due respect, I mean—*Anna*," Carol said, eyes on Virgil. She was next to a man who'd done all manner of things.

"He's *repentant* now, Gil is." Anna napkined the damp off her forehead. She turned to Virgil, disturbed in her eyebrows. "Those days—" Anna stopped, likely because she didn't know a damn about those days. "Well, I can say one thing. I'd have no toleration for that foreign-peopled city New York." She shrugged. "I like America."

Virgil cleaned off his chin with a napkin. The air in this house was stale.

"Oh," Carol said. Her eyes looked much older than the rest of her. "*I*'d love to hear about it, Gil, anyway."

He looked at Carol, round-faced Carol. No, this wasn't love at first sight.

"Father went up there and came back much different," Anna was going on. "He called that city the seat of Satan." She talked at a very laggard pace. "He's sorry about what he did, he is."

Virgil didn't realize at first who Anna was speaking about. "I am!" he said finally, his voice shaking with sincerity. "I *am* sorry about what I did."

"And"—his half-sister shook her head—"people in *this* town don't often leave, like he did, and that's for a reason." She squinted with overexcitement. "Or lie about who they are, like he did. Or make a fuss over themselves. Or—"

"Yes," Virgil said, "all right." He gave Anna a frown and, her cheeks gathering drably toward her mouth, she shut right up. Shutting right up was a woman's lot in life in the Nineteen Aughts.

"So, Carol," he said, breathing deep, trying to sound like—who?—both his father and Johnnie Gold, "Bertram Abbott is *your . . .*"

After a long while she said, "Yes." And among themselves the three girls were dealing out glances like playing cards. Virgil understood what was going on. He imagined the backroom discussions that had brought Carol here. He bit on his lip, squeezed one hand in the other. Did they think they could flimflam him? Imagine the feeling when a band of Lilliputians shoots catapult pebbles and toothpick arrows at you.

He looked for his reflection in that room. It lived in the smudged knife he used to stir his tea and it undulated along the surface of the tea itself, and he thought, hope against hope, if even for a moment, that he saw someone he recognized; he saw the glow of McCoy. Cocksure, he gave that winning smile. He did this just for himself; soon Virgil smothered his happiness and returned to the girls.

"So . . ." he asked absently, "is Bertram working at the bank?" *Would they even recognize me, with the McCoy smile? I bet they wouldn't know it's me.*

"I don't want to talk about Bertram and the old bank." Carol waved her hand in a supple arc. "Oh, pishy *pish* to that."

Virgil gave a start. "*What* did you just say?"—his arms tapping restlessly on his chair. Everyone looked at him.

"I don't, I mean, I don't want to talk about the bank?" Carol spoke as if she feared that she'd revealed something without knowing it.

Virgil let himself gaze at her awhile. Well, her eyes were bright, swift-darting blue flies. He wondered how *he* looked to her.

She smiled.

"Carol, New York is a city burning with change," he began with a smile of his own, over his porcelain teeth. "I'll tell you all about it."

Small Town Folks

That's the way it started. Not love at first sight. Virgil did begin to court her, or began to let Carol's courting of him look like its opposite.

Oh, how?

They would take walks, and pleasure from homecooked dinners—what else was a couple to do in that town, in that time? With no flicker theaters, no theater-theaters, restaurants, amusement parks, no athletic events, store windows, sights to see, museums to muse over—well, you took walks. Occasionally, he'd read aloud, poetry from Maeterlinck, or from his own pen, and she'd pretend not to get sleepy. He married her.

Months seemed to pass. Around the country and the world people continued to use the phrase *the real McCoy*. They just forgot why. Meanwhile Virgil Selby got a $6,000 job working loans at the bank. The Bluffton Creek Library, once he'd left it, closed its doors.

He settled in. He tried to find some satisfaction in life. For the most part closedmouthed Virgil wasn't McCoy in the least. He stopped keeping himself fit; the skinny scientific fighter grew a potbelly.

Seasons seemed to pass. Here came the Indiana winter, difficult and cold; then summer, halfhearted as any daytime moon. The house that Virgil and Carol bought on Mulberry Avenue filled with sweet smells and quiet; she was a good cook. If most women kept fairly silent for the first day and a half after they were married, Carol held her tongue for much longer than that. Then it was winter again, and Virgil put his shoulder to his life and worked at acting a better loan officer and husband, that being the New Year's resolution of a man who didn't realize, for a whole Saturday, that his wife had been out of the house until she'd disturbed his nap by slamming the door and saying: "I'm back." By autumn he was only miscalling Carol by the name Susan one or so times a month.

Susan Fields had taken up the entire, lighted flicker screen, sway-hipped and her hair bouncing.

Virgil Selby bore in mind that he was a failure.

But I'm pretty sure he did find consolation in the sky. What Indiana had that New York didn't: the wide, pacific overhead. And all of that grassy America spread out, silent as if covered by a quilt. Also he liked his house, the long porch that faced east, as far east as his eyes (if not his imagination) might roll. After a while Virgil Selby could again navigate this town blind, a quick right before that bluff got you onto Mulberry Avenue, another sharp right after about a hundred steps took you free of those several buildings, then past that shallow creek, up the incline to the unending prairie—and he felt some comfort in that, too. Even a lone cloud against a blue sky can be full with meaning to a man living with an unfamiliar woman and growing flabby around his middle. He did learn to care for Carol. She wouldn't have turned on him. As the nearing of adulthood let some of the stuffing out of her face, she grew almost pretty—lanky and bold and vulnerable. She tried to hide the bashfulness of her kisses with a kind of desperate mouthwork. At first Virgil assumed that she was pretending, but in fact Carol was in love.

"You're sweet, though," she'd tell her husband, *just mad* about what she thought she made out in him. "I can see it by the kind face you have." But what did he see in himself? A face ghostly calm in the looking glass, shadows gathering under his eyes, wrinkles fanning out around the corners of his broad, unmoving lips; his porcelain teeth.

In their marriage they had a few nights of desire. Carol always slept soundly and woke at dawn to fix his breakfast. Then she made herself busy ironing, sewing, washing—and she still held to every young American girl's need to be both wild and proper: she'd found a once-famous scoundrel who'd become a loan officer, the rogue Selby in her town of respected Selbys.

Virgil came to understand his wife was no simpleton. She'd read Harriet Beecher Stowe, and *Little Women*. After a while she spoke easily—asking questions in her earnest voice—and she listened whenever her husband found the need to talk to her. She liked in theory to help people, and had once hoped to become a nurse. Still, he decided Carol was an immature spirit. She covered her room (she and Virgil didn't share one) and most of her effects with girlish velvet ribbons, and so, it seemed, was her personality decorated to excess with frilly velvet, effete frilly velvet. He regularly found himself, out loud as well as in his head, asking her to scale back on her many questions.

Years seemed to pass.

After all this time he'd absolutely forgotten he could be charming. He'd grown shy of expressing opinions. And he skulked around town like a thief, avoiding people. What he continued to feel about this life was too calm, slightly too calm to be panic. He tried anxiously to focus on the world around him and could barely concentrate. Once in every great while he'd find himself sneaking outside in the morning to cry for no reason. Mostly he felt in a state of mild confusion that was like smoke in the head.

Not that he was restless. If ever the fire of ambition spread in him—as from time to time it would, after he'd catch sight of a major newspaper, or word of some occurrence in a city, any city—his insides no longer went up like twigs and tinder; the flame just didn't catch. Maybe that accounted for the smoke.

Sometimes, walking down Mulberry, he'd for an instant be in some other place, say, Times Square at sundown or a lighted boxing ring before the winner is announced. But then he'd be right back in Bluffton Creek. There was the death of Johnnie Gold to consider, the great sadness of loss that shot through every memory.

One day in 1909 he found himself mowing his lawn, unable to remember much of his last five years, the way you sometimes say hello to your neighbor and then end up in your own kitchen, unable to recall the details of the intervening minutes.

Well, that wasn't entirely true.

Certain moments had life for him, certain details did. Once, when he'd arrived home after a late solitary walk, Virgil opened his front door onto a tired, pretty young woman gaping at him. Her shoulders, Carol's, were naked, and her careless hair fell over her breast. "Gil!" She gulped, starting to blush. "I didn't think you'd be home so soon, is all." At moments like this he'd startle and remember—*Oh, yeah, Bertram Abbott's sister is my wife. She wants to be a nurse, or some such thing.*

Another moment stood out, too. This one had happened three weeks into the marriage. They'd been in his bed, late. With Carol's head on his chest, Virgil's rib cage had felt uncomfortable. He didn't—he never—made the effort to ask her to move.

"So." Carol's eager voice didn't sound familiar. "I mean, you never told me about your other wife." She waited, breathed, and then: "You've never told me a thing about her."

Which one? Which wife? he thought. *Really I had only one. There was no Lottie. And no Rosella.* "Well," he said—*And no you*—"Not much to tell, Carol."

He moved his chin chestward to look at her tangled hair. He closed his eyes and watched the black-and-white flicker actress in his head.

"Why is there not much to tell?" Carol's voice like a doddery hatchling. "I mean—Virgil?"

She needed him to say: *She wasn't you, that's why.* Virgil could feel this like a fat Chinese flimflammer sitting on his head.

"There just isn't much to tell" was all he could manage. He did feel for Carol—if not love, then a desire to love her.

Eventually he bought Carol a Victrola (she'd asked), and even after his long days helping bumpkins to sign their names on bank papers that he didn't understand, either, and no matter how tired he felt, she would invite him to dance to the thin dinky music that stumbled—pop, hiss, *screech*—from the contraption's horn. She'd invite him, and he'd usually say no, thank you.

He was now thirty-one.

Imagine the humor of Bluffton Creek toward its infamous son. It was a bad humor. Carol had friends, but fewer than before. Virgil had none. Because of him reporters had once come to town, something no one had wanted or liked.

You have to understand there were three types of people who made up the population of Bluffton Creek, such as it was—whether they were women or men, and regardless of social rank, they fit into one of these main types (with minor differences and shifts):

(1) the disappointed associate of Virgil
(2) the angry neighbor
(3) the pretend well-wisher

The disappointed associate category could be split further:

(a) the regretfully disappointed
(b) the coolly disappointed

And the angry neighbor:

(a) the truly angry
(b) the counterfeit angry

There's not much point in my breaking down the pretend well-wishers for you.

Many in Bluffton Creek—the least unlikable—were counted among the *disappointed* associates. These were, at least, people who had the virtues you'd expect from small-town America: concern for your fellowman, etc. The *regretfully* disappointed seemed pretty embarrassed that they couldn't look Virgil in the eye or hide their bitter expressions whenever he talked to them. This group included his half-sister Anna, herself now a trembly, forty-fiveish twenty-five.

The *coolly* disappointed were grumpier, if less moved, and included Anna's only male friend, one Ben Crick, a livestock-breeding, pint-size widower and veteran of the Spanish-American War.

Now, the angry neighbors included all the people who'd stop in their tracks to give Virgil malignant looks, licking their teeth, shaking their heads, squinting. The *truly* angry included Chuck Velen, a wisp-haired, remarkably honest bootmaker who lived next door to "the Long and the Short," and whose portly wife (herself one of the pretend well-wishers) had been a childhood playmate of Virgil's. And the *counterfeit* angries behaved the way they did because they thought a show of hostility toward Virgil Selby was expected. Virgil's own sister Bea now fell into this category. She'd begun to feel ashamed when her friends, especially her fiancé, gave her a hard time about Virgil; and so Bea kept a hint of apology behind her snide public comments and her cold stare. Even her scowling eyes appeared to say, *I have nothing to do with this.*

The pretend well-wishers were, like hypocrites everywhere, probably the most common. Virgil's obnoxious boss and father-in-law, Isaac "the King" Abbott, placed himself in this group. A busy man, a hard worker and respected town father—"Country life may be dull," he'd say, "but it lasts longer"—he'd always take the time to lay a hand on his son-in-law's shoulder. "How are you? You'll feel right at home again soon, I know it." But Virgil could sense the unease in that hand, the contempt that jittered those skinny old fingers.

Living in that town, Virgil was so lonely in his gloom—especially in company—that it felt sometimes like his air had been cut off.

Of course, he had Carol, who loved him. How on earth would he join her in that?

Most of Bluffton Creek came out—local feuds broke off whenever a marriage was announced—to see Virgil's sister Bea get hitched in the moss-grown backyard of "the Long and the Short of It," October 20, 1910. Few if any of the guests lived outside of Moscow County.

Everyone, including Virgil, looked the part: the men in their

once-a-year "occasion suits"; the ladies in that kind of tall, grim
bonnet not worn fashionably in cities like New York since the
Chester A. Arthur administration. It was a breezy afternoon; many
of those bonnets skimmed right off heads and bounced, floaty as
balloons around the grass, chased down by their owners' husbands.

The actual ceremony was at its finish; Bea at twenty had become
Mrs. Robert Kemp, carpenter's wife.

It was six in the evening, the time when Indiana's colors smooth
off and the land and buildings and the sky combine under the glow
of daylight slipping away. The sycamore tree across from the house
threw its old man's bent-over shadow.

The wedding guests at the string of tables that coiled around
the yard ate their dinners of chicken and corn. The bride and
her groom hovered in sight of the party, he youngish, chewing his
lip, and scared; she grinning, thanking everybody as her blond hair
in the wind streamed out above one shoulder to taper like a frayed
pennant.

The guests were not seated according to family relations,
which meant Virgil could avoid his half-sister Anna. He also
would be spared Anna's friend Ben Crick, who, despite all Anna's
hopes and effort, would never have even considered marrying her.
(The Spanish-American War may seem quaint to you, not the slog
that was World War I, or the horror that was World War II. Those
wars were more terrible only because they involved more people.
The dark circles under Ben Crick's eyes showed that war is war if
you're unlucky to be caught in it.)

Nor were guests seated in keeping with business associations.
Safely on the other side of the party, Virgil's father-in-law "The
King" Abbott chewed with his mouth wide open and drank himself
wobbly. And Virgil, stuffed to bellyaching, sat alone with Carol.

Carol held her bonnet in her lap. Her hair was tangled, half-
done. The outline of her full legs in her dress was pretty to look at,
but she was so fragile and flushed, unseductive and fidgety: she had
the posture of a child onstage for a grammar school play. Her little
girl's pink mouth was always moving. (Lately, he kept trying to remember how he'd felt about her the first time he'd ever seen her.

Had he found her pretty? If it hadn't been love from the very first, had he at least enjoyed a bodily thrill?)

Carol saw him scrutinizing her and gave a brief smile, similar to a hesitant pout. Then she put her hand on the side of her face. This blocked his view.

The wind, like a scattering of snakes, made the grass move in patches. A sunset was just now clotting above the sycamore tree. Carol turned to Virgil for a moment, a half-moment, before stirring again toward the other guests. Her eyes went in for a lot of blinking and her arms crossed over those lovable breasts that she never in her life waved under anyone's nose. Virgil knew what it was like for Carol to be married to him, and a surge of protectiveness for her swelled his heart.

He rubbed his eyes and let the quiet go on until he started to feel her gaze on his cheek like a swatch of velvet. Sometimes he was sure her eyes said things like: *You've met the President, and here you sit like a lump!* Virgil was really pretty sure that's what they said sometimes.

His leg'd been bouncing, rabbit-thumping active. His shoe'd fidgeted a rut in the ground. (After five lazy years, an athlete's grace of movement still lurked inside that heavied body.)

Voices in a daze of boredom were humming lightly on the outskirts of his attention. There, near the house, Ben Crick wore his glasses low on his nose and seemed to be pointing right at Virgil. And some twenty feet away, now ten, the rosy-cheeked Ellis Ralphson approached. As he got closer, Virgil saw that the man's face was twisted and his eyes had flared up like clouds with sudden light. This was the start of something.

Cousin Isaac Selby—standing just behind Ralphson—also began to gawk at Virgil. *All right, what now?* Even Bea, wearing her white, was gawking at him, as was "King" Abbott.

Why?

His half-sister Anna, sitting at the far corner table, gawked, her oatmeal eyes big with concern as she broke off fussing with her now-grayish hair. Likewise the young groom Robert Kemp gawked. So, too, was Chuck Velen's wife, the dull tinge of a just-finished pregnancy on her cheeks, gawking. At him, without a doubt at him.

Everything around Virgil rustled at once, the dead leaves that opened out across the cool grass rustled, and those fading leaves still on their branches, the napkins on the tables rustled, and the trimmed dresses of the ladies who now headed for Virgil; all the world rustled in his ear. *They're coming at me!* he thought. There must have been fifty of them. His whole town—or so it seemed—had crawled its way inside his head.

"Virgil, what is it?" And now his wife, too! "Why're you looking around like that, Virgil?" And her eyes—going on about his past again, going on and on. . . .

Across the lawn the bootmaker Chuck Velen stood, rolled his sleeves, and ran full-bore toward Virgil.

Our boy gave a quick glance to his own hands, his bulgy-veined, splotch-knuckled bony hands, and he curled them ready. He could hear the irritable thump of his own heart and nothing besides. His instinct told him to stand, but he didn't stand. Chuck Velen reached him—the bootmaker's gaze widening over his own mumpy face— and Virgil drew a breath so deep, it needled across his lungs. *All right, Chuck Velen.* Virgil, making a fist, got to his feet. *I'll show you all a little McCoy, as much as I remember.* But something didn't feel right. As if the pull of gravity were easing. Meanwhile Chuck Velen had sped past him, to the sycamore tree.

Bea and Anna's gray cat, Wilhamena, was hanging by its forepaws from a wickerwork of leaves and branches at the treetop. The gathered clouds framed that cat hanging there in jeopardy, and a gaggle of taunting white pigeons made a great flapping noise on every side. All the guests now gathered to watch Wilhamena, who was drawn out like a twopenny gymnast and showing the whitish hair of her underbelly.

Women wept; men barked. At Virgil's side Carol, now almost beautiful in the charitable twilight, eyed him very intently. Yes! Maybe he could save the cat! *Okay, pal,* our boy told himself. *This just might be your way into their hearts.*

Chuck Velen, craning his neck far back, said, "We'll rescue your Wilhamena, Anna." But Velen, like everybody else, only stood there.

Meanwhile, McCoy was admitting to himself that there'd been

something pleasant in having believed that all these folks'd been staring at him. It'd been both pleasant and the opposite of pleasant.

Velen was knuckling the trunk of the tree, which stood tall and branchless most of the way up. "I just don't know how anyone would climb this."

A stitch of bark landed at Carol's feet. She stood quiet, urging her husband on with her eyes. McCoy looked at her hopeful face—that quality being one more crop that grew strong in the Midwest—and at the open distressed faces of his neighbors. *Over a cat!* He thought. *One stupid cat in a tree!* He understood that no world that had seen the changes of a New York, of skyrises and immigrant slums and Dogsbody Flats, could allow Moscow County to remain in its pigheaded seclusion for long.

And McCoy understood something else, too.

What if I died here? he thought. *In mild Bluffton Creek?*

Anxious Carol said, "Oh, pish! Virgil can climb up there and get her!" She always prized the idea of helping out. She'd wanted to be a nurse. "I know he can. Can't you, Virgil?"

The wind touched McCoy, remindful of a caress under warm bedclothes—or, he wanted it to remind him of that. *Oh, Susan,* he thought, *has it really been five years?* A woman's voice off his left shoulder was crying out, "Dear God," as the gray cat shook in the tree.

Chuck Velen, under his breath, said, "Well, Virgil." The hair lay over the man's forehead like the curl clouds that shade the lower mountaintops: wispy and colorless. "Looks like we're waiting on you to save your sister's cat, Virgil." These were among the only words Chuck Velen had said to our boy in five years.

All eyes were on McCoy and they made him blush and warmed him. His sister Bea was blinking and nervous and eager. Her new husband nodded, waiting for something good to happen. McCoy's wife was looking into his face like a beam of sunshine.

So he made his way to the tree slowly. The trunk was broad all the way around. He walked up to it, and then past it. The wind blew stronger on him. He kept walking. In the end a man's ambition stays tangled up with his life. Nobody can untangle those two. As McCoy passed the cat he stuck out his tongue at it.

"Virgil?" This sounded like Carol, but McCoy was hurrying away from everyone and he couldn't see who'd said it. Not too far ahead of him the end of the grass waited. And after that the street. What in the world had McCoy been thinking, returning to Bluffton Creek? What diamond ever tried to repeat its lump-of-coal days?

"Virgil?" Childish, kind—yes, this was Carol. "Virgil?"

Almost halfway to Mulberry Avenue, breathless, his shoulders pretty well back, looking almost slyly at all the nothing laid out before him, his face taking off into a leer—that seemed the right facial expression to be making, though nobody could see his face—McCoy crossed the cool, twilit, grass-smelling yard with near-skipping steps. The evening stars had come out weak; the mottled, white-painted side of the house added some indifferent light.

"Virgil!" Carol cried now, "Virgil, where are you *going*?"

He tried not to hear her, not to let her familiar voice gnaw at his heart. He didn't want to turn around and see her this last time. He didn't want to. When he did, she already looked changed, her hunched shoulders and her face struck by despair and surprise. Turning again toward the street, McCoy brought a guilty pity to this escape; the feeling was like when a hungry man reaches for an apple and sees a worm in it.

At home, McCoy collected his money and what few possessions he'd take to Manhattan, among them his silver locket that Susan Fields had given him. His heart was hurrying as it had before championship fights and little else. Sure, he had felt terrible about what he'd done as the real McCoy, and now about Carol. But he would not die here in Bluffton Creek.

Manhattan

After three train-bound days and nights: New York.

Another two weeks—an earsplitting, frenzied pair of Manhattan weeks—and McCoy was backstage at the close of a Friday evening performance of *One More Go-Round, William H. Taft?*, trying to get to Susan Fields's dressing room. He was in no hurry. One way or another he was going to see his ex-wife tonight.

The usher said that, well, as bad luck would have it, in view of the fact, and what have you. It seemed a lot of men tried to talk their way into meeting the Elephant of the Proscenium. The usher's snivel-pitched voice condescended at McCoy.

Every minute of McCoy's short time back in New York had brought anxiety. The world's largest city had topsy-turvified. "The real McCoy" had been replaced in the popular imagination by the unreal magic of Houdini, who in 1908 had published the knockout success *The Unmasking of Robert-Houdin*. Or maybe it was just that McCoy had changed during his time in the sticks.

He couldn't afford to think about that now. He was backstage, leaning his whole body against the theater's cold brick wall, menacing the usher. "You don't know who I am, son." McCoy tried to sound greatly offended. "D. W. Griffith, the flicker chief. Director. I'm the moving-picture director."

"Yes." Bathed in perfume, the usher had the lavish, shellacked hair of Lionel Barrymore. "I'll ask you to leave now, Mister"—the kid's pause was deliberate—"Griffith."

True, if McCoy'd felt more at ease in this changed New York, he would've known better how to flimflam such a dunderhead. But the city had grown severely different in five years. From the very first, his train had entered into an unfamiliar giantess of a new building— Pennsylvania Station, all bosoms of arching steel and glass, with spindleshanks of cut stone—and when he'd emerged, free and easy and ignored, onto turbulent Seventh Avenue, the fiery unknown faces out in the street and in every apartment window and the cold firmness of the granite earth hadn't been as comforting as he'd hoped. No horses anywhere. Likewise, electrified signs now told him when to walk through the feverish streets and when not to. The air purred and crackled just overhead, thick with a million wires vibrating. At night, too many anxious light-bulbs gave rise to vowels and consonants that ran up walls; blinking words branded the steaming atmosphere before vanishing; hot glowing lies. And in sight of McCoy's hotel, the newest, tallest building in the world shot fifty swaying stories directly upward. Called, rightly, Metropolitan Life.

Sucking in his breath now, stepping close to the backstage usher, McCoy drew his revolver, which had lain against his stomach. Of course, McCoy did not feel well doing this. What he felt was his own face going white, an apology of sorts. (He'd come by the gun some days earlier, by way of a Jacob Stromobofsky, one of the flimflammers he'd met recently.)

In any event.

Stepping up to Susan's door, the one with her glitter-board star on it, McCoy paused a moment. *Knocking on yet another door*, he thought, rapping with the back of his knuckle. What would Susan look like? Would she be unfair to him again? She'd been very unfair.

Regardless, he'd made it here, and was about to see Susan Fields one more time.

It hadn't been an easy crossing. He'd arrived from Bluffton Creek with money only to stay for six nights at the Shepherd Meadows occupancy hotel on the Bowery. After some hasty training, disguised by cheek bristles and a mustache, half-afraid he'd be arrested for the murder of Johnnie Gold, he boxed under the name St. Corkscrew LeFist (inspiration, when it works, works in strange ways). He pulled some of the "one-man swindles" Johnnie'd taught him ("Truly, kind madam, if you'd be good enough to entrust me with two hundred dollars to make my way to my palace in Basel, why, I'll send you back an undiminished *twice the sum* by post!"). Such flimflams paid humbly, and his eroded ring skills and past recognizability in the fight world had forced him to box chumps for "chump change." Still, after two undefeated weeks, he'd been able to move into a three-room flat at the Galina Hotel on the corner of lower Broadway and Bourne where the flies liked to march across a man's pillow at night.

Now Susan Fields opened her dressing-room door to him and his heart jolted awake after years of cold storage. She wore an embroidered green Chinese dressing gown, her hair dangling loose. Her eyes didn't widen, nor did her brows lift with surprise. The air smelled a little from the burn of the stage lights a few yards off.

"Virgil." Susan's inflection dragged and wasn't kind. She could've called him McCoy.

But he—well, he'd laid eyes on his beloved. He said nothing, however (his choices were either to say nothing, or to go teary). Her hair trapped the light that wavered behind her.

My girl is still beautiful, he thought. *Even if she's got more of a tired look around her eyes.*

The smile he offered felt propped up with toothpicks. Meanwhile, Susan dimpled half her face by gnawing on the inside of her cheek. If she wasn't quite shaking her head at him, its offhand, side-to-side movement had him worried.

McCoy, standing there idiot-style, knew that a silence like this one was awful; things couldn't seem any worse. It was now that he noticed her wedding band.

The ring was extravagant and polished, and sad McCoy, hope-crushed McCoy, lost his breath over it. *Who?* he thought. *Who took her from me? Spencer Todd? Frederick Huntington?*

He looked away, down the shadowy narrow backstage corridor,

where that usher still made a point of facing in the other direction. McCoy's clothes felt very clean on his body; this was the nicest suit he owned, a close-fitting blue one. His revolver tugged at his belt, made his belly skin itch. At every turn she'd disappointed him—unlike pleasant Carol Abbott, the wife he missed now.

"So." Susan's voice arrived grim and surprising like a new shadow. "Did you come merely to stand here like—"

"Hello, Susan." McCoy didn't say this quickly; not breakingly or high-pitched or accompanied by fidgeting. His posture was close to exceptional. After years of being Virgil, he wasn't going to let a little nervousness keep him from acting out-and-out McCoy. He was wearing the silver-heart locket.

Susan eyed him, up and down and calmly. Under her long green dressing gown she had on a low-necked white camisole, and under *that* the crown of her chest buoyed up in sight, pale and rounding full; a place where his hands had many times been happy.

"He*llo*, McCoy." She sighed. "Quite an interesting growth of cheek bristles you've attempted." She didn't move to usher him inside.

His chin flared just a stroke higher than hers. With the years, the gray of her eyes had started to run just a bit into their whites, like half-spent coals in the snow. They gave nothing of what Susan was thinking now.

How thrilling his nights with Susan had been! *Imagine how awful life would've turned out, if I'd never known that.* The taste of the skin of her neck . . .

He felt too dammed up to say that he'd come back mostly because her eyes deepened when she said, "Pishy *pish*." And because her stomping bare feet used to startle him awake every morning. And because he'd never felt more famous than when he was with her. *No, I mustn't think of all that.* McCoy brought himself back to the present. Susan's gown purled out at her knees and snared at the best curves of her body, smoothing all the moldable lumps of womankind. She bent one leg behind her, the muscles of her exposed calf standing erect to hold off the sliding censorship—the approaching hem of her dressing gown.

What if I never know that soft skin again?

He told her that he was back permanently. (Back to discover *this* New York, this howling wilds done up in concrete.)

"Oh? How wonderful for you, McCoy." This seemed like more apathy. She was, however, patting down one red curl that didn't need any patting down. He hadn't asked about her ring; she hadn't asked him anything at all. *My pillow person*, he thought. *My charlotte russe with legs.*

McCoy was gazing into Susan's face. He took her in slowly. Her cheeks, jawline, etc. He looked and he looked. This was giving her cause to blush.

"What," she said, while he just stared like a mad bull.

"What," she said again.

But he was taking in her lips (turbulent, loose), and her nose (straight) and brows (arched, damp, lovable). Her eyes went wide, and she brought her hand absently to cover her throat.

McCoy took his forever beloved by her wrist and he drew her to him. Next, he let her hand go with a theatrical drop. Then, bringing his finger to her chin, he raised her face. Susan, in a furtive voice, said only: "Hello."

They kissed and the years since he'd last known her lips flamed into nothing. His heart was a spurting hot water bottle everywhere in his chest. Then she smacked him across the face, very hard.

"On top of it all, McCoy," the sophisticated Susan Fields said as she drew her own knuckles across her lips, "you've lost your reflexes."

It was a long time before McCoy turned away, even though he didn't want Susan to see the emotion warping his features. Listening to her fast breathing amid all the quiet that framed it, McCoy knew Susan had hated her slap, too. Her breath came very loud.

He might've left, but stayed put. She hadn't asked him to go. The facing brick wall stood charred; soot overlaid its natural red. And now came McCoy's overdue despair, smothering and intolerable, dropping over him like a heavy blanket.

"I'm married," Susan was saying, in her most dreadful voice. McCoy received these words with tears in his eyes. "I did not kiss

any other man when I was your wife, McCoy; I shan't kiss one now."
But the splintering formality of her tone, her agitated breathing,
that fine white hand that whisked around at the brink of his vision,
the goosefleshy splotches breaking across the crown of her chest,
even the affectionate, split-second lingering of her palm on his
cheek following her slap—McCoy was sure *all* of these gave the
same message: *This isn't the way it should be between us who still love
each other*.

"Aren't you going to leave now?" is what she said aloud.

"Could be," he said, feeling a great deal of tenderness for himself. He knew—maybe she did, also—that he'd be back; that soon
he'd end her current marriage, no matter who her husband was.
The old feeling was returned. He'd have Susan and the world, too.
McCoy was in a rush to start that process, and so he bowed his head
and quickly left.

Would he need to remake himself again?

What'd lent him power as an impetuous teenager now exhausted
him even to think about. For a grown man to remake himself . . .
What would that mean? When he looked in the mirror, he didn't
see St. Corkscrew LeFist.

Couldn't it have been this changed Manhattan *itself* that was
holding him down? The roaring home of millions, the city now felt
as desolate as the bottom of the ocean.

Elbowing through the hurried, electric swarm on First Street
he'd thought to ask one young, shawl-wearing woman what time it
was, and she gnarled up her face with such disdain that McCoy's
tongue lay slack in his mouth like a dead fish in a grocer's crate.
"Why you ask me?" she spat.

Unkindnesses came daily, sapping his strength. What he'd once
seen as the newest ways of life had already antiquated; last year's
wonders of Coney Island had closed in favor of weirder, steeper
roundabouts and higher-flying horses; old ladies now urinated on
swarming street corners; innocents were cheerful to rob you in a
broad daylight made grimy by the hiccups of new industry.
Stageshow women who'd blushed to show a naughty ankle now ex-

posed their breasts at noon, while the sky was no longer to be found overhead. This taller Manhattan had surrendered the old's patchwork mixture of bright and dark, beautiful and ugly, for an all-over gray; week after week of that had turned McCoy's heart into a gray-walled tenement house.

But it wasn't just the gloom; McCoy'd seen certain things, disturbing things. He'd seen Jacob Stromobofsky in action.

A week before he'd gone to Susan, McCoy'd met Stromo in the downstairs barroom of O'Shaugney's Pub on the Bowery. Each man had spotted the crafty other for a flimflammer, the way a dancer might ferret out a peer by his light-footed grace on a crowded street. And in a matter of minutes the two had decided to pull some scams together. (Emmanuel Babel, Stromobofsky's partner in crime, had recently died.) McCoy had introduced himself as Corkscrew LeFist, the boxing flimflammer out of Jersey City. But Stromo had recognized him as McCoy at once.

Before long they hit on a Western Union swindle involving a fake teletype machine and six hired actors to be found later. McCoy hoped to con up enough money to propose to Susan by the New Year.

From the start, he and Stromo were an imperfect match.

"So," McCoy asked him at the end of this first meeting. "How did Manny Babel *go*, exactly?" A ceiling fan was kneading the muggy air overhead. Union workers and bluecoats, stevedores and flimflammers, were making their deep-voiced noise all around. Cigar smoke twisted about the ceiling fan blades in white-wisp tassels like threads of cotton candy. Our boy and Stromobofsky stood at the bar. A framed drawing of the Wright brothers' airplane and nothing else hung on the wall, over a line of colored bottles. O'Shaugney's was a basement bar: no windows. "Did he go quick?" McCoy was asking.

"He should burn up! That's how he went." This Stromo had a body—slim hips, short, a big belly—like a schoolgirl eight months into a mistake. "A dumb head, my partner was."

"Manny *Babel*? Was he dumb?" McCoy'd heard—every flimflammer had heard—of Manny Babel. Manny Babel had scammed five g's off of J. P. Morgan in a false-pretense flimflam with a forged Roosevelt signature on real presidential stationery.

"Dumb like *every*body dead is dumb." Jacob Stromobofsky leaned with his hands on the bar, his peanut head a little dropped. "A dumb person is a dead person." He sighed toward his hands that he braided together. "An unlucky person is a dead person."

"Okay." McCoy thought of Johnnie Gold and felt a bolt of sadness. He blinked at his new partner, who looked weak as an old elf. McCoy was drinking beer, and he took a sip now. "Okay, Stromo."

The pause in the conversation was interrupted by the jarring growl of a passing subway train. It was a rumble specific to New York City and expressive in its way—*You're an animal underground; so am I.*

"He had a boil, Manny. It turned into a sickness that hung on," said Stromo. "He should get a stomach cramp in hell, that one." Stromo came from Russia, a place called Odessa. New York, which now let in some ten thousand immigrants a day, had become nearly half foreign. Old customs were being reborn in the shade of the new kinds of buildings.

A thickset, scar-faced bartender approached and asked Stromo if he wanted a drink.

"Go peddle your fish elsewhere." Stromo's lips glistened when he talked. He wheeled on McCoy, more quickly than you'd have thought such a body could move. "For what are you worried?"

"Me? I'm not." But McCoy had a feeling that plans with Stromo were going to turn out in a way he couldn't prepare for. "I just wanted to know about your old partner, that's all."

"Don't imagine a lung and a liver on your nose!" Stromo's little red craggy face was not unlike a boil. "Go drive yourself crazy!" He edged toward McCoy.

The ex-champ's body took on every tautness, starting with his fists. "Just what are you talking about, Stromo?" Looking down on the Russian's head, he could see between the strands of the old guy's hair. "Calm yourself now."

"This is not a safe business we're in." Stromo was squinting, nodding, already smiling. He spoke, if not quietly, then at least reasonably. "What do you need me to tell you, in my *gebrochener* English? Did I ask you about your old partners?" He yawned. "Now it's getting dark in my eyes; I need to go to sleep."

Their very first scam together was the scariest McCoy had ever done.

The idea had been Stromo's: they'd convince a rich businessman, newly arrived to the Lower East Side, that McCoy, or "Mr. Smith"—as whitely American as "that honest Avraham Lincoln they talk about"—had run into trouble after an affair with a young Jewish girl. More, they'd say this Mr. Smith now had to sell his prospering haberdashery "for a song"—as he needed money in his pocket to flee the state. The dupe, who'd made his money in the hat trade in the old country, was told he could buy a $17,000 business for $950.

This was a simple flimflam to set up—just forge some documents of business ownership, bribe a late-night worker in an existing haberdashery to play along during a tour of "one of Mr. Smith's three successful shops"—and McCoy and Stromo would get almost a thousand, in cash.

The new flimflam partners met the dupe, a Chaim Fishbein, at the corner of Hester and Essex Streets, where low tenements and lower makeshift wooden storefronts pitched blue shadows over elderly women in sleeveless cloaks, beggars in black, pushcarts with fruits, pots and pans, shirts and pants, fabric swatches, eyeglasses, buttons, stationery, scissors, and underwear. There was a peppery smell, and saloons and hanging laundry everywhere, a few religious stalls overlaid with Hebrew letters, and the choleric faces of so many aspiring young men.

Stromo and McCoy stood on the curb, Fishbein on the street itself. Fishbein was saying, "Don't twist my head." He had skinny legs and a chest like a small boat. "I gave you my answer, which it happens to be 'no.'"

"What is this?" Stromo actually snorted. He strained his chapped pale lips to half their normal fullness. He wore a bow tie and a straw hat in the sun. "Such good luck *I* should have! Mr. Upside-Down! Don't be stupid, you do everything backward."

"Hey," McCoy put in quickly, "it's all right," touching Stromo by the arm. *Never let a dupe see how badly you want him.* "We'll just simply find someone else, Moishe, okay?"

Stromo hadn't turned his enraged eyes from Fishbein. "He grows like an onion, this one—with his head in the ground!" That little red craggy face once again a boil. "A new life, Fishbein! This American man is offering you *a new life*!" Stromo looked to the sky and laughed as if with good-natured envy, but his obvious anger made the gesture less than believable. "Such good luck I should have!"

Maybe McCoy had overestimated the city's new drabness: this morning's high unclouded sky was topped by a sun big with cheer.

"For instance, sirs, I don't have a thousand dollars." Fishbein seemed a thoughtful man, his round clean face turning a smile at his top lip, his hands deep in his pockets. "I wish I had it, sure." And as he whispered, he batted his eyes like a flirty woman when she starts to coquet. "Forgive me, Moishe, for saying this. But listen, for what should a Jew have more than one haberdashery store? This I am telling you from experience. A Jew with more than one haberdashery store will forget the Torah."

"You listen!" The old elf Stromo's hands went flying up. "Asses on the table now! Let's conclude this!" he yelled in a rasping voice.

Fishbein raised his eyebrows and motioned his thumb at Stromo. "He's a cooking ladle, this one. Trouble he stirs up."

What are these people talking about? McCoy thought, while in the street a black motorcar swerved around the produce truck that'd stalled at the stoplight. Also a long-gaberdined peddler, not old but with white in his beard, smiled at Fishbein and stepped with his little son toward the intersection. Others walked by, too, some of them spitting at the ground, and McCoy noted that, even on this busy corner, a few started to gather across the street. There are worse things to watch than a brewing commotion. Fishbein was still talking: "At business I do not so good, but not so bad, either. I put food every day out on the table and that's that."

"This you call a living?" Stromo took the lapel of Fishbein's mangy jacket in his fingers. "This piece of knitted dung, pardon my saying." How could McCoy have been ready to make such a nutjob his partner? Had he lost his sense of the world? "They don't let you live!" Stromo was yelling.

"Okay, ok*ay*, Moishe," McCoy said abruptly. Then: "I understand why you're concerned, Mr. Fishbein." He smiled one of his old-time fierce wide smiles.

A shadow covered the bottom of Fishbein's face. Some young limper who held his bowler hat against the wind nearly knocked into Stromo. The bells from a church a few blocks uptown started nervously to titter; and an old man bent underneath a load of coats joined the crowd that grew across the street.

"I can lend you some property, too, Mr. Fishbein," McCoy said. "As collateral. Because, you see, I have a nice, two-story place in—"

"You're afraid, Fishbein?" Stromo seemed happy to be enraged; he was even smiling. "In heaven there's a big fair! Do you know what I am saying to you? You're making a big deal out of nothing! Give us the money, or else!"

Fishbein looked a little worked up himself now. "Listen to me. You're right. I have a stomachache in saying no to a bargain." He avoided Stromo's eye. "But I do not have the money. I do not know you from Adam for you to yell at me."

"You should choke on it!" Stromo's cheeks suddenly went so inflamed he might have been having a heart attack. "You should get killed! In Russia they called me the Pogrom!"

"Go threaten the bedbugs!" Fishbein was screeching all at once. "You don't frighten me!" But his pale eyes showed clearly how frightened he was; their whites caught more than enough sun so that the pupils reeled.

McCoy said, "Okay, Moishe." He failed to get Stromo's attention. "*Moishe!* Let's just—"

"Go take a shit for yourself, Fishbein!" Stromo's own eyes were glittering, too, as if with tears. "Go fight with God."

A young woman carrying two loaves of bread walked by, making sure not to look at Stromo just before he drew a small dirty revolver from under his coat and shot Fishbein in the face. The blast rang on the air like a single throaty bark from a vicious dog.

Then Hester Street held very quiet and still. Fishbein lay faceless at McCoy's feet, bent from the waist backward at an impossible angle. Nothing moved: the scene just like a photograph, but full with color. The sun, like a cut circle in a blanket, was blocking out its shape on the blood that covered the pavement.

At last the neighborhood awakened to scream and run off. Stromo, who'd dropped his pistol, scuttled with the crowd, his hat flying away, his legs working stiffly as he made his way up Hester Street and out of this story. Then it was quiet again. Only now did McCoy start to run, too, slipping in Fishbein's puddle, terrified.

Running past people, elbowing his way through the walkers on the street, running east, knocking over a fat immigrant boy and not stopping, the wind on his face: *Is Fishbein dead or not?* He ran on his toes; he'd been running less than a minute, but already he was past the pushcarts; past the peppery smell, the Hebrew letters. *Dead or not?* He kept on until he was short of breath and still he ran. Of course Fishbein was dead. And McCoy started to feel tired and slow, tired and slow—and finally, walking now, he made his way down the stairs of the Essex Street subway station.

When he reached the platform McCoy bent double with his hands on his hips to catch his breath. He saw no sign of any police.

Another body! he thought as he pushed through the turnstile, looking around, very sad, hardly breathing. He was ill at ease but trying to fake a look of unconcern. *So much death!* He was struck with the belief that for a flimflammer, he had pretty strict ethics. Those of us who knew McCoy tended to agree.

Mrs. Utnap

Am I brainsick? he asked himself. The *New York Herald*'d run a week-long series about the "new illnesses of the mind." Well, if a man *never* felt satisfied, what was he but touched in the head? If only he could find an idea bigger than just grand; an idea grander than the real McCoy, an idea as grand as . . . as—*what*? He believed that time was running short. But as usual, McCoy's fear was shot through with some elation. He shaved his cheeks.

And then he saw Johnnie Gold on a sunless December noon.

Thousands were out walking lower Broadway, literally thousands rushing to and fro, more frantic droves hurrying in the shadow of the monumental new Palagets skyscraper. It was a week after McCoy's meeting with Susan, and two after he'd last seen Jacob Stromobofsky; this morning's warmish air gave occasional cold clutches. Still, the first snow of the season was melting away here at everyone's feet. And right across the avenue, glimpsed between so many passing bodies: Johnnie Gold. In the widespread shadow of that skyscraper, the old flimflammer leaned against the building's uptown wall. Johnnie'd always stood in shadow.

"It can't be!" McCoy cried. Everything was melting away here.

There could be no doubt: Johnnie Gold. Heavy, Chinese looking, foppishly dressed in a black suit that was too thin even for this milk-warm December day.

No, McCoy thought, *I saw him die.* And he went blear eyed and staggery like someone leaving a dark cave for the sunlight. Because McCoy had killed Johnnie Gold with his hands. (Not that anyone had bothered to investigate the murder of a foreigner killed in his tenement.)

And yet, there stood McCoy's oldest friend, impossible, yet a breathing figure all the same. Imagine seeing an unreal thing, a building rise without end, swallowed up into a gray sky; or imagine a gigantic reflection of a face—is it your face?—spreading above, warped as in a funhouse mirror yet brightening the gray overhead. The face in the sky rolls with clouds, there it glares, here it shimmers. . . .

Without Johnnie Gold, McCoy'd had no purpose. No, it was Susan Fields he needed most—everything got confused in his head. His life had been like the gray sky: dark, empty, maudlin. No wonder, then, that as McCoy saw Johnnie Gold, alive and leaning fatly against the wall, the sight bewildered him to visions and daydreams.

Maybe a good flimflammer can die anytime it's convenient, McCoy thought.

And he went to him.

It didn't even matter that as soon as McCoy crossed through the agitated tide of passing people, the man who sloped against the building was no longer Johnnie Gold but a heavyset Occidental with cheeks as pale as linen. The fat leaner's hair had turned fair once McCoy'd gotten into the shadow with him. Like Johnnie, he wore a daisy in his lapel and showed a cantaloupe slice of belly skin where his shirt couldn't quite reach to his belt. Still, the man could've turned out to be a cannonball pyramid or a large rosebush and it wouldn't have mattered. It didn't matter. McCoy knew who he'd seen. Or, rather, the message of what he'd seen.

"*Guten Tag?*" This portly man was thin-lipped and small-footed, his whisper faint like a seashell's. He sucked on a corncob pipe and must've felt McCoy staring at him for some time. "Speken ze German?"

"No," McCoy said. "Excuse me."

The next afternoon, wearing a new tan jacket bought on credit, he made his way to Susan Fields's brownstone on Madison and Warrick (McCoy'd read the papers, found where she lived, who she'd married). An unfamiliar woman with a big nose answered the wide green door.

"Welcome." The big-nose woman used an official tone: "Utnap residence." She stood almost McCoy's height.

"Are you the—maid?" He swallowed, nodded. "I'm here to see"—not easy to call his Susan this—"Mrs. Utnap."

The Utnaps' foyer was the size of McCoy's bedroom at the Galina Hotel, and its floors were a reflecting black marble. McCoy held his hat while the big nose sniffed past him in a hurry.

"I shall be back after I check if Madame Utnap can see you, sir."

Alone, he looked in the hatstand mirror and saw more McCoy than Virgil. Still a wiry pug, if less so around the waist. The skin on the side of his neck had remained a little discolored from his fighting days. Also, he wore a fake mustache and fake glasses.

"McCoy."

Susan stood all in green at the junction of her foyer and what looked like the start of a blind hallway. Her earnest oval face held so stiff and self-possessed, it appeared she felt nothing at all in seeing him. If he'd been near enough a wall, he'd have leaned against it. But McCoy stood in the middle of the room and didn't even know where to to put his hands. He missed Carol Abbott all at once, her sweetness, and he regretted the mistake of how he'd left her.

The only sound in the foyer was the dainty tweet of Susan's breathing.

"Susan, I know you." This, a fairly Virgil tone of voice: mundane pitched, as he hadn't caught it in time. "Your walk, Duck. Your skin. I know the way you laugh." (Susan's laugh always went: Ha *ha* ha.) Why hadn't he just said hello? Susan narrowed her eyes; the glow at her temples might've been sweat. She was waiting for something.

"Susan," he said. "Susan." If wit is a bag of tricks, McCoy's had fallen open and all the contents had dropped out. "I—think you know why I came, Susan."

"Why not tender me a favor," she said, her face as empty as a blind woman's, "and spell it out. And afterward you may leave. What's that pelt over your lip?"

He set out to say he loved her, but stopped: that'd be inadequate. He laughed nervously, stammered in Virgil's voice, and then relaxed. Much later he remembered this moment for how clear his world got. He had one chance to win her for good, also one last chance to unburden all that ambition.

"I've arrived here today," said ardent McCoy, holding his ex-wife's stare, "knowing you love me, Susan Fields. You always have *and . . .*" He spoke, if not unwaveringly, then at least with some composure. When he saw she didn't understand the fullness of what he'd meant, he added: "Will. You always will. We can't help but keep coming together, even if we always go apart." It was the time of evening when Mr. Utnap would not yet have left work, or so McCoy assumed. "This Utnap, whoever he is—"

"McCoy." Susan's face lit up flushed.

"Mrs. *Ut*nap." A tentative jab.

But Susan wasn't in the mood. "You've finally made it to the big leagues," she said. "But it's a short visit, because this is not your splendid house, is it?"

It might've been that, just by looking at him now, Susan understood that he'd shown up here with a plan, a plot excessive, immoral, and ridiculous—but just possibly miraculous, too. The lipstick Susan wore made a brief gluey pop of red between the lips as she opened her mouth. She'd always been able to tempt him, the way little seaside girls can lure a boy out into deep water. But could he lure *her* now? His own judgments had always proved so deceptive; he didn't know if those really were safe waters he saw ahead, or one last trap in shimmering blue.

He let a moment pass so he could fill it with a look he hoped was weighty. Couldn't she have been more kind to him? Couldn't she have cheered him now the way Carol would have, with a few comforting words, after how they'd loved each other? "Susan," he said, pressing his mustache so it wouldn't fall off, "I have an idea." He almost added something flirtish. But then he thought: not yet.

"An idea?" Her face, as a rule so composed, now flashed a lost expression. "I assumed as much."

He told her the broad outlines of a flimflam, a huge flimflam, the grandest in history, and it would involve her. He left out the details. The most important detail McCoy didn't say was that this'd be the first-ever scam in which the end prize would be less important than the act itself. The act itself would be everything.

"You want to involve *me*, McCoy?" They'd gone into Susan's living room to sit on the huge, red, cane-backed sofa nearest the open hearth. "What about your confidant, the fat Chinaman?"

"Susan," McCoy said, a little too loud. "I need for you to be a part of it."

"You must leave now." And as quick as that, all signs of Susan's struggle with her own feelings quit her face. "I should not have invited you in." And never before had McCoy ached so badly to touch her face.

He told Susan that she couldn't love this man, this Utnap. "I've seen his photograph, Duck." Still, he tried to sound courteous, respectful. He even kept his voice from coming off as overly familiar, which required work; in 1910 the average man had just one intimate with whom he shared his whole life—having an ex-wife seemed rare and ultramodern as owning an airplane. But McCoy knew he needed the calmest possible tone to charm the stubborn—here, its head peers out of its basket; there, it ducks away again—snake of revived love into the open. "I've seen your Mr. Utnap in the papers, Duck," he said. McCoy couldn't help but happen into a little bit of a smile, and his smile carried over to Susan's lips without dwindling much. He was sitting with his wild-haired elusive love in her colossal living room, where the Persian rug stretched all the way to the fireplace, and where a stuffed lion's head on the wall roared a silent roar from behind shining glass eyes.

"The point is, I am married to someone else," she said, and for a moment McCoy and Susan seemed both to think about their own marriage, its days and its nights. You might have even called her face tender.

She went on: "I would never consider starting any transgression with you, especially not a *flimflam*." She sat up straight with a dark, aloof calm. "Really, you should leave before I call the police." She seemed afraid to look at McCoy. Then she did look. "Out of curiosity, what is your plan?"

McCoy closed his eyes. His mind soared as if he'd thrown it in the air, high where the mists of an idea came together into a terrible cloud. The ex-champion, ex-husband, ex-symbol of truth or something like it—he had only now found out what he really was, and what he'd always been after. No more suffering this life, over which he had no control. McCoy was going to flimflam and flimflam and flimflam until he'd made a complete, perfect world of his own. To do what Johnnie Gold couldn't do.

And piece by piece the flimflam to end all flimflams took shape. Trick mirrors and prankish paintings appeared in his mind; a phonograph record played to great sly effect; electric lights going on at the throw of secret hidden switches; a mound of jewels twinkling in a dark room somewhere; guns hiding in jacket pockets; telephone wires that led into fraudulent vocal machines; mask after mask. Pulleys, levers, fake skyscrapers. Mazes, mannequins, wigs.

Up till now the only thing he'd ever done whole hog was to think of himself as McCoy. He'd drawn near all else with half-averted eyes. If his right hand were to reach for a political career, his left would covet the heavyweight championship. If he took one step toward being Johnnie Gold's flimflam partner, his other foot had gone to a sanitarium and D. W. Griffith flickers. Now McCoy would pervade every last aspect of his new-made reality: his eyes would see through the mirrors and the phonograph horn would speak with his voice; each of the masks would in turn become his real face. . . .

This reverie dissipated. McCoy opened his eyes once again on the reality of Susan Fields sitting by his elbow. He hadn't said a word to her in half a minute. But to his surprise the struggle was back in her high-boned face. He looked at her, hard, and she started to blush. A gambler scooping up his chips, McCoy knew the frenzied, pure elation of victory. "You're with me, aren't you?"

At this point Mr. Utnap came home.

Together McCoy and Susan heard the front door click open,

then slam shut; next came a rasping, oldish man's "Hello?" They waited out the tap of approaching footsteps.

Mr. Utnap swung into the room, a pink-cheeked robber baron with a forehead that wouldn't quit. Either the filthy money the man had made in the set-gems business, or the surprise of his wife sitting here with a trim stranger in a new tan jacket, lent his eyes a blazing, overtheatrical wideness. Now Susan took in a short, audible breath. Utnap had a walrus's torso. This was not a man a woman like Susan could love easily.

"Hello, darling darling." Susan's voice didn't sound close to right. "This is—"

"I," McCoy said, quick and calm, "am Connor Alterman." And he shot Susan a frantic look: *Play along.*

"Very well," Utnap said. "Hello." He stared blankly at McCoy, trying to form the appropriate next question. And over his shoulder a crowded Madison Avenue at nightfall unfurled outside the window, flowing and wavering, squirming, changing the colors within its overall gray. Utnap, Susan, even McCoy himself, were waiting for what McCoy would say next. Susan's lips contracted with what appeared to be rage.

"I knew your wife back in New Jersey," McCoy/Alterman began. (I don't know how the name Alterman had come to him so quickly.) "It seems your wife's forgotten me, Mr. Utnap, but, oh well." The smile he gave was his attempt at something more dull than the usual McCoy good cheer, but still it shone too bright, possibly too winning. "The point is I now work for a charity. . . ." And from there McCoy went into a flimflam.

He made up a world, tale-telling like a virtuoso, piling detail onto bogus detail, revealing a bold, mysterious, *complete* imagination—Susan could only watch openmouthed—and the whole time Utnap was looking at him a little askance. Because he'd been a famous man who'd been married to Susan. Now he sat there, a humble, mustachioed guy, friendly, telling Utnap that he was someone else, and that he'd come to enlist Susan's help for his charity, the Immigrant Foundling Association.

Utnap strode right up to where McCoy sat and he stared down

at him. He was known to the New York tabloids as "the Color-Blind Money-Grubber."

"Take this," Utnap insisted, reaching into his wallet and starting to tease out a ten-dollar bill. Susan might have shaken her head a little, but she didn't blow the scam.

McCoy smiled. "Really, I couldn't."

"For the barbarian children," said Utnap. He must have been thirty years older than Susan; thirty-five. The bill quivered before McCoy's face. The old man wanted to show this stranger and his wife just how kind he was. Or was that the wrong reading? Maybe shoving a bill into someone's face was just the robber baron's answer to everything. Or maybe he knew that McCoy was lying and he wanted to show our boy up?

"Well, there are other ways in which you and your wife can help, sir," McCoy said. "No, thank you. It's a kindly offer, just the same."

The money was still there. Finally, McCoy took it. "All right, Mr. Utnap." He winked. "But I'm going to ask you for more than that, before I'm done, ha ha."

Utnap laughed, too, but at the same time he narrowed his eyes at McCoy. The robber baron kept up that squint, eyeing McCoy the whole time that he and Susan walked him out to the foyer.

"I'll be seeing you, Mr. Utnap—and Mrs. Utnap," McCoy said with a smile. He searched Susan's face for the features he loved so intimately. His desire for her was like a damp cold that penetrates to the bone.

He shook her hand, which just now felt as tender as a broom handle, just before the door clicked shut behind him.

What Johnnie Gold Died Not Knowing

Days later, Susan was asking, "Why did you choose the name Connor Alterman?" This was in McCoy's room at the Galina—afterward. "Wasn't Connor Alterman the name of a friend of yours? I know I've heard of him." The annoyance in her voice, if that's not too strong a word for it, had little to do with McCoy's assumed name.

Understand, this had never happened to him before. He absolutely couldn't believe that it'd happened today. It was too embarrassing to think about. "Yes," he answered her finally. Why was she asking this *now*?

He started counting all the places where the paint on the wall had gone yellow. Because he couldn't look at Susan at the moment, of course. This had never happened before, not with any woman. Now he lay stretched out beside his ex-wife, not touching her at all.

Because she had risked so much to come here, and he—

Had McCoy gotten too used to Carol Abbott and her indifferent body? The wall of this room seemed at its most yellow above the window frame. He tucked the cold sheets around him. Neither he nor Susan made a move. He imagined this as a scene in a flicker; the audience not knowing whether to laugh or cry.

Why had it happened, when this had all felt so familiar? It was hand-in-glove! This was love! Minutes earlier he'd filled with a terrible longing for Susan's body even as he'd felt it twisting against him. . . .

I wish I was Connor Alterman, he thought. *Then I wouldn't have to be so humiliated.*

Now she gave a sigh that sounded just like the radiator's hiss. She ran a finger over the exposed part of his arm. "McCoy," she said, "I decided to come here, of my own power, and had my reason to do so." She hadn't kept all the contempt and aggression out of her voice.

I ruined it, he thought.

"I'm deeply sorry, Susan." That's what he said—deeply sorry. Self-pity drove over him like some thundery old-time automobile.

"McCoy, it was hardly my plan merely to be unfaithful to my husband, all right?" In one motion she threw off the covers, got up from the bed—unveiled—and bent to pick up her black dress. "Do you understand that much, McCoy?" And her stooping body couldn't have looked any more alluring. "This is not something I've ever allowed myself." Susan sighed in undertones, as people often do when they talk to themselves. "Not I."

Next she breathed, with a squeak, through her nose, as if she kept a little fife in her nostril.

McCoy sat up and pressed his eyes for a while. How she breathed may have no longer been any of his concern.

"I don't want to be Mrs. Utnap," Susan said, just a little more faint than she'd been saying it for weeks in McCoy's dreams. "You have to understand that I came here to see you because . . ."

Well, this was exactly what he'd wanted to hear. (Only, had she interrupted herself to talk like a flimflammer, or because she felt unable to go on?) But McCoy's embarrassment was so huge that he'd only partially heard her. His self-pity and his desire had their turns with him, one after the other. He was unworthy of Susan Fields. With sidelong glances he saw that she was dressing in a hurry.

How silly that they acted unlike husband and wife—even now! Just because she had this Utnap of a husband? Why did he feel shy as a virgin with his own Susan?

. . . It had been lucky that she'd come here at all. He'd sent her a note, signed "Alterman," asking to meet him at Plume's on Broadway. She'd been late, her smile had been like an etching gone many times to the printer, but at least she'd smiled. He'd told her how beautiful she was, how kind and funny and sophisticated, and what a jackass he'd felt himself to be. Everything would come together for them, he'd said, if she would only let it. And now here they were. . . .

He opened his mouth and tried to tell her: "I have nothing in the world except you," but the words dried up in his throat. It was one of those high winter afternoons when cold spreads even into the breaths of your radiator. The drapes were down. The air held the narcotic, slightly sour scent of Susan.

Swallowing, McCoy—devil take the hindmost!—gathered the nerve to sweep his eyes over her slim-legged body; he expected her to give him a long, searching, ecstatic look of her own. But she, standing wobbly in one black shoe, aimed her eyes at the floor. Her lowered face was almost as pink as her lips, which she was chewing on.

In a flash of lightning McCoy could see there was something un-Carolish and vulgar about her. Mostly it was her marriage to successful, filthy rich, ugly old Utnap.

But what was it she'd said? That she wanted to *leave* Utnap?

Right now Susan was lifting her leg, stumbling, regaining her balance, putting on that other shoe. McCoy couldn't find words to end the rotten silence. But he hadn't taken his eyes from her body.

"Say something, McCoy." Susan's voice came all at once, like an ending. The expression of her face, of her scowling brow, changed. She looked almost afraid. (Every time he thought he knew how she'd look, another Susan showed up.)

Just as she appeared to tense, McCoy relaxed. His ambitious plans, instead of retreating, marched up to the front line. Confidence boosted him; more, he felt physically excited; even more, he was happy, driven close to elation by the mysterious voice that seemed to be talking to him now. McCoy and Susan were going to steal Utnap's jewels—worth six million dollars. It turns out the Why hadn't been about the fame of deathless fame, or even money.

If McCoy didn't fully understand these thoughts, he didn't need to. He'd always been guided by a feeling, and he leaned on that feeling now. No two ways about it, the answer was stretching out, it lay right there on Susan, it spread across the room, it fanned out everywhere. McCoy just had to get it to speak more clearly.

All at once the now fully dressed Susan, looking as sweet as you please, said, "Why in God's name are you staring at me like that?" Her tone was familiar, at least. "What the blazes are we going to do now? Do you have any idea at all?"

Feeling kind of foggy, McCoy couldn't put it into words himself; how could he explain it to her? But he saw it coming together, just beams and girders, like a skyscraper at the beginning of its construction.

Here, I'd have thought that McCoy would explain this. But he said, "Don't worry, Duck," and followed that up with the poignant rule of the speechless moment. Naturally, he was a little pleased.

Here's one way McCoy defended his fancy-built aims over the next few weeks: Friendships wither, passions wither, our bodies and angers and our satisfactions wither, and like successes, the people we love die or abandon us in other ways. Living at all is basically a flea-bitten way to live.

"How charming," said Susan, not yet willing to listen to reason. "Where did you get such drivel—it doesn't even sound like you."

If he'd found that reddish bags had appeared under his eyes these last few years, he'd regained his winning, dogged boyishness. At least, he assumed that he had.

"Would you rather be here with some Connor Alterman, some dullard—or with McCoy, as I am?" he asked.

"I don't follow," she said.

Christmas came; the New Year, too. McCoy would often come to fetch her in a taxicab four blocks from her home. She'd curl her fingers around his elbows, gaze into his face as if it were a view of the New York skyline. Then her lids would come down, slow like draw-bridges, and she'd lean gradually to him, buckling forward at about the pace of the Tower of Pisa. "McCoy," she'd whisper with an al-most sad face. "What do you think you're doing?" And he'd touch her, away from the eyes of anyone he would touch her, and try to convince her to help with his scam.

Flimflam, if done as he imagined it—and no one had ever flim-flammed as he imagined it now—would turn a man into a little girl; a small, jimmy-rigged room into a concert hall; a flat poster into a countryside; even a mannequin into a living person. If you were bold enough, the prospects flew to the endless. And he blushed even to admit it to himself, but he felt as if he were changing, as well. He needed to think bigger; bigger. He boned up on the newest Ameri-can gadgets and how to use them.

Sometimes, he'd relate a few of the details to Susan as they came—the hidden ropes and winches, for example—but the oddest touches he kept to himself. How could she understand his need for the thunder and flash of a great counterfeit storm that'd serve no purpose other than to add an element of mystery? Still, she didn't grasp even the *basics* of his scheme.

"Like Houdini?" she said.

It was not like Houdini. She'd lived a life onstage, but the flim-flam was something beyond theatrical performance, beyond what existed already. It would be the orchestration of life itself. Even if it would mean extra risk, he couldn't make his plan safe and easy; stooping to perform a commonplace flimflam would do nothing to quiet the Why now. He imagined his body as the head of a phono-graph arm, his mouth the needle. . . .

"Yes, a bit like that," he said. This was at the end of another late afternoon at the Galina. "A bit like Houdini."

Susan made a strange face. Here was an occasion for a dramatic moment, and she wasn't going to miss it. Lordy, what flashing eyes!

"I think"—the tone of her voice was like an admiring curtsy—"that you are crazy." And then she gave an unexpected, irritated nod. He realized now what he should have known hours, days, maybe even years before—she was an unhappy woman. McCoy's eyes like the fingers of a blind man went over every inch of her face: her pale skin, upcast nose, her lips.

"You are so—perseverant." Like a flimflammer she was finessing the difficult thing she was about to say to make it sound unplanned. "Wonderfully perseverant. What's most flattering is that, time after time, you reappear, with love for me." She rolled over to face the wall; the sheets whispered until she settled in place. She said, "Do you know I love you?"

He didn't hesitate at all: "Yes."

"But how can you know? I mean, oh pishy *pish*—I certainly do. However, if I have no idea *why* I do, then how can you be so sure that I do?" Turning back to him, she frowned. Or, he thought that she might have. "Please don't take that as an insult, McCoy." Then her voice really clouded over. "You are crazy. You have always been that way—which, to be honest, has been my great disappointment in life."

Maybe, by adding to the silence, he might reject what she'd said.

They never talked about what had happened in their years away from each other. Maybe that was why they weren't as familiar as they had been—they *had* been very familiar once upon a time, hadn't they?

"McCoy, I'd have liked to think I could've counted on you. But I never could."

Looking at her now, he saw most clearly how she'd aged. The private feminine tricks died away as her grimace set in vexation; Susan's mouth fell pinched at both ends. He thought, *I've got to take her away from her present life.*

"Oh, why can't a girl choose who she . . ." but she trailed off.

"Marry me, Susan Fields," he said. Susan wouldn't only be throwing away certain wealth with Utnap for the hope of a possible wealth with McCoy; she'd risk going to jail. But he was sure it was their only chance at happiness, and his last and only chance to remain McCoy. "Wouldn't it be wonderful to change into someone new, Duck?"

And she laughed a sorrow-struck laugh. "How would it be new? It's not new."

Soon, though, she agreed to help him.

He worked full tilt; he'd feel bad if he didn't rob or scam something every day—bullets, several large mirrors, a little seed money, tools. He had a street artist draft a forest scene, and he spent a suspect amount of time at Uruk Voice Studios on Forty-third, recording phonograph after phonograph of himself as he talked in voices. With a stolen movie camera on a borrowed tripod, he had Susan capture him walking Central Park in guises. And when Utnap was out at work, McCoy—often right under the nose of that maid— would sneak into the color-blind robber baron's office to prepare for the flimflam. And naturally, there was all that scientific research.

"Well, are you ready?" asked McCoy, still fairly slender, still pretty energetic—more so now than he'd been in years. The next day, February 2, 1911, would bring the scam and determine the balance of their lives. Looking back on this I wish I could feel as happy for him as he did for himself.

"Yes," Susan had said. "I am ready."

The Flimflam to End All Flimflams

On that momentous day at the front end of 1911, the sky appeared less overcast than the almanac had predicted, and the temperature at forty-two Fahrenheit was off by almost two degrees.

At 4:34 P.M. the phone rang. McCoy'd planned on 4:35, but he wasn't going to nitpick, not now. With a groan the aloof Utnap rose. "Excuse me, Mr. Alterman. Always answer your own phone, no matter how rich you get."

"Certainly," said McCoy, slouching into the cane-backed sofa, blinking, looking as unlike a champion as he could. *Don't smile!* he thought. He'd made sure to sit directly in front of the window, and two inches left of center on the sofa.

"Hello?" Utnap's capillaries showed as a dainty red lacework across his nose and his flaccid jowls. And for a moment he gave the facial cast of an orangutan as he fussed his tongue along his front teeth. He squinted at his cup of coffee, which may have tasted queer because of what McCoy'd slipped into it.

Glancing around at the room's stuffed lion head, the Chinese gong, and the fancy paintings—especially the precise reproduction of the *Mona Lisa*—McCoy thought that Utnap had a life like that of the gods. He saw the old guy as a creature of ambition, no different from himself. And yet Utnap might as well have spent his time on his back. It was this slow-moving man's cunning, rather than any heroic deeds, that stamped him as exceptional, McCoy thought.

"Hel*lo?*" Utnap's voice was getting loud into the phone. The skin of the man's cheek sagged. "*Hello?*" Though he lived color-blindly, Utnap was wearing a business suit of a dark blue fabric so rich that it shone like crude oil.

McCoy checked the clock: 4:36 P.M. Why the delay? Already, the flimflam was failing!

"Hello? Operator?" Utnap stood confused. In 1911 there were no wrong numbers. Trained telephone officers placed each call.

McCoy's fake mustache itched the left side of his lip. His cheeks were shaved closer than ever before—they'd need to be, for a later phase of the scam. Just behind Utnap the *Mona Lisa*, suppressing a smile, appeared curious about how this would all turn out. Back then we all loved a good flimflam.

Shaking his head, Utnap bent to start hanging up the receiver. Even from across the room McCoy heard a crackling voice begin its pulse through the speaker of the receiver: "Mr. Utnap? Please hold for your caller—"

Utnap breathed loudly through his nose as he brought the phone back to his ear. He probably hadn't been forced to wait for anything in years. "*Now* what's the blasted delay!?"

And after the time it took for the unseen Susan to replace one phonograph record with a second, there crackled some other voice out of the phone—hopefully not a voice recognizably McCoy's. The *pop-pops* of a 78-rpm record, McCoy hoped, wouldn't sound different from the *thock-thocks* of the earliest phone lines.

McCoy knew by heart the message Utnap was getting in his hairy earlobe:

"*Mr. Utnap? This is Edward Fealty at your bank—*"

"All right, yes this is Utnap, what is it?"

"*—to bother you today but you have to come immediately, it's very importa—*"

"Who is this?" Utnap was tapping his foot without much rhythm.

"—*thing's happened to your jewels. All of them.*"

"What's happened? What? My jewels? Hello? Hello? Where have you gone?" Utnap, his face churning, hung up the receiver, waited a second, then picked it up again.

McCoy, meanwhile, had bent at the waist. He wasn't rubbing a scuff off his shoe, though it looked that way. With a little stealth he pulled the near-invisible thread that ran from the window to the floor.

"Wait a minute!—what're you tugging there, Alterman?" Utnap had wheeled around, the phone still against his ear.

One swift yank, two, and McCoy felt something give on the other end, like a sigh.

Utnap's old and rugged features grew tighter. He was stunned about something else and forgot about the thread (which had at its other end a razor blade). "Dadnabit! Now the phone's dead!" Utnap looked dispirited. "The blasted, blasted phone is dead."

Right on cue.

Dramatic "thunder" sounded, as slivers of the newly cut telephone wire fell from the building's receiver box and onto the thin leaf of sheet metal that McCoy'd earlier draped across the alleyway outside. The effect rang more out of place than climactic, because the sky was not stormy as the almanac had predicted.

McCoy, trying to nudge the thread back under the couch with his heel, told himself that keeping calm was the first rule—this was how we did things in that era before male sensitiveness had spread like a fungus. And McCoy seemed to be thinking of someone very far away.

Weeks earlier, when McCoy'd realized he was mistaken about having seen Johnnie Gold against the wall of a skyscraper, he'd imagined the old flimflammer saying: *You've wept enough for me.* When the image of Johnnie showed itself really to be a fat German, McCoy was alone, but not with loneliness or the memory of death. There'd been something implied by Johnnie's words and that had driven him to this shadowy, preposterous quest.

* * *

Utnap hurried McCoy from the house. "We'll consider your little orphans another time, Alterman." And then from across the street McCoy watched Utnap scurry out to his garage.

It was not as difficult as you'd think for a man like McCoy to trail a car on foot. He'd chosen this day because it was supposed to have rained; that it wasn't raining made his job harder. Still, with the congested traffic along the cobblestone avenues, the potholes and pedestrians, McCoy was able to keep stride with Utnap's Packard Laundaulet as that jewel magnate's tommy-gun-carrying driver and protector drove toward Wall Street.

McCoy's face glistened. He tried to see and know everything around him: the tendencies of a Packard Laundaulet on a bustling street; how fast could he get downtown; Utnap's exact weight and the make of the driver's gun; and all else that was to matter in the flimflam. When McCoy closed his eyes, he saw a gigantic house of cards collapsing right on top of him. He hadn't slept in two and a half nights.

Utnap's Packard, gleaming huge and white almost like an iceberg on wheels, reached the D'Aulaires Bank at 5:24, which might have been early enough to ruin everything. By now the blue overhead was thin skinned, a dyed parchment with a black sheet behind it.

McCoy stopped running, looking at the corner of Wall and Costin Streets for Susan. Would she be ready this early?

As soon as McCoy came to a stop a thousand pedestrian faces began to crush around him—where was Susan?—a press of bodies and shouts and car horns and smells: street smoke and dog squalor and roasting chestnuts for sale and there stood his truelove, in profile and done up like a little Italian boy next to a wooden cigar-store Indian. Her breasts were taped small under a baggy white shirt, her hair pinned beneath a swaying gray newsboy's cap. (A perfect disguise except for the one ungathered curlicue that, as she hurried up the street, danced in a precise figure over the back of her long thin heartbreaking snow-white neck.)

That she was doing this for him! Emotion came thick in his throat.

McCoy let his nose fill with the sweet aroma of roasting chestnuts. What other woman would be so refined? He'd given up trying to find an explanation for their persistent, stick-to-itive love. *She has saved my life*, he thought. Then he ducked into the shadow of a market awning as Utnap stepped from his car.

The wooden Indian started to bellow: "Utnap! Listen to your doubts! Save your wealth!" Susan had timed it well, having dropped the hidden needle inside the wooden headdress at the right moment. "Believe the unbelievable, Utnap!"

Utnap spun around, looking confused. The voice of the phonograph had come muffled out of the hole in the Indian's "mouth," and so maybe Utnap hadn't heard it at all, except in the way you hear a whisper on the edge of dream. Which was okay, too.

Utnap scuttled like a crab into the bank.

And McCoy's reflection swelled and mutated inside the burnished white surface of the Packard as he approached the car. "Hey, there," he said, flashing his smile at the driver. Pigeons at the curb looked up.

McCoy'd removed his fake mustache. Of course, he now wore a blond wig and carried a flask of "whiskey" in his shirt pocket.

The driver rolled down the window. He was a weary-looking Goliath whose jacket gathered too tight around his shoulders. His small eyes were trained on McCoy, but they gave no sign of actually seeing anything. The pigeons took off and flickered into the raw afternoon.

"Hey, there," McCoy said again. He waited. The chill was flicking at his ears. Utnap's driver had a face like an unpaved street.

The driver tapped his fingers on the steering wheel.

McCoy bounced a bit. "Your car is snug as a bug," he said. For this to work, he would have to come off more amiable than he'd ever been. He said, "That is some car, boy oh boy"—his face as open as day. The driver watched him with small red-rimmed eyes.

"Must be a real ran-tan to drive it, eh?" McCoy gave a little wink with his words. No time to spare. "A labor of love."

"Big deal if it is." The driver's voice was hard and gray as cement.

McCoy checked his reflection in the car door. Was the smile not bright enough? the face not enjoyable enough?

"What," the driver sighed, "do you want, bub?"

"Me?" McCoy laughed like a rusty hinge. "Just admiring your car." He drew his flask and pretended to take a swig. He gave his best rendition of a man enjoying the most delicious whiskey anyone ever tasted. The driver kept tapping the steering wheel distractedly.

"Hey!" McCoy looked very much like someone hit by an inspiration. He motioned his flask toward the driver. "You want some?"

"No." The driver's breath puffed from his mouth in a frost.

This was taking too long. Utnap would be out any minute.

McCoy said, "Whiskey'll warm you up," motioning with the flask, which naturally held some valerian sleeping potion (a flimflammer's best friend).

The driver slid his vacant eyes from McCoy—"Don't want any, bub"—and leaned down to start rolling up the window.

Do just one thing right for a change! McCoy thought, and suckerpunched the driver in the side of the head. McCoy's hand stung as if he'd stabbed it into a beehive. The driver was out cold. McCoy's twist-fist hadn't failed him.

Our boy slipped off his jacket and even his pants to reveal a blue uniform similar to the driver's. Then he ran to the cigar-store Indian, unlatched its back, and removed a hidden stage-prop head. He slipped it over his own face as a mask. It didn't look realistic from the front, but McCoy believed that, from the back, he'd be indistinguishable from the driver, whose body McCoy now dragged a little too conspicuously into the alley behind Cowles Yarn Market.

I don't think it was the thrill that now caused McCoy's happiness, though the spark that comes with risk did shiver his backbone a little. But a solitary spark is never the whole of a roaring flame of happiness. No, McCoy hadn't ever—even winning his championships—known any joy to set him on fire in this way. I'll bet what burned now within his heart was like a forest gone up, the kind of bonfire that churns for days.

* * *

Utnap strode into view, holding a sheaf of note paper as carefully as
if it were a lighted match. He walked toward the car tensely, a very
good sign. In the rearview mirror—even from far off—McCoy
could see that the man's eyes were frantic.

Utnap opened the door and fell into the Packard's backseat in
one motion. He sat there a moment, slouching.

"William." Utnap parted his dry lips and spoke uneasily, tiredly.
"Do you know how to get to Fresh Meadows, upstate?"

McCoy nodded without a word.

"William, answer when I ask a question." Utnap's voice seemed
energized by the chance to be bossy. "Answer me *now*."

McCoy grunted.

"So then—you know how to get there?"

The grunt again. He desperately didn't want Utnap to look
closely at him; hiding his face with the hand not on the steering
wheel, he couldn't see Utnap in the rearview mirror.

Utnap leaned forward and dropped an address on the seat next
to McCoy. "Just go," he said.

At least things in the bank must have proceeded according to
plan. Earlier that day, tuxedoed McCoy as Alterman had gone to ask
the manager to give a note to Utnap when the color-blind jeweler
arrived.

"Your jewels are in grave danger here," the note read. "Go and
check them, and see if some of them don't look duller than usual.
That's because they are selling them off, one at a time! DO NOT
TELL THE MANAGER!!! He is in on the scam. If you remove
the jewels now to take them to be appraised, THEY WILL SELL
OFF ALL OF THE REAL ONES, which they now have in hiding.
As you probably know, THE CHIEF OF POLICE IS FRIENDLY
WITH D'AULAIRES HIMSELF. If you go now to the police it
will TIP THEM OFF. But remain calm, friend. I work here and I
want to help you. Come to see me now, at the address listed on this
card. DRIVE TO ME RIGHT NOW—TIME IS OF THE
ESSENCE. DO NOT WORRY. I AM ON YOUR SIDE. I'M AN

HONEST BANKER AND AM ABSOLUTELY OFFENDED AND OUTRAGED BY WHAT IS HAPPENING AT D'AULAIRES LATELY. It's criminal, literally." The address card, which now rested beside McCoy, showed: "785 Bryant Avenue, Fresh Meadows, Upstate." (Because Utnap hated the city, McCoy deemed it necessary to have the color-blind magnate's anonymous helper live upstate. And, to be honest, he'd embraced the opportunity to turn New York into a pastoral scene. Just to see if he could remake the world that much more.)

"Where are you going?" asked Utnap now, leaning forward in his seat. The path that the driver had taken seemed not at all the fastest way to the country. (It was, however, the fastest route to Dogsbody Flats.) "William, why are you going this way?"

Will you fall asleep already! thought McCoy. The sedative that "Alterman" had put in Utnap's coffee had been timed to kick in an hour and fifteen minutes after the man drank it. It was now 5:43 by McCoy's watch.

The abandoned shingle house on the edge of Dogsbody Flats that McCoy'd cleaned up had a closed stable, which he planned to use now as a garage.

"William!" Utnap said, almost savagely. "I said where are you going?"

McCoy coughed. Not a polite cough, but a furious, rough, hacking convulsion. The most realistic stonewalling tactic he could think of was to feign a black lung.

"What's going on?" Utnap demanded. He was strongly agitated. But he started to speak tiredly. "Why won't you answer me, William?"

"Coughcoughcough—*cough!*"

The sky grew darker and darker, sunlight falling in arrows here and there as if through the leftover scraps of a dream. That elegant car glided over those bumpy cobblestones smoothly as an ice yacht. Utnap was quiet in the backseat, all of a sudden asleep under the effect of the sedative.

There was no light at all in the garage as Susan changed into the costume that made her look—from the back, and in the dark—pass-ably like the driver. And as she dressed she couldn't hide from McCoy her pleading, ghostly eyes. She was scared to death. He wanted to hug her, to comfort and thank and love her—*That she would do this, for me!*—but he was too busy using his new stereopti-con to flash messages onto Utnap's closed eyelids: "Your jewels are in danger in the bank," "Believe the Chinaman," etc. The ceiling looked mottled with painted stars, and along the walls there was a cardboard forest and a horizon of hilltops painted in silhouette: one-dimensional, playhouse scenery renderings of bushes and un-derbrush were scattered here and there, and mirrors in the corners gave an illusion of depth.

This twenty-feet-by-thirty lean-to was decked out to be the wide open spaces of Fresh Meadows. The floor, at least, was real dirt and mud. He hoped it didn't smell too much of motor oil.

"Mr. Utnap, wake up!" McCoy, standing outside the car, reached through the opened back door to shake the color-blind jewel mag-nate in the backseat. McCoy was now dressed as a woman. He wore an attractive calico dress, perfume, rouge, but no lipstick, as that would be difficult to remove quickly enough.

"Wha-what?" Utnap's features came to shape immediately, as he awakened into a real fear. "Where am I?"—his voice shrill and more girly even than dolled-up McCoy's. "What's going on here?" He looked around, blinking to get used to the dark. "William? *William?*"

"Your driver's asleep," said the girl-dressed McCoy, motioning to-ward Susan, who wore her padded driver's getup in the front seat. Susan hunched over the wheel and, as far as anyone could tell, snoozed.

McCoy went on: "You must have nodded off, too, sir." This was a voice he'd worked on. Sure, he hadn't shaken all of the masculine intensity from each word, but Utnap would likely not have caught that. Most who get duped hear just what you want them to hear. People don't put up a defense, or even want to.

McCoy, flirty now, smiled at Utnap. "My boss has been expect-ing you."

"William, arise!" Utnap was shaking his own head to wake himself. "William!"

Susan, up till now breathing peacefully to mimic the calm of sleep, started to tremble.

"He's expecting you—Mr. Utnap, is it?" said McCoy, bracing his body against the side of the car. The shaking of his own limbs surprised him. "Please come to see him; he's not well."

"*Who's* not well?" Utnap said, very disturbed; his nose twitched like a bunny's. "And what in blazes? What *are* you?"

A flimflammer has to know when to show his cards. McCoy said: "The man who contacted you about your jewels, *that's* who's not well." He looked into Utnap's cold eyes, and he kept up the high-wire act of making his voice stern while keeping it believably feminine. "Come with me."

Utnap stepped woozily from the car, unassisted. (A touch from McCoy's manly hands would have given the game away.) The sleep drug still had Utnap a bit groggy, which could only help.

"Crimeny, it's *unbelievably* dark outside," Utnap said.

Susan, hunched in the front seat, voiced one loud, masculine snore—a nice, actressy touch.

McCoy ushered Utnap to the door that led into the abandoned shingle house attached to this garage. On every side of the door the wall had been painted, in black on black-gray, to look like the shadowy outside of a house—and this side door was made to seem a front door. It had a brass knocker.

Good, thought McCoy. *At least I got him inside.*

Unfortunately, dust mites danced in the run of light that beamed from the hidden projector toward the movie screen on the far side of the window. Instead of looking out on Dogsbody Flats and, beyond that, the tall buildings of Manhattan, the window now played the flicker of a pastoral scene, in black and white. The projector was hidden on a rafter, high enough so that no one would interrupt the scenery by walking through the ray of light. And the thick pillows that McCoy'd put around the projector muffled its loud *tick-tick-ticking*, but not nearly enough.

"Please wait here," said McCoy, leaving Utnap in the antecham-ber and running into the next room. He couldn't give the old guy a chance to see how manly he looked in this light. Of course it was hard for McCoy to scurry in high heels. His flimflam, all his aspira-tions, ran with him, a centipede scuttling with its hundred legs. I can say for sure that McCoy didn't lose faith.

Once in the other room he removed his dress down to the waist and he jumped into the bed. He still wore his high shoes, but he switched his long, wavy blond wig for a straight, short black one, and he slipped on a shirt with a fat man's paunch sewn into its front. McCoy did all this while swabbing a saffron cream along his cheeks. The transformation would take about a minute. A minute in which Utnap might walk to the window and break up the flickery image of the forest. In which Utnap could notice the meandering specks of grit that floated down the projector's stream of light: acceptable risk. All the while McCoy was taping back the skin at his temples to narrow his eyes. His memory replayed the wisdom of Johnnie Gold: *The more that you were nobody—the more that people didn't see you—then maybe the more complete you were, the more every-where.* Is that what he'd said?

McCoy, loud but in a sick man's voice, spoke toward the door. "Come in, please, Mr. Utnap."

But the only noise that followed was the soft whir of the projec-tor in the room where Utnap was. Between the machine's throbs the worrisome quiet stretched out like a morass. Utnap hadn't opened the door. McCoy stared at it with an aching fear. His mood col-lapsed. Had Utnap figured it out? "Come in, Mr. Utnap."

Utnap entered, flinging the open the door. Maybe he was stronger than he looked. His eyebrows were drawn closely.

Was it an unreasonable ambition to be everywhere and everyone in the world?

"All right, what's going on here?" said Utnap. Yes, the flimflam was leaking air. But at least Utnap'd stepped directly on the strip of flooring that'd been calibrated to react to his weight. Yet an-other projector (hidden in the woodloft over the bed) set out its light.

Oblivious, the jewel magnate was shaking his head at other confusions. "This is all very odd—just who in tarnation are you?" His eyes shot daggers at the Johnnie Gold–imitating McCoy. Then he said: "Where's the ugly woman who let me in?"

Stung a little by that, McCoy pointed to the window. "Why, look. There she is."

Right on time a flickery image of the woman-dressed McCoy passed by, part of the forest scene now playing out the window. The room was lighted by candles.

"How did she get out *there*?" asked Utnap, at the end of his rope. He shook his head again. The projector wasn't quiet enough, the image out the window seemed too blurry if you inspected it closely. "Listen, just what in the—?"

"Mr. Utnap, did your jewels look duller?" McCoy, because he'd had to interrupt so quickly, sounded nothing like Johnnie Gold.

Utnap didn't answer; he seemed to be weighing everything in his brain. McCoy was close to reeling him back in.

McCoy began into what he thought were Oriental gestures, nodding, circling a finger in the air. "Did your jewels look duller today?" Then McCoy rushed his hand back under the blanket, because he hadn't yellowed his skin beyond his face.

"Yes," Utnap said slowly, as if admitting a childish mistake. Of course, the jewels hadn't *really* looked duller. They hadn't been touched at all. Every good flimflammer knows that the power of suggestion—mixed with a dupe's inclination to overestimate the brightness of his possessions—can always lead suckers to misjudge their own property. "Yes, they *were* duller," said Utnap. "That's why I came. However . . ."

Here he stared at the bed as if first noticing how odd McCoy looked. "Are you unwell?"

McCoy coughed. He worked to make this cough different—more foreign pitched—from the throaty hack he'd sounded when he'd played the lumbering driver.

McCoy said, "Yes. I'm unwell." Near the window a discreetly hidden urn contained a pinch of rotted pork to approximate the smell of a man on his deathbed.

Squinting, Utnap said: "You almost look like a Chinaman or something."

"I am," said McCoy. *What do you know of Chinamen?* McCoy thought. *I followed a great one around, like the tail to his comet.* "I am a Chinaman."

Utnap's eyebrows rose halfway up his forehead.

"Well," McCoy added quickly, "part Chinaman."

"You are?"

"Yes." In McCoy's voice desperation shook, and burst confidence. He had to concentrate to get the flimflam back on the rails. The trouble lived in the subtleties. McCoy felt a hunger in his empty stomach, but he told himself to ignore it, and not even to think of Susan or what she was doing that very moment. And to forget the sweat that stung his eyes.

A clock chimed dramatically, or at least that's what it was supposed to sound like:

Gong.

Gong.

Gong.

So at least Susan was still doing her part. But McCoy'd not yet said his piece about the bank president, and so this recorded sound signified nothing.

Gong.

Gong.

Gong.

"Well, Mr. Utnap." McCoy had never focused so hard on anything as he now did on Utnap's soft drooping face.

"Mr. Utnap, thank you very much for coming." To speak the way he thought an immigrant would, McCoy talked around each word as if he had a very hot bun in his mouth. But Utnap didn't answer.

Because Utnap was wondering at the window.

Even for someone color blind, even for a dupe who'd never expect that he was involved in a flimflam like this—the window looked pretty suspicious. And even with the black fabric McCoy'd draped over the screen, the landscape looked too bright for nighttime. And what were probably stray little hairs on the projector lens quivered along the surface of the image. Utnap inched, squinting, toward the window.

Don't step too close! If McCoy didn't stop him, Utnap'd block out the woodland scene by catching it on his back. It was time to make him drink another valerian sleeping potion.

"Mr. Utnap!"

The jewel magnate turned to face McCoy. The drumming of the projector seemed to get louder. McCoy didn't speak. Utnap didn't speak. Then the robber baron said: "What the devil?"

Gong.

Gong.

Gong.

"Your jewels are in grave danger, Mr. Utnap."

McCoy knew he'd fallen into unsafe waters. He had to calibrate his voice as painstakingly as he'd calibrated the strip of flooring that'd started up the projector. So the flimflammer McCoy, his eyes shut tight, his heart writhing like a live bird nailed to a wall, the ex-champion and husband McCoy, contesting subtleties, increased his volume from whispery to almost-yellish. "And I can save them for you!"

It was early for this, but McCoy pulled the cord under his blanket, and the flash powder made a lightning moment, and the rocks outside fell with some thunder onto the kettledrum " 'Zounds," gasped McCoy, even as he cursed himself for being repetitive with the effects. "You see *that*?"

Utnap looked down; he seemed dispirited in the thick of his confusion. "This whole thing is preposterous."

Gong.

Gong.

Gong.

McCoy still held hope. They were so close! Almost halfway to the end of the flimflam! Sure, he and Susan still had to get Utnap back in the car for a drive home from "the country" (valerian again, and trick mirrors); and to convince him that the Galina Hotel was the D'Aulaires Bank (prankish paintings, more mirrors), where a corrupt "president" could be seen among "customers" (electric-driven mannequins, wigs, recorded crowd noise). And then they had to have Utnap think he was settling his jewels in his own strongbox when he'd actually be putting them right in harm's way (a midsized maze; one odd voice). But that was it! Except for the getaway (fake blood; revolvers that shot blanks; one lever to start an "electrical blackout," another to release the "bats"). They'd win, he knew it.

They'd win and move to a safe town.

"Mr. Utnap?" McCoy, his determination just stronger than his sudden elation, held off smiling. "Mr. Utnap?" (By God, it was going to happen, because it had to! It had to! We'd thought of everything!)

"Mr. Utnap? Care for a drink?"

But mad-eyed Utnap turned all at once and broke for the door in high gear. Two steps, and he'd disappeared. And as he did so the projector turned itself off.

Was Susan still out there? If Utnap saw her—!?

McCoy had to catch Utnap, bring him back. From the waist down he still wore a dress and high heels. He started to make his way out of bed.

The door swung open; Utnap stormed back in.

McCoy threw the covers over his legs and tried to look as if he were just sitting up casually in bed.

Utnap's voice came out clipped and begging. "Tell me how did you know about my—?"

Then Utnap jerked around, openmouthed, staring again at the replayed image of girl-dressed McCoy as she passed by the window once more.

McCoy felt tears rolling down his cheeks. His empty stomach growled.

Utnap spoke in a loudish whisper—"*What the devil?*"—steady and audible, hard hit and hoarse, and he looked around the room, slowly, thoughtfully; he saw the beam of light that issued from the projector, and his gaze followed it back to the projector itself, which was clamoring: *Tick tick tick.*

Utnap cringed away from the beam of light, from McCoy, the bed; he looked like a toddler lost in the forest who makes out wolves' eyes in the underbrush. And so he tumbled out of the room again.

McCoy flung off the blankets and reached under the bed for his next outfit: a pressed driver's uniform. Trembling, weary and limp-minded, McCoy dressed in a rush, scraping up his naked knees with the hurry of his hands. Then came the noise that sank his heart.

"I'm here!" This was Utnap's voice. He'd made it outside already. "I'm here! Help me! I've been kidnapped—"

McCoy ran out toward the voice, but not before he'd reached up between the pillows that surrounded the projector, and found his revolver.

His ambition no longer ran beside him; the centipede was losing its legs. He had failed. Everything he tried, he'd failed at. The moan that came from his lips took him by surprise. The most important thing now was stopping Utnap from finding Susan.

The garage was empty, its door was lifted up. The big Packard, too, sat open; the mannequin driver that Susan'd placed there now lay along the front seat with its unrealistic face pointing, for some reason, to the ceiling.

Outside, a wasteland yawned in front of McCoy. Early evening was touching down like a flight of bees, having stung fifty, seventy, a hundred twinkling pinholes into the wide sky. The air smelled of tar and garbage.

There was no snow, but the ground was covered in ice and frost. About a hundred yards from where McCoy stood, Utnap was running toward four men, three being police officers; the fourth looked from this distance to be Utnap's driver. They had no torches or lights. Behind them stood dark Manhattan like a painting in black on gray-black. McCoy ran in the other direction. Where the ground was free of ice, there were cold puddles and there was mud.

Shadows lapped here and here against the shingle house and its garage, and against the cracked bones of the city that elbowed up at every hole and corner, the garbage strewn along the ground. Mists drew theselves high in curtain after white curtain.

McCoy's feet kept sinking into cold wet spattery mud as he ran past the shingle house.

"Susan?" McCoy whispered through his teeth. "Susan, where are you?"

While he searched for her in the underbrush, the gloom around dark corners, as much as he tried to hurry, his nervousness and despair and anger and insecurity and self-hatred and guilt weighed on his steps, and while his feet stumbled, McCoy saw clearly the terrible devastation of his years to come, and his years past. He saw the deaths he'd caused or watched. And as he looked, grimacing, there appeared, as by a curling together of shadows, the dark but vivid shape of the *real* McCoy. An image, that is, of the club boxer that the sixteen-year-old Gil Selby had let yellow and die in North Judson, Indiana. Maybe our boy wasn't crazy—there are times when the dead force themselves on the living.

I swear our boy heard the other, real McCoy say: *I want my self back. What have you ever done with it?*

The figure moved close; it was bigger than him and he stepped away from it. "All right" was his answer (it was difficult to address illusions, if not to hear them). "Have it," he said, and not only because he felt very fearful in the presence of death.

The figure, the first McCoy, dissipated with the sound of a gunshot. The ghost'd been as fake as everything else.

McCoy found himself at most twenty feet from the shingle house.

The noise of the gunshot had him transfixed. A group of pigeons flew up. The clamor had also roused some of the destitute, the needy of Dogsbody Flats. From unlit funk-holes a few hundred feet to his left and right, between two mounds of garbage opposite the shingle house, and in the various crops of ruin outspread beneath what'd become a big, spiteful moon, dark silhouettes could be seen.

McCoy barely noticed them. He ran back toward the garbage mounds just across from the shingle house. That's where Susan might be hiding. He slipped in the slush—was he in sight of the driver and the policemen? Had the driver awakened in time to follow the Packard as it went toward Dogsbody Flats? Or, had Susan set him up? No—not Susan. McCoy flattened himself against the wall of the shingle house.

The policemen and the driver were making their way toward him. They were twenty feet from where McCoy was, maybe fifteen.

What had they shot at?

"There!" The driver yelled, seeing McCoy first—seeing McCoy dressed as *him*—and he pointed while the police blew their terrifying whistles.

McCoy wheeled around; he ran away. And a dog started barking not too far off: *Urf! Urf! Urf!*

McCoy ran without knowing where, full out into the cold darkness. Maybe he could turn back, toward where he thought Susan had hidden—too late! Was that thunder, or another gunshot? The bullet sounded, as it darted past, like a match being lit. McCoy stooped, by instinct, *after* the danger. He felt a useless surge of hope in his breast: Maybe he and Susan would get out of this. Maybe he was wrong about where she was hiding. He felt along the top of his pants for his gun. It was gone. He must have dropped it.

McCoy came to a ruin of an old four-in-hand carriage and ducked behind it. He figured he'd made it about thirty yards. All at once he saw Susan on her knees beside a stack of dingy paving stones in the weak moonlight—gasping, tense, helpless Susan, turning to McCoy her pale, drained face. A warm sensation shimmered up his back, going round to his arms and legs. McCoy and Susan sat almost close enough to reach out to each other.

Feeling at once relieved and heartsick, he studied her features, her skin, her—

She turned away, as if meaningful looks might expose them both. McCoy's socks felt like heavy tongues on his freezing soaked muddy feet. Susan was crying enormously. McCoy's throat cramped and tightened. The warm sensation reached the back of his head. The police were looking left and right as they came toward them. They were about twenty-five feet away, at most.

And, slowly now, two young guttersnipes, silent, misshaped, sickly girls, came creeping up from behind, their eyes wide with curiosity, their palms up. McCoy made a fist and shook his head *no*. And the dirty children shuffled off. And they evaporated into the mist.

And then McCoy turned back to Susan and her many tears.

And the sound of nearing policemen speaking harshly at each other reached him in pieces through the broken ruins everyplace, half-sentences, stray words.

And, and.

McCoy peeked out over the four-in-hand. The policemen— three fat ones, their guns drawn, their sweaty faces pink with enthusiasm, what bastards some people can be!—had started running around blindly after something else, some false lead. They were about ten feet away, now fifteen, now twenty. The driver was nowhere to be seen.

This was McCoy and Susan's chance to hurry away.

Urf! Urf! Urf!

McCoy turned to her. Cowering with her head down, she was all heaving shoulders and back. Even in the cold, her sweat had burned an oval stain onto the back of her driver's uniform.

McCoy whispered, "Susan." Just over the lump she made the flickery coal sky of stars batted its hundred eyes. "Susan, we can run," McCoy said in a pitiful voice; he was tapping his shoes into the ground to try to unstick the socks from his feet. "Look at me, Duck." Susan's delicate sweat-stained back as she curled over made a sad picture. And the stripe of absolute quiet between them seemed to widen; they grew farther apart with each second. "*Susan!*"

The policemen were closing in and getting closer. One looked broad at the hips and young; he was nearer than his partners and muttering in every direction from under his blue patrol hat. The two others eased up slowly behind him. None yet saw where McCoy and Susan hid. McCoy and this first policeman were as close as fighters in opposite corners of a boxing ring. Behind the police, the skyline of New York shied up like rough teeth in an open mouth.

McCoy turned to Susan, who was raising her head and staring at him. Her glassy eyes were alert with a light that would come to nothing at the end of her life. Her white face creased just as it had in the embrace of love.

Sorrow hangs saddest on a delicate face. Hers was not a look of affection.

That dog barked again. There were tramps peeking out from the shadows to get a look before plunging back into the darkness like rabbits into hiding holes. McCoy thought he saw a wounded boy— not too far off—clambering out of a ditch and pointing at them. Would this boy, these beggars, give Susan's location away?

I can't tell you how close the policeman's steps were to them now, clip-clopping on the damp cold ground like the steps of a horse.

McCoy stared desperately at Susan, squinting, because maybe even without words he'd be able to say all of it: all that it'd meant to have loved her and no one else, only his Susan. But a look is no more than a look—*clip*, went the policeman's steps, *clop*—and eyes are delicate to convey that much.

One of the loveliest things about Susan was her knees, those small perfect circles; she was looking fixedly at them, not at McCoy.

Clip-clop

There seemed only to be one policeman now. McCoy hadn't taken his eyes from Susan. Not far to their right was the shingle house. Various crops of ruin stretched out just ahead.

"Get back, all of yous!" said the policeman, probably talking to the beggars in the shadows. He spoke excitedly, high-pitched and urgent in the gloom. "This is a criminal inquest here!"

I can say for sure that McCoy felt the cannon roar of regret deep in himself.

Clip-clop. His hands, head, and his feet went cold. His whole body shook. Something terrible was going to happen.

Susan jumped to her feet and ran; just ran. And even for that harrowing instant there was real pleasure in watching her long ferocious stride, her thin calves acting with their quick animal hurry. Oh, I wanted to run after Susan then, I did! But as I leapt up to chase her, to rescue her, I kicked to life a cloud of bees that blinded and stopped me in my tracks.

But how could there have been any bees, in that cold season? The clamor of the policeman's gunshot pierced the ears like ice.

You'll never understand how brutally, how terribly I have agonized over what those bees were, if they weren't bees? Who knows? Who knows?

Urf! Urf! Urf! barking again. Also the policeman was shouting frantically. But all the noise seemed, if not to have dropped away, at least to have blunted.

Susan lay still. Her face turned to the side. Her hair was drawn across her sweaty brow in red streaks like streaks of blood. Her mouth hung open casually. But her face was just as I'd remembered it, a world of moods. I don't know how long I stood there gaping. I remember I felt cold and not myself. She lay in her own blood, her feet flaring out heel by heel, and she looked very slender. I'd seen her die at least forty times on the stage and in flickers.

Urf! Urf! Urf!

The one love of my life lay dead at my feet, shot through the breast. I was already someone else.

"Halt! You are under arrest!"

The man I had been faded from the man I was becoming the way the moon pales softly into a dreary morning. It could be that sadness had driven me out of my mind.

When the police officer, or maybe it was the police officers, converged, stepping to me cautiously, I—even under all this sadness I couldn't hold up under; even at this moment of utter failure, when I needed to know if I could reach into my chest and yank out my hemorrhaging heart—even now I tried to sound a McCoy note, maybe to see if I still could. "Boys," I actually said, "cunning is a dignified defense."

But of course it didn't work—the words collapsed, unrecognizable through my gagged, disgusting sobs. Extreme oddness sometimes makes a failure.

Then as if against my own will, I let out a cry from deep in my throat, a frantic, burning yelp of sorrow. I yelped like a dog, like fifty dogs burning at the stake. This yelp of sorrow went high over Dogsbody Flats before coming down to hang for a moment among the ruins, the gnarled train-wheels and the unused bank-doors, like drying laundry. When it met the sounds of a barking dog and questioning, official voices and nervously approaching footsteps, my yelp disappeared.

McCoy was gone.

Connor Alterman

Nowadays my bed is crowded with memories and the mattresses here at Restful Days are brutal. My name is Connor Alterman, and that's who I've been for decades.

I admit everything. To protect myself I've tried not to let on that I once was McCoy—and that lie now has failed as well. But who's going to prosecute me now? Connor Alterman is the identity I'd always been making up—in secret, and vaguely comprehended even by myself—in case I ever needed an emergency haven of escape from being McCoy.

The man I've become never lived before McCoy invented him, and there's no McCoy, not any longer.

Now I spend my life in horizontal isolation surrounded by white-haired idiots who snore together in accidental symphonies every minute day and night. Often I see Susan Fields's face, steeped to the lips in misery. It's her death face and I can't escape it. I have a photograph of her but I haven't looked at it since. I spend my evenings listening to the crooked counsel of this old rattletrap body. When I'm edged onto my back for a sponge bath, I talk McCoy to the delicate nurses, the young pretty nurses who wouldn't know an old-fashioned masculine touch on their breasts, legs, face, etc., from the cold touch of the stethoscope. I believe that all of these people live—no less than I did all those years ago—as renderings and fabrications, mutoscope projections of their imagination, dressed up in quotation marks. They just don't know it. I have such terrible bedsores. The end.

But you still want to talk about what happened that night.

The policeman, the fat young one, had got to McCoy first. He'd had a gun, a nightstick, and a fidgety look. His name was Francis. Francis came right up to McCoy's face, so close I couldn't see anything but him.

"McCoy?" Francis asked, with meat breath. He had a tight grip on McCoy's bicep and a face lost in thought. O, grief! This was killing McCoy. And Francis said, "That man"—that man being Utnap, I assumed—"said he guessed you was probably the real McCoy or something like that?"

Nobody, as far as I knew, had retrieved Susan's body.

Later, alone and weeping on a bench in a bouncing, pitch-black, windowless paddy wagon, shivering all over, jolted senseless by the lurch and shudder of this private earthquake, the man who'd been McCoy came up with one more flimflam. Whatever they'd sentence me with, I'd soon be out on bail (everyone got bail those days). I'd hunt up some dead bum's corpse on the Bowery—there were always a few, every night if you knew where to look. Next, I'd pin a suicide note to the guy's lapel and push him off a building tall enough so that no one would recognize the deceased wasn't the right corpse. This would work, I was sure of it. At the same time, brand-new memories were closing in and stifling me.

But here's the thing. You're likelier to get a gift from Fortune after she's just bitten your head off. Every yelping dog has his day. What I mean is, without even really paying attention, McCoy tried the door of the paddy wagon.

The door was unlocked.

Escape was one leap into the unknown away. A leap to be undertaken while crying.

At that moment another story began, a sad story. My story. It involves a man forced to cast aside his ambitions, his name, his life. A man with skinny legs, a paunch to his belly, and glasses worn just for show. A man who's had to live closemouthed and free of his seething vanity. A man who's suffered too many decades celebrating his first three. Suffering will overwhelm my story, the suffering of loneliness, poverty, milk-and-water obscurity, unending years of boredom, and the guilt that has been my only companion. McCoy was a part of the deaths of everyone I cared about. Also it's the story of the rise of the society I deserved all along, the bewildered century of "experts," of fame-seekers, of bold-faced lies, corrupt games, grand empty plans, portraits of portraits, "art" lacking all art; the century of America and the all-over pervasion of flimflam.

Finally, mine has become the story of a man who's refused to let go of life because he's so deathly afraid of death. And who has achieved immortality in a catchphrase. In the end, there was nothing extraordinary about me but the intensity of my desire to be extraordinary.

I don't want to tell that story. Let me tell the one I always come back to.

Once upon a time I was McCoy, and McCoy was an immaculate figment of myself.

Here was your champion before he closed his hand into a fist.

A Note Upon Finishing the Book

This book is a novel, not an attempt to repeat the historical record verbatim. All of my major characters—Johnnie Gold, Susan Fields, Utnap, Stromo, H. H. Measures, Rosella Bunker, even McCoy himself—have sprung strictly from my imagination. Not that such invention is ever a cut-and-dried feat.

In "real life" there did exist a turn-of-the-century boxer named Norman Selby who called himself Charles "Kid" McCoy, and that man is believed to be one possible source for the term "the real McCoy." Competing theories have it that the term comes from an advertising ploy dreamed up to promote McKay Scotch, or else the African-American inventor Elijah McCoy, who is best known for developing rubber heels, lawn sprinklers, and locomotive oil cups in the 1870s.

The true story of the real Selby does, of course, bear *some* resemblance to the plot of the book you hold in your hand. Norman Selby was married numerous times (although not to the same woman again and again). Also unlike my Virgil Selby, Norman did not steal the name and identity of McCoy from another man. Further, he was never a professional flimflammer, to the best of my knowledge. Likewise, his childhood relates in no way to the invented family history herein. And, as I said, he had no Susan Fields or Johnnie Gold in his life.

Norman Selby was, however, accused of being a thief—though I doubt he ever attempted a jewel heist like the one my character attempts at the end of this narrative. Before he was jailed for murder, the real Selby did battle such celebrated boxers as Tommy Ryan, Gentleman Jim Corbett, and Joe Choynsky—the last of whom brought out such ferocity in Charles "Kid" McCoy that one report proclaimed: "Now you've seen the real McCoy." One more thing: The *real* McCoy did try his hand at poetry. The poem that serves as an epigram for my chapter "The Real McCoy in Training" comes from Norman Selby's pen, not mine. The rest, as they say, is history, just not as I write it.

I researched the details of Selby's life by reading news articles from the time, and also a biography called *The Real McCoy: The Life and Times of Norman Selby,* by Robert Cantwell, which proved especially helpful when it came time to compile the list of products that were introduced when artificiality began to take root in our national life. What I did with those facts is the cornerstone of my chapter "The Real Mccoyalooza." In addition, Cantwell's thoughts on the ascension of "image" as a guiding force in human behavior influenced the end of my chapter "Golden Lessons." *The American Confidence Man,* by David W. Maurer, provided an invaluable look into the grifter's world.

Finally, the kind people I need to thank. My sister Tracey Hechler, and my parents Bernie and Ellen. Chris Noel, John Hodgman, Rae Meadows, Jeff Roda, Barbara Kerbel, and especially Susannah Meadows gave me invaluable recommendations and were better readers than anyone deserves. Brian Tart, Carole Baron, Amy Hughes, Seta Bedrossian, Lisa Johnson, and Brant Janeway at Penguin Putnam have all been bolstering and talented and goodhearted. The remarkable Sarah Chalfant, Andrew Wylie, Matthew Snyder, and Sonesh Chainiani are the hardworking secret to any success I may achieve in my writing life. And thanks to Rob Kraselnik for lending me some history books.

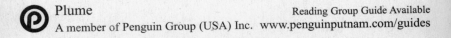